s a dead one alright

# that's a dead one alright

## a jimi smith mystery

### susan case

TATE PUBLISHING & Enterprises

Published by Tate Publishing & Enterprises, LLC
127 E. Trade Center Terrace | Mustang, Oklahoma 73064 USA
1.888.361.9473 | www.tatepublishing.com

Tate Publishing is committed to excellence in the publishing industry. The company reflects the philosophy established by the founders, based on Psalm 68:11,
*"The Lord gave the word and great was the company of those who published it."*

Book design copyright © 2009 by Tate Publishing, LLC. All rights reserved.
*Cover design by Lance Waldrop*
*Interior design by Jeff Fisher*

Published in the United States of America

ISBN: 978-1-60799-421-3
1. Fiction, Mystery, Detective, Women Sleuths
2. Fiction, Contemporary Women
09.06.25

# *acknowledgments*

I'd like to thank my pushy husband, who encourages me to write, write, and write some more; and to each of my three handsome sons for their love and laughter. A special thanks to Bev and Deb at the office for their feedback and giggling in all the right places. Also a note of appreciation to John Boothe, PA, for the medical facts I needed. Ron and Rona, thank you so much for your support. Also, my sincere appreciation goes out to all the residents of Glenns Ferry, which Ditters Ferry is somewhat modeled after. Glenns Ferry is a special town full of community-minded, caring, neighborly people, the likes of which haven't been seen since television's Mayberry. I wouldn't want to live anywhere else; we have several annual events and entertainment opportunities that big cities could never match.

Grandmama, thank you for instilling in me the love of writing.

Terri, I am grateful to you for believing in this book and for actively taking part in the future success of Jimi Smith. "You go, girl!"

Connie Wills, thank you for promoting this work with such enthusiasm. I could use a few thousand more just like you!

Mark, *stop* hiding my envelope opener. You weren't the inspiration for the murder victim!

Thank you to all my family and friends. God has blessed me richly with your presence and love.

My biggest thank you is reserved for my Dad, who told me I had "moxie" and would accomplish anything I set my mind to. I miss you, Daddy. Can't wait to see you in heaven and give you a big hug!

# *chapter 1*

As a twenty-four-year-old unemployed college dropout living with my grandparents, I can honestly say, "Life sucks!" My plans since puberty of a meteoric rise to journalistic fame would never happen, primarily due to the fact that they had never begun. After an embarrassing fiasco in high school, I determined to put my dreams of investigative journalism on permanent hold.

After graduating high school, I spent two years bored out of my mind in irksome business courses before finally dropping out. After a couple years of job-hopping, I found an opening in commercial banking. It was a high-level position as a currency conduit for vehicular occupant pneumatic tube utilizers. All right, it was a drive-up teller position, but it was much more challenging than one might think. Count money in, count money out, balance at night. *Yawn.* Eight months after the inception of this new career, my supervisor, Ms. Castille, recommended me for a promotion to credit card services.

The recommendation was surprising as Ms. Castille had been the target of numerous practical jokes, the last one being when a small African violet was thoughtfully potted in her shoe. She had a habit of taking her shoes off and keeping them under her desk. The velvety purple flowers looked stunning in her ivory Manolo pumps. Ms. Castille was clearly a woman with a sense of humor, integrity, and judging by her shoes, pretty darn good taste.

Credit card service was also a dud. I got my work done too quickly and had far too much idle time on my hands. The saying about idle hands being the devil's tools, well, that expression has lasted since the twelfth century for a reason. *It's true.* Not a day went by that I didn't find some mischief to get into. Apparently I lacked a much-needed creative outlet.

The Department Head of Credit Card Services agreed with me. After leaving a fake letter on my coworker's desk that read, '*I am unable to make my credit card payments, as I died in an industrial accident last week. Please do not try and get money from my dog, Papoochi. He died in the acid bath with me*'. Unfortunately, I made a slight error in judgment using a real customer's name and account number for authenticity's sake. The customer was contacted, and a very embarrassing conversation ensued.

My creative little missive was one joke too far. A soft-spoken HR manager called me into her office to inform me that the bank had decided to 'grant me my personal freedom to explore new employment horizons'. And this is how I arrived jobless and broke at Dibbzy and Granddad's.

Our home is located in the thriving metropolis of Ditters Ferry, Idaho, population 932. Some jackrabbits and coyotes must have been included in the census head count, as there can't possibly be more than seven hundred residents of our fair city situated along the banks of the Snake River between Boise and Twin Falls.

My grandmother—we call her Dibbzy—is a slightly reformed hippie. Her real name is Debbie, but her old hippie friends call her Doobie. I refuse to ask any questions or even ponder how she acquired that moniker. She wears her hair in one long, thick braid that is now more silver than black. She also favors loose, gauzy dresses and Birkenstock sandals. She has a flat, round Germanic face and clear blue eyes. Her face is smooth and given to a ruddiness that makes her look as if she is perpetually warm from exertion.

At our house, meals resemble weeds, seeds, grass, and the like, and we graze accordingly. If it isn't organic, salt free, chemical free, high in fiber, and tasteless, it simply isn't in our diet regimen. Luckily Granddad occasionally takes me with him on his surreptitious food excursions.

My brother, Spencer, and I moved in with our grandparents when our parents' were killed in a car crash. I was almost eleven years old and Spence four at the time of their deaths. While the pain of losing our mom and dad was staggering, we were truly blessed to have such loving and *colorful* grandparents step in and raise us.

"Juliet . . ." My full name is Juliet Montague Smith. Mercifully everyone but Dibbz just calls me Jimi. "We need to talk," Dibbz informed me. "You've been here for two months and haven't accomplished anything more than reading mystery novels and watching *The Price is Right*. Learning what denture cream costs and how to play *Pinko* are not useful job skills. You are wasting your life and talents away. You need to make some plans."

"*Plinko*," I mumbled.

"Huh?"

"It's *Plinko*, not *Pinko*," I corrected Dibbz.

"Juliet, that's really *not* the point. Get on with your life. You have a passion and talent for writing. You suffered one bad," she paused, catching my expression, "okay, one *really* bad experience and let it stop you from realizing your dreams. When you were writing you showed some drive and moxie."

"Java."

"What?" Dibbz never could follow my train of thought.

"I need a latte. Moxie reminded me of java, and java reminded me that I could use some caffeine."

"You're not funny, and caffeine is poison. Do you know how many gallons of water it takes to dilute the effects of one cup of coffee in your system?"

"No. How many gallons of water does it take to unscrew the effects of one cup of coffee from the human body?"

"Thirty-two gallons, Miss Smarty Pants. Maybe you should get a job writing for that Bart Simpson show."

"I thought you hated that show."

"I do. I figure if they use your jokes it will finally get canceled."

"Ha-ha."

"Do something with your life, Juliet. Be a better example for Spence. Take a class, go on sabbatical, join the Peace Corps, get married, whatever. Just get off the couch and *do something!*"

"All right. I'll do something," I consented.

"Good."

"I'm taking my unemployment check to the bank, cashing it, and then going to get a double-shot latte."

Dibbz took a deep breath and was ready to unload on me.

I held up my hand to deflect the verbal blow and continued, "When I get back, I'll go through the classifieds and see if there is something worth checking into."

"Two weeks, Juliet."

"Two weeks and then what?" I asked.

"You have two weeks to get your life in order and set some goals."

"No problem. I'll get right on that goal thingy." I hated disappointing Dibbzy, but I had no clue what direction to take. I felt like a failure, and sarcasm, however inappropriate, was an easy way out of a conversation.

---

Precisely two weeks later.

Having had a wonderful visit with Kirstie, my very best and only friend, I was in a good mood as I parked my car along the street curb. Walking up the front sidewalk, I saw four hugely swollen, black, thirty-gallon garbage bags with bright yellow plastic tie handles, two large boxes, and one smaller box with my stuffed wolf, Blitzer, perched atop all setting out on the front porch. Dibbz must be donating to a charity drive. I snatched up Blitzer, determined to rescue him from the Salvation Army. I tried to open the door, but it was locked.

I rang the doorbell impatiently. *What the heck is going on?* I slapped the door loudly with my palm. "Hey, open up!" Looking around for something heavy and hard to bang on the door, I spotted a white envelope on the porch swing. My name was printed boldly dead center, giving me a sinking feeling.

Ripping the envelope open, I quickly scanned Dibbzy's curling handwriting.

*Dear Juliet,*

*Because I love you so much and cannot stand by while you waste your life away, I have made the very difficult decision to give you the push you need. All your things are in the bags and boxes. Take them with you and find yourself. Let me know when you do something you are proud of. All the locks have been changed, and your grandfather and Spencer have strict instructions to abide by my wishes, which are in your best interest.*

*Love,*

*Dibbzy*

Find myself! What sort of hippie guru logic is that? What if I find myself and don't like me? The trip will have been a waste.

*Psst! Psst!*

I couldn't tell where the sound was coming from. It would be just my luck that my tires were losing air.

*Psst!* "Jimi, up here."

Backing up a few steps, I gazed skyward. There was Granddad in his undershirt hanging out of the upstairs bathroom window. I would lay ten-to-one odds that he had no pants on. Retirement had not done well by Granddad . . . or *was it the other way around?*

"Jimi, catch." Granddad threw a wadded-up sweat sock at me, smiled, and disappeared.

The dingy sweat sock landed with a thud at my feet. It was heavy and oddly shaped. Curiosity got the better of me, and I unrolled the sock. Inside was a roll of cash in assorted denominations. Using my past banking skills, I sorted and counted the booty, which totaled $1,237. I sat down on the stoop, looked at my belongings indignantly stuffed into trash bags, and promptly proceeded to sob. Not a single, noble tear, but a torrent of mascara-permeated salt water ran amuck all over my face. I had officially hit rock bottom, and it was time to pull myself up. Thanks to Granddad, at least I wouldn't be sleeping in a tater field tonight.

Dibbzy would not be happy with Granddad if she found out about the money. The two were so unalike in personality and philosophy of life. Dibbz was artsy yet pragmatic, still only referring to Granddad as "Jonathon" because Jon Smith is simply too common for her to consider. She probably thought she would marry an environmental activist named Raindance Paisley Peace, and together they would save the world one granola bar at a time. Instead she fell in love with Jon Smith, a round-faced civil engineer and Republican to boot. Granddad had a soft heart and more idealistic mindset, and thankfully a very generous nature. The lumpy sock in my hand was proof of that.

---

"Come on. It will only be for a couple of weeks," I begged.

"No!"

"Please. I have nowhere else to go," I begged.

"Sure you do. Go find a YWCA."

"In Ditters Ferry?" I asked incredulously.

"In wherever. Your loser butt is *not* moving in with me. Besides, I only have one bedroom." Kirstie could be really insensitive at times.

"I'll sleep on the couch."

"You'll never get off the couch." *That hurt.*

Kirstie is a natural red head and bears all traits that red hair implies—fair skin, freckles and a fierce-some temper. She befriended me when I was still in high school. I had attempted to cut my own hair to hide an ugly bruise on my forehead.

Unfortunately, the only scissors to be found were manicure scissors, so my hair ended up looking like an abstract Picasso painting. Kirstie, recently graduated from beauty school, fixed my hair, creating a softer, sexier style for me.

Kirstie was my only friend, and at the moment I was in desperate need of her help, *again.*

"You'll never even know I'm there, Kirstie."

"Yes I will, and you know it. I won't have any privacy, and I've heard you're a real slob."

"Where did you hear that?" I asked more curious than indignant, because it was true.

"From *your* grandmother. She said when you went away to college she found used dishes, trash, empty pop bottles, and dirty clothes all over your room."

"I won't be messy or a bother. I promise. Just let me get back on my feet."

Kirstie looked down at my feet with an expression of incredulous revulsion. "Getting on those feet might be too big of a job."

Ignoring the jab at my shoe size, I continued to plead my case. "I'll even cook for you."

She hesitated. Maybe I had discovered her Achilles' heel. Kirstie went out for every meal except Sunday supper with her mama. "You can cook?"

"I'm a terrific cook." Such a lie. "In fact, I love to cook." Full steam ahead on the fibber's express train with a one-way nonrefundable ticket to wherever sinners go. "Please. I'll make Mexican food tonight—tacos, beans, rice, enchiladas; all your favorites." I gave her my most pitiful look.

"Listen, Jimi. You have one month to get a job and find a place to live. You *will* pay me $250 rent and half the utilities. And if I catch you on the sofa during the day, I'll kick you out onto the street without so much as a backward glance. Got it?"

"Got it." I threw my arms around her in a grateful bear hug. Kirstie talked tough, but she wouldn't let me down. I knew for a fact she babysat for several young mothers in her apartment complex, and she did it for free. Kirstie was also the first one to donate money, clothes, blankets, or whatever necessary to every relief fund the town held. She always did it anonymously, I assumed to protect her *bad-girl* image, but I'd caught her in quiet acts of generosity several times.

"Get off me." Kirstie shifted her shoulders up, down, left, and right to loosen my hold. Kirstie pretended she didn't like hugs or people invading her personal space, but I had been granted a reprieve and needed to demonstrate my gratitude. "Now get out of my shop. I have a client coming in. She was in here earlier but said she needed *reinforcements* before she got pierced."

As if on cue, a teenage girl entered with her arm slung over a nervous-looking young man. She leaned heavily on him and was obviously joyously, stinkin', slaphappy drunk.

"I jesh needed a little shumshing *(hiccup)* before thurr peershed." She giggled up at her escort and patted his cheek. "This is all for you, baby baby baby. Have I told you how mush I loves you?"

The poor guy was turning so red I thought his ears were going to catch fire.

"You don't have to do this, Tiff."

"Course I do, shilly. I tole you I loves you."

"Come on to the back, Tiffany," Kirstie said.

"Can Joshy woshy boo boo boo come with me?"

Joshy woshy boo boo boo looked like he was going to pass out.

"Uh, no. Idaho state beautician rules require that only the client and aesthetician may be present during piercings."

Kirstie's lie had Joshy looking very relieved.

"He can help you to the back, though."

Now was a good time to make my escape. Whatever Tiffany was getting pierced was her business.

"They won't loosh feeling, will they? Hee hee hee. Joshy woshy wouldn't likey wikey . . ."

14

Thankfully the door shut and I couldn't hear anymore of the Tiffany–Joshy holes in the whatever saga.

The sun was so bright that I put a hand up to my forehead and was about to step off the curb to cross the street when I saw *him*. Jet was back in town and behind the wheel of a shiny new black Lincoln Navigator. Apparently Jet's taste had moved to the high end of the Ford Motor Corp. line. In high school Jet had driven a well-maintained but used Bronco. The current SUV was "ghetto style," with darkly tinted windows and special order premium wheels. The breath went out of me in a whoosh. I needed to find a place to hide. Too late. Jet turned his head and his gaze locked with mine. Recognition registered at the same moment his brake lights illuminated. I ran next door into Litton Auto Parts, hoping he didn't see me go in.

I'd never been inside the auto parts store before. Not one item on the shelves looked even vaguely familiar. It was dimly lit with an old ceiling fan whirring overhead. The shop was full of shiny thingamabobs and shelf after shelf of whatchamacallits. Scurrying to the farthest, darkest aisle, I began perusing little boxes. Bending down, pretending to inspect the labels, I made sure my head was well below top shelf level. I picked up one of the little boxes, trying to look like a real shopper.

"And what exactly do you plan do to with those?"

Warm breath blew on the back of my neck, sending a tingling sensation throughout my body.

"Hmm?" I stalled to compose myself and then turned around. "Why, Jet," I said, feigning surprise, "when did you get back to town?"

"I arrived right when you saw me." He smiled.

Jet moved closer, backing me close against the shelf. Somehow Jet had managed to get even better looking. He had transformed from a good-looking, cocky seventeen-year-old boy into a devastatingly handsome, self-assured man. His rich, brown hair with natural gold streaks that used to curl past his ears was now cut short and styled. He had filled out some too, but was

15

still all lean, hard muscle. His expensive Borelli shirt was neatly tucked into his faded jeans that accentuated his athletic hind asset to perfection. His shirt sleeves were rolled up, exposing muscular, tanned forearms. Jet's skin was the color of caramel, and his eyes the color of a Hershey's kiss. He was, simply put, delicious.

"Why wouldn't you answer my calls?" Jet asked.

"What calls?" *Good move. Play dumb.*

"How about the half dozen calls I made to your house after our unfinished *interview?*"

"Uh, I was busy. You know, searching for the right college, applications to complete, people to meet, and things to do."

He moved a step closer, and there was nowhere for me to go.

"Uh huh. Right. So why do you need these?" He tapped the box in my hand.

I finally *really* looked at the box in my hand. Of all the things to pretend interest in, I had to choose *Butt Connectors for 10-Gauge Wiring.*

"Oh, you know. This and that. A girl can never have too many butt connectors."

He laughed out loud. It was, without a doubt, the sexiest sound I ever heard. His head was tipped back, and his throat looked absolutely appetizing. I couldn't shake this *thing* for Jet. It teed me off though, because he was laughing *at* me.

"What is so funny?" I demanded.

"You." Edging even closer, he leaned down and whispered, "But that's what I like about you. You make me laugh even when you're not trying to be funny."

Placing the flat of my palm in the middle of his chest, I intended to push him back a bit. That was the plan until I felt the heat and muscle under his shirt. I stopped moving and, unfortunately, stopped thinking and stood there mesmerized with my hand on his chest.

He put a curled index finger under my chin and lifted my

face. The look on his face made me momentarily forget my indignation.

Then the memory of him and Candy the night of the *interview* came crashing back. "He just feels sorry for you," Candy had said. Placing the butt connectors back on the shelf, I tried to dart around Jet. "I'm late. I gotta run."

He hooked my elbow with his hand and turned me around. "You can run, Jimi, but it's Ditters Ferry, where are you going to hide?"

"I'm not running or hiding. I'm just late."

"Jet, is that you, boy?" a voice bellowed. We both turned to see George Litton, the store owner, barreling toward us. At sixty-five, George was still an imposing figure with a base drum for a chest. His shoulders were at least three feet across. "Hey, Jimi. Never seen you in here before."

Jet grinned at that remark, probably because it confirmed his suspicion that I ducked into the first door I could find. Turning his attention to Jet, George slapped him on the back and started rapid firing questions about college football. Making my escape, I dared a glance back at Jet.

"I'll see you later," he mouthed at me.

Shrugging my shoulders as if to say 'we'll see', I headed off to Kirstie's apartment, where he'd never find me. I wasn't sure if this made me feel secure or depressed.

---

As does everyone in Ditters Ferry, Kirstie kept her front door unlocked, something that I would later wish I had made mental note of. I unloaded my belongings into her small and *formerly* tidy living room, then went back to the car to retrieve the groceries for tonight's dinner. The deception I was about to perpetrate wasn't very nice, but desperate times call for desperate measures. I took some solace in that cliché.

Two frozen Mexican dinners, a tomato, one bunch of green onions for garnish, and enough shredded cheese to cover everything were pulled from the bag. Chips and salsa would round out our gourmet meal. My finale would be homemade apple pie for dessert. Good thing I know Marie Callender's recipe. Kirstie was going to want me to stay forever.

It was only a little after four o'clock, and Kirstie wouldn't be home until around 6:00 p.m. There was plenty of time to put everything into pots or pans and then hide the dinner boxes and salsa jar. I planned to claim the salsa as homemade also.

It was time for a nap. This had been an arduous day, and I deserved a little siesta. Clicking a talk show on, I turned the volume down and stretched out on the couch. I never even made it through the first set of commercials before falling asleep. The loud trill of a ringing phone woke me.

"Hullo." Still groggy, I cleared my throat.

"Were you sleeping?" Kirstie sounded annoyed.

"No. No. Just a little frog in my throat. What's up?"

"I wanted to know if you needed me to bring anything home from the store for dinner tonight."

"You're on your way home?" *Panic!*

"Yeah, soon as I lock up here."

"Uh. Yeah, I really need some fructose." Dibbz had to go all the way to Boise for this unique item. Hopefully that would tie Kirstie up at the store for a while.

"*What* is fructose?"

"It's for my homemade apple pie."

"Oh. Well, okay. Be there in a bit." And she disconnected. Kirstie still had a habit of never properly ending a phone conversation.

Flying into action, I thanked my lucky stars for the foresight to leave everything on the counter to thaw. It shouldn't take long to cook. Opening the dinners, I saw they looked a little squishy. I slid the soupy enchiladas from each cardboard tray into a huge pot. The tacos went into the only other pan I could find. All this went onto the burners set at nine. The highest choice on the dial was ten, but that might be too hot. I mixed the rice and beans together into a bowl and placed it in the microwave for five minutes.

The enchiladas looked like they were liquefying in the pan. They didn't smell good either. Thinking they should be flipped over, I realized my mistake of not greasing the pan first. They were firmly stuck. The tacos didn't fare much better. I diced up some large hunks of tomato in a bowl and poured the salsa over it in a vain attempt to make it look homemade. Unfortunately, the diced jar tomatoes were a distinctly different color and consistency from the fresh tomato.

The pie was going to have to save me. I mushed down the once perfectly fluted edges and sprinkled sugar over the top. Voila! Homemade pie. No store would sell something this ugly; Kirstie would surely believe this pie was homemade. I shoved the deformed pastry into the cold oven.

I snatched up all the boxes and evidence of processed food and ran out the back door to Kirstie's next-door neighbor's trash bin and threw everything away. I could be a career criminal I was so cunning.

Running back into the house, the realization hit that with the pie box I had also thrown out the baking instructions. It needed to cook quickly, so I set the oven to the highest temp of five hundred degrees. Surely it would be done by the time we finished dinner.

*Dinner!*

The smell of smoke was beginning to permeate the kitchen. The black cloud confirmed my suspicion that something was indeed burning. I turned both burners off and opened the kitchen window just in time for Kirstie to make her entrance.

"What's the stench? You settin' fire to my kitchen?"

"Hi, Kirstie. How was your day?" I asked sweetly, ignoring her question.

"Why it was just fine, Mrs. Brady. Where's Greg, Peter, Marsha, and Bobby?" Kirstie's tone was pure sarcasm.

*susan case*

19

"Have a seat at the counter. Dinner will be served up in a jiffy."

Kirstie crinkled her nose in disgust. "If it's what I smell, no thank you!"

"It'll be great. The chips and my salsa will be right up. Can I get you a diet soda?"

Kirstie sighed with fatigue and nodded. She sat down at the one and only bar stool. Guess I'd have to eat standing at the sink. I pulled a diet cola from the fridge and got a glass out of the cupboard to put ice in. Twisting the ice tray produced no action on behalf of the cubes; they were immobilized. I ran the bottom of the tray under hot tap water just long enough for the cubes to fall into the sink. The cubes might have been salvageable, except there were still bits of tomato and green onion butts in the sink.

I poured salsa onto two plates then put the taco and enchiladas on top of that. It was no longer distinguishable which was taco and which enchilada. A huge handful of cheese covered the entire dish. Remembering the rice bean mix, I retrieved the bowl from the microwave. Two-thirds had exploded out of the dish and was splattered on the sides and top of the microwave's interior. The remainder in the bowl had a crust formed over the top. It looked like when mud dries out in the vast wastelands and curls into tiles of thinly dried earth—not particularly appetizing.

The salsa and chips now sat before Kirstie, along with the can of pop. She took a chip and dipped a good amount of salsa. It must have been okay, because she grabbed for another chip.

"Homemade thaltha?" Kirstie asked.

It took a minute to translate *thaltha* into *salsa*. "Yeah. How did you guess?"

She opened her mouth and pealed a store vegetable sticker off her tongue and held it out to me. "You're supposed to rinse your vegetables and remove their name tags before serving."

"Sorry."

I presented Kirstie with her dinner. She was eyeing it a little critically and very cautiously. "You think you got enough cheese on here?"

"Cheese is calcium, and calcium is good for you; builds strong bones."

"D'ya get a bonus from the united dairy council for endorsements?"

We both took our first bite at the same time. We both spit the food out at the same time.

"Are you trying to poison me?"

*Gag! Gag! Spit! Spit! Spit!*

I would have had a snappy retort, but I was too busy trying to scrape the top of my tongue off.

Kirstie took one swig from her cola and gargled with it then snatched her purse and keys off the counter. "C'mon."

"Where are we going?" *Was she going to drop me off in the desert somewhere?*

"The Pig Out or In. You are buying me dinner, and we will be discussing the consequences of lying."

I slunk out behind her, locking the door.

---

We arrived back at Kirstie's after consuming some good greasy food. I groveled and begged for Kirstie's forgiveness and promised never to lie, *to her anyway,* again.

There were lights, sirens, and emergency vehicles everywhere. The town's only two fire engines were parked out front catawampus in the middle of the street. A Hilltown cop car was there, and EMTs were milling about.

"What the—" Kirstie ran for the building entrance.

Bart, the volunteer fire chief, was just exiting the building and stopped her with a perfectly executed NFL stiff arm.

"Sorry about your door, Kirstie. You may want to turn your oven off before you leave the apartment next time."

"*Wha—Wha—*" Kirstie was having difficulty forming a coherent sentence *or word.*

"You want the good news or the bad news?" Bart asked.

Kirstie just stood there confused and mumbling while angry tenants shot glares at her. They were probably upset to have their dinner and *Wheel of Fortune* interrupted.

"Okay. Good news first," Bart said. "There was no fire damage 'cause there was no fire, just a lot of smoke."

"More good news. You'll be glad to know the sprinkler system in your apartment works." He hesitated. "Uh, now for the bad news. You got some serious water damage, and Bill smashed in your back window while we were breaking down your front door. Did you know you're probably the *only* person in Ditters Ferry to lock a door? Guess that's the price you pay for safety."

Kirstie turned round on me, and I experienced the fear that a Matador must know when he has run out of spears and is being charged by a bull with vengeful malice in its eyes.

"You!" she said, pointing a shaking finger at me. "You!"

I tried to get behind Bart, who was busy brushing particles of dead door off his pick ax.

"Get over here!" Kirstie meant business.

With my head hung low, I slowly shuffled over to her. The emergency crews and gawkers were dispersing and leaving the scene.

"I'm so sorry. Truly, truly sorry. I'll make it up to you. *Really.*"

How in the world to make up for this fiasco, I couldn't imagine. The only reason I stood before Kirstie now was because I was fairly certain she wouldn't kill me in front of all these witnesses. Half the town of Ditters Ferry had come by to see the spectacle.

"Get inside."

*Where there would be no witnesses? I don't think so!*

"It's a nice evening. Let's go for a walk," I helpfully suggested.

"Get your lazy, loser, lying, door-locking ass in there now!" She snapped her fingers and pointed simultaneously just like

22

Dibbz used to when she sent me to my room to clean it. I had never seen Kirstie quite so rigid.

Stepping over the jagged door pieces, we went into the apartment. There was a lovely breeze coming from the broken back window and blowing out the front door frame. Trying to put a positive spin on the situation, I decided this was a good thing, because the acrid smell of smoke and incinerated apples stung my nose and burned my eyes. The dampness did not improve the aroma in the room. Little droplets of water continued to sporadically fall from the sprinkler overhead. Every surface in the house was sodden. If Kirstie had a few more plants, her apartment would look a lot like the rain forest.

Gesturing to the sofa, she said, "Sit."

I headed to the barstool.

"No. Sit on the sofa."

"But it's all wet," I whined.

Kirstie made a low growling sound like a pit bull guarding its dinner bowl, so I sat. The water from the cushions instantly soaked uncomfortably through my jeans.

Kirstie began to pace. The carpet beneath her feet made sounds like a mud sucker gulping air.

"Here's what you are going to do." She paused and turned to me. "Tomorrow, you will clean this apartment top to bottom, side to side, front to back, and then clean it again. *Do not* even think about forgetting the oven. You will take the cushions and curtains and anything else that needs cleaning to CapaCity Laundry and have them professionally cleaned. You will haul the sofa frame and chairs outside to dry. Anything that is wood, you will dry and shine with lemon oil tonight. You will wash and dry every wall and surface in this place. Tonight you will sleep in the doorway so if a burglar stops by, hopefully he'll only steal *you!* Of course, it would have to be a burglar from out of town 'cause everybody here knows what a disaster you are. I am going to my mother's. When I get home from work tomorrow, this place better look as if it has never seen any catastrophe and

23

be fit for a layout in *Home Beautiful* magazine. Do you understand me?"

"Yes, ma'am." Although Kirstie is only five years older than me, yet a full nine inches shorter than me, I felt like a wayward child.

"When I get home tomorrow night, we are going to sit down and discuss your future."

"But I—"

Kirstie held up her hand. "Don't say a word. Not one single word." With that, she harrumphed out of the apartment.

*Some friend you are,* I thought. *Kick me while I'm down, why don't ya. After all I've been through recently, she could at least cut me a little slack.*

I looked up at a knocking sound. There was Jet standing in the open door frame.

"Uh, looks like you had some excitement here," Jet stated the obvious.

Perfect. Just perfect. The final straw of humiliation that was bound to break this camel's back.

"Need some towels?"

His half smile was my undoing. I cried like I'd never cried before—and I'd had a lot of practice the last few years—very unattractive, bodywrenching, loud, hiccupping, blubbering sobs.

"Looks like the dam busted." Jet put an arm around me and pulled my head to his chest.

"D-d-don't." I tried to pull away. "I'll m-m-mess up your sh-shirt."

"It cleans," he said, and he held me tight.

I don't know how long we stood there or which emotion to settle on: embarrassment because he was a spectator to my meltdown, or comfort because, well, he was here. Finally, the hiccupping reduced to a minimum.

"What brought you here?" I asked, staring at the floor.

"I followed the parade of emergency vehicles and trail of

smoke." I looked up and made a face. "Just kidding. I told you at the store I'd be seeing you."

"Why? Why do you want to see me?"

"We have unfinished business."

"Uh, I decided not to write the article seven years ago," I said, attempting to end the conversation. *I had such a crush on Jet during high school that I invented a reason my senior year to interview him about his football scholarship to BSU. The evening turned into an embarrassing disaster as he brought his girlfriend, Candace Kane, along with him. Candace threw a few degrading comments my way, making it clear that she knew the real purpose behind the meeting and that Jet only consented to the interview because he felt sorry for me. I quickly made an excuse to postpone the interview and end the evening.*

"That's not the business I'm referring to." He hesitated. "Later, we'll talk about why you ran out of the restaurant and then wouldn't answer my calls. Tonight, let's just see how much of this mess we can clean up."

We both looked around at the drenched ruin that was once Kirstie's flawlessly clean apartment. It was too big of a job, and I didn't know where to begin.

"I'll go get a wet/dry vac and some fans for the carpet. Why don't you find some towels and dry off all the furniture. I'll be right back." He turned around. "By the way, where are you sleeping tonight?"

*Wah!*

The sobbing started all over again with a ferocity that surprised and scared us both.

"I guess we'll talk about it when I get back."

Catching a glimpse of myself in the sooty foyer mirror, I considered my mascara-streaked, swollen-eyed, red, mottled face and came to the logical conclusion that he was never coming back.

I toweled off the last of the wood in the living room, thankful that Kirstie's extensive movie and CD collection were safe and dry inside a glass front cherry cabinet.

"Hey." Jet appeared in the doorway towing a wet/dry vacuum behind him like a stubborn puppy. He cradled a stack of extra towels in assorted colors and sizes with his free arm.

"Gotta go get the fans. Be right back." And he dashed back out.

I just stood there shocked, not believing he had returned to the scene of my crime.

After a few trips to his car, there were four huge, box-style fans parked in the hallway, whirring away. A plaid sleeping bag and pillow was set atop the newly cleaned and dried counter.

"Looks like you got a lot done," Jet complimented me.

"Hmm," was the most enthusiastic response I could come up with.

We both just started moving our own way to set about making the apartment right again. We worked until 3:30 the next morning, when I told Jet I couldn't do anymore.

"You gonna be okay here?"

"I'm fine. I'll lay a couple of plastic garbage bags under the sleeping bag to keep the water from seeping in. No worries."

He gave me a "yeah right" expression and hesitated. "Well, if you're sure, I guess I'll head out. I'm tired too."

Jet rested his chin atop my head and hugged me. "Sleep tight, and don't let the water bugs bite."

I let the water bug comment go. Placing my hand on his forearm, I looked up at him. "Jet, you've been terrific. Thank you for the help." This was said with every appreciative, sincere fiber of my tired being. I stood on my tiptoes and kissed his cheek.

"Jimi, the next time you kiss me . . . use better aim," he said and then left.

The sounds of footsteps on the walk and streaks of early morning sunshine awakened me. How many neighbors had walked by seeing me asleep in the plaid bag? I was too tired and stiff to care. Just hoped I hadn't been snoring. There wasn't a muscle or bone in my body that didn't ache with a burning intensity. Sitting up in my makeshift bed, I looked over the railing to the street below.

Still parked at the curb was Jet's Navigator. Inside, Jet rolled his head from side to side, apparently trying to work the kinks out of his neck. He started the SUV and pulled away. I couldn't help smiling. Jet had spent the night outside the apartment complex to ensure my safety. Either he *really, really* felt sorry for a pitiful geek like me, as Candy indicated our senior year of high school, or he was worried about me and truly cared. The motive didn't matter. Jet was no longer the enemy. There was also no going back, for a certainty; Jet Mitchell was going to break my heart.

*Resolution to self: next time Jet's in close proximity, use better aim.*

# chapter 2

The phone in Kirstie's apartment was demanding my attention, so I picked up the receiver.

"How's the apartment?" Kirstie barked into my ear.

"Good day to you too, Kirstie," I responded.

"Humph."

"The couch cushions and curtains are back from the laundry. I'm getting ready to hang the curtains now. The place will be perfect when you get home."

"Will you still be there?"

"Of course."

"Then it won't be perfect." *Click! Dial tone.*

"Good-bye to you too, Kirstie." I stuck my tongue out at the handset.

A large floral arrangement was centered beautifully on the pristine kitchen counter. The apartment sparkled with order and cleanliness. Store bought spaghetti sauce simmered in a newly purchased pot on the stove, and the garlic bread was ready to go in the oven when Kirstie arrived. The salad was in the fridge. It was very handy that a complete Caesar salad in a tidy little bag was available for the culinary challenged.

A large pot of salted water on the back burner waited to come to a boil, at which time the pasta would be added and the cooking time watched *carefully*. There was still a slight smell of smoke, but it wasn't too bad. The lemon oil I found in the linen closet had a clean, homey scent. The complex super had sent someone over to replace the door. The window was sealed with saran wrap-looking stuff and tacks. The glass guy would be here tomorrow to fix the back window.

All my belongings were neatly stacked in the hall closet out of the way, and not even a used drinking glass or errant magazine was in sight. Chocolate cake and vanilla ice cream would be presented for dessert. Maybe Kirstie wouldn't kick me out tonight. I was hoping the offer for a full month was still valid. When the Sunday classifieds arrived, I would be in hot pursuit of a job and a place to live. The unexpected cost of repairs had put a severe dent in the sock money Granddad had given me, so I was going to have to be very careful with my finances.

Kirstie arrived home a little after 6:00 p.m. She immediately started going through the apartment with an eagle eye. I followed her everywhere, hoping for a word of encouragement. She checked every nook and cranny, even running her finger over furniture to check for dust, as if everything hadn't just been thoroughly washed by the sprinkler system. She closely inspected the interiors of the oven and microwave. She made a face at the plastic covering the window where glass should be.

"The window guy will be here tomorrow afternoon."

"It still smells like smoke."

"Just barely, and everything is dry and clean," I offered. "Dinner is even cooking: spaghetti, garlic bread, and salad. There's even chocolate cake for dessert."

The look she gave me would have wilted a lesser person.

"Mmm-hmm. Did you steal Garfield's dinner, or will I find empty Spaghetti-O cans in the neighbors trash bin?"

"It's jar sauce and store-bought cake, but I did everything else. And there's no mess anywhere." I did a TV spokes-model impersonation and spread my arms wide, indicating the showplace around us.

Kirstie seemed resigned, if not pleased, with my presence. "Let's eat then. I had so many clients today I didn't get lunch."

"Business is that good?"

"Yeah. I'm actually thinking about building a bigger shop and taking on a tattoo artist. I get lots of requests for tatts. I might even take on another stylist."

"Can I help you at the shop? Maybe answer phones or sweep hair or something?"

"No," Kirstie said emphatically.

"No?"

"No," she said with more firmly resolute emphasis.

"Why?"

"You nearly destroyed my home, and you ask me why. I plan on building my business and saving money until I have enough to leave this town forever. I'm not taking the chance of you blowing up all my hard work. You are like all four horsemen of the apocalypse rolled into one."

I let that slide, mostly because I didn't have a sound defense. "Where will you go?"

"New York."

"Why New York? It's so far away."

"Being 'far away' is part of the attraction. Besides, I want to do hair and makeup for models and actors. Someday I want a whole line of products with my name on it."

"You've never mentioned this before. When did you decide to do all this?" I was surprised and impressed by all her goals.

"*You've* never asked. And I decided a long time ago. It's why I made the decision to go to beauty school. I have a talent and want to keep developing it and see how far it'll take me. It's not a dream; it's a goal. Talent is a gift you're born with. It's what you do with that talent that makes it yours. Unused talent is a waste that disgusts me."

She was looking me level in the eye, as if there was a point in there somewhere for me.

"Been writing lately?" Kirstie asked.

"Where did that come from?"

"You know exactly where that came from. *You* are a coward. One little setback and you give up without so much as a whimper. It makes me sick."

"It was no big deal then or now. Investigative writing was just a kid thing. I'm way past it now."

"Liar."

"You don't even know if I had any talent at all. What makes you think you know everything? Do they hand out psychology degrees at beauty college these days?"

"Yeah, it takes a real genius to figure out you haven't been happy with any job you've ever had. You have no passion whatsoever."

"You been talkin' to Dibbz?" I shoved my half-eaten spaghetti dinner away from me.

"No, but maybe you should be listening." Kirstie curled more strands of pasta around her fork and calmly continued to eat.

"I'm looking for a job. I promise."

"I'm not talking about a *job,* you idiot. I'm talking about doing something that gets you excited, something you love that will drive you to succeed, something that you wake up looking forward to each morning."

"You know what? I may need a job and a place to live, but what I *don't* need are people needling and nagging me about stuff they know nothing about."

"Well, at least I hit a nerve. I haven't seen you this worked up in years."

I stood to leave. "I'm going for a walk."

"Don't be gone too long. You have a kitchen to clean."

I let the slamming of the newly hung front door do my speaking for me.

# chapter 3

The receptionist at the *Ditters Weekly* newspaper office held up a finger to let me know she would be with me when she could. Only one job was posted in the paper this week. My luck seemed to be holding, because it was for a writer at the Weekly. Maybe God was trying to tell me something. He'd apparently been whispering in Dibbz' and Kirstie's ears to nag me incessantly about resuming my writing. And now the only job available in town was for a writer. Providence. I mentally waved the white flag of surrender in God's direction. Heaven knows listening to my own instincts hadn't turned out very well for me.

"He didn't?" The receptionist breathed aghast into the phone. "No!" Apparently, the other send said something shocking. "What are you going to do? You're *what?* Does he know?"

I was losing interest in the one-sided conversation. I sat down by a large grimy window in the only chair the room offered. Obviously there was a pressing issue to be concluded before the secretary would be turning her attention to me. Several large flies lay about in different postmortem poses across the window seal. A couple of flies were on their sides, while several were on their backs, feet straight up. One looked as if it were alive, so I gave it a little flick. It didn't fly, but I flicked it hard enough to send it soaring into the window frame. There it fell onto its back, feet straight up in the air. The preferred death position for flies, I gathered.

A thick layer of dust covered a plastic tree. It was a sad-looking tree in a plastic container with fake brown moss where potting soil should have been. It was a fake tree. I was a fake writer. We made a good pair.

I felt silly with my sample book on my lap. It contained

*susan case*

all the articles I had written for my high school paper. I also put in Mr. Davis's, my high school journalism teacher, letter of recommendation. At my age, there should be articles from established papers or magazines. But high school was the last I had written.

Why had I cared enough to bring the book? I didn't want to work for the Weekly. Still, it was a job, and after a lot of soul-searching, I decided to listen to the people who loved me. It was my burden to bear that the ones who loved me were a cold-hearted, sniping, vicious lot. Looking up, I mouthed, "That doesn't include you, God." I figured it would be good to keep Him on my side.

"Jimi Smith, Mrs. Greene will see you now. She pointed behind her to a scarred wooden door with a *Keep America Beautiful* poster taped to it. The tape had yellowed, and the edges of the poster were torn and curling. The irony made me smile. I tapped lightly on the door and waited.

"Just go on in," the receptionist said.

I stepped forward into the room and backward in time. The sculpted carpet was a faded olive green. Mrs. Greene's desk was made from heavy metal and painted turquoise. It looked like a leftover from WWII. There was an old wooden chair across from the desk. The only other furniture was a small divan and rickety-looking brown metal filing cabinet. The divan was upholstered in taupe-ivory with pictures of rust colored wagon wheels and sagebrush. The filing cabinet had seen better days. Two of the drawers were partially open with papers sticking out. One of the drawers was at a tilt and couldn't be closed even if there weren't files sitting higher than the drawer could accommodate.

Mrs. Greene also looked to be pre-WWII. She was fifty-fiveish with mousy brown hair streaked with frizzy gray and pulled back into a severe bun. Her cat-eye tortoiseshell glasses were a throwback to the early fifties. And where she found a mint-colored, double-breasted, bubbly, polyester suit in this day and age completely mystified me.

"Have a seat," she said crisply.

I sat in the wooden chair. One of the legs was shorter than the rest, which made the chair rock back and forth.

"Stop fidgeting," Mrs. Greene snapped at me.

"Yes, ma'am." I leaned hard to the back right to keep the chair in place.

"You're here about the community events writer's job," she stated.

I nodded in case I was supposed to concur.

"I don't think you're qualified for the position, but the new *boss* told me to give you a chance." She spat out the word *boss* as if it were a swear word.

What should a person say to that?

"What's *that* on your lap?" She pointed to my work portfolio as if it were rancid garbage.

"It's a book with samples of my writing." I was truly wishing now that I hadn't brought it.

"Like it matters how you write," she said sarcastically, dismissing my book with an abrupt wave. "The job is yours if you want it. You'll start at $1,850 per month. No benefits for the first six months. If you last six months, you will be eligible for medical insurance. The employee pays $175 of the premium each month. An optional retirement plan will be offered at the end of a year. But a year is a long time away."

"You're offering me the position?" I asked, confused.

"Don't give me that innocent why-am-I-getting-this-job look. We both know better. Do not ever underestimate me or my intelligence," she retorted.

"Look, Mrs. Greene. I have no idea what you are talking about or why you have a problem with me. I saw the ad in the paper for the position and submitted an application and résumé. If I'm not qualified *don't* hire me."

"If you think I'm going to let a manipulating little snip like you get me in dutch with the new boss, you're crazy. But don't think for even a second that your employment here is anything

*susan case*

35

more than a joke. We both know why you're here and how you got this job over more qualified people."

I was dumbfounded.

"You'll start on Tuesday. That's the first day of our next pay period. Be here at 7:00 a.m. sharp. Of course, if you're late, who'll care? It's not as if you'll get fired now, is it? But sooner or later he'll tire of you, and then we can hire a real writer."

"Who'll tire of me? You're not making any sense." I was standing now with hands on hips, feeling angry heat burning my cheeks.

"Sweetie, you should go into acting. You'd have a fine career. Couches make great launching pads for careers in Hollywood, I hear."

"That's it. I'm done." I turned to leave.

"I'll tell you what, Miss Sweet and Innocent. If you really need answers, go ask the new editor in chief."

I stormed out of Mrs. Greene's office and asked the receptionist where I could find the editor in chief.

"He's in a meeting right now with the production assistant. Would you like to wait in his office?"

"Sure." Steam was surely misting off the back of my neck.

The receptionist ushered me into an obviously newly remodeled office. The décor was rich and masculine, but not in an intimidating way. I could picture a mature man in a tweed jacket smoking a pipe and sipping fine brandy while perusing a classic Dickens tale. I liked the room and the faint presence of a man's cologne. The distinctive scent of the cologne reminded me of someone.

"What may I do for you, Jimi?"

I turned to see Jet enter the room. "I'm waiting to see the new editor in chief. What are you doing here? Do you have an appointment with him too? I can wait outside until you're done."

"I apparently do have an appointment. What can I do for you?"

The light bulb was not illuminating, the hamster in my head having paused mid-stride on the wheel.

"I just told you I need to see the editor in chief." Was the man daft or hard of hearing?

"Have a seat. May I get you anything? Sweet tea perhaps?"

"No. I'll just wait for the editor. Thank you." *Poor guy is having mental problems.*

"Jimi, *I am* the editor."

My newest resolution came back to me full force. *Next time you're around Jet, use better aim.* I was looking for something to throw at him *with perfect aim.*

"You feel so sorry for me that you're giving me a job? While Mrs. Greene thinks I got the job from doing 'couch' time. I am *not* a charity case, Mr. Mitchell, editor in chief, and you can take—"

"Jimi, before you get to the 'sun don't shine' place, you need to know that you did not get this job because I felt sorry for you. You got this job because I remember what an excellent writer you are."

I took a deep breath, preparing to unleash a verbal attack.

But Jet held up his hand and continued. "Just in case I remembered incorrectly, I had the school send over every article and essay you had ever written. The truth is, Jimi, you have real talent. Or at least you did, and I'd like to find out if you still have that talent and the same passion for writing."

If one more person used the word passion, I was going to explode. Jobs were paychecks, nothing more.

"Yeah, Jet? Then why aren't you living *your* dream. You have a talent, and I heard you got a great offer from the Pros as a wide receiver. So why are you back here in Ditters Ferry?"

Jet sat down on the edge of the mahogany-colored leather chair and lifted his pant leg. *Where was this going?* Then I saw the ugliest scar I had ever seen. It was about six inches long, raised, and a dark, purplish red with dots of the same angry color on both sides of the scar. It looked like a huge centipede.

*susan case*

37

"I didn't give up on my dream or talent. I blew out my ACL during training camp. After two operations, I can walk just fine, even jog. But I will never be able to play football again, especially not professional football. My dad is planning to retire in a few years, and he asked if I would oversee some of his business ventures. Since I majored in Business Administration, it seemed like a good fit. I took stock of my life and made new goals."

I was such a schmuck. "Jet, I am so sorry. I should have asked."

"Yes, you should have." Jet held out his hand to me. "Will you take this job and help me grow this paper into something to be proud of? I need you, Jimi. The business part I can handle, but I want vision and drive and a writer with personality and flair. I believe you are that person." His thumb, gently rubbing over my knuckles, was very distracting.

"I'll be here at 7:00 a.m. sharp on Tuesday. But Jet . . ."

"Yeah?"

"If I don't cut it, promise me you'll get rid of me fast. No special favors."

"Jimi, for the good of the paper, I'll fire you if I have to, but I have no intention of getting rid of you."

His phone rang and he moved to answer it. I waved good-bye and headed out. What have I gotten myself into now? But at $1,850 a month, I would definitely be able to afford my own apartment. Independence. What a beautiful word. Having Jet for a boss seemed a little tricky though, because I wasn't sure that was the type of relationship I wanted with Jet. That was a lie; I knew exactly what type of relationship I wanted.

---

Turned out it was a moot point. I'd been at the paper for more than a week and had yet to see Jet. Mrs. Greene, my immediate supervisor, still hadn't warmed up to me. She avoided speaking to me for the most part. When she absolutely had to talk to me, she used an acid tone and made numerous cutting remarks.

However, on a more positive note, I had moved out of Kirstie's apartment and into my very own studio unit. The leasing agent confirmed my employment and with first and last month's rent and small cleaning deposit paid, I had my own place. Sutter's Complex was my new abode. The name sounded more like a psychological ailment than an apartment building, but at $485 a month plus utilities, it was perfect. I had exactly $13.54 left and was going to have to eat on that money for the next two weeks, at which time I'd be receiving my first check from the paper.

"Smith!" Mrs. Greene yelled harshly.

"Yes, Mrs. Greene?"

"Where's the dog show article?"

"In your kennel," I muttered under my breath. "The article is in your new copy basket."

"I'm sure it's crap," she snapped.

*Then I'm sure you'll circle it, sniff it, and try to bury it.*

"I'm assigning you Evening Lawn Chair duty tonight. Have your article ready by 7:00 a.m. tomorrow."

Mrs. Greene was a real piece of work. The Evening Lawn Chair Gathering along the banks of the Snake River didn't even start until sunset and usually lasted until past midnight. Then I'd still have to convert my notes into a story.

How the heck was I supposed to make the Lawn Chair gathering interesting? A bunch of old farts sat around in outrageously decorated chairs at the river's edge, swatting at hordes of gnats and mosquitoes. They told farfetched stories by firelight and watched the river flow by. The gathering was held each month during the full moon from April until October. Obviously, the threat of West Nile Virus was of little concern. The Gathering show must go on.

Actually, I'd never been. There was an unspoken fear in the back of my mind wherein I envisioned a cauldron by the riverbank and the attendees performed ritual stray cat and/or badger sacrifice ceremonies. I'll just have to garner some courage, bug repellent, an industrial size garlic necklace, and buy the bright-

*susan case*

39

est flashlight available. There was absolutely no way I would be caught in the dark at . . . ominous background music was playing in my head . . . *the Gathering.*

"Smith!"

I jumped at the piercing sound of Mrs. Greene's voice.

"What?"

"Take Daniel with you. We'll need photos of the different chairs and people," Mrs. Greene commanded.

Mrs. Greene was walking toward me with a sour look when she glanced toward the door. An actual sincere smile spread across her face when she saw the woman entering. The smile made her look ten years younger and almost attractive.

"Sylvia, thanks for coming. I really needed a night out," Mrs. Greene gushed.

"Hello, Harry. I wouldn't miss a night out with you. It must be a special occasion for you to call me twice in one month."

Whomever this Sylvia person was, she was dressed to the nines. She also had a lot of courage to be calling Mrs. Greene "Harry."

It was difficult for me to imagine anyone calling Mrs. Greene by a first name, but a nickname like Harry?

Sylvia was presumably in her early fifties also, but stunningly attractive. Her thick, chestnut, shoulder-length hair was perfectly coiffed and held back by a decorative gold clip. Sylvia was chic, elegant, and formal from the top of her lustrous head of hair to the designer silk pantsuit and down to her expensive, pointy-toed, high-heeled shoes. Sylvia's buttonless wrap blouse would open when she moved a certain way, exposing a tiny bit of lacy lingerie. She wore an ostentatious ring on her index finger that went from her knuckle to the first joint. It was a large opal surrounded by six fairly good-sized diamonds on each side of the oval stone, all set in heavy antique gold. This was a woman who exuded confidence in her sex appeal. Basically, she was the antithesis to Mrs. Greene in her dated, buttoned to the throat, pilled polyester suits.

"I'd really like to try that new Italian restaurant in Boise I've heard so much about. The chef is getting rave reviews, and the wines are supposed to be unsurpassed in the area," Mrs. Greene suggested.

"That sounds wonderful." Sylvia's head tilted in my direction. "Aren't you going to introduce me?"

I had been sitting there in rapt attention, looking like a Wimbledon tennis match attendee, turning my head from speaker to speaker during their brief conversation. Mrs. Greene had a friend? This seemed unfathomable, and yet here was someone willing to spend time with her, and apparently *twice* in one month.

Mrs. Greene grunted a reluctant introduction. "Sylvia, this is Jimi. Jimi pretends to be a writer here. Basically, she wants an easy paycheck. Of course, she does have an important and generous friend in a high position."

Sylvia trilled a laugh at the obvious connotation of *friend*. My anger was boiling just beneath the surface.

"Let me close up my office and get my keys; then we'll head out."

As soon as Mrs. Greene was out of hearing range, Sylvia laid a perfectly manicured hand on my forearm. The ring felt cold and heavy on my skin. "She can be a colossal pain, huh? She could suck the joy out of a two-year-old getting a first taste of ice cream." Sylvia sighed as if carrying a heavy burden. "She needs a friend though, so here I am."

Although Mrs. Greene was my arch nemesis, it was sickening to hear Sylvia betray her. Kirstie may be a sharp-tongued beast at times, but I would never verbalize that thought out loud to anyone. *One,* I couldn't be that disloyal, and *two,* Kirstie would kill me.

"I'm sure you are an excellent writer because you know how to use and parlay every advantage, including using *friends* in high places. I'm on my fourth husband, each one more powerful and rich than the previous." Sylvia was chock full of character—unfortunately, all of it bad. Mrs. Greene was on her way back. "Be smart and bide your time. A resourceful girl like you will replace a hardworking shrew who relies on ethics alone any day."

Sylvia could star in her own television mini-series: *Touched by a Devil.* I definitely needed to exorcise my arm where this she-demon had touched me, and with her garish finger amulet no less. Sylvia was faithless treachery wrapped in a pretty designer package. What's worse, she seemed to think I was just like her and appreciated her deceitfulness.

"Don't forget to call Daniel for those pictures," Mrs. Greene barked at me, returning to the room.

"Maybe you should write it down for her in purple crayon on a sticky note, Harry." Sylvia giggled to Mrs. Greene.

They both laughed and walked away arm in arm. Sylvia winked at me behind Mrs. Greene's back. Beyond certainty Sylvia must be on a first name basis with Lucifer.

*Dear God, please protect me from all life's evils, in particular, Sylvia. Amen.*

I decided to get my call to Daniel out of the way. He was the newspaper's freelance photographer. Daniel's parents were extremely well off financially and very generous to their only son. His only working contract was with the Weekly. When Daniel was bored, which was often, he hung around the office. Resting a hip on the corner of my desk, he'd chat incessantly until I shooed him away. He was evidently not offended, because he just kept coming back. Truth was, he was an outrageous flirt, and I couldn't help but like him. Daniel was a very good-looking guy with the bad-boy charismatic smile of a pirate out to secure (*or procure*) his next wench. He was tall, blonde, tan, athletic, blue-eyed, basically your modern day Adonis. His hair was messed up so perfectly that it must have been artfully and purposefully arranged, giving him that naughty all-American boy look. A person couldn't take him seriously, but he was a lot of fun.

"Hello."

"Hey, Daniel. It's Jimi."

"I knew you'd breakdown and come chasing after me," he teased.

"Yes, yes, yes. I couldn't take it anymore. I must fulfill my lifelong dream of chasing down a rarely employed, arrogant playboy—emphasis on *boy*—to trifle with my emotions and then set me aside. Ooh, baby. Ooh, baby. Yeah."

"All right." He laughed. "What do you want?"

"I got Lawn Chair Gathering duty tonight, and the Mean Greene Crushing Machine wanted me to call you. She thinks we need pics of the event."

"Gotta love the small town flavor, don't ya," he said. "I'll pick you up at 8:45."

"You know where I live?" I just barely had moved in.

"Jimi, it's Ditters Ferry."

As in all small towns, everyone seems to know everything about everybody. This factor could be a comfort or an intrusion depending on the given situation.

"I'll see you at a quarter to nine. I'll wait for you out front."

"By the way, Jimi, you're wrong about me being a boy. I'm all man."

There was a sexual undercurrent to Daniel's tone. I hung up. Carrying on that dialog would definitely be a mistake.

*Ahem!* A throat cleared behind me.

Glancing over my shoulder, I found a furious-looking Jet.

"Who were you talking to?" he demanded.

"Daniel Forsythe. Why?"

"Are you making a date on company time?" Jet made it sound more like an accusation than a question.

"No, Mr. Nosy. Mrs. Greene wanted me to call him. I was assigned the Lawn Chair Gathering tonight, and she wants photos."

"What was that '*Ooh, baby*' stuff? And why does he need to pick you up. You have a car." His words came out sounding like the staccato firing of a 1920's tommy gun.

"Well, excuse me, Mr. Mitchell. Are you telling me I can't ride in a car with Daniel?"

His tone and stance relaxed a little, but only with concerted effort. "No, Jimi. What I'm trying to tell you is that not every guy is a nice guy. Daniel is a competent photographer, but he's also a womanizer."

"I think I can take care of myself. Daniel is a harmless flirt."

"You don't have a clue, do you?"

"No, Tarzan. Me just empty-headed little Jane who doesn't recognize jungle beast using bad pick-up vines."

"That's not what I meant. *Pick-up vines?*"

"You know what? I'm leaving. I've been here since 6:45 this morning, haven't had lunch; plus I have to be at that stupid Gathering until probably after midnight and my story in by 7:00 a.m. tomorrow. I'm tired and quite frankly a little sick of being ordered around." I got my purse and keys out of the side drawer and proceeded to shut down my PC.

"Why do you have to have it in by tomorrow? Deadline isn't until Thursday."

"Ask Mrs. Greene. In the meantime, see ya." I headed for the door.

"Jimi, wait. Let me take you out to dinner."

Mrs. Greene came back into the office to retrieve her jacket at exactly that moment with Sylvia trailing right behind her. Mrs. Greene pursed her lips in a smirk, while Sylvia gave me a knowing, approving smile. This was too much!

"No, thank you, Mr. Mitchell. I already have a dinner engagement." I pushed past Greene and Sylvia and stormed out.

---

Sticking my head in the door, I said, "Yoo-hoo, Dibbz, Granddad."

"We're in the kitchen," Dibbz called out.

Granddad was sitting at the table and to my astonishment

*fully clothed.* Granddad had a propensity for sitting around the house in his t-shirt and underwear. Granddad in his BVDs is a sight no one should have to behold. He looks a lot like Humpty Dumpty with his bald head, white body, skinny legs, and round belly. I bent to kiss his cheek. I was surprised to realize just how much I had missed seeing my grandparents every day. "What's for dinner?" I asked, directing the question to Dibbz.

"Gluten-free pasta with roasted cherry tomatoes and spinach pesto."

"Yum."

Dibbz, standing at the sink, looked over her shoulder to see if I was being sarcastic. *I wasn't.* I was sincerely thankful for any free meal. Especially now that I only had eleven dollars and change left after the two Klondike ice cream bars I devoured after leaving the office in a huff.

"Thank you for the invite to dinner. I've really missed you guys. Where's Spence?"

"He's out with Karli," Dibbz answered.

"Wow! They've been dating for an entire three weeks now, haven't they?"

"Four. She's a nice girl, and he seems fond of her. Of course, he's so busy with football and homework that they don't get to go out much, which is a good thing if anyone cares for my opinion. Karli seems like the kind of girl who wants to get married and start a family right out of high school. Spence has other plans."

"Did his scholarship come through to Oregon State?" I asked.

"You haven't heard?" Dibbz looked surprised.

"Spence got a full ride. Between his academic and baseball scholarship, he won't have to come up with a dime." This was from Granddad, who looked so proud he could burst.

"Well, good for Spence," I said, meaning it. "Wish I got to see him more." I missed my little brother. We lived in the same small town but rarely got together.

*susan case*

45

I heard the back door open, and Spence came in through the mudroom.

"Hey, Jimi. Burned down any buildings lately?" Spence flashed a smile.

"No, brat, and I've never burned down a building."

"Well, not for lack of trying." Spence grinned. "How's the new place?"

"It's great. Come visit me sometime, why don'tcha."

"I try not letting anyone know we're related since you're known as the town kook."

"Oh, you're just a million laughs." I gave him a playful shove.

"What's for dinner, Dibbz?" Spence wanted to know.

"I thought you were going out to dinner with Karli. Where is she anyway?" Dibbz inquired.

"She wasn't feeling well, so I took her home," Spence answered.

"Did you put gas in the car?" Dibbz asked.

"I only went a couple of miles."

"Did you put gas in the car?" Dibbz demanded for the second time.

"No. I'll give you five bucks, okay. Jeez." Spence sat at the table.

"I just don't want you to become irresponsible or selfish." Dibbz leveled a look at me.

"Hey, I'm working and have my own place. Don't give me the evil eye," I responded to her glare.

"We're so proud of you, Jimi, working at the paper and all." Granddad could always be counted on to pour the proverbial oil on troubled waters.

"Thanks, Granddad. My pieces are fluff, but hopefully something interesting will come my way eventually."

"You just keep working hard, sweetie. Good things will happen." Granddad is such a peach. JJ, full name Janice Joplin, waddled in with her tail wagging ferociously. Her corpulent belly swayed like a pendulum from side to side. JJ is Dibbzy's fat little gray and brown wirehaired terrier with giant plastic daisies on her collar. "I guess she missed you."

I bent to pet her.

"I don't know how that dog gets so fat on the diet dog food I feed her. Just look at her." Dibbzy gestured toward the dog.

Spence and I exchanged grins, while Granddad studied the floor intently. Granddad frequently takes "fast-food finding excursions" disguised as a walk with the dog. Both master and dog reap the regular rewards of Twinkies, cookies, potato chips, and french fries.

"I guess I'll have to find another brand of dog food with fewer calories and less fat." Dibbz switched topics. "Put a pot-holder on the table, Juliet. I'll have the pasta out in a jiffy. Oh, and set out some plates, silverware, and glasses."

I went to the cupboard and got the dishes out to set the table. "Spence, get the silverware."

We all sat down at the little table after Dibbz put the color-ful mosaic ceramic casserole dish in the center.

"No meat?" Spence asked.

"There's tofu in the fridge," Dibbz replied.

"Dibbz, tofu isn't meat," Spence stated the obvious.

"It's a better protein."

"Couldn't you scrounge up a free-range, no hormone, organic chicken somewhere?"

"Why, when firm tofu is just as good and a whole lot health-ier and cheaper?"

"I'm going for a walk after dinner, Spence. Wanna join me and JJ?" Granddad asked.

Spence perked right up. "Sure. That'd be great."

I sensed there was going to be a greasy burger from the Pig Out in Spence and Granddad's near future. Granddad on a walk could only mean one thing: a reconnaissance mission for fast food.

"Good for you, Jonathon. A walk is so healthy for you. I'd

*susan case*

47

come along, but I'm just plain tired out from working in the garden all day."

Sighs of relief echoed in the room.

Granddad patted Dibbzy's hand. "Just you take a nice little rest, Doobie. You already get plenty of exercise."

She had an almost smile, which was the equivalent of a belly laugh for anyone else. These two eccentric opposites really did love each other. I felt lonely all of a sudden. I had never made time for dating and hadn't really missed it, but lately, well, suffice to say something, or someone, was definitely missing from my life.

At a quarter after eight, I said my good-byes and headed to my apartment. I'd call it a home, but with no pictures and no furniture other than one chair and a couch purchased from the thrift store, it really couldn't be called a *home* yet.

I changed into a faded pink tank top with a sheer, long sleeve blouse over it. It was still pretty warm out even in the evenings, but I'd need something for protection from the bugs. Old worn jeans, ratty tennis shoes, and a John Deere ball cap completed my ensemble. This outfit was created especially so Daniel wouldn't interpret any wrong signals.

Outside standing on the curb, I waited looking for Daniel's fire engine red Corvette. He pulled up at precisely 8:45.

"Right on time." I raised my voice to be heard over the revving engine.

Daniel gave me the once over and, judging by his expression, found my outfit *lacking*. "Hop in. We don't want to miss anything."

We both laughed at that. He handed me his camera bag to hold.

We headed out old airport way and took the dirt cutoff road to the river. "Why is the boss following us?" Daniel asked after checking the rearview mirror.

"Huh?" I turned to look back and, sure enough, there was Jet's Navigator right behind us.

"You got me." I shrugged.

"Yeah, that's probably why."

"What?" For the life of me, I could not imagine why Jet would come out to this ridiculous town affair.

"Jimi, you're such an innocent."

"Compared to you, Hugh Hefner and Larry Flynt are innocent. So I won't take offense."

He tried to sound sincere. "I'm not a player."

"Yes, you are. But I like you anyway."

Daniel waggled his eyebrows at me. "How much do you like me?"

"Enough not to take you seriously."

"Jimi, you wound me deeply." He placed his hand over his heart in a melodramatic fashion that made me laugh.

We got out of the car, and I handed Daniel his camera bag. He bent to retrieve the lighting equipment tucked behind the front seats.

Ten acres of empty field, but Jet parked right beside Daniel's Corvette. Jet got out and went to the back of the Navigator and extracted two lawn chairs and a cooler.

"Jimi, wanna give me a hand with these chairs?" Jet asked.

"Sure. Where do you want them?" I picked up a chair in each hand.

"Somewhere in the mix of things, I guess." He nodded toward the gathering crowd.

"Your chair is a little tame for this gig, isn't it?" I noted the plain blue- and white-striped folding chairs.

"I'm here to observe, not *compete*."

Daniel snorted a laugh of disagreement then tried to cover it up by coughing.

"Forsythe," Jet acknowledged Daniel with a curt nod.

"Boss." Daniel nodded back. "What brings you here?"

Why do men look like Pez dispensers when they greet each other? Head back, nod, head back, nod. I'm always waiting for the little pastel candy to pop out of their necks. There was a

*susan case*

pause while Jet and Daniel stared at each other. They looked as if they were sizing each other up the way boxers do when they're told to tap gloves before heading to their neutral corners.

"I thought I should mingle with the community, get them used to me being involved in the happenings around town," Jet said by way of explanation.

"Uh-huh." Daniel sounded skeptical.

I had to admit it did sound a little feeble.

"Boys," I attempted to get their attention, "shall we get moving? I have a story to write, and these chairs are getting heavy."

"Let's sit over by Emma's chair," Jet suggested.

Daniel and I looked ahead, squinting.

"She has the chair decorated like a covered wagon." Jet motioned with his head because both hands were occupied supporting a cumbersome picnic cooler.

A hundred yards up to the left was rail-thin Emma Sinclair, bent in half as she set up her chair. Her spine was not curved from task but from years of hard living. Emma was ninety if she were a day old. Her wooden folding chair had a slat bench-type seat. On either side was a replica of a wagon wheel that neatly hid the chair legs. Some crafty carpenter had made a tan canvas cover that truly resembled a covered wagon top.

Emma was busy tying a faded, flower print, ruffled prairie bonnet under her papery turkey neck as we approached. The bonnet's tie strings drew emphasis to her brown, mottled skin and deeply etched network of wrinkles. Emma even had on a layered pioneer-style dress that she surely must have been sweltering in.

"Jarret Mitchell, as I live and breathe. How are you, son? And how's your daddy? I hear tell he upped and retired. And him being so young and all. Don't understand that nary a bit."

Jet's dad was sixty-three and still ran several of his business enterprises. Not quite the lazy young pup Emma made him out to be.

"Hello, Ms. Sinclair. It's a pleasure to see you. Your chair is quite something. Who made it for you?" Jet neatly sidestepped Emma's questions.

Emma preened at the implied compliment. "Hoody Jacks made this for me. I told him what I wanted, and he made it right up. That boy's dumber than a box of rocks, bless his heart, but he sure can do fine woodwork."

Emma felt it was her right to say *anything* so long as it was followed up with "bless its/his/her heart." I overheard her once at the grocery store tell a flustered cashier, "Your momma sure is getting fat, bless her heart." Another time she told a new young mother that her baby "Sure is a homely little critter, bless its heart." As far as Hoody was concerned, I didn't know if he was dumb or smart. I never heard him say anything more than "hello" or "fine day, ain't it?" He was also never without a big, friendly, gap-toothed smile.

Hoody Jacks lived behind the local convenience store in a one-room house that had seen a lot of weather without the refreshment of new paint. Broken windows were boarded up, and several pieces of roofing were missing. The front porch sagged, and the yard was nothing more than waist-high weeds and rusting discarded appliances.

Hoody survived off odd jobs like pulling weeds and white-washing fences. Unfortunately, he never applied these working skills to his own place. Town gossips said he made homebrewed liquor with corn he stole from local fields. Every day Hoody wore the same dirty black coveralls with a stained handkerchief wafting out of his hip pocket and a red plaid shirt. He always let one strap of the coveralls hang down his back so the front corner of the bib flapped forward at an angle. The cuffs of his sleeves were filthy and frayed. He was also one of those people whom you couldn't put an age to. He could be anywhere from thirty-five to sixty. When he'd arrived in town about fifteen years previous, no one could find out where he came from, and believe me, every busybody had tried their best. Hoody was secretive

*susan case*

about his past. But heck, in Ditters Ferry characters aren't just welcomed; *they're expected.*

"Well, he did a fine job on that chair of yours, Ms. Sinclair," Jet remarked. "Mind if I set up our seats next to yours?" he asked, indicating the two folding chairs.

"Them's pitiful looking things." Emma was looking askance at the generic seats. "It's darned embarrassing."

"This is Jet's first time at the gathering," Daniel explained. "Why don't you give him some ideas and maybe a blueprint for a special chair? Jimi and I have work to do, so begging your pardon, Ms. Sinclair," he gave a two finger salute from his right eyebrow, "we'll excuse ourselves. You and Jet have a nice chat. We'll be back later."

Jet looked like he was going to strangle Daniel first chance he got. As we were moving away, Emma could be heard prattling on and on about potential chair designs.

"You could have one that looks like a fairy . . ."

*Fairy?* This gave me a good giggle as I pictured Jet in a fairy chair complete with sparkly wings and pixie wand.

"Get a pilot wheel and pontoons for legs . . ."

Oh, *ferry,* like the boat. The light bulb went on, but I still preferred the other image.

"Jet's gonna have your hide for leaving him alone with Emma."

"He'll be fine." Daniel snickered. "Why don't you start milling around and getting nosy while I snap some shots?"

"Sounds good. Catch up with you later." I headed toward the river's edge where the most outlandish chairs were arranged. There was a giant potato; a bathtub-looking thing; and a short, stubby tree with a seat notched into it. Ditters Ferry is beyond eccentric; it's just plain weird. The bathtub chair, however, was the most disturbing. The occupant was sixty-seven-year-old, pasty, pudgy Mr. Grinnel sporting a nude colored Speedo and waving a purple nylon-netted dainty wash puff. I tried beating a hasty retreat before he spotted me. There was no way to interview him with a straight face and maintain my gag reflex as well.

"Yo, Nancy Drew. You here to interview the gathering clan?" Mr. Grinnel hollered at me. He was so loud that I couldn't possibly pretend not to have heard him.

"Yes, and I have a lot of ground to cover, so if you'll—"

"Come look at my tub. It's a pip, isn't it?"

I kept my eyes firmly focused on his nose, intending to look no lower than his chin at the utmost.

"This is my finest chair yet. Took me almost six weeks to get it completed, but it sure is worth it. Jenny said she wouldn't be seen with me in my tub. I don't understand that woman a bit. So I made her a fine outhouse chair complete with swinging door and crescent moon cutout. Did she appreciate all my hard work? *No!* When she saw it, she kicked me in the shin and said she wasn't gonna be squatting in public in no outdoor crapper. The woman has no imagination whatsoever, and my shin still smarts."

That was probably the only "smarts" Mr. Grinnel possessed. Personally, I would have kicked him in the head and burned down his workroom. "That's a tub, all right," was the best comment I could come up with for his nightmare monstrosity.

I remember once reading that Janet Leigh, after filming Hitchcock's *Psycho,* was unable to take a shower for years. Now I understood how she felt. I'm a shower person myself, but because of Mr. Grinnel's get-up I would never be able to take a tub bath again. *Ever!* Anthony Perkins wielding a butcher's knife is far less disturbing than Mr. Grinnel in a puckered-up Speedo.

"Before next month's gathering, I'm gonna paint the side of my tub with the name I gave it."

You'd think I would know better than to ask, "So, what are you going to name your chair?"

"Stud in Suds." He grinned.

*susan case*

53

Elmer Fudd in Suds would be more appropriate, but it wasn't mine to christen. Better just leave him to his delusions.

"Well, Mr. Grinnel, it's been nice speaking with you. I really should go talk to some of the other folks, though."

"Do you think fancy boy will put my picture in the paper?" Mr. Grinnel asked hopefully.

*Fancy Boy.* Daniel would love that.

"I'll send Daniel over to take your picture. Ask him to take several pictures in numerous positions. We want the best shot, don't we?"

Mr. Grinnel looked ecstatic about the idea and was already trying out poses.

"Bye, Mr. Grinnel."

"Buh-bye, Nancy."

*Let it go,* I told myself before getting trapped into another conversation with him. I was also terrified that my gaze might inadvertently drift to the hairy white paunch above the Speedo, and then I'd be sick.

There was a secluded spot at the river's edge surrounded by shrubs and a couple of scraggly trees. That would be a good place to collect myself and cowgirl up the courage to interview a few more whacked out chair designers. Stepping carefully, as the sun had fallen below the mountaintops and it was getting dark, I headed toward an isolated location. A few feet before the bank, I tripped on an exposed tree root and fell face first, just missing the water's edge by inches.

Directly in front of me, caught up in a tangle of reeds and shrubs, was something resembling a giant, tube-shaped buoy. Wait a minute. Was that a belt buckle? Still lying flat on my tummy, I parted the shrubs to get a better view. There amongst the flotsam, floating face up, was a middle-aged male body with a shiny metal object sticking through his horribly bloated chest. The eyes were open, but there were vacant sockets where the eyeballs used to be. His feet were bare, and purple rings were visible around each ankle. A large, black slug had made a home on his cheek. I couldn't scream because it was taking too much effort not to throw up.

Scrambling to my feet, I ran toward where Jet was still sitting with Emma, falling twice before reaching him. There were twigs in my hair, and my blouse was torn. My jeans were filthy and my knees had taken a beating and burned like fire. The palms of my hands were scraped and bleeding.

"Jet, come here. Quick," I hoarsely whispered.

"What happened to you? Are you hurt? Where is that jerk?" Jet was up in a flash in a fighter's stance.

"What jerk?" I paused for a moment. "You know what? Never mind. You've got to come with me now." I grabbed his hand and began dragging him toward the spot where the eyeless body bobbed in the reeds.

"Excuse us, Emma," Jet said apologetically.

"What's going on? Are you okay? Did someone hurt you?"

"Shush!" I began pulling him along.

As soon as we were out of Emma's hearing range, I said, "Jet, there's a dead guy floating over here."

That got his attention, and he started moving a lot faster. When we got near where the body was, I pointed it out.

"Right through there." I was unwilling to take another step. One encounter with the eyeless bloated bobber was enough for me.

Jet made his way the last few yards. "Call the police, Jimi. But do it from where no one can overhear you."

"I don't have a cell phone."

"Jimi, *everyone* has a cell phone. We'll discuss later why you need one." He tossed me his set of keys. "My phone is on the console in the car."

The run to Jet's Navigator left me completely out of breath. It took three tries to get the key in the door lock because my hands were shaking so badly. Then I looked at the clicker key chain and mentally berated myself for not simply pressing the unlock button.

Jet's car smelled so good; expensive sexy cologne, leather seats, and new car scents intermingled. I wanted to take my time and have a good sniff fest. *Oh, yeah! Dead body!* Grabbing the cell phone, I dialed 911.

"911. State your emergency please?"

"I'm at the river, and there's a dead bobby here. Uh, body."

"Ma'am, have you been drinking?"

"No, I haven't been drinking. I'm at the Lawn Chair Gathering in Ditters Ferry. There's a dead body in the river caught up in some reeds and stuff."

"Calm down, and tell me your name," the emergency dispatcher intoned.

"Jimi Smith."

"Spell your first name please."

"J-I-M-I, but actually my first name is Juliet."

"I see. Jimi/Juliet *Smith.*" By the way she said *Smith,* I could tell she thought I was a prankster giving a false name. Thankfully she decided it was worth checking into further. "Exactly where you are?"

"I just told you. It's out old Airport Way about three miles past the water tower. You can't miss the group of bizarre chairs."

"Where precisely are you calling from?"

"A field next to the gathering place. I'm only a few yards from the road in a black Lincoln Navigator."

"I'll send someone out. Stay where you are, and wait for the deputy."

"I'll wait."

This gave me a chance to take a much-needed break in the Navigator's luxurious seats. I turned my head around and stuck my nose into the headrest to inhale deeply. I'm not sure which scent I found sexier—new car, expensive leather, or Jet's cologne—but the combination was beyond description and unsurpassable. If I could bottle this blend of scents, I'd never have to work another day in my life. Every woman in the world would want their man to smell like this. And every man in the world would want a bottle, because it would make them irresistible to women.

I turned on the hazard lights to hopefully assist the deputy quickly locate the Navigator. Then it hit me: *a murder in Ditters Ferry.* I had a story, a real story, a big story. There had never been news this salacious in the town's history. Excitedly, I got my little notepad from my back pocket and started scratching out notes with the miniscule pencil I kept lodged in the spiral rings of the pad.

*Who was the victim? How long had he been dead? Who stabbed him? What were the purple rings around his ankles?* So many questions shuffled through my head, I couldn't wait for the authorities to get here. Maybe some of my questions could be answered tonight.

It was almost thirty minutes before the deputy sheriff's car pulled in beside me. The officer had a high-beam flashlight in his hand because it was pitch black out now. He flashed the light in my direction. "I'm Deputy Sanchez. Are you Jimliet, the person who called in the report of a dead body?"

"Jimi, and yes, Officer, I called in the report. Follow me, and I'll take you to the body."

We started toward the river. It was so dark that the narrow path the flashlight illuminated wasn't enough to get my bearings. The Gathering people had circled their chairs and had a good-sized bonfire blazing away. I tried to see if there was a cauldron over the flames. It was too dark to tell precisely where Jet and the body were, but I knew it wasn't near the fire. After leading the policeman around for several minutes, I gave up and called out to Jet.

"Jet. Psst! Jet."

No response.

"*Jet!*" I yelled.

"Stop screaming, Jimi. I'm right over here."

His voice came from my left not too far away. Deputy Sanchez and I stumbled along toward where the sound emanated from.

The officer flashed a beam back and forth across the shrubs until we saw Jet waving.

"What took you so long?" Jet glared at me.

Biting back a sarcastic retort, I said, "Why don't you show the officer the body, Jet?"

Deputy Sanchez moved forward in the direction Jet indicated and parted the shrubbery. We heard a gasping intake of breath. "Yep, that's a dead one alright, for a while too. He's been in the water long enough to give the fishies time to eat his eyeballs out. Pretty bloated too. Stick a pin in this cadaver and he'll take a spin around the river like a jet propelled tub toy."

*That's it!* Between Mr. Speedo and Bobber, the human tub toy, I sincerely would *never* bathe in a bathtub again.

The deputy chuckled at his own disgusting joke.

His insensitivity got my ire up. "May I quote you on that, Officer?"

"Quote? What're you talkin' about?"

"Jimi Smith, investigative reporter for *Ditters Weekly,*" I said. I held out my hand, which the deputy purposely ignored.

Jet gave me a look I couldn't interpret.

"No, you may not quote me, little missy." He sounded peevish. "We need some more light over here."

"I'll go get Daniel," I offered. "His lighting equipment should help." Going to find Daniel made a perfect excuse to get away from the bobber.

Daniel was by the fire laughing and chatting up a pretty redhead. She was probably the only gathering attendee, besides the newspaper staff, under age sixty. I tapped Daniel on the shoulder.

"Excuse me," I said in the direction of the redhead, then turning to Daniel, "I need to speak with you a moment."

"What's up?"

The redhead didn't look too pleased at the interruption.

I pulled Daniel just far enough away to whisper in his ear, "I found a dead body. We need more light, so I thought we could use your equipment."

"Cool. I'll go get my gear." He looked like a kid at Christmas and ran for his gear. Men can be so peculiar and creepy. He never even gave a good-bye glance to the redhead who was now openly glaring at me.

When Daniel and I got to the bobber, the deputy was just finishing up a radioed request for coroner's wagon and forensics unit.

"Where is it?" Daniel asked again with excitement.

*Yuck!*

"Over here," the deputy said. "Let's see if your lighting will help."

Daniel quickly set up the lighting equipment, and a twenty-foot area was soon brightly illuminated. Daniel started furiously snapping pictures, even going waist deep into the river so he could get a shot from every conceivable angle.

Then it happened; my greatest fear closed in on me. Their gnashing little teeth were taunting me. One of the devil's swooped me, and I screamed so loud that everyone stopped what they were doing to stare at me. The lights had drawn the enemy in. Several came at me with "Death to Jimi" in their beady little eyes.

"What the—" Jet ran over to me. "Are you okay? What's wrong?"

I was batting my arms around my face like a lunatic trying to keep the furry flying beasts at bay. "Get them away from me!"

"Get *what* away from you?"

My arms were flailing wildly about me in an effort to protect my head. I accidentally smacked Jet in the chin.

"Those nasty moths. I hate them!" Every time one of them hit me, I let out a yip or an eek, but at least the volume of my yelps was lowered somewhat.

"Let me get this straight. You find a dead body in the river and don't make a sound. Then you see a couple of harmless moths and scream bloody murder."

"Dead bodies behave. They lay there like they're supposed to. Dead bodies don't swoop at you charging and retreating, leaving disgusting silvery fleshy scales behind. Dead bodies don't fly at you unpredictably. You can't trust a moth. They're ugly, deranged kamikaze butterflies."

Jet laughed at me. "You're nuts."

"It's not funny." Why couldn't I be afraid of something normal like spiders, heights, blood, or death? No, my mortal fear had to be *dive-bombing moths.*

"Go wait at the car." Jet was trying, unsuccessfully, to keep the laughter out of his voice.

"I can't see my way back," I whined, sure that more vile killer moths were evilly circling overhead in reconnaissance units, plotting my demise.

"I'll go get you a flashlight. Stand just outside the circle of light so the man-eating moths will leave you alone."

I fled the illuminated area while Jet went in search of a flashlight.

Three more deputies and the coroner finally came on the scene. "Let's pull the body out of the water," Deputy Sanchez said.

For the sake of my story, I charged straight ahead toward the bobber. My curiosity was marginally stronger than my fear of moths. I pushed my way through the gathering onlookers who were trying to get a glance of the body. Two of the three newly-arrived deputies were trying to keep the spectators at bay. The third deputy grabbed me by the arm.

"Stay back." He barked the order.

Jerking my arm free, I said, "I'm with the press. I'm also the one who found the body and reported it in."

"Lady, I don't care who you are. I'm telling you to stay back."

A commotion interrupted us.

"*Get off of me!*" We both turned to see Mr. Litton, the auto parts store owner, shouting at Mr. Grinnel.

"What's yer problem, George?" Mr. Grinnel yelled back.

"My problem is you're a freak show and you're touching me. Put some clothes on. You're disgusting."

"It's part of my theme. Do you bathe fully clothed?"

Mr. Litton poked a finger in Mr. Grinnel's doughy chest. "*I* don't bathe in public. Don't touch me."

Mr. Grinnel started bobbing and weaving, leaping from foot to foot like some sort of psychotic court jester, poking Mr. Litton with his dainty purple wash puff, chanting, "I'm touching you. I'm touching you. Na-na-na. I'm touching you." He puffed Mr. Litton in the chin then puffed him in the belly.

George Litton let out a roar and charged at Mr. Grinnel. They fell to the ground with a *whoompf.* The deputy who was trying to keep me away from the body went to break up the fight. The officer was being careful not to touch the nut-job in the Speedo. With the deputy distracted, I made a quick dash for the bobber.

I arrived in time to see them attempt to pull the bobber up by his arms and legs. Deputy Sanchez, who had been first on the scene, had a hand placed on each side of an elbow. I crept up right behind him, inches away, staring in morbid fascination.

"On three," he said to the other deputy, who had his hands around the dead man's ankles. "One, two, three."

With a grunt, they attempted to haul the bobber ashore. Instead Deputy Sanchez had only skin in his hands. He dropped the bobber's arm like a hot potato and vigorously wiped his palms on his pant legs. The deputy who had the bobber's feet blanched white and was swaying dizzily. The bobber's skin had neatly peeled right off the bone. The torn skin folded in a blob around the man's pale, puffy hand. Muscle tissue and white bone were openly exposed.

With no time to turn my head, I began to heave. Unfortu-

*susan case*

61

nately, I heaved directly onto Deputy Sanchez's pant leg, throwing up until there was nothing left to expel; yet my body continued to violently wretch in an effort to eject nonexistent contents from my stomach.

A warm hand started rubbing the small of my back. "You shouldn't have looked." It was Jet's voice. *Why does he always see me at my absolute worst?*

I tried to push him away, mortified that he had seen and *heard* me throwing chunk puddles onto a seriously angry officer of the law. Deputy Sanchez was still trying to shake the bigger hunks off his pants. Jet propelled me away from the deputy.

"Will it make you feel any better if I could tell you the identity of the body?" Jet said when we were out of earshot.

That perked me up enough to try and stand straight. "They've already ID'd the bobber?"

"*They* didn't; *I* did." Jet sounded pretty proud of himself. "I recognized the tattoo on his forearm."

That started my stomach churning again. "Who is it?"

"It's Herb Greene."

"Never heard of him. Is he from around here?" I asked.

"He's Harriet Greene's long lost husband."

"You mean *Mrs. Greene? Our Mrs. Greene?*"

Jet nodded.

I was incredulous. It was hard to imagine that Mrs. Greene had ever been married. She seemed the man-hating spinster, career-type woman. Then, of course, I didn't even know until recently that her first name was Harriet. Mrs. Greene didn't mingle much with the locals in Ditters Ferry. And she made her distaste for me purposely apparent at the office.

"I met him once late at night when I was working at the paper during high school. He had the weirdest tattoo—a dragon with a bleeding heart in its jaws. It read 'Wenches' underneath in medieval script. I always wondered what the significance of it was. Anyway, he left Harriet about thirty years ago. He came to the newspaper office one night and asked to talk to Mrs.

Greene. I asked his name and he said, 'Herb Greene.' I knocked on her office door and told her that Herb Greene was out here and would like to see her. She flatly refused to see him and yelled through the door that she was calling the cops so he better get out."

"Why were you at the paper late at night?"

"You ask the most random questions." Jet paused. "Because Dad would have had my hide if I didn't get the place cleaned before morning, and sometimes other pursuits got in the way and I wouldn't get there until after midnight."

"You were the janitor?" My tone didn't make it sound very flattering.

"So, something wrong with that?"

"No, no. I just always thought you led the charmed life of a rich boy. It's hard to picture you mopping floors and emptying wastebaskets."

"There's a lot you don't know about me. You assume too much."

Our conversation was interrupted when the bobber, a.k.a. Mr. Greene, passed by in a black, zippered, plastic bag. They wheeled him on a large gurney toward the coroner's wagon, bumping and thumping along. Most of the Gathering began to lose interest, now that the body was covered and being taken away, and were making their way back to the bonfire.

"Wasn't that cool? I got some great shots, even close-ups of the empty eye sockets. Wicked awesome." Daniel had come up beside us. "I'm gonna get my gear and head out. Jimi, you ready to go?"

"She's riding with me," Jet said as if he were the final authority. I gave him a look, so he explained, "I want to talk to Jimi about the direction I want the story to take."

"Sure, Boss." Daniel leaned down and kissed my cheek. "See ya around." He winked at me and headed toward his Corvette.

Jet turned on me. "He in the habit of kissing you?"

"No. It was just a friendly gesture of good-bye. It didn't mean anything."

Jet started to say something, then apparently thought better of it. "Let's go." He took my elbow and steered me along. When we got to the Navigator, Jet opened the passenger door for me.

We rode in silence. When Jet pulled up to my apartment complex, he got out and came around to open my door for me *again*. "Come on." He held his hand out to me, and I took it. We walked up to my second floor unit: 2B. Every time I thought about my apartment number, 2B, Hamlet's soliloquy would drift through my brain: *2B, or not 2B: that is the question: whether 'tis nobler in the mind to suffer the slings and arrows of outrageous fortune, or to take arms against a sea of troubles . . .* That Shakespeare sure knew how to turn a phrase. I lifted the doormat to retrieve my key.

"You keep your key under the doormat?" Jet hollered at me.

"I don't carry a purse. What's the big deal?"

"The big deal is that everybody knows to look for a key there. What are you thinking?"

"Good grief, Jet. It's Ditters Ferry, not south central Los Angeles."

"You're a woman living on her own. You need to start using your head for something other than a hat rack."

My back was to the door and I was facing Jet, ready for a good shouting match. Then he removed my ball cap and put one hand on either side of my head and leaned forward with intent. I quickly dipped under his arm and turned to get the key in the lock. If Jet was going to kiss me, the first time would certainly *not* be after I had recently vomited.

"Jimi?"

I opened the door and went in, then turned to look at him. "I'm tired, Jet, and it's been a really long day."

"Yeah." It sounded more like a sigh than a word.

"Are you going to call Mrs. Greene?" I asked.

"No. I don't want to wake her up, and it would be better if

the police made a positive ID first. I'll call Deputy Sanchez first thing in the morning to see if I can be the one who tells her."

"Jet," I said softly, "you really are one of the good guys." I shut the door before he could respond. In complete fatigue, I leaned my back on the front door and slumped there for minute.

From the other side of the door was Jet's muted voice, "Are you going to lock your door or what?"

Smiling, I snapped the dead bolt over with a clang. This was shortly followed by the sound of retreating footsteps. Moving over to the window, I parted the curtains just a bit. He stood at the driver's side door and looked up as though expecting to see me watching him and waved. I let the curtains fall shut.

*What a conceited man he is. How did he know I would be looking? Then again, what kind of fool woman wouldn't be looking?*

# chapter 4

*Bzzt! Bzzt! Bzzt!*

Six a.m. came much too quickly. Annoyed, I slapped the snooze bar on my pink plastic alarm clock. Staying up until past 2:30 in the morning organizing and typing my notes made getting up this early untenable. Maybe I could get away without showering; that would buy an extra fifteen minutes of precious sleep. My eyes felt gritty and heavy, and it was an effort to breathe. Remembering my fall from the night before and the twigs in my hair, mixed with the knowledge that there was moth goo on me, I forced myself to get up. My knees were bruised and achy.

The shower *was* reviving, and after washing my hair with my favorite scented shampoo and giving my teeth a double brushing, I felt a little more ready to tackle the day. Mrs. Greene had a problem with me wearing jeans to the office, so I decided to cut her a little slack and opted for pleated khaki Dockers and a crisp, white blouse.

Generally I walk to work since it's less than a mile from my apartment, but my knees decided the car was a better idea for today. Arriving at the office minutes before 7:00, I noted a lot of activity in the parking lot. Two cop cars sat at opposing angles in the handicap section of the parking lot at the stoop outside the front door. Before I had time to even formulate a question in my head, out came a stunned-looking Mrs. Greene with her hands behind her back, escorted by a cop on either side of her. The officers accompanied Mrs. Greene to one of the police cars and put her in the backseat.

That was when I saw the handcuffs.

Jet was at the doorway frantically motioning for me to come

in. One last look at Mrs. Greene showed a woman I had never seen before. Confusion and vulnerability were clearly etched on her face. Encountering my bewildered gaze, Harriet abruptly looked away.

"What in heaven's name is going on?" I asked Jet.

"Come into my office," was his curt reply.

Once inside Jet's office, he closed the door. "Mrs. Greene has been arrested for the murder of her husband."

"*What?* Why would they think it was her?"

"Remember the metal object sticking out of Herb's chest?" Jet asked.

"Yeah. So?"

"It was Harriet's letter opener. The Weekly had it engraved on her tenth anniversary as head editor. The engraving reads, "Harriet Ann Greene, Editor ten years dedicated service ~Ditters Weekly April 1, 1985."

"Harriet *Ann* Greene?" I was definitely buying her a set of monogrammed towels for Christmas—nice, thick, plush, black towels with gold-stitched initials. *H.A.G.* And an anniversary date of April Fools' Day—too perfect. A small chuckle escaped me.

"You may not like her, but this isn't funny," Jet scolded. "Harriet has been a fixture around here for years, and I learned a lot from her. She was almost like a grandmother to me. Not the warm *let me bake you some cookies* kind of grandmother, but she really looked out for me and made sure I learned everything possible about the newspaper business."

"I'm sorry," I said, lowering my gaze in false contrition.

"I know you didn't get much sleep last night, but I need you to focus."

"Okay. What can I do?"

"The deputy I spoke with said it will be three to four hours before she gets through the booking process. First thing I'm going to do is hire an attorney for her and see if we can get her bonded out. I need you at the jail talking to anybody and everybody who will share any information with you. In other words, nose around. Surf the net and see if you can dig up any information on Herb—where he's been living, working, etc."

"What do you want for last night's story?"

"Let's wait to see what kind of information you gather before determining the focal point of the story."

"Isn't Herb the focal point of the story? It's not every day someone is murdered in Ditters Ferry." The locals would be panting for information about the murder.

"Just the basic facts, unless we are able to substantiate more facts than we have now. Speculation and gossip will be running rampant, and we don't want to add fuel to the fire with conjecture."

"Jet, why not arrest her last night at home? Why wait until she gets to work?"

"I asked that same question. Apparently she wasn't at home last night."

"All night?" That seemed more than a little peculiar.

"According to the deputy."

We both paused to consider that. She wasn't the type to be out all night partying. Then I remembered that she had gone out with Sylvia to Boise for dinner. Maybe she stayed with her for the night.

"I'll get going. You have an attorney to hire," I said.

"Jimi, do your best. Okay?"

"Of course," I responded, slightly insulted.

"Don't take offense," Jet said. "There are so many variables and ramifications to this story. It's the biggest piece in the paper's history, and it involves a long-time employee."

"Jet, I'm going to do my level best not to let you or the paper down."

"Keep me posted on what you dig up."

"Will do."

Jet was already at his computer, probably searching online for the best attorney Idaho had to offer.

The giant, round clock on the wall read 7:22. I planned to spend the next few hours researching Herb Greene's background, but where to start? I didn't know his full name, birth date, or Social Security number. Cautiously, I made my way to Mrs. Green's office. Maybe there would be something in her files to help me get started.

The rickety old filing cabinet squawked and grated loudly when I attempted to pull the top drawer open farther. I paused, waiting to see if anyone was going to investigate the noise and catch me snooping around in here. After a few moments, I expelled the breath I'd been holding.

Rats! The top drawer yielded nothing except work-related files. My search of the other three drawers was as useless and unproductive as the first. Moving across the room to her desk, I sat in Harriet's chair and hesitated only a second before opening a side drawer. A file marked "medical" and another labeled "personal" were the only two items that showed any potential whatsoever. I didn't want to take the time to review everything in the files. Fortunately, Mrs. Greene had her own copy machine. I loaded all the papers from both files into the feeder and grabbed up the copies as they spat out. The folders went back into the desk precisely as I had found them.

Mrs. Greene's top middle desk drawer only contained pens, stamps, etcetera, and was meticulously arranged. *Eureka!* In one of the cubbies sat Mrs. Greene's keys. A car key, what appeared to be a house key, office key, and a small key that probably opened some type of padlock.

Pocketing the keys, I held the paper copies close to my chest, took a deep, bracing breath, and walked out of Harriet's office as if there had been a perfectly good reason for my being in there. Rhonda, the personal phone call junkie who sometimes masqueraded as the Weekly's receptionist, bumped into me on my way out. Rhonda appeared very flustered and distracted. She didn't even realize we had collided. She continued to walk zombie fashion to wherever she was headed.

The phone book yielded Mrs. Greene's home address and number, so I headed out. Her home was in an area I had never been to before. It was past several farms outside the township of Ditters Ferry proper. She owned a forty-acre parcel along the river. There was a wooden arch made from rough-hewn logs with a placard in the middle that read "Greene'r Pastures." The home was set back about fifty yards from the dirt road. My presence would be very conspicuous if anyone happened to venture this far out, because there was nothing else in sight except Mrs. Greene's home and my car. There was a flowered mailbox with "Air Mail" stenciled on it atop a pole some forty feet high. I was having a difficult time correlating this picturesque home and humorous mail receptacle with Mrs. Greene. Obviously, there was another side to her other than the venomous viper who reluctantly interacted with me at the office.

I pulled my car around to the rear of the house and got out. Cheery little potted plants in a myriad of sizes were placed haphazardly around the flagstone patio floor. Several ferns and baskets of geraniums hung from the wood-beamed, netted canopy covering. An oversized thermometer, which had no numbers, was nailed to a support post. Instead of temperature digits, next to the mercury level was scrawled "just right". A beautiful oak rocking chair and matching chaise lounge were the only two items of furniture on the patio.

Several ceramic animals peeked out of flowering bushes. Among them were a lop-eared bunny, a cute little pig, and a chubby burro with a serape blanket across his stout back. There was even a striped tiger playfully crouching by a miniature fountain. Should I look for a door or a knothole entrance in the wall? Because, just as surely as Bruce Wayne is Batman and Clark Kent is Superman, Mrs. Greene's alter ego must be Winnie the Pooh.

Okay. Time to stop being silly. There was police tape across the sliding glass door. At least the cops had already tossed the place. That actually relieved me because I didn't want to encounter any unexpected visitors, least of all the long arm of the law.

The front door had a strip of police tape also, as if that would slow me down. Of course, I rationalized, it's not as if I were breaking and entering. *I* had a key. While inserting the key with one hand, I stuck my other hand inside my shirt to use it as a glove—no sense leaving any telltale fingerprints behind.

The interior of the home was as serene and enchanting as the patio. The living room was my idea of a paradise retreat. Welcoming, overstuffed chairs, comfy couch, smooth, high gloss cherry coffee table and end tables, tiffany lamps, and shelf upon shelf of books—the room begged for the occupant to relax, have a glass of iced tea, and spend some time with a good book. There wasn't a television in sight.

The kitchen walls were a mellow yellow, and shiny copper pots hung from a wrought iron overhead rack above a tiled island. A floral ceramic canister set of descending sizes sat neatly under the cabinet to my right. The cabinets were cherry, which offset the yellow walls nicely, giving the room warmth. There was a small desk table with a phone on it. Unfortunately, only a local Ditters Ferry phone book and one pen were in the single drawer. A couple of barstools and a small, two-person dinette was the only seating in the dining area.

The kitchen was obviously not where to find anything useful, so I headed down the hallway. Miniature paintings and hand-stitched, framed samplers decorated the walls, but no photographs. The first door opened to a guest bath. Next to it was a sparsely furnished guest room. The closet and chest of drawers were empty. The linen closet produced nothing but what one would expect to find in a linen closet.

Farther down the hall was the home office. The desk was organized and Spartan, only sporting a wooden, cup-like holder that contained a pen, pencil, highlighter, and black permanent marker. The only other item on the desk was a large monthly planner set to the current month. There were two notations on the planner: one for a doctor's appointment, and the other was for a dinner date with Sylvia. I turned the page to the next month, and a folded piece of paper peeked out from the bottom right corner. I carefully unfolded it and saw that it was a receipt for a furniture dolly dated two weeks earlier. Something about the receipt from the Boise rental company bothered me, but I couldn't put my finger on it. The only item notated on the following month was another dinner date with Sylvia.

The bookshelves and a filing cabinet completed the matching office furniture set, all in burnished walnut. The filing cabinet held old newspaper stories with Mrs. Greene's byline, assorted billing statements, and receipts in chronological order and stapled by month. Now why would the furniture dolly receipt not be stapled with the other receipts for the month? That's what bothered me; the lone receipt was out of place and character for Mrs. Greene. I jotted down the rental company's name and office phone number together with the date of the receipt and receipt number. There were at least three locations to rent a dolly, much closer than Boise. In fact, one was located right in the heart of downtown Ditters Ferry.

*Why go all the way to Boise?*

The next drawer held home loan papers dating back to 1977. The paperwork listed the owners/borrowers as Herbert M. Greene and Harriet A. Greene, who purchased the forty acres and home for sixty-seven thousand dollars. Harriet had made the final payment on the house just three months ago. The mortgage company sent the paid in full statement together with a deed of reconveyance, which had been filed and recorded with the county assessor. In the same file as the loan papers was a recent home appraisal dated six weeks ago, which valued the home and land at $1.4 million. Not a bad profit—even for thirty years. Three fat drawers and nothing useful in them; I was beginning to think I was wasting my time. But at least I now had Herb's full name.

The master bedroom was behind the last room at the end

of the hall. The door opened to the center of a spacious room. To the right was the master bath, to the left was a huge walk-in closet, and in the middle was the biggest bed I had ever seen. The mattress on the four-poster bed was at least three feet off the ground. There was a step stool beside the bed. Unless one wanted to pole vault onto the bed, the steps would be necessary to reach the summit. Getting on my hands and knees, I looked under the bed. Nothing there; not even a dust bunny.

Mrs. Greene's vanity and dresser yielded nothing except the usual accoutrements. The closet was my last hope. I flipped the switch by the door to the wardrobe. The closet was almost as big as my studio apartment. I couldn't reach the top shelf, which held a promising number of assorted boxes. I retrieved the step stool from the bedside and was just able to reach the lowest boxes on the shelf. The box closest to me was extremely heavy. I shifted it side to side several times, trying to maneuver it forward enough to afford a good grip. When it was hanging about halfway off the shelf, I placed one hand on each side and brought it toward my chest. Unfortunately, the shelf was no longer supporting the weight of the box, and it was too heavy for me to handle. I tried to catch my balance and keep hold of the box. Instead I lost my balance and dropped the box. Everything, including me, hit the floor with a loud thud. I lay there for a moment admiring Mrs. Greene's plain, square-heeled pumps in a variety of bland colors, trying to get my breath back and hoping nothing was broken.

Loose photographs, personal letters, documents, and several photo albums surrounded me. *Pay dirt!* Proof was now in my possession; Mrs. Greene indeed had a personal life or was storing someone else's memorabilia, which didn't seem plausible. Sitting cross-legged on the floor of Harriet's closet, I removed the last of the contents out of the box that hadn't already spilled out then began methodically going through each item. A couple of heavy photo albums caught my attention first. There were pictures of bikers of the hell's angel persuasion in numerous social settings.

Some were taken from a moving motorcycle. One picture had a tough-looking guy at the handlebars with a free-spirited, smiling girl with long, flowing brown hair on the seat behind him. Her arms were wrapped possessively around his waist. Then I noticed the tattoo on the driver's arm: a dragon with a bloodied heart in its jaws and the word "Wenches" scripted beneath. I turned the picture over, and written on the back was "Herb and Harry, Calif. '74." Good thing I was already sitting down when the realization hit me that uptight Mrs. Greene used to be a biker chick. A few pages later in the album was another photo of young Mrs. Greene. I immediately closed my eyes.

*Oh, dear Lord, please let me be mistaken. Eradicate forever the things I think I saw. Amen.*

Cautiously, I opened my eyes; my prayer had not been answered. There was Mrs. Greene and another girl who looked like she could be her sister standing atop a bar in leather pants, motorcycle boots, and unfortunately, *topless.*

On the list of things I wish I had never seen and could permanently remove from my memory bank, definitely *numero uno* was seeing my supervisor's naked little bubbies. The eyeless dead body floating in the river was now a distant second on that same list. I was doomed to weeks and weeks of nightmares over this; quite possibly I would need long-term therapy. Looking away from the album, I drew in several cleansing breaths. The facial features of other girl seemed a little familiar. Flipping the picture over, in the same handwriting as previous pictures was "Harry and Syl." Sylvia. That's why she looked familiar. Perfectly coiffed Sylvia was a biker chick too! Well, rock my narrow, pedantic world. This meant their friendship went back to the mid 1970s at minimum.

The album contained more of the same, yet thankfully everyone was fully clothed in the remainder of the photographs. I reached for the second album. The first page contained a receipt for ten dollars from the Addel County Courthouse. It was paper-clipped to a marriage certificate. Herbert Malcolm

*susan case*

75

Greene and Harriet Ann Porter wed May 22, 1975. The next page was a birth certificate for James Herbert Greene, October 12, 1975. There were several photos of little James at various stages up to toddler. Several snapshots contained a smiling Herb playing with James, and a couple of photos featured a tense, uncomfortable-looking Harriet and her son. It appeared the biker couple had settled down and decided to try to live the suburban dream. They looked like any young, working, middle-class couple of the era.

The last page of the album contained a meticulously folded piece of paper. I peeled the cellophane covering off and unfolded the official-looking paper. My heart wrenched, and my breath left me. It was a death certificate for James. Cause of death was determined to be sudden infant death syndrome. Date of death: April 15, 1977.

There I sat in Mean Greene Crushing Machine's closet, crying for a child I didn't know and who had been dead for thirty years. My feelings toward Mrs. Greene altered a bit. She was still a royal pain, but possibly I had discovered the reason a once smiling, carefree girl could become a coldhearted, closed-up woman.

Next, I picked up a packet of letters bound with a lavender ribbon. There were at least a dozen or so. No return address; just "H. Greene" printed in the upper left of the envelope. All were sent to Harriet Greene at her current address in Ditters Ferry. The first was postmarked July 10, 1977, from Phoenix, Arizona.

*Dear Harry,*

*I'm sorry for leaving without saying good-bye. It had nothing to do with the affair; I ended that permanently. I just couldn't stay in that house a moment longer with all the memories of James coming at me from every room.*

*I have a good job with a construction paving company. It's hotter than hell here, but I can drink away my nights—which sometimes helps keep the demon nightmares away.*

*I know how much you like your job at the paper, but please think about forgiving me and coming out here to live. We'll ride the Harley to wherever the highway takes us. You know we'll get by.*

*Love always,*

*Herb*

The second letter was postmarked November 11, 1977, from Amarillo, Texas.

*Dear Harry,*

*I guess you decided Phoenix wasn't for you. How about Texas? You know everything is bigger out here. Maybe you could come for a visit. I'm doing some roofing work. It's a bone-tiring job, but the pay isn't bad.*

*I'd like to hear from you and know how you are doing.*

*Love always,*

*Herb*

The letters continued on about every six months to a year or so apart, always from a different city and state but with the same invitation for Harry to join him. One of the last letters was dated April 15, 1979.

*Dear Harry,*

*I guess it's not the location, but me. I still haven't heard from you. This being the second anniversary of James's passing, I know you must be hurting also. I wish you would take a chance and start a new life with me, but that doesn't seem too likely. Our relationship wasn't strong enough to endure my cheating or especially the void that James's early departure created. I won't tell you where I am anymore because fear has set in that the only probable thing I might get from you is divorce papers.*

*The world is still a beautiful place to be explored from a Harley.*

*Wishing you well,*

*Herb*

The last letter was dated just four months ago from, of all places, Harmony, Idaho, just sixteen miles from Ditters Ferry.

*Dear Harriet,*

*I've been working on a ranch near Harmony for six years now. It's hard to believe we haven't run into each other at least once. We're so close, yet it seems like a thousand years since I saw you last. I'd like to see you to discuss the house and property.*

*Herb*

Well, this didn't sound good for Mrs. Greene; recent appraisal and reference to the jointly owned real estate. Placing everything back into the box, I carefully climbed the step stool to replace the box on the shelf. I had just maneuvered the box into place when a door creaked open.

"This is the police. Who's in here?" an authoritative male voice shouted.

I thought about hiding under the bed, but that would make me look guilty of something.

"Come out with your hands up."

Menacing footsteps were approaching from the hall. I grabbed a decorative pitcher resting in a porcelain bowl from atop the chest of drawers and carried it overhead into the doorway.

"It's Jimi Smith. I'm coming out with my hands up."

I peeked around the corner, still holding the pitcher high, when I came face-to-face with Deputy Sanchez.

"Drop the vase," Deputy Sanchez said in his best *Law and Order* cop voice.

"It's a *pitcher*," I said, stating what I thought was the obvious.

"I've got my .38 pointed directly at your chest."

"I'm putting the *vase* down." It was difficult to fight his logic.

Finally, recognition set in for Deputy Sanchez. "Hey, it's Jimliet something or other from the river. She found the vic's body and called it in." This was said over his shoulder in the direction of two other officers.

"Jeez. You better put your gun down, Sanchez, before she pukes on you again."

The officers laughed.

Deputy Sanchez's humor was short-lived. "Just what do you think you're doing here?"

"I'm watering the plants."

"You always ignore crime scene tape? I mean, I know you're with the big city press and all, but you do know enough not to cross police tape. I'm sure you also know I could arrest you right now for breaking and entering."

"I had permission and a key." Well, a key anyway.

"Obstruction of justice, tampering with evidence . . ."

Forcing big, fat tears to my eyes, I bawled to beat heck. "I was just trying to help poor Mrs. Greene. I couldn't stand it if one of her precious plants died and I did nothing to help." I was laying it on a little thick. "Besides, I figured you had already gone through the place and that's why there was tape around it."

"Quit yer boohooin'. Jeez. If you aren't pukin', yer crying like a baby."

"Should we shoot her?" one of the deputies joked; at least I hoped he was joking.

Sniffling a few more times, I angled sideways, hoping my profile would make a smaller target just in case.

"May I leave now?" I said in a shaky voice. I didn't have to try and sound scared; I *was* scared.

"I don't know . . ." Deputy Sanchez seemed to be mulling it over.

I started bawling all over again, *loudly and obnoxiously.*

"Get her outta here before I really do shoot her," one of the junior officers said.

"Yeah. I can't stand her catterwallin'," the other deputy complained. "Stray cats in heat fighting in a back alley aren't as noisy as her."

"Or as annoying," the other officer chimed in.

"Get going, Miz Smith, but if I find you've tampered with anything or taken so much as a tissue from here you'll be in the cell next to Harriet Greene."

"I didn't take anything or tamper with anything." I attempted to sound insulted at the accusation and let some more crocodile tears well up.

Deputy Sanchez sighed with resignation. "Just go."

I left as fast as my shaking legs would carry me. In the relative safety of my car, it occurred to me that if the police *had* gone through Mrs. Greene's house they wouldn't have left it so tidy—an observation that would have come in handy earlier.

*Sanchez carried a .38 revolver. How small town is that? Isn't it obsolete for cops to carry a revolver? Didn't they pack 9mm these days? Well, that's TV for you. Of course, I guess either gun would get the job done at close range.* That's when random thinking gave way to rationality. *Get the job done.* What an idiotic thought, considering his revolver had been pointing at *my* chest. Pulling away from Mrs. Greene's, I decided that this job might not be right for me. Perhaps I should be learning how to say, "Welcome to Wal-Mart. Would you like a sticker?"

# *chapter 5*

Back at the office, I decided to get a few calls out of the way. My first call was to the Boise rental company where Mrs. Greene had obtained the furniture dolly. A young man answered on the second ring.

"Rent It All. This is Jason."

"Hi, Jason. I'm hoping you can help me with something."

"I'll try. What do you need?"

"I have a receipt for a furniture dolly and was wondering if you could tell me anything about the person who rented it."

"Ma'am, we rent several of those every day, but give me the receipt number and date. I'll see if there's anything I can do."

I gave Jason the information he requested and was put on hold for what seemed like fifteen minutes, but given my lack of patience it was probably closer to three minutes.

"Still there?" Jason asked.

"Yes. Are you able to remember anything about this particular transaction?"

"Actually, yeah. I'm the one who helped this customer." Jason paused for a second. "I remember this lady because she was so nervous. She was really anxious and wanted to make sure she could move a lot of weight by herself. Wanted to know what type of dolly would someone her size use to lift and move approximately two hundred pounds."

I waited for him to continue.

"I felt kinda sorry for her 'cause there didn't seem to be anyone she could ask for help. Anyway, I assured her with the proper dolly, like the heavy duty one with straps, that with good leverage she might be able to lift and move two hundred plus pounds."

"Do you remember what this woman looked like?"

"Yeah. I'd guess she was between fifty and sixty, had brown hair, slim build, and probably around five feet four or so."

"Did she sign a contract?"

"Of course," he said, as if any idiot would know that.

"What is the name?"

"It's signed." There was a hesitation while he searched. "Here it is. Harriet Greene."

*The noose was tightening around Mrs. Greene's scrawny neck.*

"Did she return the dolly on time?"

"Yeah, on time, but the wheels were caked with mud. I asked her if she was able to use the dolly by herself, and she said it had worked perfectly."

*I think I just heard the trap door dropping out from underneath my supervisor.*

"Well, thank you for the assistance."

"Sure. No problem."

I was about to hang up when he said, "One other thing."

I pulled the phone back closer to my ear.

"I don't know if it was because she was nervous or what, but she didn't sign anywhere even close to the signature line. But then, she did seem to be in a real hurry."

"Could you fax me a copy of the contract?"

There was an extra long pause as if he finally thought perhaps he'd given out too much information. "I'll have to check with the boss and he isn't here right now."

I gave him the Weekly's fax number in hope that he would be given permission to send me a copy. I wanted to compare signatures with the ones of Mrs. Greene's here at the office. I thanked Jason again and disconnected. I made a note to call back in a few days if I didn't receive a fax from Jason.

Next call I made was to Jet's cell phone.

"This is Jet."

"Hey, Jet. It's Jimi. Any word on Mrs. Greene? Is she through with the booking process?"

"I don't know, but you should probably head over there any-way. I found her a highly recommended attorney who is well-respected in criminal defense. How about you? Were you able to find out anything helpful about Herb?"

"I got some information, not sure how helpful it is to Mrs. Greene though." I paused for a moment then decided I'd rather have this conversation in person with Jet. "I'll tell you about it when I see you next."

"Okay. I'll be back at the office later this evening. If you're not there, I'll stop by your apartment."

I panicked at the thought of my messy apartment. "I'll meet you at the office later."

"You either don't want to be alone with me, or you left your apartment a pigsty and don't want me to see the clutter. Which is it?"

"Both."

Jet grumbled something that may have been good-bye. There was no sound now except the hum of dead air, so I hung up. How did Jet know I was on the untidy side? Maybe he'd been talking to Dibbz or Kirstie. One quick glance at my work area gave another clue as to why Jet might know about my penchant for clutter and disorder. I was either going to have to: 1) learn to clean and become organized; 2) never invite anyone over to my apartment; or 3) get a thick skin about the littered chaos that usually surrounded me. The path of least resistance would definitely be option number three. Therefore, I determined to acquire a thick skin. It was also a choice I would be able to stick with over the long haul.

Now was as good a time as any to head over to the jail. It was a fairly short drive to Hilltown, barely allowing time to decide my course of action. I pitched the idea of saying I was with the press. That would only get me a few basic facts and put everyone on their guard not to speak with me. It definitely wouldn't get me in to see Mrs. Greene. I didn't even know if they allowed visitors this early into the incarceration process. I'd act like a concerned friend. I was a little unsure that my thespian skills were up to this. The concerned part maybe, but a *friend* to Mrs. Greene would require a performance worthy of an Oscar. I had already used up most of my dramatic talent on the deputies at Mrs. Greene's house, and they wanted to shoot me.

I left my car parked at the elementary school directly across the street from the county courthouse. Walking briskly, I accessed the breezeway between the courthouse and jail.

There were two armed guards at the entrance manning the metal detector. Placing my keys and pocket change in the scratched, tarnished bowl, a gruff-looking officer gave me a two-finger approach signal to proceed through.

"Where do I go to visit a prisoner?" I asked the less stern-looking officer.

"We don't house prisoners here. This isn't a prison; it's a corrections facility—where we house integrity-challenged, dis-agreeable patrons of the correctional system, otherwise known as inmates."

This got a big laugh from the other officer.

"Would you direct me to the inmate visitation area, please?"

"Go down the hall and take the stairs to the basement level. Just follow the signs from there."

"Thank you."

These guys must be really bored, as the whole routine felt a little rehearsed.

The basement area had signs directing visitors to the entrance of the jail facility. I came to a halt at a window where a sour-faced woman sat. The steel door to her left posted the following instructions: No weapons; State your purpose; Have valid ID ready; Persons with contraband will be prosecuted; and No food or drinks allowed in visiting area. I wondered if the Snicker's mini candy bar in my pocket could get me prosecuted.

"I'd like to visit Mrs. Harriet Greene," I said to the dour-faced woman.

"Carrying any weapons?" she snapped.

"No."

"State your purpose," the window woman said without looking up.

"Uh, I'd like to visit with Mrs. Greene," I restated.

She sighed heavily and pursed her lips. "Friend, family, or attorney?"

"Friend, I guess."

"You don't know."

"I'm a coworker, so yeah, friend."

"Thank you for the history lesson on your relationship with the inmate," she barked at me. "Which inmate are you here to see?"

"Harriet A. Greene. She was brought in early this morning."

"ID." This was an order, so I handed over my driver's license.

She flipped through some computer screens and made a call. "22756, finished with processing yet?" There was a moment's pause, and she slid my license back to me. "Okay."

A buzzer went off.

I stood there waiting.

"You wanna see number 22756 or not?" she asked impatiently.

"Yes, please."

"Then try turning the door handle when you hear the buzzer."

"Uh, I have a mini Snicker's in my pocket." I really didn't want to do jail time for a chocolate bar.

Her face lit up like the Fourth of July night sky. "You'll have to leave it here; it's contraband."

I reluctantly gave up my afternoon snack and had the sneaking suspicion that window woman's breath was soon going to smell like chocolate, caramel, and peanuts.

The buzzer went off again, so I quickly turned the handle

and entered a room with six plastic chairs and one plastic tree. The lights overhead were casting a grayish tinge and flickering rapidly. This was one depressing place.

A weary-looking woman came through the opposite doorway, accompanied by a girl in tattered clothes who looked to be around nine years old. Both had been recently crying.

"Didn't daddy look good? I'm sure he'll be home soon."

The girl didn't look as optimistic. Her eyes were as old as her worn-down mother. They left, using the door I was just buzzed in through. I made a mental note that you had to ask window woman's permission to be buzzed out.

I sat waiting to be called for my visit with Mrs. Greene. An elderly Hispanic couple was buzzed in and sat two chairs down from me and began rapidly speaking Spanish in hushed tones. Everyone who came through these doors appeared to be depressed, except me. I was just curious and sorely in need of my mini Snicker's bar.

"Juliet Smith," an enormous female guard called out to me.

"Here," I said, sounding like a third grader responding to roll call, even foolishly raising my hand.

"This way, Ms. Smith." She turned and strode down the hall.

Although I judged her to be in her late forties to early fifties, she was an intimidating presence. She stood at least six feet three and weighed in at an impressive two hundred and fifty plus pounds. She was one solid, scary mass packed into a bland, tan uniform. Her rubber soles didn't make a sound on the polished cement floor.

Before me was a bank of individual windows, each with a small, round orange stool and heavy, black phone attached to the cubicle wall. Everything looked so pristine and new. I decided to sit at the far end, as it afforded the most privacy.

"22756, you have five minutes."

Mrs. Greene was ushered in, completely dwarfed by the gigantic guard. She was wearing no makeup, and her hair hung limply down her back in a ragged ponytail. The orange jumpsuit she was wearing was made for someone three times her size. Her shackled ankles clanked and rattled as she approached.

Mrs. Greene didn't look all that thrilled to see me. I gazed back at her through glass that looked too clear and clean to be believable. I stuck my hand out to touch the glass, but instead my hand went past where the glass was *supposed* to be. A shrill whistle sounded, and Ms. Greene and I both jumped.

"Keep to your own side," the guard ordered, still holding her whistle at the ready. "22756, *stand* for pat down of contraband."

Apparently the guard thought some contraband had been passed to Ms. Greene. The pat down took up three precious minutes of our five-minute allotment. The feminine alter ego of Hulk Hogan—a.k.a. the guard—did not miss any part of Ms. Greene's anatomy during the body search.

Ms. Greene glared at me for subjecting her to this further degradation.

"I'm so sorry," I started to say when the sound of the whistle pierced the air again.

Again, we were both startled.

"What?" I squeaked out.

"You *must* use the phones," the guard snarled.

"But I can hear her just fine," I argued.

Again, the whistle sounded. Neither Ms. Greene nor I jumped too much, having become accustomed to the shrill noise.

"Use the phones," the guard restated.

"I feel silly; there's no glass here."

"The glass will be installed soon; however, we're operating as if the glass were actually in place. Follow the rules and use the phone, or you will be escorted from the premises."

Ms. Greene picked up her phone and gave me a look that suggested I do the same.

I picked up the phone on my side of the nonexistent Plexiglas and waved it at her with a smile.

"What?" For some obscure reason, Ms. Greene seemed a little put out by my visit.

"I came to see how you are doing."

She made a face, and I had to admit that was an incredibly stupid thing to say. She was incarcerated, for heaven's sake. How did I think she was doing?

"I'm just peachy keen. How are you?"

Okay, I deserved that.

"I want to help you. I'm doing some investigation on your behalf."

"Well, this is definitely the icing on my *Death Becomes You* cake—Jimi Smith, child reporter, as my own personal private investigator. They're probably revving up the amperage on the electric chair as we speak."

"If you don't want my help, fine, but at least let me tell you the things that I found out, information I'm sure the police have also uncovered by now. It will give you time to prepare some explanations."

"Prepare explanations?" She raised her voice alarmingly. "You think I'm guilty!"

"I found some evidence which doesn't look too favorable on your behalf. I wanted to give you a heads up."

This got her attention, and her shoulders sagged in surrender.

"Jimi, I've been robbed of almost every human dignity." She paused for an awkward moment with her head down. "Two guards stood staring at me while I had to strip naked and receive a *full* body search and then shower. I have nothing of my own, no privacy, and no rights. I share a ten by seven cell with a drug dealer. What I'm trying to say is I guess your help is not the worst of my problems."

*Was that an apology?* "Listen, I was out at your place trying to find out anything that might help you."

"And what did you find?" Harriet asked benignly.

"Well, there were the letters from Herb."

Mrs. Greene gasped with a loud intake of breath.

"You read my personal letters?"

She appeared as if she were about to cry. I'd rather deal with her acid tongue or anger.

"I was trying to find out about Herb."

There was a long, uncomfortable pause. "What else did you find?"

"Your original home loan papers and recent appraisal," I said.

"So, you think I murdered Herb for money."

"I think the *police* will think you murdered Herb for money, yes." I couldn't lie to her.

"And?" She waited expectantly.

"I found a receipt for a heavy-duty furniture dolly dated two weeks ago."

"Time's up," Big Body Bertha the Guard announced.

"Furniture dolly?" Mrs. Greene appeared completely nonplussed.

"Time's up! Put the phones down, and exit the visitation room immediately," the guard reiterated, her tone indicating a plea for a couple more minutes wouldn't get me anywhere.

I hung the phone up and mouthed that I would be back. Mrs. Greene shrugged as if she didn't care. She looked pathetic and defeated as she hobbled out of the room. Mrs. Greene didn't have a single redeeming quality, and yet I felt sorry for her.

I went back toward the waiting area. When the harsh-faced woman behind the thick glass window looked up at me, I asked if I could have my Snicker's back.

"What Snicker's?" she said, and the door buzzed. Turning the handle, I gazed back over my shoulder.

"You have something in your teeth."

She rubbed her index finger over her teeth then bared them at me for inspection.

"Don't worry. You got all the chocolate and caramel off them now." I smiled and exited quickly.

*Resolution to self: I will do my best to make new friends wherever I go—unless, of course, they steal my candy.*

# chapter 6

It was getting late, and I hadn't made any more headway with Mrs. Greene's case. A quick glance at the clock showed it was well past time to go home. Apparently Jet had gotten caught up elsewhere. It was a quarter after nine and I was, as Granddad likes to say, plum tuckered out. The few facts garnered I would have to tell Jet in the morning or whenever I saw him next.

The parking lot was completely empty with the exception of my car. For some reason, the skin on the back of my neck was tingling, like the feeling you get when you're watching a scary movie and you know something bad is about to happen—mostly you know because eerie background music forewarns you. Of course, there was no soundtrack playing. I simply had a bad feeling. I got into my car as quickly as I could and locked myself in. No boogeyman was going to get me.

A hand grasped my shoulder from the backseat. I screamed so loudly that my own ears were ringing. I ripped two fingernails off as my hand slipped through the door handle. The stupid door was locked. Then I jammed my knuckles into the window while frantically trying to unlock the door. It was amazing with so much time passing that my assailant hadn't already strangled me. I jolted out of the car and landed painfully on my hands and knees, one foot still inside the car. As I was scrambling to get up, the back door opened. I rolled over onto my butt because I once heard that a woman's legs are the strongest part of her body and could be used to effectively kick at an attacker. I tucked my painfully throbbing hands under each opposing armpit.

"Geez. You're as coordinated as you are observant." A woman's legs may be strong, but the tongue is more likely to inflict the most pain. "I've been sitting in the backseat of your car for

91

the last two hours." I recognized Sylvia's disdainful, pretentious voice immediately.

"Why were you in my car? You scared me half to death!" I was struggling to stand and not getting an accommodating hand up from Sylvia. No wonder the hairs on the back of my neck were standing straight up—the devil had come for a visit.

*Dear Lord, I thought I asked real nice for your protection from this evil being. Well, anyway, here I am asking again. Please protect me from Sylvia. Amen.*

"I was waiting in my car across the street and was afraid I'd fall asleep and not get a chance to speak with you." I looked across the street and saw a new white Cadillac. It was the only car on the street, so it had to be hers.

"Why didn't you just knock on the office door and ask to come in?"

"Because what I have to say is private. There's no reason the whole world needs to know about our little chat."

"You could have called." I stated the obvious.

"Listen. I want to save you a lot of trouble."

*Sylvia wanting to do me a favor?* My knuckles were feeling slightly better, but I was in a rotten mood over the continuous burning sting of having the fingernails ripped from my index and middle fingers.

"I imagine you're running around trying to prove Harriet's innocence."

"I'm looking into the situation. Do you have some information that can help provide evidence that she's not guilty? "

"Hardly," Sylvia said emphatically, "because she's guilty—guilty as sin."

Maybe I should hear Sylvia out. If anyone could recognize sin, I was fairly certain it would be this woman.

"I thought Mrs. Greene was your friend?" Hating to show weakness, I still couldn't help placing my injured left hand under my right armpit. Somehow the warmth and cocooning protection made my fingers feel a little better.

Sylvia gave a short, sarcastic laugh. "No one is Harriet's friend."

"Why are you so anxious to believe she's guilty?"

"Because she is." Sylvia paused for a second. "Herb was going to ask her for a divorce and half of everything they owned."

"How do you know Herb?" I asked, fishing, considering I already knew about their biker history.

"Our friendship goes back to the '70s."

"Wow. That was a long time ago, before I was born even."

Sylvia made a face. I couldn't resist the little dig. Sylvia was fighting the signs of advancing maturity with a concentrated vengeance. I reluctantly had to admit that she appeared to be winning the battle. As usual, Sylvia looked flawless and was impeccably dressed to accentuate her best assets.

*Perhaps demons age at a slower pace than us mere mortals.*

"Anyway," Sylvia continued impatiently, "Harriet isn't about to let Herb get half of everything, so she killed him."

"Who told you about the alleged divorce and property settlement request?" I asked, preening with pride because I sounded like a real investigator.

"Have you been watching old reruns of *Murder She Wrote?* You sound like a bad actor delivering a cliché line."

That wounded me a bit.

"I suppose you have proof of Mrs. Greene's guilt." I waited.

"I don't need proof. She's a vindictive, miserable wretch. I know she did it. I know she killed Herb." Sylvia looked as if she were about to cry.

"Sylvia," I lowered my tone, "why do you care so much about a deadbeat husband?"

"You don't know squat about anything," Sylvia spat at me. "I gave you too much credit for intelligence. You're going to follow her trail of crumbs like a puppet, not even realizing Harriet is pulling all the strings. She's a master manipulator, and I can guarantee you that she had everything—down to the most miniscule, seemingly insignificant detail—thought out ahead of time."

I ignored her crumb/puppet mixed metaphor.

"Sylvia, our little chat has been a barrel of fun, but unless you have some concrete evidence to prove what you are implying, this conversation is over."

"Stupid. That's what you are: stupid and useless," Sylvia hissed.

"And you are a venomous snake with no conscience. I guess we each have our own burdens to bear."

"She's using you." Sylvia stalked off toward her sleek Cadillac. She opened her car door and turned to level a gaze at me. "You better watch your back!"

I got a chill and shivered, but it wasn't from the temperature. There was something final in Sylvia's warning to me. Was I supposed to watch my back from Mrs. Greene, or was Sylvia making her own personal threat? All I knew for sure was that I was tired and wanted to get to the relative warmth and safety of my home.

I checked the backseat of my car for unwanted intruders—a little late for this precautious measure—and was comforted when no one else was hiding there, waiting to scare the buhjeebers out of me. The streets were dark, and the only lights came from the occasional bluish glow of a television set visible through a curtained window.

At my apartment complex, I wearily climbed the stairs to my unit. Opening the door, I started to cross the threshold when a hand grabbed my wrist and violently pulled me inside. My attacker pressed his body into mine and had effectively pinned me to the wall. His other hand was pressed hard over my mouth.

A gravely voice whispered into my ear, "You have no survival skills whatsoever, do you?"

It was pitch black, so I couldn't make out a face. Suddenly

the scene from *Ms. Congeniality* popped into my head. When attacked, sing. *S-I-N-G:* Solar plexus, Instep, Nose, Groin!

My assailant moved back just enough to allow me to throw a short, hard punch with my elbow to the solar plexus. I heard a grunt of pain, so without missing a beat I stomped onto his instep. My attacker yelped, so I bit the fleshy part of his hand hard. When he took his injured hand away from my mouth, I was too terrified to scream. Not knowing where his nose was, I decided to skip that step and turned around to deliver a swift knee to the groin. With a woof of anguished pain, the invader released me and was rolling on the floor in the fetal position. Running for the front door, a hand caught my foot, and I fell painfully down to my knees for the second time tonight.

"Wait, Jimi."

My attacker knew my name! He sounded weak and breathless. Kicking viciously with my free leg, I caught him square in the forehead with a satisfying thud. He released my foot and curled back into a ball. Half crawling, half standing, I pulled myself through the doorway. Limping as fast as I could down the stairs, I turned to see if my assailant was following. No one was behind me, but my apartment light was on now. There silhouetted in the doorway was Jet holding one hand to his head and the other around his midsection. He came stumbling out, slightly bent over.

"Jet?" I ran back up the stairs. "What do you think you're doing?"

He leaned feebly into the doorframe. "Apparently, taking a hell of a beating."

"Were you trying to scare me to death? What gives you the right to break into my home uninvited?"

I was mad at the imposition on my privacy and embarrassed imagining Jet's horror at the sight of my messy apartment. Then I noticed an alarmingly large lump on Jet's forehead. Brushing past him, I went back inside my apartment.

"Come on. Let's see if I can find something for your head."

"I think I need to go to the hospital."

"Quit being a baby and get in here," I ordered.

"If I go in there injured, I'll need a tetanus shot too," Jet whined.

"You can't be too injured. You still have your caustic wit intact."

"Yeah, but I've been separated from my testicles. If you find them on the floor, bring them to the ER and maybe they can sew them back on. I think my foot may be broken too."

"Oh, for heaven's sake. Stop whining. I'm sure your foot isn't broken. Let me take a look at you."

The bump on his head looked ominous. I got some ice from the fridge but soon realized there was nothing to put it in. Dropping the ice into the sink, I looked around the kitchen for something soft and flexible to use. A loaf of bread caught my eye. I dumped the last few slices onto the counter and filled the plastic bag with the cubes from the sink, together with a few more from the freezer, and twisted the tie back into place.

"Lay back on the couch," I ordered Jet.

"You mean lie back on the pile of clothes that are lying on the couch?"

"See. I can tell already that you don't have a concussion."

Jet sat on a pile of discarded clothing and leaned his head back. I noticed he needed a haircut. I pushed a large, curling lock of hair back and plunked the lumpy bread wrapper onto his forehead.

"Ouch! Are you trying to kill me?"

"Maybe, if you don't give me a good reason why you were hiding in my apartment in the dark."

Jet sighed. A little rivulet of water was cascading past his eye and down his cheek. He must be in serious pain.

"Are you crying?" I asked softly.

"No, I'm not crying. The bag is leaking." He moved the bag to his lap and I pretended not to notice.

"Oh." I knelt onto the floor and pulled a past due library

book out from under my knee and tossed it over my shoulder. "Let's get your shoe and sock off and inspect for damage."

"Where did you learn your defense skills? Maim Foe Dojo?"

"No. I learned from Sandra Bullock."

Jet looked confused.

"I've watched *Ms. Congeniality* at least a half dozen times. You know the scene where she kicked Benjamin Brat's character arrogant butt on national TV? Anyway, that movie is a favorite of mine." Truth was I had probably watched the movie well *over* a dozen times. "Your foot is a little, shall we say, *puffy*." It was actually a lot swollen and a lovely shade of periwinkle. "Why don't we go ahead and get you to the hospital?" It was a little chilly outside, so I attempted to put his shoe back on his foot.

Jet screamed so loudly it put my girlie scream from earlier to shame.

"Sorry."

"I gotta go." Jet sounded tired. "Hand me my shoe, and I'll get out of here."

"Jet, why were you here? I told you I'd be at the office late."

"I didn't think you'd be there *this* late. Anyway, I came by to see what, if anything, you had learned about Herb. When I found your door unlocked, I decided to teach you a lesson."

"Well then, you'll be happy to know I've learned my lesson."

"Yeah. Well, I learned you do have some survival skills after all."

We both paused for introspection.

"I'll take you to the hospital if you want," I offered, holding out the olive branch.

"No. I just want to go home." He handed me the leaking bread bag and hobbled to the door.

"I really am sorry, Jet. I didn't know it was you."

"I sure hope you didn't know it was me," Jet said. Then, as

an after thought, he said, "I'm going to hire someone else for the office."

"You're firing me? I said I was sorry. It wasn't my fault. You're to blame more than—"

Jet put a hand up. "Relax. I meant that with you and I trying to fill in for Harriet's duties and still get our own jobs done, we're going to need a little assistance."

"Oh," I said, feeling a little silly.

"Put an ad in the next issue for office help."

I arched an eyebrow.

"Please."

"Sure thing, boss." I smiled and snapped a salute.

"I'll get with you tomorrow about Harriet. Goodnight, Jimi."

"Goodnight, Jet. I truly am sorry about, well, you know, beating you up and everything."

"Jimi, beating me up implies I fought back. If I had been a real intruder with evil intentions . . . You know what? I can't even think about it right now. Just lock your door, all right?"

"Okay."

Jet left, and I could hear his halting gait fading off toward the stairs—*Clump! Drag! Clump! Drag!*—reminiscent of the sound that Quasimodo made while shuffling around in the bell tower. That's when I noticed the little bouquet of trampled flowers that had fallen to the floor. The card read "Jimi, Thanks for all your hard work. Jet." I breathed in the sweet fragrance of miniature roses and lacy carnations.

*Poor Jet. I think Ms. Congeniality may have broken his foot.*

# chapter 7

Arriving at the office early, I made a strong pot of coffee in the big carafe. A continuous onslaught of caffeine should help me get through the day. I quickly created an ad for an office assistant. Jet hadn't given me too many details, so "general office duties" and "salary DOE" would have to cover it.

I needed to get in to see Mrs. Greene again. Her shock over the dolly rental seemed genuine. After placing a call to the county jail, I was informed that visiting hours for Mrs. Greene's (a.k.a. inmate #22756) housing unit were only on Wednesdays and Saturdays from 8:00 a.m. to 11:00 a.m. and Thursdays from 6:00 p.m. to 9:00 p.m. Since this was Friday, I'd have to wait until tomorrow morning to visit again.

Daniel ambled over to my desk. "Hey, Jimi. What's new?"

"My supervisor may very well be a homicidal maniac."

"So I hear." He leaned comfortably on the corner of my desk as usual. "I released my photos of the body to the police. You should see them."

"Uh, thanks but no thanks. Seeing it once in person was more than enough for me."

"Wanna hear something really crazy?"

"Sure. Fire away." I was distracted getting my pc to boot up and not really paying Daniel much attention.

"I heard that Mrs. Greene was hysterically demanding to see the pictures of her dear ol' dead husband."

I perked right up. "You're kidding. Why would she do that?"

"She said that she didn't believe Herb was dead. She wanted to see the pictures and prove it wasn't Herb they found."

"Did they show them to her?" I asked, appalled.

"Of course. They wanted to see her reaction." Daniel was just warming up to his story.

"And?" I waited.

"She looked at every single one of them, pausing for a long time over each."

"Gross." I couldn't imagine anyone wanting to see pictures of a corpse, especially a corpse of someone they had once been intimate with. "So, how did she react?"

Daniel hesitated for dramatic effect. "She just calmly stacked them up and handed them back to the detective and said, 'It's Herb,' then asked if she could go back to her cell. No tears—no reaction whatsoever. It made her look even guiltier."

"Well, that's not really fair because, let's face it, she isn't exactly prone to wearing her emotions on her sleeve."

"All I can say is the detective thought it was peculiar."

"How did you find all this out?" I was interested in his source of information.

"I used to be good friends with the stenographer, Stacy."

"They use stenographers during questioning?"

"Actually, I think she hits the record and stop button on a tape recorder."

"Do you know if Mrs. Greene was only questioned this one time?" I asked.

"I don't know. Why?"

"I was hoping you could get me a transcript or copy of the tapes."

"Getting an old girlfriend to tell me a few details is a far cry from stealing evidence from the police."

"Is that a no?"

"It's a *hell no!*"

"You don't have to swear at me. I was just asking."

"Sorry." He didn't seem all that contrite. "How 'bout you let me make it up to you?"

He waited for me to respond. When I didn't, he continued with his makeup offer.

"Do you like seafood? I know this fantastic restaurant in Boise. All the crab legs you can eat."

"I don't eat seafood since I found out fishies eat the eyes out of dead bodies."

"Those are river fishies. Ocean fishies have a much more discriminating palate."

Daniel was so easy and uncomplicated, and not too hard on the eyes either. I wished I understood why I wasn't more attracted to him.

"I'd rather have a good, juicy burger and a funny movie."

"You're on. I'll pick you up at six tonight."

"I hope you realize this isn't a date. It's just two coworkers going out to dinner and a movie because one of the coworkers is too chicken to steal records from the local police."

"I promise to be on my best behavior." He crossed his heart and held up the Boy Scout salute promise fingers.

"I can't imagine what *you* consider to be good behavior." I laughed.

Daniel waggled his eyebrows at me and then meandered off. If possible, there was a little more swagger to his step than normal. What the heck. I hadn't done anything fun in a while. Kirstie was so busy expanding her new shop, and Dibbz and Granddad never did like to go out much. Even my brother, Spence, was too busy to socialize with me. A night out would be great. I was surprised by how much I was looking forward to it.

Turning my attention back to my computer, I started a background and public records check of Herbert M. Greene. The first search produced a big, fat goose egg. His birth date and marriage date was the only information I gleaned. The criminal background check didn't provide much more: a drunk and disorderly in 1972 and an aggravated assault in 1979, resulting from a barroom brawl in Balch Springs, Texas. Herb had pled guilty to both and spent a minimal amount of time in the county lockup for each offense.

I was going to have to leave the comfort of my office and investigate the old-fashioned way: visit the places he lived and worked. I thought I'd start in reverse order, at his last known whereabouts in Harmony, Idaho. Too bad the letter from Herb didn't mention the name of the ranch where he was working.

I printed out all the directory listings for ranches in the Harmony area. It wouldn't be a complete list, but at least it would be a start. Then I decided to print the listings for local bars and farm and ranch supply stores. *Now, that's thinking like a detective,* I thought. *I just wish I had a photo of Herb.* Picking up the phone, I dialed Daniel's mobile number.

After the third ring, I was about to hang up, when I heard Daniel's voice come on the line.

"This is Daniel."

"Daniel, it's Jimi."

"Let me guess. You want me to pick you up now instead of six o'clock tonight. I knew you'd fall prey to my infinite charms."

"Daniel, shall I tell you why your charms are most definitely finite?"

"Maybe you should just tell me why you called."

"Do you have any photos of Herb, where you can tell it's him but without the gaping empty eye sockets?"

"Well," he paused while he thought about it, "I think I may have a couple of profile shots and some close-ups of his tattoo. I even have a really cool picture of his arm with the skin peeled off."

"Could you get me a copy of the profile shots and the tattoo, while the skin is *still* on the arm?"

"When do you need it by?" he asked.

"Five minutes ago."

"I'm turning the car around as we speak." I heard the squeal of tires and horns honking.

"Daniel, are you okay?"

"The semi truck I made my U-turn in front of must have been speeding. I hate reckless drivers."

"Uh huh. Just get here safely, okay?"

"Be there in ten minutes," he said, and he clicked his phone off.

I gathered up my notebook and directory lists and headed outside. It really was a spectacular day, and with fall fast approaching I wanted to take advantage of the sunshine. Exiting through the back door of the office, I went to the parking lot. Jet was just pulling in. He got out of his Navigator with more than a little difficulty. One foot was encased in a medical walking boot. I guess *Ms. Congeniality* may have fractured his foot after all. As he headed toward me, I noted the huge, ugly bruise on his forehead.

"What happened to you? Get run over by a truck?" I asked innocently.

"Very funny." He didn't sound like he was laughing.

"I really am sorry about what happened, but you have to admit it was your fault."

"I'm certainly never hiding out in your apartment again."

"You wouldn't be able to anyway. I lock the door now."

"At least something good resulted from this," he added, shaking a crutch in my direction. "So, what are you doing out here?"

"Waiting for Daniel."

"Why?" His foot must have really been bothering him, because he sounded very unhappy at the moment.

"I'm going to Harmony to see if I can find the ranch where Herb worked. Thought I could show some of the pictures Daniel took around with me. Maybe someone will recognize Herb."

"You're using the photos Daniel took of the body? That should raise more than a few eyebrows, not to mention the contents of a stomach or two."

"He said he has some profile shots that aren't too gruesome and a close-up of the tattoo."

"Might work. Good thinking," Jet complimented.

"Why, thank you, sir." I gave a little bow of my head in mock humility.

"Jimi, I was thinking. Why don't you come over to my place tonight to discuss Harriet's case? I'll even make you dinner."

I thought about my semi-quasi, non-date with Daniel tonight.

"I can't make it. Unfortunately, I already made plans." *Dear Lord, please please please don't let him ask me what my plans are. Amen.*

"What do you have going?"

"A trip to Boise for a burger and movie with a friend."

"I thought Kirstie was too busy with her new shop to go anywhere." Jet made an assumption based on my very limited circle of acquaintances. "I think it will do you great to get out and relax a bit. Maybe tomorrow night then?"

"Tomorrow would be great. I'm going to try and talk to Mrs. Greene again. Visiting hours are from 8:00 a.m. to 11:00 a.m. I figured I'd head over at about 9:30. That will give me at least an hour with her, assuming she will talk to me that long."

"It will also give you another hour of sleep, I'm guessing. Why not head over at eight o'clock?"

"No one should meet with Mrs. Greene unless they have had a full night's sleep, a hearty fast-food sausage breakfast biscuit, and at least three cups of java coursing through their veins."

Jet smiled. We both knew I simply wanted to sleep in. Daniel stopped his Corvette but didn't pull into a parking space. Without even bothering to shut off the engine, he got out and went over to the passenger's side of the car and retrieved a soft leather brief case.

"Jet." Daniel gave Jet the *guy* nod.

"Forsythe." Jet returned the *guy* nod.

Daniel opened the case and retrieved a manila folder of photographs. He took three pictures out and handed them to me. The pictures were unpleasant, but I didn't think anyone would faint or throw up over them. Actually, using me as a litmus test was a good idea since I had such a low threshold for blood and gore.

"Gotta run. I'm taking some pictures of the high school's football preseason training at Bannock Field and need to get going," Daniel said. "I'll see you tonight at six, Jimi." Daniel got into his car and pulled away with a wave.

*It's gonna hit the fan now.*

"I'd better get going," I mumbled, turning toward my car.

"Stop!" Jet bellowed.

"I have a lot to do and better get to it." My back was to Jet as I clumsily attempted to open the car door. Some people stutter when they're nervous; I get klutzy.

"Turn around."

This sounded suspiciously like an order. I *hate* being ordered around.

"Yes?" I turned to face Jet, trying to control my irritation.

"You're going out with Daniel?" He made it sound as if I were having tea and crumpets with Osama bin Ladin.

"No. I'm going to dinner with a friend."

"And that friend is Daniel." The bruise on his forehead was certainly standing out now. Perhaps it was the large vein pulsating next to the bruise that made it appear more prominent.

"Well, yeah. I told him it wasn't a date and he said, 'Fine,'" I explained. Then it hit me; why should I account for my actions anyway? "What business is this of yours? Just who do you think you are?"

The vein on his forehead was ferociously throbbing. "I'm your boss!"

"Excuse me, but I thought that title was exclusive to office hours. Anything unrelated to work is not your concern." My voice was shrilly.

"The paper doesn't permit office romances."

"First, this isn't an office romance, and second, the handbook states that it's discouraged, not prohibited. I checked." I read that paragraph twice, mostly with thoughts of Jet in mind.

"Jimi, Forsythe is a great photographer, but I've tried to tell you that he's not known for his ethics with women."

"And I have told you that it's not a date. Also, as your present injuries should attest to, I *am* capable of taking care of myself."

"You're delusional." By his prolonged, indrawn breath, I could tell Jet was trying to calm himself and would now attempt to reason with me. Little did he know, I was feeling rather *unreasonable.* "Forsythe is a practiced professional at the art of seduction."

"And I'm the reigning princess of avoidance and deflection." Jet ought to know that by now. The few times I thought he might get close to me, either my anger or other extenuating circumstances always got in the way.

"You know, you still haven't given me details on what you found out about Herb, or what Harriet told you either. Don't you think that's more important than a night out?"

"Two minutes ago you told me a night out would 'do me good', why the change in attitude?"

Jet started to answer then shrugged his shoulders and headed for the office. "Do whatever you want. It doesn't matter in the slightest to me." His unfounded anger indicated otherwise.

"You were trying to control my choices."

"I wish I could." He limped into the office without so much as a wave or a good-bye.

Jeez. He was so temperamental. And here I am so easy going and accommodating, generally speaking. In retrospect, I wish I hadn't accepted Daniel's offer. An intimate dinner with Jet was much more appealing. *Intimate, what made me think of that particular word?* Who was I kidding? I'd been attracted to Jet since I was sixteen.

*Resolution to self: next time Jet asks me to spend time with him, don't prevaricate; just say* yes!

The trip to Harmony only took about fifteen minutes. I decided to try the farm and ranch store first. Pulling into the packed dirt parking lot of the Plow 'n Herder, I noticed I had the only *car* in the lot. There were several pickups in various stages of age and disrepair. Each truck had a thick layer of dust, and all but one had a rifle in a rack mounted on the rear window. The other truck probably had a shotgun on the front seat for easy access, but I wasn't going to check it out.

A bell jingled overhead, announcing my arrival. This was much like the auto parts store in that absolutely nothing looked familiar.

"Kin I hep ya, little lady?" the portly, grubby man behind the counter asked.

"I hope so," I said, pulling out the manila folder containing Herb's death photos. I was suddenly very self-conscious about my mission. "I was wondering if you would look at some photographs and tell me if you know who the subject is."

He looked eagerly curious. "Why, sure."

"I'm Jimi Smith, reporter for the *Ditters Weekly* paper," I said, extending my hand.

"Pleased to meet ya," he said, grasping my hand with his filthy one. His fingernails were jagged, broken, and encrusted with dirt and grime. "I'm Gerald Goode, owner of this here store."

I shook his hand cautiously, trying to avoid contact with his fingernails.

"Before you look at the pictures, I need to warn you that the man in them is deceased."

"Then he won't mind my a'lookin' at 'em, will he?"

"What I mean to say is these pictures were taken post mortem."

"What's thet?"

*Ah, Gerald, Gerald, Gerald, you just can't make this easy for me, can you?*

*susan case*

"Post mortem, as in he's already dead in the photos."

Gerald looked positively jubilant at the prospect of viewing the pictures now.

"I don' mind a bit. I gots me a strong stomach." He patted his generous midsection girth.

I opened the folder and slid the close-up of the tattoo across the counter to Gerald. He looked extremely disappointed in the shot.

"Cain't tell nuthin' from this. Ya got sumthin' better?" he asked hopefully.

If he didn't recognize this highly unusual tattoo, he probably didn't know Herb. "Well, here's another." I slid the profile photo across.

"Looks all bloated. Hard ta tell. Did he drowned?"

Before I could answer, he was bellowing for someone named Maybelle.

"Maybelle! C'mere!"

In walked the exact opposite of what I expected. A woman named Maybelle should be round, jolly, and wearing a shapeless floral dress. Instead, Maybelle was about five feet tall and weighed on the shy side of eighty pounds. She moved quickly and had sparkling blue eyes. She positively buzzed with radiated energy.

"Gerald B. Goode, stop that hollering!"

Gerald winked at me. "My middle name don't start with a *b*. She's a-tellin' me to *be* good."

"Come over here, Mother, and look at these pictures."

"I'm trying to get the books done," she said. Then Maybelle noticed me and gave a welcoming smile. "May I help you?"

"She wants us to identify a dead body," Gerald inserted excitedly.

"Oh. Okay," she answered as if she were asked to ID a dead body every day.

Gerald was extremely disappointed with her lack of enthusiasm, but he handed the photographs to his wife for inspection.

After carefully looking at the pictures, Maybelle said she didn't recognize the man in the photo. Gerald didn't either.

"Wasn't there anyone who could identify the poor man?" Maybelle asked with sincere empathy. "What made you look in Harmony, if I may ask?"

"We know who it is and that he worked at a ranch around Harmony, but we need more background information for our investigation."

"Investigation?" Maybelle's curiosity was aroused. "Was he *murdered?*" She whispered the last word.

"Yes. He was stabbed and then dumped into the river."

"Oh my," Maybelle said.

With his pasty, round, white face, Gerald's eyes looked as big as two Oreo cookies floating in a bowl of milk.

"Thank you both so much for your time. I really need to check out some other possible leads," I said.

"Where are you headed, Miss—?"

"It's Smith. Jimi Smith. I'm a reporter for the *Ditters Weekly* newspaper."

"Isn't that something, and you being so young and all." Maybelle sounded impressed. Obviously she didn't subscribe to the paper.

"I'm headed over to the mini-mart, then the local store and the two bars in town. If that doesn't yield anything, I'll check out the larger ranches in the area."

"What kind of vehicle do you drive, Miss Smith?"

"It's Jimi." I smiled. "I drive a 2003 Mazda Protégé. Why?"

"The roads are too rough and dirty for your car."

"Maybelle, you don't even know what a Mazda Protégé is," Gerald scolded his wife.

"I know every make and model of heavy duty truck and four-wheel drive ever manufactured, and a Mazda Protégé isn't one of them," Maybelle shot back to her husband, completely without rancor.

*susan case*

It was obvious the two adored each other but liked a little spark of debate now and again.

"Good point," Gerald responded.

They both looked at me expectantly.

"I'll give it my best shot and see what happens," I said.

"Jimi, I'll take you around in our truck. It'll be easier if have someone with you that people recognize, and my truck can handle any type of terrain. Besides, most folks around here are more careful," Maybelle said as she looked pointedly at her husband, "than to just start talking about their neighbors . . ."

"I couldn't put you out like that. I'm sure my car will do fine, and if not I'll find a truck and come back tomorrow."

"Nonsense. It isn't any trouble at all. In fact, I could use the fresh air." Maybelle settled the matter.

Gerald looked so disappointed. His bottom lip was even sticking out. "Maybelle, don't you have to finish the books? I kin take Miz Smith 'round." Gerald looked hopeful.

"Those books can wait until tomorrow." Maybelle pulled Gerald's face down to her and kissed him affectionately. "I'll be back soon."

Gerald blushed to the roots of his hair and smiled at his wife.

"Let's get going, Miss Smith." Maybelle was already half the distance to the door. "We've got a lot of ground to cover."

I couldn't say "no" to her offer now, and it would be nice to have someone with me who was familiar with the area and townspeople.

I extended my hand again. "Thank you, Gerald. It's been a pleasure meeting you."

Gerald shook my hand firmly. "You too, Miz Smith."

Maybelle escorted me to the rear of the building. Together we approached the biggest, baddest, tallest truck I had ever seen. It was a mud-encrusted Ford F350 that had been lifted to the heavens with tires that looked like they belonged on a tractor. Not only did the truck have a step down, the step down folded out to another lowered step. There was a handhold on the side of the cab to help hoist oneself up into the truck. Maybelle's Ford was just a hair smaller than a semi truck. Tiny Maybelle swung herself in with ease, while I looked like a newborn colt with awkward, wobbly legs. Once seated, though, I had to admire the view. Not much could block your line of sight in this rig.

"Let's go to Smitty's Bar," Maybelle suggested. "It's the most frequented place for ranch hands on Friday and Saturday nights. It's too early to talk to any regular patrons, but we might have some luck with the bartender."

Smitty's Bar was less than a mile away, and Maybelle parked at the hitching rail out front. I wondered if people still rode their horses into town and tied their horses to the post. The inside of the bar was dark and smelled of stale smoke. Scarred wooden chairs sat around matching scarred wooden tables. The bar was adorned with a line of tall, chrome barstools with black vinyl seats. The jukebox in the corner was playing a country and western song. The gravel-voiced female singer was lamenting the loss of a tooth and potential love while praising the virtues of Jack Daniels by the bucketful, thus reinforcing my theory that country and western music causes loss of brain function.

Maybelle walked directly to the bar and ordered a Coke with lime, then looked at me expectantly.

"I'll have the same." Never tried Coke and lime before, but it sounded interesting.

The bartender poured the teaspoon of cola over the ice packed into a tall, slim glass, then squeezed a sliver of lime into each. He set out two small, white cocktail napkins and set our drinks before us.

"That'll be $5.50."

I reached for my wallet, but before I could even pull it out, Maybelle told him to put it on Gerald's tab and to add a $1.50 tip as well.

"Thanks, Miz Goode." The barkeep smiled.

"Maybelle, please let me pay for our drinks," I insisted.

"Oh, horsefeathers." Maybelle gave a dismissive wave of her hand. "Gerald keeps a running tab here. He doesn't drink much, but he likes to come in here on Saturday nights for some nickel ante Texas Hold 'em and to drink a couple of beers with his buddies."

"Mickey, this is Miss Jimi Smith, a reporter from the *Ditters Weekly*," Maybelle said by way of introduction. "She'd like to show you some pictures."

I opened the manila folder and slid the picture of the tattooed arm over first.

"That's Herb's arm. What'cha got a picture of Herb's tattoo fer?" Mickey asked.

I wanted to jump up and down with glee. It was difficult to contain my excitement. "I'm trying to find out where he worked."

"Worked? Was he fired?" Mickey was a little more cautious now. "Why are you lookin' fer him?"

"Well, Mickey,"—I decided to jump in with the truth—"he was found dead in the river, and I'm trying to find out some details for an investigation. Herb was, by all indications, murdered."

Mickey shrugged his shoulders. "Not surprised. He was a mean SOB, always startin' fights just so's he could bloody someone up. Never saw anyone who enjoyed inflictin' pain more 'n him. He even seemed to enjoy the hits he took. See this here?" Mickey pointed to an ugly jagged scar on his right cheekbone, just below his eye. "Herb cut me with a broken beer bottle while I was trying to break up one of his fights."

For a moment I thought Mickey might be a potential suspect, but it made no sense how he could get access to Mrs. Greene's envelope opener.

"Like I said," Mickey continued, "Herb was a mean SOB."

This simply didn't jive with the Herb I knew from his letters to Harriet. Maybe he was mean only when drinking. I still puzzled over the incongruity between Mickey's description and the man who wrote heart-wrenching letters to Harriet.

"Do you know where Herb worked?" I asked hopefully.

"He was a ranch hand for Mr. Conway at the 501." I noticed Mickey had no problem referring to Herb in the past tense.

"Thank you, Mickey. You've been a tremendous help."

Maybelle took her cola from the counter and motioned me to follow her over to a table in the far corner. Maybelle had her forehead furrowed and nose scrunched up. We sat and enjoyed a few sips of our drinks before Maybelle started talking about what seemed to be bothering her.

"Mr. Conway hates Gerald, so I'm not too excited about going out to his ranch," Maybelle stated.

"Okay. Well, I appreciate everything you've done. If you give me directions to the ranch, I'll head out there by myself."

"Now, don't go getting your britches in a bunch. I'm only contemplating how to handle this. I'm taking you to the 501; I just need a couple of moments to gather myself."

"Maybelle, you've already gone far out of your way to assist me. I don't mind going alone."

"Little girl, you'd probably get yourself shot. Levi can be nasty and not prone to being helpful."

We sat each in our own thoughts for a while. Finally, my curiosity got the better of me.

"Why does Mr. Conway dislike Gerald? I can't imagine anyone disliking him," I said honestly.

"It's a long story, and an old one to boot," Maybelle said, "but here it is in a nutshell. I am an only child and was raised on a large ranch that borders the equally large and impressive 501. The Conways had one son, Leviticus, or Levi for short. Both ranches were well-run and turned around good profits. My folks and the Conways were best friends. I used to run around with Levi. We grew up playing together, catching frogs by the river, tipping cows, and even getting my first kiss at fourteen in the hayloft at the 501. Both sets of parents were determined to marry

113

us off to each other. I guess Levi wanted that too. But I needed to explore the world outside Harmony a bit. So, at eighteen I left for college in Nevada. Levi assumed I'd get homesick and come back in a few months. Instead I came back two years later with a husband in tow. Gerald and I got married in a quickie ceremony in Las Vegas. I wanted to marry him before my parents could interfere. Eventually my folks grudgingly accepted Gerald, but Levi never got over it. Levi was used to getting his own way and couldn't stand to be second to anyone. He was furious and has never gotten over his little tantrum. It's not me he wanted; it was winning and, of course, owning what would have been the largest ranch in Idaho."

"With how Mr. Conway feels about Gerald, maybe you shouldn't go out to his ranch with me."

"Nonsense. It's about time Levi gets over his pout anyway." Maybelle thoughtfully crunched on a piece of ice. "Let's go."

"Are you sure?" I didn't want to cause any trouble for Maybelle.

"I never say anything I don't mean."

I believed that about her.

With a good-bye to Mickey, we went back outside and climbed into her truck. "It's a twenty-minute drive out to the 501."

"Well, then you have time to tell me how you met Gerald."

Maybelle smiled at my prompting for another story.

"You believe in love at first sight?" Maybelle asked.

"I believe in attraction at first sight."

"Fair enough," Maybelle declared. "During college, I got a job waitressing at a truck stop. The tips were great, and the owners allowed me to work around my class schedule. Anyway, I'd been there about a month when this filthy, grimy trucker came in and wanted to use the phone." She paused. "Mind you, this was years before everyone and their dog had a cell phone." Maybelle continued with her story. "I asked the trucker if it was a local call, and he replied, 'Miss, I don't know anyone in this town, but if I was to know someone here I'd want it to be you.' He had the softest brown eyes and the sweetest smile. He even blushed when he said it, so he wasn't the typical polished flirt. I told him the payphone was outside and for small change he could call someone he knew. He pulled out a dollar and asked for ten dimes. I gave him the dimes, and he went outside to the payphone. About three minutes later, the phone at the diner rang.

"When I answered, the voice on the other end said, 'Is this Maybelle?' Apparently he had made note of my name tag.

"I said, 'Yes, this is Maybelle. May I help you?'

"He said, 'Since I spent ten cents to find out the diner's phone number and then spent another ten cents to call you, I thought you might say yes to having dinner with me tonight.'

"I looked out the window, and there was the filthy trucker with the beautiful, bashful smile looking back at me. I turned my back to him because I didn't want him to see I was smiling too. I said, 'You think I'm impressed that you spent twenty cents trying to get my attention?'

"He said, 'Sweetheart, you tell me what it will take to impress you, and I'll make it happen.'

"I said, 'I guess if you could dance like Gene Kelley, sing like Sinatra, and were carrying a dozen yellow roses, that might impress me a little.'

"He said, 'Done.' He hung up and I laughed. Two hours later there was a clean-shaven lunatic with an old umbrella in one hand and a dozen yellow baby roses in the other hand. He was singing—badly, I might add—at the top of his lungs. The goofball was attempting to perform Gene Kelly's famous *Singing in the Rain* bit. Anyway, he's spinning the umbrella and then gets his foot caught up in the spokes. He falls teapot over kettle, drops the roses, and breaks the umbrella. Instead of slinking away embarrassed, he gets up, noticeably limping with a torn pant leg, and continues his song and dance. Bleeding and embarrassed, he took a bow and, still smiling, begged me to go out with him.

"Now I ask you, how could I not fall in love with him immediately? Anyway, he quit his trucking job and moved to Las Vegas where I was attending university. We've been inseparable since. We got married as soon as he made enough money for a down payment on the feed store in Harmony. He knew how much I missed my parents and the town where I grew up. Gerald wanted to wait to get married so I could have a big church wedding with friends and family. He wanted my father's permission first too. I was so afraid that my folks would try and end our relationship and scare Gerald off. Oh, honey, how I cried and carried on until Gerald finally gave in. We got married on a Thursday and were in Harmony, Idaho, by the following Sunday."

"How did your parents take it?"

"Not well. In fact, not well at all. It took years before they accepted Gerald. They also weren't too happy that he didn't want to work on the ranch. Gerald wanted to be his own man and make his own living working for himself. For a man with just a seventh-grade education, he's smart and hardworking." Her pride in Gerald was endearing.

"Here we are," Maybelle announced.

We pulled up to an iron swing gate. The post above carried a sign that looked like a cattle brand, declaring "501 Ranch." Maybelle asked me to open the gate. I got out and unlatched the gate and swung it wide for the truck to enter. After she pulled through, I shut the gate and made sure it was latched and hopped back into the truck.

I couldn't see a home or any outbuildings. "Where's the ranch?"

"It's another mile from here." Maybelle pointed to an outcropping of trees at the base of a hill. "The house is tucked back into those trees. It really is a spectacular home."

In the distance were seven large, white windmills with three blades each. "Are those part of the Conway ranch?"

"Yes. Beef doesn't pay like it used to. Since there is rarely a day in Idaho without wind, especially out here on the plains, wind generation is a wise investment. Several of the farms around here have them. Most make more money off the electricity they produce than the beef they raise."

They weren't quaint little wooden Dutch windmills, but they weren't an eyesore either. They kind of looked like giant seagulls with wings spread wide, spinning on poles—well, if seagulls had three wings anyway.

The clearing of trees was approaching, and I could see a few outbuildings: barns, sheds, and what appeared to be small bungalows, and then one spacious building with large windows on every side and a huge chimney rising from the corrugated roof. Farther into the haven of magnificent old trees, the dirt road made a gentle curve, and a huge, sprawling, one-story ranch-style house appeared. Maybelle was correct in her description; the home was truly spectacular. A twelve-foot-deep porch wrapped around three sides of the home. Large baskets of flowers in a rainbow of colors and textures hung from the eves every couple of feet. Whiskey barrels overflowed with more flora. An old wagon wheel was tipped onto a large boulder and was shaded by a lush pine tree. The home itself was made of rich, sturdy, hewn logs. Decorative wrought iron dormers framed each window. A ruffle of faded gingham curtains could be seen through the windows. Rocking chairs and assorted benches made the porch a welcoming place to chat and maybe have a tall, cold glass of lemonade. A huge brass spittoon was placed next to the front door. I was expecting Ben, Hoss, or Little Joe to greet us at any moment. This was a home of a time gone by. You could sense the history in every scar of the wood made by heavy boots and spurs.

Maybelle broke my reverie. "I told you it was grand."

"Wow. I didn't expect this." The porch seemed to go forever in each direction.

Maybelle smiled at the awe in my voice.

*susan case*

"Wait until you see the ranch where I grew up. It's very different, but equally impressive."

I was touched that she would even think to take me there, as it had nothing to do with my investigation of Herb. Maybelle had a way of making a person feel accepted.

"Mom still lives there. Dad passed on a few years ago, but she and Manny, the foreman, still run the place with precision and a love of ranching. There are a few less horses and a lot more four-wheelers, but other than that the ranch runs much as it has for over a hundred years."

Maybelle grasped the iron knocker and gave it a few quick raps on the door. Before anyone could answer, a voice boomed from behind us, making us both jump.

"What the hell are you doing here, *Mrs. Goode?*"

We were confronted by a tall, lean cowboy who had seen more than his share of wind and sun. He might have been considered handsome in a cigarette commercial sort of way if it weren't for the nasty scowl on his face. His dusty Levis hung on slim hips. He had long legs that ended in leather boots that weren't worn for style but for hard, dirty work. Around his squinted, intense blue eyes were slashes of deep crow's feet. The blue of his eyes was not of the soft summer afternoon sky variety, but more in a steely there's-a-storm-approaching shade.

"Good afternoon, Leviticus."

Judging by his face, the name Leviticus didn't set too well with him.

"Don't you remove your hat in the presence of ladies anymore? And I *know* you were raised better than to swear at a woman," Maybelle scolded. Her tone was firm but not too harsh.

Leviticus spit a stream of coffee-colored tobacco juice onto the ground not too far from where my feet were on the porch. "Don't see any *ladies.*"

What a disgusting habit. I tried not to stare at the spittle on the dirt in front of me.

Maybelle moved to the edge of the porch, placing her hands

on nonexistent hips. "Levi Conway, it's been thirty-four years and you're still pouting like a spoiled, four-year-old boy. Now, take your hat off this instant and greet us properly."

The cowboy's face flushed, and his square jaw clenched tight. They stared each other down for several seconds before his gaze lowered and he reluctantly removed his hat. The sweat-stained brim was being mauled by large, calloused, brown hands. Mr. Conway was trying hard to control his temper.

"Very well," he said tightly. "To what do I owe the honor of this visit, *ladies?*"

The sarcasm was lost on no one. However, Maybelle chose to ignore it.

"Levi, this is Miss Smith. She's a reporter for the *Ditters Weekly,* and she'd like to ask you some questions about an employee of yours."

He looked at me as if he had just noticed my presence for the first time.

"And why would I be talking to a reporter about one of my men?" Mr. Conway graveled out.

"Because this employee of yours was murdered," Maybelle stated flatly.

This took the wind right out of him, though he tried hard to mask his expression with indifference. "Who you askin' about?" he said in my direction and spat another flow of liquefied tobacco.

"I was hoping you could tell me something about Herb Greene." I rushed on. "I understand he's worked for you the past six years."

"Herb's dead?" He didn't even blink.

"Yes, sir. His body was found in the river a few days ago—definitely a victim of homicide."

"He was a mean cuss and given to wandering off every now and again. But he kept to himself and worked hard, so I was always takin' him back on."

"May I see his quarters?" I asked hopefully.

There was a long pause while he continued to study Maybelle.

*susan case*

119

He shook his head as if to clear it. "Suit yourself. It's bungalow eight." He pointed to the row of individual housing. "I've got work to do, so get your investigating done and then get off my property." He was already walking away. "And don't forget to shut the gate behind you."

Maybelle was already briskly walking toward the bungalows. I took a few steps and then looked back. Leviticus Conway had stopped and was staring at Maybelle with the most tortured expression of unrequited love I'd ever seen. He caught my gaze and stuffed his gray Stetson angrily onto his head then glared at me before striding off. Maybelle was wrong about Leviticus Conway; she wasn't something he wanted to win or a prized possession he lost. Maybelle was and continued to be the love of his life. It wasn't her family's ranch he wanted; it was Maybelle herself—facts to which she seemed completely oblivious.

Maybelle was walking up the steps to bungalow eight. She opened the door and let me pass to get inside. It was a very small room, but kept tidy. The wooden plank floors were swept clean of any dust or debris. A multicolored, braided rag rug was the only covering on the floor. The single bunk was neatly made with a scratchy-looking wool blanket. One chair and a small night stand with two thin drawers completed the furnishings. There were hooks on the wall where an extra pair of jeans and two western-style shirts hung. A chipped, beveled mirror was bracketed to the wall opposing the bed. No pictures on the walls, no books—nothing personal was anywhere in sight.

I opened the top drawer of the nightstand only to find a deck of playing cards, a neat stack of folded handkerchiefs, one pen, and an empty notepad. The second drawer contained some rolled-up socks and underwear and a matchbook from a Twin Falls hotel, which I pocketed. And that was it. There was nothing under the bed or hidden floor or wall compartments. What a bust.

"Where does he keep all his personal effects? Surely this can't be everything."

"He probably keeps his shaving kit in the shower house," Maybelle offered.

A razor, toothbrush, and deodorant weren't what I was looking for, but I didn't want to hurt her feelings.

"Do you think we could interview some of the other hands?" I asked Maybelle.

"Most will be out working. It's only a little past noon, but we can stop by the mess hall and see if Cookie is around."

"You know the cook here?" I asked.

"Every big ranch has a cookhouse and dining hall, and every cook is called Cookie." I was gleaning a lot of new information about ranching.

We left Herb's bungalow and went to the large building with the chimney. There were numerous tables and chairs and a buffet-style counter. Off to one side by the picture windows was an area with comfy couches and low tables in a semicircle around the biggest fireplace I had ever seen. I wished I'd had a cup of tea and a good book with me, because I'd make myself at home. The cozy corner alcove was an inviting retreat.

There was a rustle of pots and pans behind the buffet counter. Maybelle went to the swinging doors and pushed them open, entering the kitchen with me following closely at her heels. A stout, muscled figure was busy stirring something steaming in a large pot. Several cast iron fry pans were out, and a board with fresh vegetables, about half of which were already chopped, waited for someone to finish the job. A huge chef's knife lay to the side.

"Can I help you?"

I had no idea if the voice or body belonged to a man or a woman. Perhaps a name would help me discern if the cook was male or female.

"Hi, Cookie. I'm Maybelle Goode. Mr. Conway said we could visit around the ranch, so we wanted to stop by and see the dining hall."

"The name ain't Cookie; it's Terry. You been readin' too many western novels," the cook said. Terry for a name certainly did not help the ambiguous gender question.

Maybelle blushed at her blunder but recovered quickly. "We were looking for anyone who might be close to Herb Greene."

"Most folks don't get close to a rattlesnake," Terry commented as he/she tapped the long-handled wooden spoon against the rim of the giant iron pot. Terry then began finishing the vegetable chopping job. I'm ashamed to say I was looking for traces of an Adam's apple or bra strap marks to solve the gender mystery.

"You didn't like Herb?" Maybelle asked Terry, the he/she Cookie.

"Didn't like him, still don't like him, won't ever like him. Herb's only decent trait was that he loved my apple spiced-walnut double crust pie. All that sugar, you'd think it would sweeten him up a bit. But he is an ornery, nasty varmint. More'n one good hand left this ranch because of him." The words were feminine, but the voice was low and masculine. Not much help there.

"Why do you dislike Herb so much?" I asked, still checking for signs of mustache or mascara.

"Never has a nice word for no one. Gets in fights all the time and has no respect for no one or nothin'. Once had me a crooked-headed yellow tabby cat that followed me everywhere. The stupid thing was always a curlin' himself around my ankles and trippin' me up." Terry went on to describe the cat. "Something was wrong with his neck, and its head was stuck in a crooked position. He always looked at you like he was a questionin' ya. Ya know, curious like. Anyway, I had me this no-good cat for several years, and Herb says, 'The filthy thang don't belong in the cookhouse." Even complained about it to the boss, but Mr. Levi says for Herb to mind his own business, that the cat weren't doin' him no harm. This made ole Herb furious." Terry stopped to dab at his/her eyes. "I hate these onions; they make me tear up so bad."

I didn't want to point out that he/she was chopping cabbage.

"Anyway, two days after the blowup, Crooked Head's body was left on the stoop at the back of the kitchen. Somebody had

122

broke his little neck. His poor old head was finally on straight." Terry paused for a while longer, staring at the mound of vegetables. "Useless, dumb cat. Don't know why it matters no how."

I looked at Maybelle, who had tears streaming down her cheeks. She gave Terry a hug and said how sorry she was about Crooked Head. It didn't sound like Herb was a very likable character, and I was beginning to lose hope that we would find anyone who knew much about him.

"Thank you for your time, Terry," Maybelle said.

The cook never looked up; just moved on to another kitchen chore, deep in thought.

Back out in the bright sunshine, I told Maybelle we might as well leave. Didn't think there was much here to help the investigation. She nodded, and we went to her truck. As we left the ranch, I glanced back toward the hill overlooking the homesite. A lone figure on a horse was facing our direction with the sun to his back. Both arms were up to either side of the silhouette's head, as if holding a pair of binoculars. I had the feeling that Levi Conway was trying to utilize every possible moment to catch a glimpse of Maybelle, even from afar. Although I adored Maybelle, it had been a rather depressing afternoon, and I was anxious to go home. The mood during the ride back into town was subdued. When we arrived back at the feed store, I thanked Maybelle for her time and trouble. She told me to come back for a visit anytime. I desperately wanted to ask Maybelle if she felt beard stubble or bra straps when she hugged the cook, but it seemed in poor taste, so I held my tongue *for once.*

# chapter 8

During the drive back to Ditters Ferry, I ruminated over everything I had and hadn't learned about Herb. Before leaving Harmony, I stopped by the local convenience store for a soda and a few questions. The cashier at the mini-mart had one possible useful tidbit for me. She said she saw a man who looked a lot like Herb get into a luxury car driven by a woman almost every Saturday night around dusk. They always met in the parking lot near the phone booth. The cashier had never seen the driver, because the driver never got out of the car. However, she could tell by the silhouette that it was a female driving. She didn't know the type of car, just that it was "sparkly white and expensive-looking". At least she knew that the plates were Idaho. I gave her my phone number and asked her to call me if the car were ever to show up again. This didn't seem too likely, however, now that Herb was no longer among the living.

A quick glance at my watch showed it wasn't even two o'clock, though it felt much later. I no longer looked forward to my dinner date with Daniel either. On second thought, perhaps a night out might be what I needed to get out of my deep blue funk.

Arriving back in Ditters Ferry, I decided to go visit Kirstie for a while. Her new shop was located centrally in town, and she had designed an attractive front façade. The sun was brightly reflecting off the white cement and made my eyes tear up. I quickly walked into the shade and tapped on the glass door. Kirstie was on a ladder with a paint bucket in one hand and a brush in the other hand. I could tell she was growling at the interruption. She had a tendency to make a sound like a dog guarding its food dish when disturbed from a task.

*susan case*

125

Kirstie climbed down the ladder and carefully set the paint bucket onto the drop cloth and put the lid back on the can. Then she set the paintbrush in water before wiping her hands on her coveralls and heading to the door.

"What's up?" she hollered through the door.

"Let me in."

Kirstie rolled her eyes but unlocked the door. "Don't you work?"

"Good to see you too, Sunshine," I quipped.

"I'm busy, so unless you want to grab a paintbrush and join in . . ." She let the rest of the implied request trail off.

"Well, I'm not really dressed for painting," I prevaricated, "but I wanted to know if you would like to go to Hilltown with me tomorrow morning."

"I'd planned to keep working on this place," Kirstie said.

"Take a break and come with me. I'm going to some yard sales to look for furniture for my apartment."

Kirstie couldn't resist a yard sale.

"Well, I would like to find a bench for out front, give the customers a nice place to sit outside when the weather is good."

"Perfect. I went by a place last Saturday where a man sold his own handcarved furniture. There were some incredibly beautiful pieces."

I had her now.

"Okay. What time do you want to pick me up?"

"How about nine thirtyish?"

"All the good stuff will be picked over and sold by then. Pick me up at eight," Kirstie demanded.

Eight a.m. seemed a little earlier than necessary, but as they say, "Beggars can't be choosers." I wanted some company when I went to the jail again. People have a tendency to push me around, but Kirstie was a different story.

"See you at eight. Guess I'd better let you get back to painting." Perusing my surroundings, I noticed how Kirstie had made the space look inviting. It was bright and airy yet with a modern *edge*. "You're doing a great job decorating," I said.

Kirstie looked around at her handiwork. "Thank you. It's going to be nice working in a larger place with better lighting. I'm taking on another stylist too."

"I'm impressed. You can tell me all about it tomorrow."

Kirstie turned her back to me and proceeded to open the paint can and shake the water out of the brush.

"See ya tomorrow," I called over my shoulder.

With still about three hours left before my date with Daniel, I decided to visit Dibbz and Granddad. There was a message on my voice mail from Dibbz a couple of days ago that was short and to the point: "You have a family, you know. Did you forget where we live?" I decided to stop by the mini-mart and pick up Granddad a box of powdered doughnuts. He and JJ loved sugary baked goods, but they would have to be snuck past Dibbzy of the junk food KGB.

After purchasing the contraband goods and a cola slushy for me, I headed to my grandparents' house. Not wanting to risk a health talk from Dibbz about the dangers of high fructose corn syrup and the FDA's conspiracy to hide the facts, I tried to finish my slush quickly. The resulting ice cream headache was so intense that I had to pull the car to the curb and stop. I pinched the bridge of my nose, willing the pain to cease. It took a full minute for my sinus passages to defrost and the sting to go away.

A loud knock on my window scared me to death. There stood Hoody Jacks with a concerned look on his face.

"Are you all right, Miss Jimi?" he said through the glass. Hoody was wearing his standard dirty black coveralls with the prerequisite dirty handkerchief in his hip pocket and red plaid shirt frayed at the cuffs. As always, one strap of the coveralls wasn't hooked into place.

I rolled down my window. "Hey, Hoody. I'm fine. Just needed to stop for a second."

"You looked like you was in pain."

"Nah. A little headache. That's all."

Hoody eyed my slushy and smiled. "Ice cream headache?" He drawled the question.

"You know, Hoody, that was a beautiful chair you made Emma Sinclair for the Lawn Chair Gathering. You do real fine work."

"Thank you, Miss Jimi. I sure was glad when I got that chair done. Didn't think she'd ever stop pickin' and fussin' over every detail."

"Well, I'd better get going. I'm on my way to see my grandparents."

"Give 'em my best," Hoody said, then added, "You may wanna sip a little slower. Those slushies can be a dangerous thing whilst driving." He headed back to his run-down house with his shoulders trembling in laughter.

*Perfect. Now I'm a source of entertainment for the town character.*

Granddad was walking out the front door with JJ on her leash when I pulled up.

"Hey, Granddad." I gave him a big hug and JJ a loving pat on her round rump. Her tail was wagging vigorously as she sniffed at the doughnut bag.

"I brought you some contraband," I said, handing over the bag.

Granddad peeked inside and then licked his lips.

"JJ sure is gonna enjoy these," he said.

"Make sure she shares a couple with you," I managed with a straight face.

"I'm taking JJ for a walk now. We'll be back in a few. Go on in and see your grandma. She's been missing you." The last comment was said with the tiniest hint of censure.

"I've been real busy at work." I tried to excuse myself.

"You're here now, and that's all that matters." Granddad smiled.

"Make sure you wipe any powdered sugar evidence off your faces before you come back home."

Granddad winked at me and left with JJ in tow. I'd bet a month's salary that a half dozen doughnuts would be consumed before they even got to the end of the block.

Entering the foyer, I called out to Dibbzy.

"In the kitchen," she responded.

Dibbz was at the kitchen table painting a ceramic yard gnome. I don't know how anyone could like those ugly creatures. Personally, they give me the creeps.

"It's nice to see you, Juliet." She gazed up at me. "How have you been? Haven't seen or heard from you in a few months."

It had been closer to three weeks, but since I felt guilty over even that amount of time I decided to let the matter drop and try to distract her with another topic of more interest.

"I've been so busy with the murder investigation."

"Do you have any leads? I'm sure poor Mrs. Greene was arrested because she has the only obvious tie to Herb. I'll bet they wanted to get a quick apprehension, and they found a perfect scapegoat. Wonder if they are even trying other leads to find the real killer. When all is said and done, Harriet should sue for wrongful arrest. Does she have a good attorney?"

*Oh, goody.* Twenty Questions. *We haven't played this game in a long time.* "I have a couple of leads, but I'm not sure how helpful they will be. Jet is hiring Mrs. Greene an attorney. I don't know who he contracted, though, but knowing Jet it will be someone with expertise and a winning record for murder trials."

"Can you stay for dinner?" Dibbz asked out of the blue.

"Sorry. Can't. I already made plans for tonight," I said, and the door to the Spanish Inquisition was opened.

"What plans? Who with? What are you doing? Where are you going? Hope you aren't hanging around with that Kirstie person."

"Do you have any herbal iced tea made?" I prevaricated. "I'm thirsty."

"It's in the fridge. You know where the fructose is if you want to sweeten it."

Taking my time, I got my favorite dark blue glass from the cupboard and spooned two generous spoonfuls of fructose in, then poured the chilled tea about two-thirds of the way full and stirred vigorously until the fructose dissipated. For some reason, fructose takes a lot longer to dissolve than regular sugar. I got the ice tray from the freezer and gave it a good twist to loosen the cubes. As usual, two ice cubes landed on the floor. I filled the glass to the top with the remaining ice. I have a rule for a very precise amount of fluid to ice that must be adhered to. I won't drink anything at room temperature or from a can or bottle. All cold drinks must be poured over large quantities of ice. I would gladly suffer dehydration rather than break my rule of proportionate ice-to-liquid ratio.

"Mmm. Great tea, Dibbz."

"Where are you going tonight?"

*Rats! Why couldn't she have a mild form of short-term memory loss?* "Boise to grab a hamburger and see a movie."

"Oh? Who with?" Dibbz wanted know.

"Um, Daniel Forsythe, but it's not a date."

"Sounds like a date."

"No. He's just a coworker, and we both thought a break from Ditters Ferry would be nice."

"Why would anyone need a break from here?" Dibbz honestly couldn't figure that one out; she was so content with her life here with Granddad and her precious garden.

"Actually, it's a break from work," I said, not wanting to hurt her feelings.

"If it's not a date and you are only coworkers, then your only common ground of conversation would be work, and therefore you're not actually getting away from work then, are you?"

Attempting to wrap my mind around her logic, Dibbz continued painting her horrible little yard gnome.

"How's Spence? Seems like he grows another foot taller and adds an extra layer of muscle every time I see him."

"Maybe you should see him more often then." Dibbz looked at me. "His first football game is this Friday. He's starting quarterback again this year."

"I'll be there."

"Maybe you could bring Jet with you. He'd probably enjoy visiting his old stomping grounds."

"We'll see." My response was non-committal at best.

We chatted awhile longer, then I said my good-bye with a hug and went home to my apartment.

---

Daniel arrived at precisely 6:00 p.m. Not wanting him to come up to my apartment, I headed out the door. We met halfway on the stairs.

"You look *terrific*," Daniel said, taking in my swirling gauze thigh-length skirt, white tank top, tanned legs, and strappy sandals. I had even painted my toenails a pretty, sheer pearlescent pink. His gazing perusal missed absolutely no detail.

Although Daniel was only a friend, the masculine approval made me feel very feminine and slightly flirty.

"You don't look half bad yourself."

Actually, Daniel looked quite handsome in his pressed white shirt opened at the throat, perfect jeans, and casual jacket. He really was too attractive, too wealthy, and too charming for his own good—or for a woman's own good anyway, because there wasn't a serious bone in his body. I was sure.

The drive to Boise was relaxing and enjoyable. Daniel left the top down on his Corvette and had soft pop music playing. Conversation wasn't necessary. It was a beautiful day, with the barest hint of the cooler fall temperatures to come. It was nice to shake off the heaviness of the Greene murder investigation. Maybe I could even put Crooked Head, the dead cat, out of my mind.

We pulled into the parking lot of the Gulch Moose. This

restaurant was completely new to me. The interior of the Gulch Moose had the mellow ambiance of a well-loved neighborhood tavern with a mix of sports bar thrown in.

"The hamburgers are the best in the state. My favorite is the SOB," Daniel informed me. In response to my quizzical look, he added, "It's the South of the Border burger. If you like spicy, you'll love it. The Spruce Moose Original burger is good too. Too bad it's not Wednesday; that's when they serve two-for-one burgers."

"If that's your way of trying to get me to go dutch treat for dinner, you can think again. My level of pride is equal to my level of cash flow. And right now I have only $4.54 of pride to last until next payday. Generally I can afford to be snooty and prideful about six days a month."

Daniel smiled. "I'll pay for dinner anytime you want to go out with me."

"Even just as friends?"

He leveled a look at me for some time before answering, "I'll buy my *friend* a meal anytime, but I will hold out the hope for something more."

He sounded so serious. I wasn't used to this side of Daniel. I was glad the waitress approached at this very opportune moment.

Daniel ordered an SOB and dark ale. I played it safer and ordered the Spruce Moose and an iced tea.

"You don't drink?" He didn't look surprised.

"No. I don't like the feeling of not being fully in charge of my brain. Besides, what if alcohol made me say what was actually on my mind? The world would not be a better place knowing all the errant thoughts that bounce around in my head."

"Might be amusing. I'd like to see you with your guard down."

"You think I'm guarded?" I asked, not particularly liking that description.

"I think you are too virtuous for your own good and need

more vices. But you're also klutzy, a poor dresser, and a little self-centered."

"Now, that just hurt." This was said with a smile, but it did hurt—not the klutzy part, or the poor dresser, but the self-centered comment.

"Honey, perfection is highly overrated and supremely boring. I like you the way you are, except I'm hoping someday you'll pick up a penchant for blonde photographers who drink dark beer and drive red Corvettes."

"Daniel, I'd be just another girl in a long line of conquests." This was said in a teasing tone, but he looked injured nonetheless.

By mutual consent we drifted to less serious topics of local news, gossip, and of course the investigation. When we finished Daniel paid the check and left a generous tip. I assumed it was because the waitress was quite good-looking and had no qualms about flirting with Daniel. However, much to his credit, he didn't flirt back or even seem to take notice.

At the theater, I chose a chick flick. The promotional trailers looked amusing, which was perfect because I really wasn't in the mood for drama or bloodshed. As it turned out, the movie was full of drama. The female protagonist loses the love of her life within the first ten minutes of the movie. I cried throughout the entire movie. It got a little chilly at one point, and I rubbed the goose bumps on my arms. Daniel put his arm around me and pulled me close to him. Since it felt more like a friendly gesture than an overture, I didn't pull away. The second the credits began to roll, I ran for the exit. I knew my face would be streaked, and my nose was running copiously.

Along with about fifty other women, I fought for use of the bathroom mirror to repair the damage. It actually wasn't too bad, so I blew my nose on a paper towel and headed out to look for Daniel. I didn't have far to go. Daniel was casually leaning on the wall outside the women's room waiting for me. He didn't say anything, but I knew he wanted to laugh at me.

"Would you like to go anywhere else? We might as well take advantage of the big city," Daniel said.

"Nah. It's after ten, and I have an early morning tomorrow," I responded.

"Okay. C'mon then." He took my hand, and we walked to his car. He put the top back in place because the evening had turned chilly. He unlocked and opened my door.

"Daniel?" I paused turning to look at him. "I want to ask a favor."

"Ask away." He smiled. He had a hand on either side of my arms and pulled me slightly toward him.

"May I drive? I've never driven a Corvette before."

He looked as if I had asked him to donate both his kidneys to a stranger.

"No way!"

"Please. I'll be careful," I begged.

He paused for a moment. "I'll tell you what, if you will kiss me—and I don't mean a sisterly peck on the cheek—then I'll let you drive a few miles once we're out of city traffic."

"I'm too tired to drive anyway."

Daniel laughed and helped me into the passenger seat and firmly closed the door. The drive home was quiet but not uncomfortable. It really had been a very nice evening.

When we got to my apartment building, Daniel came around, opened my door, and proceeded to walk me to my second-floor unit. I pulled the key out from under the mat, then turned to face Daniel to thank him for the nice evening.

My back was to the door, and Daniel put his hands to either side of my head then closed his eyes and leaned in for a kiss. I ducked just in time for him to kiss my door.

"What the?"

I extended my hand and said a polite thank you. He looked askance at my extended hand and then smiled.

"You really are an anachronism." It was mercifully said with no rancor, just humorous resignation.

"And you are now going steady with my door. You can't just kiss it and walk away like it meant nothing."

We both laughed.

Daniel was stepping down the stairs then looked back as I bent to retrieve my *hidden* key. "You know, it's kinda dumb to put your key under the mat. Every burglar and wannabe bad guy knows to look there."

Obviously I hadn't learned from my tussle with Jet after all. I merely hated carrying a purse. Maybe I should get a long chain for around my neck and put my apartment key on it.

I went in my apartment, and Daniel got in his car and drove away. Unbeknownst to either of us, Jet was a half block away standing under a tree, his Navigator parked two blocks over. Jet had witnessed the whole goodnight scene and enjoyed a small laugh at Daniel's expense.

*susan case*

# *chapter 9*

The unwelcome buzzing of my alarm clock rudely awakened me. Seven forty-five a.m. had come much too early. There was a message on my cell phone the night before from Kirstie saying she would be picking me up in a borrowed truck. She wanted the extra room in case she found a bench for her new shop. Considering my gas tank was near empty, as was my bank account, this sounded like a fine arrangement to me.

I washed my face, combed my hair, brushed my teeth, and put on some lip gloss. That should do it. Then I slipped into my favorite pair of jeans, accompanied by a simple sweater top, and stepped into a pair of comfy loafers. Kirstie, as expected, was right on time and impatiently honking the horn to get my attention. I grabbed my cell phone and debit card and headed out the door.

Kirstie was waiting behind the wheel of a late model Chevy Silverado long-bed truck. Her purple fingernails were tapping a rapid beat on the steering wheel.

As I settled into the passenger side, I asked Kirstie whose truck this was.

"My mother's new boyfriend," she answered curtly. "Jeez. Did you just get out of bed? You have pillowcase crease lines on your cheek, and the back of your hair is a mess. You also don't have a stitch of makeup on."

"Good morning to you too," I replied. "Perhaps we had better get some coffee. Thank you for bringing this truck instead of picking me up on your broom. This is probably a lot more roomy and comfortable. Besides, I'm afraid of heights."

This at least brought an almost smile to Kirstie's face. "We'll get some coffee in Hilltown," Kirstie said. "I want to get to the

*susan case*

yard sales quickly. You know, you really should be there by 7:00 a.m. to get the good stuff."

"I wouldn't even be able to focus on the good stuff that early in the morning."

"You're so lazy." Kirstie said completely without rancor.

"Well, we balance each other out nicely then, don't we?"

I nodded off on the way to Hilltown and woke up as we were going through the drive-up for coffee.

"Two large coffee's, please," Kirstie ordered. She didn't ask if I wanted anything else, which was fine since I never eat before 10:00 a.m.

We each placed our coffee in the console, which accommodated two cup holders. The coffees needed a minute to cool. I gave Kirstie directions to the home where I had seen the beautiful, hand-carved furniture.

When we got there, several people were already milling about. There were the usual stacks of hideous outdated clothing, partial dishware sets, knickknacks, books, DVDs, etc. Over closer to the garage was the furniture. Kirstie was rifling through the CDs, so I went to look at an oak bench. It had a wet paint sign on it. That was obviously a mistake, as the bench wasn't painted; just beautiful, natural wood grain reflected the mellow shine of the morning sun. I tossed the wet paint sign aside and was going to sit down to test the bench for comfort when Kirstie walked up.

"Jimi, you were right. This furniture is beautiful," Kirstie complimented. "You know, there were some great mystery novels over there for a quarter apiece."

That caught my attention.

"I'm going to sit my butt here so no one can buy this bench out from under me. It's absolutely perfect for outside my new shop. Go ahead and look through the books. I'll wait here until I see the owner and can negotiate a deal."

Kirstie sat down and folded her arms across her stomach and tilted her head back toward the sun and closed her eyes.

That's the most relaxed I had ever seen her. Usually she was bustling with activity or bristling with annoyance.

There were stacks and stacks of mystery novels and old *Reader's Digest* multibook sets. I only had a couple of dollars to spend, so it took me almost a full hour to pick the eight books I wanted most. It near broke my heart to leave the other books behind.

Kirstie was still in her relaxed position when I ambled up next to her. "Have you bought the bench yet?" I asked.

Kirstie opened her eyes. "No. I still haven't seen anyone who looks like the owner."

About that time, an older man in coveralls was coming out of the garage. He was carrying a cash box.

"Wait here a sec. I think I see someone," I offered.

The man in the coveralls was the owner. I paid for my books and took him to meet Kirstie.

We were a few steps away when he shouted at Kirstie, "What the heck do you think you're doing?"

Kirstie looked dumbfounded.

"Girl, can't you read?" he demanded.

"Read what? What are you hollering about?" Kirstie looked bewildered by his angry outburst.

"Where's the sign?" he said, looking around.

"What sign?" Kirstie said, still confused.

"Honey, I just put the last thick coat of clear polyurethane on that bench."

Kirstie started to get up but couldn't move. "Mister, you better get me unstuck off this bench pronto. It's pure negligence to allow someone to sit down on wet varnish."

I debated whether or not to be honest. Then remembered the promise I made to Kirstie when I almost burned down her apartment, vowing never to lie to her again. I hate my stinkin' conscience.

"Um."

They both turned to look at me, annoyed at the interruption.

*susan case*

"Uh, I saw a wet paint sign, but since clearly this bench isn't painted, I removed it to sit down."

"You did *what?*" This was in stereo surround sound as they both said the same thing simultaneously.

Once again, Kirstie tried to stand. We heard the sound of cloth tearing. She was definitely and completely stuck to the bench.

"How long you been there?" the man asked.

"I don't know. About an hour, I guess." Kirstie was looking daggers at me now.

The man began to chortle. The harder he tried not to laugh, the madder Kirstie became.

"Well, little lady, looks like you bought yourself a two hundred dollar bench."

"And just how am I supposed to get off this bench?" Kirstie snapped.

"There appears to be only one way," he said, then hesitated. "You're gonna have to step outta your clothes." With that, he laughed until he had tears streaming down his cheeks. Out of some small amount of courtesy, he headed back to his garage. Nervous laughter was welling up inside of me, but the threat of death at Kirstie's manicured hands kept the laughter buried deep inside.

"Jimi, you are worse than a plague. You are a menace who will surely single-handedly bring about Armageddon!" She paused for a moment and took a deep breath. "You have two seconds to figure out how to get me off this bench."

I remembered seeing a Scooby-Doo comforter for sale, and of course there were some clothes. Leaving Kirstie adhered to her new bench, I scurried over to the clothing pile. Most of the items were men's polyester pants and western-wear shirts, but there was one floral dress. It was a size twenty-two and about the ugliest thing I had ever seen. I took the blanket and the dress to the owner, all the while wondering how I was going to pay for them since my last two dollars had been spent on the books. I supposed I was going to have to swap my bargain trea-sures for the ugly dress and cartoon blanket.

"Honey, you can have those free of charge. Can't remember when I laughed this hard." He waved me away and then added, "Let me know if you need any help holding up the blanket or dressing your friend." This was followed by another bout of laughter.

I cautiously approached Kirstie with my freebies.

"Uh, I'll hold up the blanket while you get out of your clothes."

"And just what am I supposed to wear?"

"I bought you a dress."

I held the floral monstrosity out to her. She refused to take it.

"I'd rather go naked."

We were at a stalemate for only a few seconds before Kirstie realized she had no choice.

"How do you sucker me into going anywhere with you?"

"Cause you love me?" I suggested.

Levity was evidently not called for here. I dropped the dress to the ground behind me and held up the blanket to protect Kirstie from curious eyes and to shield myself from Kirstie's burning glare. There was a lot of grunting, mumbling, and a few more tearing sounds.

"Hand me that *dress*," Kirstie ordered.

I tried to look between my legs for the dress but couldn't see anything, at least not without being able to bend. Still holding the blanket aloft, I used my right foot to feel around for the dress. Maybe I could scoot it forward then kick it under the blanket to her. It didn't feel like I had the dress, so I tried the same thing with my left foot. Apparently I did get the dress with my right foot. Unfortunately, my left foot soon became entangled in the voluminous garment. I shuffled my feet back and forth and somehow got the dress wrapped around my ankles. When I attempted to step out of the dress, I fell forward with a

*susan case*

141

thump, taking the Scooby-Doo comforter with me. Looking up, I saw Kirstie in all her pale, freckle-skinned, solidly compact, and tattooed glory, wearing only a skimpy black bra, matching black thong, and high heeled sandals. Her expression of horror defied description.

Everything went still. The birds stopped singing. The wind quit whistling through the trees. The people ceased their conversations and perusing yard sale items. For a moment, we were in a vacuum of peace. Then the ferocity of the laughter hit us full force.

I was rolling on the ground, trying to get the dress unraveled from my feet, and Kirstie was bending over me, pulling at the floral nightmare. This caused more laughter, and we were drawing quite a crowd. There were even cars stopping by the side of the road. Passengers were gawking at the sideshow act of a klutz and a near naked woman wrestling over a garment that should have never been manufactured.

Kirstie finally appropriated the dress and quickly slid it over her head. It was inside out and backwards, not to mention severely grass stained, but I decided not to mention these observations. She never said a word. The crowd, though still laughing, began to disperse, and the cars were moving on now that the show was over. The man in the coveralls approached us and held his hand out to help me up. He gave a quick, cursory glance at Kirstie, and then gazed at the bench for a long moment. Kirstie's blouse and skirt were still stuck in place. It looked like the invisible woman was sitting on the bench having a nice break in the morning sunshine. Through much more laughter and tears, the owner stated that the bench was now $150 and "Please come back any time."

How Kirstie was able to write the check with as much dignity as she did was beyond me. The neckline of the dress kept slipping, and the gaping hole was big enough to allow the dress to fall completely off her small frame. Kirstie gathered several inches of material and kept it firmly grasped in her white-knuckled fist. She strode to the truck and barked an order over her shoulder: "Load the bench." The truck door slammed with impressive velocity, and Kirstie slunk low in the driver's seat. I was sorely afraid that "load the bench" might very well be the last words I would ever hear from Kirstie again.

Fortunately, coverall man assisted me in loading the bench, as it was too cumbersome and heavy for me to have managed alone. Once the bench was in and the tailgate folded back into place, I said a hushed thank you.

He noticed my contrition and distress and said, "Don't worry, honey. In a few days, well, years maybe, you two will look back on this and have a great laugh."

As I was never going to mention to anyone what happened today, I sincerely doubted we would be sharing a laugh about this episode—*ever*. I just hoped Kirstie would still be my friend.

Nodding my thanks for his sentiments, I climbed into the truck actually surprised and grateful that Kirstie hadn't left me to find my own way home.

I buckled in and took a breath, about to apologize, when Kirstie said in a voice of dark malevolence, "Don't say a word. Not one word. I don't even want to hear the sound of your breathing."

*Was Kirstie going to drive me out into the boonies, kill me, and then leave my body for the vultures?* I kept my breathing as shallow and quiet as possible.

I was amazed when we arrived at the jail. She was keeping to her side of the deal and allowing me to visit Ms. Greene. If the situation were reversed, I was uncertain I would have been quite so magnanimous.

"Thank you, Kirstie. If you'd like, I can treat you to lunch at the Big Onion after I'm through here."

Kirstie's jaw clenched, and her knuckles whitened on the steering wheel. Her face was mottled red as she stared straight ahead. She looked down at the dress, which was now below her bra line and threatening to fall even lower. She turned to me with a look of sheer rage. "Go." Her voice sounded threatening. So I left Kirstie without another word or backward glance. I could feel her glare on the back of my neck and shuddered with a ghost-walked-over-my-grave type of chill.

---

Inside the jailhouse, I went through the identical procedure as before, but with two different armed guards. After being cleared, I went straight to the inmate visitation area. It was the same woman behind the thick, glass window. This time I had my ID ready and slid it through the small opening to the registrar of visitors. She wrote my name and the time in her little schedule book.

"Carrying any contraband or weapons?" she asked.

"No, ma'am." I was, however, carrying a grudge over her stealing my candy bar during the last visit.

"Inmate you wish to visit?" she demanded.

"Uh, Mrs. Greene, number 22756. I'm a friend."

She marked something down on her book, and when the buzzer sounded, I quickly turned the handle. I felt like a pro now. I knew all the ins and outs of visiting the local jail.

I didn't have long to wait before Big Body Bertha the guard called my name. I followed her to the familiar bank of tables and pretty, neon orange vinyl stools. I wondered if they had had a chance to install the Plexiglas. Again, I sat at the farthest end, away from the prying eyes and ears of the guard. Ms. Greene approached and sat down. She looked a little better than during my last visit, but not much. At least she wasn't in ankle irons this time.

Ms. Greene picked up her phone. Out of curiosity and without thinking, I put my hand through where the Plexiglas should be. A whistle blew loudly. I jumped, but Ms. Greene had her head down and was banging herself in the forehead with the phone's handset.

"22756, *stand* for pat down of contraband!"

Déjà *flippin'* vu. Big Body Bertha the guard certainly loved her job. Again, there was no part of Ms. Greene's anatomy that escaped inspection, *twice.*

"I am so sorry." I started to offer an apology.

Ms. Greene held up her hand to stop me from speaking. Unfortunately, her hand had gone too far in the guard's estimation. Bertha's whistle went off with an ear-piercing trill. "22756, *stand* for pat down of contraband!"

During another full and thorough body search of Ms. Greene, I was escorted from the premises. Although not a very charitable thought, I actually hoped she spent quite a bit more time behind bars so she could have time to cool off.

I found Kirstie still slunk low behind the steering wheel of the borrowed Chevy.

"That was a quick visit," Kirstie drawled, never looking my way.

"Uh, I guess Ms. Greene is having a bad day. I wasn't allowed to speak with her."

That wasn't a lie—slight prevarication perhaps, but definitely not a lie.

"The bad day seems to be contagious, but congratulations to Ms. Greene for not having to speak with you. Heaven only knows the trouble you could cause her."

I bowed my head in conviction. *Heaven knew. Mrs. Greene knew. The painstakingly meticulous jailhouse matron knew. Certainly Kirstie knew.*

*Dear Lord, please bless everyone I came into contact with today with an abundance of forgiveness. Amen.*

*susan case*

# chapter 10

Around 4:00 p.m., I decided it would be a good time to visit the Twin Falls hotel advertised on the matchbox appropriated from Herb's bungalow. Maybe some helpful information could be gleaned from the desk clerk.

It was a beautiful day, so I rolled down my window instead of using the air conditioning or vents. In less than an hour, I pulled my Mazda into the Lux Hotel on Blue Lakes Boulevard in downtown Twin Falls. Since it was Saturday and the cashier at the convenience store in Harmony said that's the day of week she regularly saw Herb get into the white sedan with the mystery woman, I was hoping my hunch could be proved that Herb and the woman were lovers having a tryst at their regular hotel. It was a long shot, but then I didn't have any other leads to work with.

Walking across the foyer, I wished I had taken the time during the drive to develop a story that would make the clerk want to give out information. No one was in the lobby or behind the counter. Taking a deep, calming breath, I rang the bell for service. A kind-looking, middle-aged woman greeted me with a genuine smile. Her name badge read, "Doris, Night Manager."

"May I help you?" Doris asked.

"Yes, please."

"Do you have a reservation?"

"No. Actually, I was hoping for some information," I said. "Are you usually the night manager on Saturday nights?"

"Yes."

"Well, um, see, I, uh, am conducting a murder investigation," I stammered out. "Actually, I'm a reporter for the *Ditters Weekly* newspaper. Our supervising editor was charged with murdering her estranged husband. I'm trying to piece together his final months to determine what really happened." Well, that was blurted out nicely.

Doris looked confused. "So how may I be of assistance?"

"I believe the victim may have been a regular here on Saturday evenings." I took out the least offensive post mortem photo of Herb and handed it to Doris.

Doris paled and put her hand to her chest. "That's Burt White."

"Burt White?" Pay dirt! "Was he a regular guest?" *Herbert Greene, a.k.a. Burt White—not a very imaginative alias.*

"Yes. Every Saturday. Burt always requested room 137. I had recommended that particular room to him when he told me he needed quiet. He is, uh *was,* a traveling salesman. After the first visit, he always requested room 137."

"Did he check in alone?"

"Well, he always signed for a single, but—" Doris didn't seem inclined to finish her thought.

"But what?" I gently urged her on.

"Well, guess it can't do any harm, although I can't see how it might help either, but once he called the front desk to ask about restaurants that deliver food and spirits." She paused for only a moment. "I told him there was a section in the back of the guest lodging book on the dresser which contained several restaurant choices with delivery service. He said there wasn't a book on the dresser. I told him I'd bring him a book, but he said for me not to bother."

The phone rang, interrupting our conversation. Doris answered a few questions then made a reservation for the caller. "Where was I?" She looked up as though her last sentence were printed on the ceiling. "Oh, yes. I felt sorry for him probably being tired and hungry, so I got an extra guest information book and took it to his room. When he answered the door, he seemed agitated or embarrassed; it was difficult to tell. Anyway, I could see a light under the bathroom door, and there was a pair of women's high-heeled shoes at the foot of the bed. He looked uncomfortable, so I pretended not to notice the shoes and just handed him the book and left."

"Did you ever see the woman?" Maybe I could finally get a description.

"No, I never saw her."

*Darn!* "Do you know what kind of car Mr. Greene, uh, I mean Mr. White was driving?"

"Well, there was only one car parked back there that evening. I remember it was an expense-looking car and white."

"Do you know the make of the car?"

"You know, now that you mention it, I remember looking at it closely because it was so pretty. I wanted to know what it was." Doris was looking up at the ceiling again, tapping her chin with her index finger. "I don't remember the model, but it was . . ."—more ceiling staring, more chin tapping—"a *Cadillac!*" She looked so pleased with herself for being able to recollect the auto manufacturer. "It wasn't a model I had seen before. It was sporty, and I remember thinking that I didn't know Cadillac made a sports car."

"When Mr. White registered, did he fill in the model of car and license plate number?" This information would be akin to finding gold.

"He may have, but we destroy those at the end of each month." Doris looked sorry that she couldn't provide me with any more information. I was feeling pretty sad about it myself.

"Doris, you have been a tremendous help, and I really appreciate you taking the time to speak with me." I extended my hand, and she took it in both of hers. Her grasp felt more like a *hand hug* than a handshake.

"I'm glad I could help. I hope you find out who murdered Mr. White. I wondered why he hadn't been around in the past two months."

"*Two months?*" Herb had only been dead a couple of weeks.

"Yeah. I remember it was the weekend after the Fourth of

July. It was a real slow weekend here, hardly even had 25 percent capacity of the rooms filled. Mr. White didn't need to worry about quiet on that Saturday."

"Thank you again, Doris."

The last bit of information was an interesting morsel to speculate on. Why hadn't Herbert Greene, a.k.a. Burt White, continued with his regular Saturday night tryst? Perhaps he and his mystery lady had a falling out. Now, how was I to find out who the anonymous woman was? My only clue was the Cadillac.

*Late model, sporty, white Cadillac; that sounded vaguely familiar, but I couldn't put my finger on it.* I knew I had seen one recently. I was halfway home to Ditters Ferry when it hit me. *Sylvia!* Sylvia drove a late-model, white Cadillac. *Could it be?* I tried to remember our last encounter when she claimed Harriet was the murderer and that Herb was asking her for a divorce and half of what they owned jointly. Herb didn't have money, so it never occurred to me that Sylvia could be the mystery lover.

I knew this was my first important clue. After all the disasters that had befallen me today—well, befallen the people who came into contact with me today—something good had happened. I couldn't wait to see Jet on Monday morning.

---

I wish I had waited to see Jet. Monday morning was not what I had anticipated.

Walking into Jet's office unannounced was a mistake of monumental proportions. There he was clinched in the embrace of none other than Candy Kane. The image of Jet hugging Candace tightly was burned into my brain.

Upon seeing me, Jet appeared embarrassed, whereas Candy looked maliciously triumphant, like the well-fed cat who had recently masticated the proverbial canary, feathers and all. As usual, Candy was overly and, in my unbiased opinion, garishly made up and wearing too tight and too skimpy of a dress. Candy's clothes never left much to the imagination.

My face was heating up, and I was feeling a little nauseated. It felt as if someone had punched me in the gut; it was difficult to breathe normally.

"Sorry. I'll, uh, come back later." I started to close the door when Jet called me back.

"Jimi, you remember Candace Kane, don't you?"

*Unfortunately.* "Yes. How are you, Candace?" I asked—as if I cared.

"Why, Jamie, I didn't know you worked here." Candy simpered out, still clinging to Jet.

Some people never change, but in Candy's case she really ought to think about it. Her personality was one the world, or at least my world, would be a better place without.

"Her name is Jimi, not Jamie," Jet corrected, then added, "Jimi, I hired Candace for the temporary office support position. You need to pull the help wanted ad from the classifieds before the next issue prints."

"I'll take care of it," I stated a little abruptly. "Is there anything else?"

"Did you need to see me?" Jet inquired.

"It wasn't important. It can wait." I shut the door and left quickly before anymore conversation could ensue.

Work with Candy? I don't think so. But could I afford to quit? Again, I don't think so. I wondered if Jet and Candy had something going aside from the new *working* relationship. It made me sick to even contemplate such a union. Truthfully, Jet with anyone, except me of course, would cause heartache. But Candy was by far the most painful choice he could make.

At my desk, I pulled the help wanted ad as Jet requested and finished the few local interest pieces that would go into the next issue. Not wanting a chance run-in with Candy or Jet, or worse Candy and Jet, I left the office. The local library had a computer with high-speed Internet access, so I'd try and get more research done from there. I didn't know Sylvia's last name or where she lived, if she worked, and more importantly if she was having an affair with Harriet's estranged husband, but it was amazing what one could find out from the assistance of the Internet.

I went into Harriet's office and appropriated her rolodex. It was stuffed to capacity and beyond. The cards were in various sizes and condition. Some were completely yellowed with age, others pristine white, and there were assorted business cards loosely interspersed amongst the properly secured cards. Going through these would take quite some time, unless of course Sylvia's name began with an *a*. I stuffed the rolodex into a canvas bag in case any business cards were to fall out.

Since it was just past nine on a Monday morning, the library was nearly empty. Ms. Schumacher, the librarian, and I were the only two in the library. Seated at the computer station, I dumped the rolodex out of the bag and began sorting through the cards. What I hadn't considered was that Harriet used a lot of initials. L. Aarons, C. Adams, S. Azevado, and so on. I removed all the *s* first name initials and placed them into a separate pile. I hadn't run across the name "Sylvia" yet.

After exhausting 90 percent of the alphabet and spending approximately an hour and a half searching, I was in the *w's* before the name Sylvia finally appeared. Whitworth, ~~Scott, Russell, Landmore~~, Campbell, Sylvia. This had to be her. I noticed Sylvia had married in alphabetical order. I surmised that husband number five, if she continued the marry, divorce, marry, divorce trend, would be someone named Zachary Zuercher. Several addresses and phone numbers were crossed out. There was only one phone number that hadn't been lined through, and it was handwritten in pencil.

The PC had already been booted up, so I clicked on the Internet symbol for connection from the desktop. Using a website for reverse order directory lookup, I typed in the number penciled on the index card. *Eureka!* The phone number belonged to Whitworth, Bertrand A. III and Sylvia M., 19871 Montrose Drive of Eagle, Idaho. I researched each of Sylvia's married names. There were wedding announcement notices on the last two husbands. Bertrand A. Whitworth III owned a nationwide chain of furniture stores. His predecessor, Donald H. Russell, is a well-respected surgeon in the northwest states. I was unable to find anything about Sylvia's first two husbands, but I didn't want to spend too much time on it either.

I used my favorite website for providing directions and a map and hit the print icon for the information on how to get to the Whitworth home. After stuffing all the cards back into the bag, letting the loose ones fall where they may, I approached Ms. Schumacher for my print out.

"Hello, Juliet. How are you? I heard you are working over at the paper. Do you like it? You haven't been in here in a while. You must be *buying* mystery novels instead of utilizing your much more practical and valuable library card. That's such a waste of your money, dear, especially with such a nice library in town," Ms. Schumacher rattled out. "I suppose you want your printout. That'll be fifty cents."

I wasn't sure if I was supposed to answer any of her questions, so I decided to beat her at her own game. "It's nice to see you again, Ms. Schumacher. Are you still reading stories to preschool children in the afternoon? Do you still live over on Elmwood? How soon do you get new releases? I've been dying to read the new Stephanie Plum novel. How's your son? Is he still running a sheep ranch in Montana with his friend, Craig? Here's the fifty cents I owe you." I held out two quarters. While she was still trying to figure out which question to answer or which comment to comment on, I made my exit.

My car was going to need gas before I headed to Eagle, which was about eighty-five miles away from Ditters Ferry. To my good fortune, I could use my work credit card. After filling the tank with *premium* unleaded—I figured the paper would want my car to have the very best—I went inside and got a large grape slushy and candy bar, which would serve nicely as my breakfast/lunch. I paid the clerk in cash for my snacks and then

*susan case*

153

used the company credit card for the fuel. I'm not a total bum. Besides, it wasn't worth losing my job over $2.12.

My newly-acquired cell phone, courtesy of Jet, was ringing insistently. The caller ID showed the paper's number, so I ignored it. I didn't want to speak to Jet and couldn't imagine why anyone else from work would be calling. Of course, a few minutes later my phone was beeping that I had a missed call. I looked at my phone and, sure enough, there was a new voice mail. *Surprise, surprise.* Jet knew better than to text message me, because I had yet to figure out that feature. I had only recently learned how to retrieve voicemails. I still didn't know how to put a number into my cellular phone book. *Why do people like to be so connected?* I lived fine for twenty-four years without a cell phone and was sure I could live another twenty-four years without one.

Pressing number one connected me to a computerized voice that demanded I input my security code. I punched in those four numbers and waited. A very disgusted-sounding Jet left the following message, which sounded distinctly like an order. "Call me now." It wouldn't do any good to continue avoiding it, so I dialed Jet's cell phone number.

"Jet here," he answered.

"Hi, Jet. It's Jimi. What's up?"

"I need to explain about Candace."

"Why?" I wasn't up to hearing the explanation.

"I don't want to discuss this over the phone. Why don't you come into the office now?"

"I can't. I'm on the freeway headed to Eagle." I was actually still in town headed in the direction of the freeway on-ramp.

"Jimi, you just drove by the office. I can see you."

Well, that was just embarrassing.

"Jet—ur—eaking up—I—n't—ear—ou," I stuttered out in halting, partial words.

"Jimi, you're in town and can hear me fine."

"et—are—ere?" *Click!* I hung up. I hadn't really fooled either of us, but it felt good to postpone our conversation.

My phone rang, and I picked it up on the first ring. Using my best monotone, computerized voice, I said, "Error message 527. The subscriber you are trying to reach is out of area network. Please try your call again."

"Jimi, I know that's you!"

I folded my phone shut. Maybe he thought it was me, but he would never truly know for sure. I let the next call go directly to voicemail. I'd listen to it later after my trip to Eagle.

The pain was just as intense as it had been seven years ago. My chest ached, my stomach cramped, and it was difficult to breathe. Seeing Candy hanging all over Jet brought back a lot of bad memories. I honestly thought she was gone for good. It felt like high school all over again. As a matter of fact, I was acting like a lovesick high school girl rather than the adult I was supposed to be. I needed to forget about the little love triangle and get on with the business at hand: my mission to find the truth out about Herb's murder.

I didn't have any specific plan in mind other than to cruise by Sylvia's home and see if her car were parked there. Maybe a call to Sylvia prior to my visit would be a better idea. I could tell her that I was interested in her theory behind Harriet's supposed guilt. What I was unsure of was how to get Sylvia to admit to a relationship with Herb. I'd just have to play it by ear; so far winging it seemed to work best for me anyway.

Dialing the phone number located from my web search, I only had to wait two rings before the phone was answered.

"Weetworth reseedence," a woman's heavily accented voice answered.

"Mrs. Whitworth, please."

"Meece Weetworth no en casa, uh, no at home."

This wasn't going well. Spanish 101 was a long time ago, and I remembered almost *nada*.

"Do you know when Mrs. Whitworth will be home?"

"Meece Weetworth no at home."

"Thank you." I disconnected the call.

This didn't bode well for my surprise visit, but perhaps Sylvia was out for only an hour or two; maybe getting her talons manicured and painted. It was difficult to imagine that Sylvia worked a regular job. Her line of employment appeared to be trading up husbands.

It was still more than an hour drive to Eagle, so I decided to stick with my original plan. The wind had suddenly picked up, and I had to tightly grip the steering wheel to fight the ever-changing air currents that wanted to toss my little car hither and yon. A large herd of tumbleweeds rambunctiously crossed the highway ahead of me, playfully bouncing up and down while rolling on. Some of them were as big as my car. Most of the herd made it safely across the road only to get stuck in barbed wire fencing. The herd was effectively corralled, except the two I hit. Bits of dead tumbleweed flew up behind my car. It sounded like I had run over a tree. Some residual tumbleweed carcass was stuck to my front bumper. Thin, tan, spiky arms would randomly appear over the hood, waving in distress.

A large thunderhead cloud ominously loomed on the horizon. Huge lightning bolts lit up the sky, and the resulting thunder let me know the strikes were close. All this fanfare of nature only produced a drizzle sufficient to moisturize my car enough for the blowing dirt to stick to it. My wipers spread mud over my windshield and made visibility nearly zero. I twisted the little squirty button thingy, but it only made a loud whirring noise. No spray of water was forthcoming to clean the mud-caked glass. It came to me that I hadn't refilled the wiper water container since the last rain and wind storm. Oh well. It wouldn't be the first time I had to rely on Braille driving methods. I listened for the loud vibrating noise that meant I had wandered slightly off the road. Hopefully, there weren't any stranded motorists on the shoulder of the highway trying to fix a flat.

Resolving it was better to stop and clean the windshield than potentially kill someone, I pulled completely off the road. The only thing I had to clean the glass with was my melted-down grape slushy. I didn't have any paper or napkins to wipe the mess off, so I turned the windshield wipers on high. I poured the slushy on the windshield only to have the ungrateful wipers spit the grape colored water right back on to me. Being splattered in speckles of a mud-colored, faint purple hue was not helping my disposition any. The wipers were making a funny noise as they dragged across the now drying sticky sugar coating.

I crawled up on top of the car and lay down, deciding it would be best to pour the little bit of liquid I had left in my cup from the top, since the previous splash went over to the driver's side. It never occurred to me what passing motorists must be thinking, until the first few horns started honking. Well, I was already sprawled on top of my car, so it couldn't get any worse. I dumped the remaining slushy onto the windshield, only to have it spray up into my face. Nature seemed to be saluting me with a toast, saying, "Here's mud in your eye, stupid." I blinked several times, trying to clear my vision. Clumps of hair were sticking to my face, encased in sweetened mud. About that time, the thunderhead finally opted to do its proper job, and a torrential downpour ensued. Before I could get back into my Mazda, I was completely and thoroughly soaked. My mud-streaked blouse became translucent and clung uncomfortably. Why oh why had it not occurred to me that the top of my car would be covered in the same mud as the windshield?

*Dear Lord, Please don't let any of the passersby who saw me on the roof of my car be people who know me. Amen.*

Fortunately, the rest stop was only a couple of miles ahead. There were some new pink sweats in the trunk of my car, still in the shopping bag with the purchase receipt. Also in the bag were a pair of new aerobic tennis shoes and pretty sports socks with pink edging to match the sweats. These items had been in my trunk for several months. It was fortuitous that purchasing the sweat suit was as far as I ever got in my fitness intentions.

*susan case*

At the rest stop, I went into the women's bathroom to change into the sweat suit and new tennis shoes and wash my face in the sink basin. I rinsed my hair and used the hand air dryer with vent directed upward to fluff my hair in the warm air stream.

"Ahem." There was a woman standing behind me apparently waiting for the dryer.

"I'm sorry." I said, stepping to the side.

"That's okay. You've got more than your share of troubles." She seemed sincerely sympathetic. "Were you, um, napping on top of your car when the rain storm started?"

Since there was no good excuse as to why I had been on top of my car, I nodded yes and tried to look pitiful. The woman dug in her purse and pulled out a five dollar bill and handed it to me.

"Here, why don't you take this? Maybe you could get some change and call some family or friends who could help you out. It's a shame for you to be living in your car."

"No, thank you. Really," I said, pushing her hand and the money gently away. "Honestly, I'm fine."

She continued holding Mr. Lincoln out to me.

Sighing with resignation, I realized once again that the truth was going to have to be told. Why did the truth always have to be so embarrassing?

"The reason I was on top of my car was because I couldn't see out the windshield and my wiper fluid container was empty. I didn't want to get sprayed with water from the wipers so I got on top of my car to pour my slushy on the glass. You know, to try and clear some of the mud off."

"Honey," she said, tucking the five dollars into the hand warmer pocket of my sweatshirt, "you're a terrible liar. Nobody would ever believe a cockeyed story like that."

And Kirstie wonders why I make up stories. It's because my reality is most people's idea of fanciful, far-fetched fiction.

The rest of the drive was uneventful, and I enjoyed some news talk radio. My thoughts still reverted back to Candy and

Jet's embrace, but I stuffed that to the back of my mind to deal with later.

Maps are a wonderful thing for men, but driving directions—i.e., left at this street name, right at that avenue, 1/5 mile ahead, etc.—are a woman's best friend. The most lost I have ever been was the result of a map. One may think it's the reader/diviner of the map who is at fault, but it isn't; it *is* the map's fault. By design, one must flip a map to the right then to the left then upside down to read the street names; by the time you've done all that, you're headed backwards to where you originally started from. Truly *anyone* could inadvertently turn a map over and start using the directions from a different state. I once drove from Spokane headed toward Newport, Washington, according to the *map* a relatively short distance. I, however, ended up in Sandpoint, Idaho, and drove into the middle of a Neo Nazi Parade. Alas, I didn't have my pointy-headed shroud or swastika-quilted sweater vest. But since I glow in the dark and could easily be lost in a snow bank, I was allowed to pass through unharmed. I was thankful that no one went *Deliverance* on me and tried to kidnap me for breeding purposes. Honestly, I don't know where these thoughts come from, but they certainly help pass the time.

I was already turning onto Montrose Drive, looking at the house numbers. The homes were massive and impressive, each an architectural masterpiece. They were so huge that I was certain if I could sneak into one I could probably live there undetectable for months, maybe even years.

19871 Montrose Drive, a.k.a. the Whitworth home, was magnificent with its perfectly manicured lawn. The home resembled a castle for royalty. The Whitworths should put a moat and drawbridge in. I parked my car at the curb and called Sylvia's number again.

"Weetworth reseedence."

*Dolly Parton was singing in my head* 'Here We Go Again'.

"Mrs. Whitworth, please."

"Meeces Weetworth no at home."

"Thank you."

A wait wouldn't be too bad, as there was a yet-to-be-read John Grisham novel on the seat beside me. I started to read the novel, but only halfway through the first paragraph the sound of a car pulling into the Whitworth's drive interrupted me.

It was Sylvia in her sporty Cadillac. Her garage door was slowly opening, so I darted out of my car and ran to the passenger side of the Caddy. Keeping pace with the car, I rapped on the window, startling Sylvia, who stomped on the brakes. She put the car in neutral and rolled the window down.

"What do you want?" She clearly was not pleased to see me.

"I was hoping for a few minutes of your time." Then, ever the diplomat, I said, "I felt like I didn't hear you out the last time we talked."

She was wavering a bit.

"I'd really like your take on why you think, or, uh, believe that Harriet killed Herb."

"Come into the garage. We'll enter the house through there." Sylvia still didn't sound pleased, but at least she was acquiescing to my request. Her garage was bigger, cleaner, and nicer than my apartment.

We went through what I assumed was a rich person's idea of a mudroom. It was the most opulent mudroom I'd ever seen. Soft, ambient lighting, Italian tile floors, mahogany cabinets, marble vessel sink, and brass coat hooks adorned the room. The washer and dryer must have been hidden behind the closet-type doors. A short hallway led to the kitchen area. If I were a gourmet, I was sure this would be a dream kitchen. In the center of the kitchen was an island that housed a barbeque pit with a massive range hood over it.

*Indoor barbeque! Cool!*

"May I get you something to drink?" Her question sounded more perfunctory than accommodating, so I declined the offer.

"Rosario," Sylvia called out.

"Yes, Meece Weetworth." A small Hispanic woman entered, replete in gray maid's uniform with a white, frilled apron. Sylvia certainly went all out on the uniform for the domestic help.

"I'd like a glass of wine, please. And Rosario, I want the Joseph Phelps 2003 Insignia Cabernet Sauvignon. Throw out the inferior Niebaum-Coppola 2002, and don't ever serve that in this house again."

"Yes, Meese Weetworth."

The wine cabinet was immediately to Sylvia's right, and the glasses were in an opaque cupboard over her head. Sylvia had to move out of the way, albeit begrudgingly, for Rosario to get the wine and glass. And Kirstie calls *me* lazy. She ought to meet Sylvia.

"Are you sure you won't have a glass with me? Perhaps you could learn to appreciate fine wine."

"Do you have any 1994 Chapoutier Ermitage Le Pavillon?"

I could tell that Sylvia was impressed with my wine palate. Thankfully she was also blissfully unaware that I had recently written an article on local vineyards and wines and in my research come across this expensive red wine. Truthfully, I wouldn't know the difference between homebrewed swill and the uppity Chapoutier Ermitage.

"That's $150 a bottle!" Sylvia squeaked out in surprise. "What I mean is, uh, actually, we are out of that particular wine. However, I'm sure you'll find the Joseph Phelps Cabernet a suitable substitute."

"No, thank you. The Joseph Phelps Cabernet Sauvignon is a little too, shall we say, oaky for my palate." Gosh, I hoped it was an oaky wine, which was just another term I gleaned from my research but had no real knowledge of whatsoever.

Rosario served Sylvia her wine in a beautiful crystal glass and quietly backed out of the kitchen. Rosario and I had something in common. I didn't like to turn my back on Sylvia either.

"Let's go into the library. It's nice and quiet there."

*susan case*

161

The kitchen wasn't noticeably noisy, but I was dying to see her library. In my dream home, my imaginary library is a fifty by fifty room, two-story high masterpiece of opulent comfort. Floor to ceiling bookshelves would be filled to capacity with all the classics, novels, biographies, history, and commentaries my heart could desire. There would be plush furniture to sink into for a good afternoon's read. A stone fireplace big enough to roast a cow in would also be blazing away on chilly evenings. Maybe Rosario could work for me so I would never have to leave the comfort of my fantasy library.

The Whitworth library wasn't my dream library, but it was a close second. The furniture was all expensive leather in deep, rich, earth tone hues. Colorful, heavy, Persian-style rugs were artfully placed around the room. I plopped into a low armchair and was immediately cocooned in soft leather heaven. It was the most comfortable seat I had ever occupied. Sylvia chose a stiff-back Queen Anne-style chair with beautiful tapestry work and scroll-carved wood. Sylvia settled herself in a very ladylike fashion. She must practice every move she makes in front of a mirror. She was so graceful and appeared as if she were sitting ready to have her portrait painted by a renowned artist.

Sylvia's voice called me from my reverie. "So, what did you want to discuss?"

"I wanted to hear the details of why you believe Harriet is guilty of murdering Herb."

"Harriet knew that Herb was going to file for divorce and request half of everything they owned together, along with half of whatever Harriet had socked away in her retirement plan and other investments."

"Well, that's certainly a motive," I said. "How do you know Herb was going to divorce Harriet?"

Sylvia looked uncomfortable.

"Oh, I heard it somewhere."

I looked her straight in the eye. "Was Herb seeing someone romantically?"

"Now, how would I know that?" Her face turned scarlet, and her tone was defensive.

"Why do you think Herb wanted a divorce after all these years?"

"He was ready to settle down and remarry. By law he was entitled to half of everything. Why shouldn't he exercise his legal rights?"

"But you just said you didn't know if he was seeing anyone."

"I don't *know* that he was seeing anyone; it was just an assumption." Sylvia was about to snap the stem of her wineglass in half.

I leaned forward conspiratorially. "Actually, Herb *was* seeing someone."

"Oh?" She feigned surprise.

"Yes. I visited the hotel where he had his rendezvous every Saturday night. The evening desk clerk was very helpful and forthcoming." I leaned even farther toward Sylvia. "She submitted an order to corporate headquarters and will be sending me a copy of the registration slip, which will have the car's year, make, model, and license plate number. I should know by next week who the car belonged to."

"Maybe it was Herb's and you're just wasting your time," Sylvia suggested. She looked really nervous.

"Herb didn't own a car. I was out at his employer's ranch, and it's been confirmed that he always hitched a ride into Harmony." Now I was headed into dangerous territory. "Herb was dropped off at a convenience store where a woman in a white, late model Cadillac picked him up every Saturday evening." I paused for a deep breath. "You drive a white, late model Cadillac, don't you?"

Sylvia dropped her wine glass to the floor, where it shattered into prisms of light-reflecting shards.

"Get out of my house!" she growled.

"Whoever Herb *was* seeing he had apparently *stopped* see-

susan case

163

ing over two months ago, long before his death. Maybe he had tired of his lover and didn't want a divorce after all."

"I said get out of my house," she shrieked. Her face and body were tense, and for the first time her age was evident; so was her anger.

"Well, it's been nice visiting with you. Maybe we can visit again sometime, perhaps from your jail cell after I apprise the prosecuting attorney of these new details come to light."

Sylvia screamed and hurled a Tiffany-style table lamp in my direction. Only the fact that it was plugged into an outlet and therefore slowed down a bit caused the projectile to fall short of its target: *my head!*

# chapter 11

It was nice to be home, and I felt a small victory from my meeting with Sylvia. It was definitely her that Herb had been seeing, but what did it equate to? Did Sylvia have a motive to kill Herb? If he broke off their relationship, could she be so vengeful as to kill him? I didn't know why, but these pieces didn't seem to fit. As hideous and evil as Sylvia Campbell-Landmore-Russell-Scott-Whitworth was, I couldn't imagine that she would risk everything to commit murder. Oh, well. Let the investigators and attorneys sort it out. At minimum, I provided a secondary suspect, which gave Harriet some measure of reasonable doubt.

Still in my comfy new sweat suit, I settled onto my sofa to go through all my notes again when there was a knock on my door.

I wasn't expecting anyone, and I really wanted to review everything I had to date on Herb's murder. I decided to pretend not to be home. *Another persistent knock.* I was wavering but still hadn't gotten up to see who was at the door.

"Jimi, I know you're in there."

Rats. It was Jet. I hesitated, still not ready to hear the truth about him and Candy.

"Jimi, open this door *now!*" Jet sounded unreasonably perturbed. "That's it." I heard some shuffling around and the front door mat slapping back into place. Ha-ha. I had used the key under the mat when I got home, and it was still sitting on the coffee table. Then the sound of the handle turning caught my attention. I sat transfixed as the handle seemed to move in slow motion. Obviously I hadn't locked the door behind me when I got home because Jet just walked in.

"What do you think you're doing?" I demanded, trying to take the offense.

"Why didn't you open the door?"

"I was in the bathroom, when you decided to commit B&E. You could have waited another couple of seconds."

"You are such a liar," Jet said, then added, "and a coward."

"Whatever." *A liar, yes, but a coward?*

Jet closed the front door and started advancing on me like a mountain lion stalking a bunny, and I was such a cute little pink bunny in my new, fuzzy sweat suit.

"I want to discuss what you *think* you saw in my office this morning."

"There's nothing to discuss. Candy is back, and you hired her for the temporary position. You're the boss, so do as you see fit."

"You can be so exasperating." Jet ran a hand impatiently through his hair. "I meant that it appeared we were, you know, hugging."

"You don't have to explain anything to me, Jet. You and Candy Kane picked up where you left off in high school. How is that any concern of mine?"

"We haven't picked up anything. Her husband recently left her, and she came back to live with her parents until she can get things settled and straightened out. I figured she could temporarily fill in at the office and, being an old friend, I could help her out at the same time. Nothing more, nothing less."

"Well, that certainly explains why you hired her, but it doesn't enlighten me as to why you were hugging her. Is embracing part of the hiring process that I somehow missed out on?"

"She was distraught when she was telling me about her husband. I was only trying to offer comfort."

"You certainly proved you are a great buddy, pal, comrade, and ally. Is there anything else? I have some work to do."

"Yes, as a matter of fact, there is." Jet took the last two steps that separated the distance between us. He took me by the shoulders and pulled me to him. One warm hand went behind my neck and the other to the small of my back, applying pressure to draw me even closer.

"Just what do you think you are doing?" The intent was to sound angry, but it came out more as curious. "Why is it you only try and kiss me when I'm mad, hysterical, or have recently thrown up?"

"Because every time I get close to you, you are either mad or hysterical, and I'm not even going to comment on the third factor. You're trying to derail me."

"I don't think this is a good idea." My statement lacked any amount of sincerity or conviction. Looking into his soft brown eyes, I trembled in anticipation.

"I really don't care." Then, on a whispered breath, he said, "I've waited a long—"

When his lips touched mine, all thoughts past, present, and future fled. It was simply Jet and me and eight years of longing finally being fulfilled. My imagination is usually so much better than reality. However, in this instance, such was definitely not the case. Jet's kiss was everything I always dreamed it would be and so much more. He brushed his lips back and forth across mine in a way that created sensual pleasure and yet was somehow pure and full of sweet promise. My arms went around his neck, and he deepened the already passionate kiss. My lips parted on a sigh, but Jet moved slightly away. Wrinkling my brow in consternation and without even opening my eyes, I tried to pull him back where he belonged. Jet rested his forehead on mine and gripped my shoulders. The back of my legs were against the sofa, so it only took a little force for Jet to push me down onto the couch. Confused, I opened my eyes to see Jet heading for the door.

*He's leaving? How dare he leave me like this?* I wasn't done kissing him. I would never be done kissing him. Every inch of me was warm, tingly, and begging to be back in Jet's embrace. Then an ugly thought invaded my ardor-clouded brain. *Maybe*

*susan case*

*he was done kissing me.* Maybe Jet found me lacking in the lip-to-lip proficiency department. Jet watched all the emotions crossing my face and smiled.

"If you can't figure out how it is between us, you're not nearly as smart as I thought you were," he said, and he left.

I sat there dazed and confused. If Jet had said his last statement *before* he kissed me, then I could assume he liked me. But he said it afterward and didn't seem inclined to continue the kiss. In fact, he left me sitting there like an idiot. And I had practically begged for more by pulling him closer. This was more embarrassing than being caught on the hood of my car in the rainstorm. What must he be thinking?

I ran to the door and called out to Jet as he was about to get into his Navigator.

"What?"

"I need to talk to you about Harriet. That's why I came in to your office this morning."

Jet closed the door to his car and came back, taking the stairs two at a time.

"What did you find out?" he asked, keeping a marginal distance.

I was standing in my doorway, so I motioned him into the apartment, but he shook his head no. Apparently he didn't want to be alone with me again.

I closed my door and leaned against it. "I found out that Harriet's friend Sylvia has been having a longtime affair with Herb. But I think Herb may have broken the relationship off a couple of months ago."

"You're kidding." He smiled openly. "Did she have any motive other than being jilted?"

"Well, she is married to a very wealthy man."

"Keep up the great work. Anything else?" I shook my head no, and he started to leave again. My mind was working furiously on how to get him to stay and come closer.

"Jet?" I whispered.

"Hmm?" He paused and turned around.

Now what? I couldn't think of a thing to keep him here any longer. My head was down, and I was shuffling my feet back and forth. Yeesh. I felt like a little kid. I was trying to erase the longing and vulnerability in my eyes before looking up at him. I tried to master a nonchalant gaze, but tears were threatening to spill. Jet took pity on me and moved closer and hugged me tightly and gave me an unsatisfactory, fatherly peck on the forehead.

"Thanks for not slipping out of my arms. I didn't want to kiss your door like that other poor slob."

It only took a couple of seconds for that comment to register with both of us. His reaction was one of shock at what he had revealed, and mine was of extreme anger at what he had apparently done.

I couldn't believe it. Jet knew Daniel had tried to kiss me but had kissed my door instead. There was only one way he could have known; he'd been watching us. "You were spying on me!"

"Now wait a—," Jet tried to interrupt my diatribe.

"How dare you! You, you, *stalker!*"

Jet appeared embarrassed and uncomfortable and looked around to see if we had an audience. "Let's go inside."

"I don't think so."

"Jimi, I was trying to protect you. I was worried that gigolo was going to try something."

"That's disgusting. What? Were you crouched in the bushes, waiting like some predatory animal?"

"He's the predator, but you're too naïve to figure anything out for yourself."

"Really? Then why was he so amicable about my not kissing him?" My hands were on my hips and my blood pressure was rising.

"He's bidding his time trying to wear you down, get you comfortable, then attack."

"As opposed to your style of just attack," I accused.

An arrogant smile played on his lips. "I didn't notice you retreating."

Putting a hand to my throat, I tried to stifle the scream that was building inside.

"Jimi." Jet moved close. "Please, I . . ." Jet tried to use the same moves as earlier, but the resulting effects were much different this time.

Without thinking, I slapped his face *hard.* The sound rang out, and there was an immediate ugly red mark imprinted on his cheek.

I was mortified at my violent instinctive reaction. Jet hadn't deserved that, but there was no way to back down now. Humiliation and anger were running too high and out of control.

Jet laughed a short, sardonic sound and rubbed his cheek. "I guess we better stick to the business relationship. Anything else just gets us in trouble."

"Do I still have a job?"

Jet looked like I had punched him in the gut. "That was below the belt, even for you. Yes, you have your job, and I promise not to *bother* you with anything other than work-related issues again."

Inside my apartment, I pulled the living room curtains aside, hoping he would look up at me and smile—even a little smile, something that would let me know everything was going to be all right. But Jet never glanced up. He got in his car and drove off. He didn't even squeal his tires or peel out, which would have at least shown some emotion. No. He calmly drove away as if nothing untoward had happened.

In the past fifteen minutes, I had been to the pinnacle of the highest mountain top and then dashed back down onto the rocks of my deepest personal anguish. One of us was such a schmuck. As the tears began to pour, I knew which one of us was the idiot.

# *chapter 12*

Rhonda the receptionist was, as usual, on a personal phone call and showed no signs of ending the conversation anytime soon. I had wanted to go through her to see Jet rather than showing up at his office uninvited. Though patience is not one of my virtues, I decided to wait awhile and approach Rhonda again later in the day for an appointment with Jet.

On the way to my desk, I noticed a light coming through Mrs. Greene's door. Curious, I poked my head in. There was Candy Kane ensconced in Mrs. Greene's old leather office chair. Candy had also taken it upon herself to do some redecorating. There were some paintings, vases filled with flowers, and some other artful knickknacks. Everything of Mrs. Greene's was hidden away somewhere out of sight.

"Jamie, what a surprise," she sweetly oiled out to me. At least she was honest enough not to say, "what a *nice* surprise."

"Uh, making yourself at home, are you?"

"Jet thought I should have a nice place to work, so he thoughtfully gave me this office. I just love a private office, don't you?" Then, barely missing a beat, she said, "Oh, so sorry. I forgot you only have that little cubicle in the *common* area."

"Well, I don't need privacy. Most people actually like to see me. But please use your door to full advantage and keep it closed."

Her expression changed in the wink of an eye from anger to smugness. She pointed to a beautiful, if not somewhat ostentatious arrangement of rare and expensive flowers. "Doesn't Jet have wonderful taste? And he's so thoughtful too. I guess the flowers were his way of saying he'd miss me while he's out of town for the next couple of weeks."

"Jet went out of town?" Unfortunately, there was a measure of regret and surprise in my tone that Candy joyfully picked up on.

"Didn't he call you? Of course, then again why would he? I'll be acting as his second-in-command for the next few weeks, maybe longer."

"Where did he go? Was it business?"

"If he wanted you to know, I suppose he would have called you."

Not wanting to put further fuel on the fire, I mumbled a good-bye and closed her door with a little more oomph than necessary.

The thought crossed my mind to call Jet, but what could I possibly say? There wasn't anything new on the Greene front, so I didn't even have a valid work excuse. I still needed to get in to see Mrs. Greene to discuss the furniture dolly and the accompanying rental receipt. Maybe after garnering some additional insight into the rental, I'd have a reason to call Jet. Until then, I would have to remain confused, concerned, and malcontent.

Looking at my watch, I had several hours to kill before covering this afternoon's high school girls' basketball game. My other story was to introduce the new business in town to our subscribers. It was a quilting shop that a middle-aged couple from Seaside, Oregon, bought. The small downtown office space had been renovated and repainted. It was quite charming from the exterior. They were expecting me sometime this afternoon to interview them about their new enterprise. Perhaps they could meet with me earlier. I really wanted to get out of the office before running into Candy the Conceited Conniving Cat again. *Meow!*

The couple's name was in my organizer somewhere. I didn't actually use the pages as intended. Instead I just stuffed papers, cards, and notes on tissues or napkins kinda willy-nilly into the book. All the loose notes and cards fell out onto my desk, so I began rummaging through the pile for the quilt shop business card. I remember it had a unique name. Finally, I came upon the card. The business card looked like a plaid quilt in soft, muted colors; the business name was bolded in deep, lavender print: *EiderDownTown*. Dibbz had to explain the store's name to me. She said that eiderdown was commonly used inside blankets and comforters for soft thickness and extra warmth. The proprietors of the store were Drew and Wilhelmina Springer.

I gave the Springer's a courtesy call. Wilhelmina asked me to call her Willie and said they would be delighted for me to come now. Wilhelmina was a cheerful sort and ended the call with a "God bless you." I hadn't sneezed, so her blessing must have been of a more general nature. I certainly hoped that He would bless me, because things hadn't been going well my way lately.

It was only four or five blocks to the quilt store, and walking seemed like a refreshing idea. It was another spectacular fall day with no wind. Any day without wind is a miracle in Idaho, so I wanted to make the most of the weather, especially since winter would be here in just a couple of months and temperatures would be dropping consistently into the twenties or lower.

Several people waved to me from their cars. Billie Sue Bailey, a local realtor, stopped her sleek, black Porsche in the middle of the street to ask if I needed a ride. I told her, "No, thank you. I'm enjoying the walk." She looked at me as if all my hatches weren't securely battened down and drove off. I guess when you drive a Porsche you want to be seen in it. Walking would be substandard and tacky.

EiderDownTown was an enchanting little place with a boardwalk front. Multicolored fabrics adorned shelf after shelf. The room was reminiscent of a beach cottage with whitewashed wood slat floors and walls. Huge windows were adorned with striped navy blue and white brocade and had gold tiebacks and trim. The high-glossed wood antique furniture was charming, as was the old treadle sewing machine on display.

Willie met me at the front entrance as soon as I opened the

*susan case*

173

door. She appeared to be in her late forties with a silvery blonde bob that framed her heart-shaped face nicely. Her open and gregarious smile made my return smile easy and automatic.

"Miss Smith?" she asked.

"Yes, but please call me Jimi." I greeted her with a polite handshake.

"I'm so excited you will be writing about our little store. We haven't had much business yet, but we've only been open a couple of weeks." She called out to her husband, who apparently was in a back room, "Drew, come out here and meet Jimi. She's the nice young reporter from the local paper."

A man sporting a long, gray ponytail, wearing a Hawaiian print floral shirt and Bermuda shorts parted the curtain divider. His smile was as gracious and genuine as his wife's.

"Hello, young lady. I'm Drew Springer." Drew extended his hand to me.

"It's a pleasure to meet you, Mr. Springer," I said, shaking his hand.

"How do you like the shop?" Mr. Springer inquired.

"It's lovely. It reminds me of a beach cottage."

Mr. and Mrs. Springer shared a smile. "That's the atmosphere we were hoping to convey," Willie said. "We love Ditters Ferry and all of Idaho that we've seen so far, but we do still miss the beach."

"I've only been to the beach one time, but I can understand how you would miss it." My one trip to Manzanita Beach, Oregon, had me hopelessly hooked on the ocean. Imposing, craggy mountains cut away into the shore. Some of the mountains poked their heads up several hundred yards off shore. In the morning it was mystically foggy around the base of the cliffs. I loved the smell of the salty sea air, the feel of the mist blowing off the water, and the sound of the crashing waves. It felt like home even though it was my first visit to the area. The surrounding towns were picturesque and full of cheerfully kind and unique residents. Boardwalk sidewalks and baskets of colorful hanging flowers were everywhere. It was as lush as Hawaii, but without the crowds and lei people.

I realized I had been standing there daydreaming while still clasping hands with Mr. Springer from our extended handshake.

"So sorry. I mentally took a trip to the beach," I said, trying to excuse my odd behavior.

Mrs. Springer giggled and said she knew exactly what I meant. She offered me some tea, and the three of us sat and talked for over two hours. They were a delightful couple with lots of interesting stories to tell. The only awkward moment came when Willie asked me if I sewed, and I answered with an emphatic *no.*

Mr. Springer went back to doing whatever it was he was working on in the rear of the store, so I related my one disastrous sewing attempt to Willie.

My freshman year in high school, for the final home economics assignment, we had to make something from a pattern. Most girls choose a simple skirt or plain blouse, but I wanted something challenging. I picked a beautiful intricate dress pattern. It took me four hours to lay the pattern out onto the fabric because it seemed there was much more pattern than fabric. Finally, the geometry of it worked out. I spent another two hours carefully pinning the pattern to the fabric beneath. Anyway, when I went to cut the pieces out, I realized the entire thing had been pinned to the living room carpet. I threw a terrific fit and ripped everything up, sending pins and pattern pieces flying across the room. Dibbz says to this day her vacuum will pick up another errant pin or two.

At the end of my story, Willie looked sufficiently sympathetic and didn't encourage any sewing efforts.

"Is Dibbz your maid?" Willie asked.

"No, she's my grandmother," I explained.

"Interesting name. Has your grandmother always lived with

*susan case*

you and your parents?" I guess that was a natural assumption, as most children are raised by their parents.

"No. My parents died two weeks before my eleventh birthday in a car accident. My grandparents raised my brother and me since then."

"I'm so sorry, dear. I didn't mean to bring up any painful memories." Poor Willie had tears glistening in her compassionate eyes.

After all these years, it's peculiar how when someone shows sympathy about my parents' death is the only time I allow myself any expression of grief, as if it's only acceptable to cry when mirroring someone else's emotions.

Willie gave me a hug, and I left feeling even more melancholy than before. I was determined, however, to write a great article for the store to do my best to bring business in to the Springer's new quilt shop.

I needed to visit with Mrs. Greene, but it was Tuesday and the next visiting day wasn't until tomorrow from 8:00 a.m. to 11:00 a.m. I wanted to discuss the furniture dolly and receipt. Also, I got to thinking that if Mrs. Greene had killed her husband, wouldn't she have suffered some injuries? The letter opener was in Herb's chest, so it was obviously a frontal attack. Why wouldn't Herb have fought back? This case got weirder and weirder, but there did seem to be some measure of reasonable doubt accumulating on Mrs. Greene's behalf.

If Sylvia had stolen the letter opener from Mrs. Greene's house on one of her visits and planted the furniture dolly receipt, then there was still the problem of Sylvia not having any wounds from Herb trying to defend himself. The body was fully clothed, so it didn't seem that he was asleep or otherwise indisposed. The questions were intriguing.

Harriet's attorney, with Harriet's permission, had provided Jet with the autopsy report. No drugs were found in the body. The cause of death had been the stab to the heart by the letter opener. It was used with such force that it was imbedded to the hilt and then some.

Due to the violence of the crime and the overwhelming circumstantial evidence against Harriet Greene, the bond for her release had been set at $5 million. Harriet was working furiously from behind bars to secure a home equity or mortgage loan for bail money. Unfortunately, the land to home value was way out of kilter, and no bank was willing to lend. Apparently the home must be more value or at least close in value to the property. In Harriet's case, the value was almost exclusively in the land and not the aging home.

None of this pondering was getting me anywhere. It was almost time to head over to the school for the basketball game, so I walked there with my notepad and the company camera. It didn't seem cost-effective to have Daniel take the pictures. I could get a good enough photograph with the ten-megapixel digital camera that the paper allowed writers to check out for such assignments. Besides, the excitement of the game would be a great diversion for my otherwise Jet-related thoughts and worries. Maybe Spence would be there too. I hadn't seen him in a while.

# *chapter 13*

At the office Wednesday morning, there was quite a commotion going on amongst the newspaper's employees. Well, at least compared to the morgue that the office usually resembled. Even Rhonda was in the thick of things instead of being on a personal call or filing her nails.

"Did you hear?" Rhonda was pulling on my arm and talking so fast that I never even saw her lips move.

"Hear what?"

"Oh, my gosh. You don't know?" In her excitement, Rhonda spit on me.

I took a swipe at my chin to remove the offensive spittle. Come to think of it, did I remove it or rub it in? It was disgusting either way. "Not yet. Why don't you take a breath and tell me what all the excitement is about?" I asked in a soothing tone, trying to calm her down.

"Mrs. Greene's trial date has been set."

"When is it?"

"*That is the big news!* The trial is set for October 12."

"This October 12?" That was less than three weeks away.

"The state was pushing for a speedy trial, but the surprise was that Harriet's attorney agreed. He seems to want it to go to trial quickly too."

"Will you excuse me, Rhonda? I have a few calls to make."

Rhonda didn't even respond. She just flitted back to the boisterous group still discussing the rapidly impending murder trial.

Jet had given me the contact information for Harriet's attorney in an e-mail. Unfortunately, I didn't set it aside or put it into my contact list for future reference. Now I had to go through my archived e-mails to find this specific one from Jet. It actually only took a couple of minutes to locate the e-mail. I dialed the number to Harriet's attorney, James Gunderson III, Esq., whose firm was located in Boise.

"Gunderson, Gunderson, Malcolm, and Reed."

"May I speak with James Gunderson the third, please?"

"Whom may I ask is calling?"

"Jimi Smith from the *Ditters Weekly* newspaper."

"One moment."

Some hypnotic elevator music played for my listening pleasure. I listened to three symphonic overtures and two movie theme songs. Finally, a deep, well-modulated voice with a British accent (a voice as rich as caramel dipped in chocolate sauce and covered in real whipped cream) came on the line.

"Ms. Smith, delightful to hear from you. How may I assist you?"

"Actually, Mr. Gunderson, I wanted to give you some information you may not be aware of." I was suddenly overly self-conscious that my sentence had ended with a preposition.

"Proceed." It was a politely intoned command.

"First, did you know that Herb Greene was having a longtime affair with Mrs. Greene's best friend and that that *friend* was herself married to a very well-to-do prominent businessman?"

"You know this for fact?" At least he sounded interested.

"Yes. I have a hotel clerk in Twin Falls who will attest to the make and model of the vehicle Herb made his regular Saturday night visits to the hotel in and will further attest that there was a woman keeping him company. Also, the woman in question admitted to me about the affair rather in a roundabout way, but admitted nonetheless."

"May I ask to whom you are referring? Who is this mystery woman?"

"Sylvia Whitworth. I believe her maiden name was Campbell."

"Interesting. Please continue," Gunderson intoned.

"Sylvia stated categorically that Herb had requested a divorce from Mrs. Greene and that he was remarrying and entitled to half of Mrs. Greene's estate."

"Anything else?" he prompted.

"Well, no. That's all I have for now."

"Thank you, Ms. Smith. You have proved to be a tremendous asset, just as Harriet predicted."

*Harriet Greene said I would be an asset?* Had the temperature in Hades suddenly plummeted to below freezing? "Please keep me informed of any other useful facts you may uncover."

"I will, Mr. Gunderson. Thank you."

"Ah, young lady, it is *I* who should be thanking *you.*"

"Yes, well, uh, you're welcome."

"Good day."

And then I heard the dial tone indicating our conversation was officially over. He and Kirstie would get along famously. Neither could wait for the other party to acknowledge that a dialogue had ended. The difference between the two, however, was that I didn't want James Gunderson III, Esq. to ever stop talking. He had a voice that could melt butter and send a woman's imagination into overdrive.

More and more, Sylvia was beginning to feel like a viable suspect. She was certainly the type not to allow *anything* to come between her and luxury. Add to that the fact Herb had stopped seeing her a few weeks prior to his death; maybe, just maybe, he was planning on taking Sylvia for some blackmail money. Given his character, Herb could have been planning to take Sylvia and Harriet to the cleaners, so to speak. Perhaps James Gunderson III, Esq. could dig up some additional information. It was certain he had more resources, especially financial, to dig up anything that could take the focus off of Mrs. Greene and provide reasonable doubt to the jury. I was still somewhat shocked that the trial was to take place so soon, but it didn't seem appropriate to question her attorney and his educated decision. Murder in the first, at least according to movies, *20/20,* and mystery novels, usually took months to even years to go to court and get resolution.

Anyway, I had done my duty and informed Harriet's attorney of the Sylvia factor. Now my mental energy needed to be focused on how to obtain Jet's forgiveness. Maybe Kirstie would have some advice. I dialed the number to Shear X-tacy.

"Shear X-tacy. How may I help you?" I didn't recognize the voice.

"May I speak with Kirstie, please?"

"She's with a client now. May I take a message, or would you like me to book an appointment for you?"

Actually, my hair could use a trim and reshaping. "Yes. I would like to book an appointment for a cut. Does she have any openings today?"

A short, sarcastic laugh emitted from the other end. "Uh, Kirstie is booked solid for the next six weeks."

"Tell you what, Miss—?" It certainly was impressive that Kirstie was booked so far in advance.

"Tiffany," she politely filled in the blank.

"Tiffany, please put me on hold and go ask Kirstie if she can squeeze me in sooner than six weeks. The name is Jimi Smith."

Hard rock music assaulted my ears as Tiffany placed me on hold. Kirstie had apparently hired someone like herself when it came to phone etiquette. After a couple of minutes, Tiffany came back on the line.

"Kirstie said for *you* it would be eight weeks."

"Hah. Very funny. What did she really say?"

"Kirstie *really* did say that, but she also said you couldn't take wait or no for an answer." There was a short pause. "She said come in at 6:30 tonight and bring Chinese takeout and an ice cold Coke with you."

I was going to have to go all the way to Hilltown for Chinese. Did Kirstie think I was made of money? "Tiffany, please tell Kirstie I'll be there with spicy Chicken Almond Ding, a side of pork and seeds, and a Coke."

"She also said to tell you not to eat her fortune cookie."

"One time! I did that one time, and she won't let me forget it." Several months ago, we had gone to eat Chinese together, and Kirstie excused herself to go the ladies room. The waitress had arrived with the check and our cookies right after Kirstie left the table. I ate both cookies. Big deal. I needed a double dose of fortune. Miss Booked Six Weeks in Advance should be more understanding.

"She said you would say that too."

"Yeah, well, she's a talented mind reader. Wonder if she knows what I'm thinkin' now."

"Kirstie said you must want something from her and you could get a little snippy when people know what you're thinking."

This was a *no win* situation. "Thank you, Tiffany. I—" Something about her name and voice seemed vaguely familiar. There was a short, mental lull before I recalled where I had heard her name. "Um, Tiffany, you wouldn't by chance be the girl who came into Shear X-tacy a few months ago with a young man named Josh, would you?" I almost said Joshy-woshy-boo-boo-boo.

"Yeah. How did you know? I got my nipples pierced then," Tiffany said surprised.

"Don't say the *n* word. It isn't polite," I instructed her.

There was a huge intake gasp of air. "I have *never* in my life said the *n* word." Tiffany was clearly insulted.

"I meant the, uh, *n* word that rhymes with *ripple*."

"You mean *nipple*," she said it again.

"Stop using that word!"

"It *is* a nipple. What would you like me to call it?"

"Chesticular pigment darkened circle for all I care. Just don't use *that* word. In fact, don't refer to it at all. I'm a perfect stranger for heaven's sake."

"You are weird. What are you, like a 118 years old?"

Now she was ticking me off. "You know what? Just tell

Kirstie I'll see her tonight, and then we can end this lovely conversation."

Dial tone. Yep, Kirstie had hired her very own Kirstie replica.

It wasn't quite noon yet, so there was time to convert my notes from the girls' basketball game into a story. It had been a fun game, and I got some great action shots. Unfortunately, the girls went from a six-point lead with less than two minutes on the clock and then proceeded to lose the game by one point.

My article for the sewing shop was already finished and ready for print. I did my best to make the shop seem like a little slice of heaven and that everyone who is anyone must go in and take a look around. Besides, sewing was a great past time *yada yada yada.*

Regrettably I was also now in charge of the obituaries since Harriet's incarceration. Harriet had held on to that duty even after her promotion to editor. She evidently liked writing about dead people. The first death to occur on my watch happened two days ago. I pulled up some old obits to review the preferred style of wording and got my notes together on his life history, his now living and dead familial relations, and of course the death and burial details.

Pastor Barry Hutt, who had shepherded his flock from the local Presbyterian church for the past twenty-seven years, had died peacefully in his sleep at the tender age of eighty-four. Pastor Hutt had actually planned on retiring in Ditters Ferry when he and his wife moved here in 1980, but once he filled in at the pulpit to help out between pastors, he found himself so well-loved and appreciated that he took the position at the urgent plea of the parishioners. It was going to be a packed house at this funeral. The entire community, as well as his flock, loved Pastor Hutt. He was quick with a smile, had a kind word for everyone, and was the first to lend a hand and take on any charitable cause.

It was shortly after 4:00 p.m. when I finished the obituary

on Pastor Hutt. I saved the obit to the disk that contained my other articles and the classifieds then closed down my computer for the day. Now the ugly part: I had to take my work to Candy, who would format and forward the articles to the printer.

Knocking on Candy's closed door, I took a deep, calming breath. I was *not* going to allow her to get to me.

"Come in," Candy cheerily sing-songed out.

"Hello, Candace." I decided to be the better person and not antagonize her by calling her Candy. "I have my articles ready for print." Suddenly I recalled the obit hadn't been saved to my hard drive and I had instead errantly saved it directly to disk.

"You know what? Never mind. I forgot to save these to my hard drive. I'll be back in a few minutes."

"You didn't back it up?" Her tone suggested she was speaking to a senseless child.

"No. I forgot. I'll be right back."

"Don't bother. I'll make a second disk, and you can save it later. Just give me the disk so I can get it off to the printer."

"I don't want to make you go to the extra trouble. This will take only a few minutes."

"Jimi, I think we need to figure out a way to work together. Please let me do this." She had actually called me Jimi instead of *Jamie.* Maybe we could both act like adults and end the animosity.

"I appreciate this, Candace," I said, handing over the disk. "Call me if you have any questions."

"I have your cell number." She put the disk into her pc, and the file was booting up as she got up to get a blank disk, I assumed to make a duplicate for me.

"Thank you again," I said sincerely.

"It's my pleasure. *Really.*" Something about the way she said that gave me a moment's pause, but when I looked at her, she was smiling graciously. I felt guilty about thinking the worst of her. Maybe *our* problems were actually *my* problems. To be honest, when it came to Jet, I found myself fiercely jealous and not

*susan case*

terribly levelheaded. Upon leaving the office, I felt a little lighter in mood and a lot more grown up. It would be nice not to have to avoid Candy and to end the hostile atmosphere between us.

Looking at my watch, I decided to go to Hilltown early and get some shopping done. Unfortunately, now I would have to travel to Hilltown two days in a row, thanks to Kirstie's food order. The paper would pay for tomorrow evening's visit to Harriet between 6:00 p.m. and 9:00 p.m. because that was official newspaper business. However, there wasn't anything to justify the trip today as *business*. I still needed to question Harriet about the out-of-place furniture dolly receipt. It was bothering me, and judging by Harriet's initial reaction, she wasn't even aware of the furniture dolly rental, much less the resulting receipt.

It hit me that I should inquire at the only title company in Hilltown to see if anyone else had requested information about Harriet's property. It would be a good idea to pay a visit to the appraiser, who valued the property at over $1 million too. The appraiser's office was conveniently located on the same block as the title company. Today's trip to Hilltown was now officially newspaper business. I truly love the way my mind works sometimes.

Listening to talk radio is a wonderful way to make a drive pass swiftly. I was deeply engrossed in the current topic of the call-in program I'd tuned in to. Hilltown was trying to get a bond passed to pay for renovation and expansion of the local hospital.

"Caller, you're on the air," the host announced.

"Hi. I can't believe I got through. I just love your show."

"Thank you, and your name?" the DJ asked.

"Adele." She paused for a moment. "I can't believe that they want to raise our taxes *again*."

"Well, that's not really this issue, Adele. The town council proposes to pass a bond to improve the hospital and provide needed emergency and diagnostic equipment. The end result would be slightly higher taxes, yes."

"That's what I'm saying. It's wrong to raise my taxes. Does the city think we are all rich?"

"I think the city wants the best hospital it may provide for its citizens. Do you realize that property values increase when a community improves its hospital or schools?"

"So now you want me to pay even higher property taxes?" Adele was becoming agitated.

"But you would build immediate additional equity in your home. Wouldn't that be good for you as the homeowner, not to mention the fact that if you became sick or were injured and needed emergency equipment, currently only available in Boise some forty-five miles away, you could be treated much faster locally, possibly saving your or a loved one's life?"

"I don't have any loved ones, and I ain't been sick a day in my life."

"So you don't believe anything beneficial would be provided to your community if the bond were to pass. I find that a little uncompassionate and shortsighted."

"Listen up, you big government communist pinko. I am never listening to your show again." The loud click of a phone being forcefully hung up was followed by a dial tone.

"Addled the Unloved has apparently disconnected from the call as well as from her community. My viewing audience is now one less, due to Adele's abdication, but my average listening audience intelligence quotient has conversely risen dramatically with her departure."

Gotta love this guy; he has a lot of chutzpah. I wondered if Adele the Addled turned her radio off or had heard the insults hurled her way. I was pulling into the parking lot of the title company, so no time for further consideration. Darn. It would be nice to hear the rest of the program. I was hoping the discussion might help the bond to pass. It was good for the entire community. The projected average tax increase was $72 per single-family residence per tax year. This seemed a small price to pay for life-saving equipment and the potential for immediate higher property values. But Adele didn't agree with me, so there were probably others who wouldn't agree with my logic as well.

The title company must have been decorated in the 1960s or so. Dark paneling covered every wall, and the carpet was muted gold and rust tones in a dizzying pattern repeated in a square every foot. A yellow bubble glass and wrought iron chandelier hung heavily overhead, and the counter was topped with obnoxious green Formica.

"May I assist you?" a harried-looking woman inquired. Multiple phone lines were ringing, demanding to be answered.

"Yes. I'd like to speak with a title officer, if I may."

"Your name?"

"Jimi Smith. I'm with the *Ditters Weekly* newspaper."

"Thank you, Ms. Smith. Why don't you have a seat while I see if an officer is available?"

She pointed to a set of three dented aluminum chairs with turquoise-colored vinyl seat cushions and backs. The chairs were welded together and bolted to the floor. I was trying to imagine why they were bolted down. Were they afraid that a 1970's television show set decorator was going to go on a furniture-stealing spree? Regardless, I took a seat and picked up an outdated, page-wearied magazine.

The phone-harassed woman who had initially welcomed me returned. "Both our officers are with clients at the moment. May I ask the nature of your visit?"

"I'm here on behalf of Harriet Greene. She would like to know if anyone has inquired about the property she owns on the outskirts of Ditters Ferry."

"Is this official newspaper business?"

"Actually, I have a power of attorney from Mrs. Greene to obtain this information." I began rummaging through my day planner. I let all the loose papers and whatnot fall to the floor in a littering mess. "I know it's here somewhere," I said, continuing to make an even bigger mess. Falling to my hands and knees, I picked up one piece of paper at a time and studied it at length, then put it back on the floor. Then I would start the same procedure with another piece of paper. After a few pieces were studied, I picked up one of the documents that I had already looked at twice before. After a few minutes of this, the woman's toe began to tap, and I could tell she was losing patience. So I began to move even slower and study the individual papers even longer. Someone in a back office hollered for the phones to be answered.

"What specifically do you want to know?" she demanded.

"Oh, Harriet just wants to know if her husband or a representative of his came in and requested information on the property that he and Mrs. Greene own jointly."

"That's easy. I handled that. Herb Greene and a woman did come in. All he wanted to know was if the property had been paid in full and if a reconveyance for clear title to the house and land had been issued by the mortgage company."

"Did you give him the answer?"

"Of course. He co-owns the property," she said as if any idiot should know this.

"And what was the answer?"

"The answer was a simple yes. The payoff had been received and the reconveyance sent to the county recorder for filing."

"Would you please describe the woman he was with?"

"Well, she was maybe late forties, early fifties and stylishly dressed, shoulder length brown hair."

"Did you catch her name?"

"No. Are we done?" Her tone was controlled exasperation, but losing control rapidly.

"Just one more thing. Did you happen to notice if she had a large, antique, opal ring on her right index finger."

"As a matter of fact, she did. Do you know her?"

"No."

She looked at me quizzically. I gathered up my notes and papers and stuffed them back into my day planner. I had ceased to call it an organizer; it was too much of an oxymoron.

"Thank you," I said, heading toward the exit.

"Wait a minute? Do you have that power of attorney for me?"

"I'll mail you a copy." With that lie I made my getaway.

The appraiser's office was a short walk down the block. There was a frozen yogurt shop between the title company and my destination. It seemed like providence since I hadn't eaten anything other than a small bag of Cheetos and a mini Snickers today. A two-scoop vanilla cone with multi-colored chocolate sprinkles was definitely in order. I got my treat and sat down to enjoy it. This was the absolutely cutest retro shop I had ever encountered. It was a replica of a days-gone-by soda fountain and ice cream shop, the kind you would see in old thirties and forties movies. The chairs were dainty, white, intricately woven metal with festive red-and-white-striped, round seats. The tables were topped with heavy glass with a white, lacy tablecloth neatly pressed underneath. There was a large magazine rack and over-the-counter medicine displays. On the counter, enormous glass globes held a huge variety of candies to appease any sweet tooth. Even the gentleman working behind the counter wore a red-and-white striped shirt with a red satin armband.

An enormous beveled glass mirror hung on the wall behind the counter, and "Mr. Sandman" was softly playing in the background. The yogurt was divine—it tasted like homemade ice cream—and the atmosphere made me feel as if I'd stepped onto a golden era movie set. I was definitely coming back to this little haven.

I finished my cone and then couldn't resist purchasing some black licorice from one of the glass containers. My purchase was put into a small, red-and-white striped paper bag that made a lovely crinkling noise when the pinking sheered top was folded over. I hated to leave, but there wasn't much time before the appraiser would be closing for the day.

The appraiser's office was in complete contrast to the yogurt shop. It was modern, sparse, and monochromatic in subdued grays and blues. There was an efficient-looking woman seated behind a massive chrome and glass receptionist counter.

"Welcome to Barnes Appraisal. May I assist you?"

"Do you only appraise barns?" It was a weak ineffectual attempt at humor.

"No. We appraise homes, land, commercial, and farm property," she stated perfunctorily.

"Actually, I was wondering if I could speak to the appraiser who performed the Harriet Greene property appraisal a few months ago. I have a couple of very generic questions. Perhaps you could help me."

"I don't know. What is it you are inquiring about?"

She sounded so stiff and formal that I didn't think the drop-the-papers/power-of-attorney scam was going to work a second time.

"I wanted to know if Herb, Harriet's husband, received a copy of the appraisal."

"Let me pull the file. You say it was within the last few months?"

"Yes."

She disappeared around a corner for about five minutes and returned with a thick file. "Here it is." She began flipping through the documents. "A duplicate copy was issued to Herbert Greene on August 5."

"Was there a charge for the copy?"

"Of course, copies cost $150."

"How did he pay the invoice?" I asked.

She turned several more pages. "With a check."

"Do you have a copy of the check?" I hoped my luck wasn't being pushed too far.

"Yes, I make copies of everything."

I believed her. She appeared very efficient and organized. I really should hate her or, better yet, emulate her. But hating her seemed easier.

"May I see the check?"

*susan case*

191

She was pondering my question, weighing whether or not it would be prudent. Thankfully, she decided it wasn't confidential information. She folded the papers back and turned the file at an angle so I could view it. The check was drawn on Sylvia Whitworth's personal account.

"Thank you so much. I sincerely appreciate all your help."

"No problem. And by the way, the barn appraisal joke you made earlier . . ." She let her sentence dangle off.

"Yes?"

"Heard it before. Wasn't funny the first time, and it still isn't terribly witty after the hundredth time."

I nodded, my cheeks warm from embarrassment. I had the sneaking suspicion that this was a woman who would excel at poker. Here all along I thought she hadn't gotten the joke. Her cool features didn't let on that she got the joke, dismissed the joke, or was even annoyed by it. I wondered if I could learn to school my expressions so carefully.

"Thanks again."

I left and picked up our Chinese food order that I had called in earlier. I bought a dozen extra fortune cookies. I would give Kirstie two cookies so she would think I was giving her mine in contrition for stealing her cookie the last time. This still left me with the extra dozen that I bought. It was a win-win plan.

# chapter 14

Dinner with Kirstie was a bust. While eating the food *I* had purchased, Kirstie verbally lacerated me with comments about my selfishness and violently over-reactive nature. She said I should beg Jet's forgiveness but not to expect it because I didn't deserve it. During her diatribe, I tried to remember why she was one of my best friends, only to have the realization hit that she was my *only* friend. There was no way I was going to call Jet and grovel or plead for absolution. The hope of a return to our unspoken flirting/mating dance seemed a very distant possibility. *Kirstie didn't get the second fortune cookie either.*

The visit with Harriet, however, went as anticipated. Happily, nothing untoward happened and she wasn't subjected to any further body searches. The glass walls separating the inmate from the visitor had been installed in the cubicles. As suspected, Harriet knew nothing about the furniture dolly rental or the receipt. Also, I asked why she had initially demanded to see the photos of Herb post mortem, and she said she simply couldn't believe he was dead. She had to see the photos to make it real. She let on that she still had feelings for Herb and even hoped they would someday get back together. My belief was beginning to lean heavily on Sylvia as the murder suspect, but I needed a way to find out if Herb had dumped Sylvia or not. I especially wanted to know if he was blackmailing her.

The latest edition of *Ditters Weekly* was due out this morning and, as usual, I wanted my copy early. I loved to see my byline, even next to the innocuous stories I was forced to write. When my big story came out about the Greene murder case, I would really take some pride in my name being associated with the sensational news story. To date, all I was allowed to relate to our

*susan case*

193

subscribers were the few known facts. *Dead body, homicide, in the river* . . . Nothing salacious or scandalous had been proven yet.

I said good morning to Rhonda when I came into the office, but she just turned her head away and pretended not to see me. The atmosphere felt as if someone had died. I wanted to ask Rhonda if she was okay or if there was anything I could do, but her body language was definitely *back off.*

The coffee was fresh, strong, and tasted heavenly. I went in search of the new issue of *Ditters Weekly.* It was kind of silly, considering I would be rereading the articles that I had written myself.

Candace approached me with a Cheshire cat grin on her face. "Mr. Mitchell wants to see you in the chief editor's office *now.*"

"Jet came back early?" My heart gave an involuntary leap.

"No. Mr. *Blaine* Mitchell is waiting to see you."

*Jet's dad? Why in the world would he want to see me?* My stomach began to roll. Something in Candy's smile made me feel ill with a sense of foreboding.

Knocking softly on Jet's office door, I nervously tried to smooth my hair and tuck my blouse in a little straighter and tighter. It felt as if two large seals were playing beach volleyball in my stomach.

"Come in," a deep voice beckoned.

"You wanted to see me, Mr. Mitchell?" I hated the telltale quiver in my voice, a dead giveaway that I was scared.

"Have a seat, Miss Smith."

Mr. Mitchell was a handsome man. Although well into his early sixties, he was tan, fit, tall, and impeccably dressed. Jet was going to age this well also. I was sure.

I sat down in the chair opposite Jet's desk while Mr. Mitchell blankly stared at me. The silence was deafening as blood rushed into my ears. It sounded as if ocean waves were crashing with each ebb and flow of my blood pressure. He continued to stare and watch me squirm. Finally, after what seemed like hours, he broke the stillness.

"Do you fancy yourself a comedienne, Miss Smith?" That was certainly a bizarre opening question.

"Uh, I think I have a fairly well-developed sense of humor, Mr. Mitchell." *Where was this going?*

"I see. Was this your idea of well-developed humor?"

Mr. Mitchell slid the current edition of the Weekly across the desk to me. It was open to the obituary page. A large picture of Pastor Hutt was prominently displayed at the top of the obit.

"I'm not following you, Mr. Mitchell. I wrote the obituary on Barry Hutt if that's what you are asking, but I didn't find humor in his death."

"Really."

His tone was sarcastic and accusatory. It felt as if I were back in high school and principal Horning was racking me over the coals for the unintended libelous and misinformed article written about Heather Minnick.

"Why don't you read the Barry Hutt obituary out loud for me?"

"Pastor Harry Butt—Wait a minute! *I did not* write this! This must be someone's idea of a joke, switching the first letters of his first and last name around, but it certainly isn't mine! I would never make a mistake like that."

"Whom are you blaming? I suppose you think our printer would take the time to rewrite an obituary at deadline. This is the same printer we have used for the past forty-seven years without a single error, omission, or *joke*. Is that who you wish to blame? Tell you what, why don't you continue reading?"

I wanted to fling the paper in his face and storm out at this vicious and erroneous attack impugning my integrity. Instead, like a whipped dog, I hung my head and continued to read, "Pastor Harry Butt, 84, died peacefully in his slumber on September 13. The community, as well as the Butt whole family, mourns his passing. Harry Butt was born July 4, 1923, in Agra, Kansas and raised on a wooly sheep ranch." I couldn't read anymore. "Mr. Mitchell, you have to believe me. I did not do this."

"Here's where we stand, Miss Smith. One: you admit you wrote the obit. Two: Jet hired you over my objections. Three: I have received no less than fifty phone calls from enraged citizens of Ditters Ferry, not to mention a call from a heartsick family member who objected to her beloved father being made sport of in his own death notice. Shall I continue to point numbers four, five, and six?"

"Mr. Mitchell, all I can do is reiterate that I did not do this. I could never hurt anyone in this manner; certainly not for some heartless, mean-spirited joke."

"Miss Smith, I'm going to be direct with you. I'm placing you on two months unpaid administrative leave. Due to public outcry a head must roll, and it will not be *my* head. Once I have had an opportunity to discuss all the legal ramifications of the obituary and your subsequent employment termination with an attorney, someone will get back with you. You have ten minutes to clear your desk out and leave this office." His expression warned that there would be no further discussion. He was judge, jury, and executioner without so much as benefit of facts or fair trial.

Taking the current edition of the newspaper, I left the office. Mr. Mitchell was obviously not going to listen to additional pleas or denials. I went to my desk and booted up my computer and e-mailed all my notes and files on the Harriet Greene investigation to my personal e-mail account and then deleted all the files from the hard drive. I hit shift/delete to permanently erase the files from the server. No one else was going to use my notes to write this story. Oh, some drips and drams had been mentioned in the paper, but the full sensational story had yet to be relayed to the public. Too much was, as yet, unsolved, and we were still waiting for the final pieces to come together.

I found a small cardboard box in the storage room and put

all my belongings into it. I went outside and unceremoniously threw everything into the trunk of my car.

*Candy!* She was behind this vicious attack. She was the only one with access to the disk before it went to the publisher. Marching back inside, I stormed into the office to confront the conniving wench.

"You won't get away with this." My tone was deadly serious.

Candy smiled. "I already did." Then she pointed her index finger at me with thumb raised to resemble a gun. She fired a pretend shot and blew imaginary smoke away from the end of the make-believe barrel. She was still smiling.

"This is going to turn around and bite you in the butt. And considering the size of your butt, it will probably leave an enormous scar." At least the verbal jab wiped the smirk from her face.

I drove to my apartment and sat in my car to read the rest of the tainted obituary.

"Harry Butt loved to get up at the *crack of dawn* . . ."

*No, no, no,* my mind screamed as I recalled his wife's name. I scanned to the end of the obituary and, sure enough, my worst fear was confirmed. "Harry is survived by his wife of 56 years, *Dawn* . . ."

I couldn't read another word, believing the obit could only get worse. Candy had destroyed my reputation, got me suspended, and embarrassed the newspaper. Here was yet another failure to add to my already blemished, infused life's résumé. I sat there feeling sorry for myself for almost an hour before a secondary thought occurred to me. How must the Hutt family feel? The obituary must have hurt them terribly.

Candy was going down. The witch was going to burn publicly at the stake if I had my way. Figuratively speaking, of course; she wasn't worth going to prison over, though thoughts of murder weren't too far from my mind.

My first priority was still the Greene investigation, but once

197

the story closed, all efforts and motivation would be used to see that Candy came to justice. Then Jet and his father would find out what an evil, depraved, manipulative, scheming creature Candy was. Jet! Did he know what had happened? There was no way I was going to call him to find out. My heart ached, but my head was full of thoughts of revenge. Where was Jet, and when was he coming home?

All I know is a story like Herbert Greene's murder didn't come along every day, and I was determined to see it through to the conclusion. This was *my* story, after all; I discovered the body, and I'd be hanged if I let someone else take it from me. This was going to be the journalism piece to get me out of Ditters Ferry. Whether it was written in the *Ditters Weekly* or another newspaper, it would be written by me.

*Dear Lord, please bless Candy Kane. I remember once reading in the Bible that to pray for blessings for your enemy was like heaping hot coals upon their head. Bless her a lot, Lord! Amen.*

that's a **dead one** alright

# chapter 15

Once again I found myself unemployed and in need of steady income. I stayed awake all night until the brainstorm finally hit. I was determined to find a job that would further my inquest into Herb Greene and his dalliance with Sylvia and put coin in my pocket as well.

There was only one bank in Harmony, the closest town to the ranch where Herb had been employed. If Herb was blackmailing Sylvia, the funds would most probably be deposited into the nearest bank, as Herb didn't own any transportation. Perhaps the local bank needed an experienced teller. I donned my best conservative banker-type outfit: navy blue suit jacket with matching A-line skirt and an ivory blouse with modest-heeled navy blue pumps. A slim, gold watch that didn't even work but looked good and small and gold hoop earrings completed the ensemble. I looked every inch the banker. It was such a short drive to Harmony that there was barely any time to think through possible interview questions and answers.

Idaho First National Bank was a small-town, friendly establishment. It wouldn't have surprised me if they made loans there based on a good ol' boy handshake as opposed to a promissory note and collateral agreement. I went directly to the teller line and asked to speak with the operations manager. A smiling young woman told me it would be just a minute. The teller approached a desk situated far behind the teller line and had a short conversation with the woman seated at the other side of the paper-strewn desk. The seated woman poked her head around to get a look at me. I smiled and waved. Another short conversation ensued between the teller and the ops manager. Finally, the woman rose and walked over to me.

*susan case*

199

"May I help you?" she inquired.

"I certainly hope so. I'd like to speak to you about any career opportunities you may have available."

It flattered bankers to hear that they have a *career* and not just a *job*. I fluttered my résumé, which was printed onto expensive crème-colored, linen stationery, to draw her attention to my career-seeking sincerity.

"Why don't you come over to my desk and we'll talk a moment, Miss, uh?"

"Smith. Jimi Smith." It sounded a lot like Bond, James Bond; there may have even been a trace of a British accent. Perhaps I should ask for a cup of coffee shaken and not stirred.

"Well, Miss Smith, I'm Lilly White, the operations manager." She extended her hand in greeting. "Tell me a little about yourself." She sat down with a flourish.

"I would like to return to a career in banking. I have teller and new account experience." I paused for a moment. "Would you like to see my résumé?"

"Thank you." She took the document and glanced briefly at it. "It states here that you are currently employed by the *Ditters Weekly* newspaper as a journalist. Is that correct?"

My keen investigator's eye caught sight of a page-wearied dog-eared paperback copy of Danielle Steele's book *Palomino* on Lilly's credenza. The book resembled a preacher's Bible. Read, read again, and then re-read a few thousand more times. I had read *Palomino* in high school and loved it. That's when the hamster on the wheel in my head started running furiously. Perhaps I could play on the basic premise of the book to entice Ms. White into hiring me.

I tried to look vulnerable but still in control. "Yes, that's correct."

"Are you still employed by the Weekly?"

"Yes." I said this softly with a sigh and a mysterious, heartsick look.

that's a **dead one** alright

"Why do you want to leave the newspaper?" she asked curiously.

"It's a long, personal story. I'm sure with your busy schedule,"—there wasn't a customer in the building—"you don't have time to hear it." I let tears form in my eyes. It was a useful talent to be able to make my eyes water on cue.

Her expression lit up. "Oh, please tell me." She realized too late that she sounded a bit overanxious for details. "I mean, uh, maybe it will help you to talk about it."

I paused for effect and drew in a deep, steadying breath. "You see, I'm in love with a coworker. He is in love with me too, but since the accident . . . he's confined to a wheelchair. He refuses to allow himself to become permanently committed to me. He doesn't want to be a burden, as if he could *ever* be a burden!" I allowed one single tear to roll down my cheek.

*Dear Lord, please forgive me for the lies I just told and the lies I'm about to tell. Amen.*

"Oh, you poor, poor dear." Ms. White was about to cry in sympathy. She groped around in her desk and came up with a rumpled tissue for my benefit. "What happened to him?"

"He was thrown from his—," I almost said *horse*, but that would be too coincidental. "Motorcycle," I continued. "It's just so, so painful to see him every day, knowing he will never be mine again and . . ." I hung my head and shuddered delicately. Needing time to work up more tears, I kept my head down for a moment to build up the waterworks.

"I'm so sorry, Jimi. Forgive me for prying and bringing up all this pain." Ms. White was so contrite that I felt a twinge of conscience.

"It's not your fault. I apologize for allowing my feelings to get out of control." I reached out and touched her hand, then dabbed my eyes with the crumpled hankie.

She repeated again, "Oh, you poor dear." She hesitated then said, "Let's change the subject, why don't we?"

*susan case*

201

My relief was palpable. I didn't know how much longer I could pull off the *daytime drama* act.

"You know, we really could use another teller. The drive-in window gets so busy, and the girls up front do their best to run back and forth. It would make sense to hire a full-time teller for our drive-up customers."

She seemed resolute. I tried to keep my euphoria from erupting into a loud *yeehaw*.

"I need to perform a background check. May I call your current employer for references?"

"No!" Oops. A little too vehement of a response. "If Charlie finds I'm looking for other work, he'll quit his job at the paper out of chivalry. He's just that kind of man."

Ms. Lilly White was now helplessly and hopelessly infatuated with the imaginary Charlie. "Well, I suppose I could just call the bank you used to work for."

"Sure, or if you want I have my last review as teller and my last review as new accounts clerk right here." I handed over the copies of my reviews.

Lilly read my bank employment reviews then picked up a large Boise phone directory from her top desk drawer. She flipped to the *bank* section then dialed a series of numbers.

"May I speak with Ms. Castille, please?" Lilly White asked whoever answered on the other end. There was a long pause. "Yes, Miss Castille. This is Lilly White of Idaho First National in Harmony. I was wondering if I could have a moment of your time to confirm employment of a past employee." Pause. "Will you confirm that Jimi Smith worked for you for just over six months and then was promoted to credit card services?" Pause. "I see, and her balancing record was perfect, not a single over or short?" Pause. "Wonderful. Thank you so much for the information." Pause. "No. That's all I had. You've been a tremendous help." One last pause, where Ms. White looked thoroughly confused. "Uh. Okay. I will. Thanks again, Ms. Castille."

Lilly looked at me bewildered. "She said to keep my shoes on and good luck, that I'd need it. Do you know what she meant?"

Apparently Ms. Castille remembered the African Violet I carefully potted in her shoe. I shook my head sadly. "Ms. Castille has a tiny problem that she simply can't help." I looked as sympathetic as possible while making the universal gesture of guzzling alcohol, inferring that Ms. Castille was a drunk.

"Oh, dear," Lilly said.

"Yes. Well, she's still a very good manager and rarely allows her *problem* to interfere with work."

"I don't believe I need to call Mr. Grunweld at credit card services." She looked as if she had come to a very resolute decision. "I'll be calling you very soon. If I get the new position approved, how soon would you able to start work?"

"As soon as you need me," I answered.

"Fine then, I'll be in touch." There was a moment's hesitation. "And Jimi, don't you worry about anything. It's all going to work out fine." She cast a glance at her copy of Steele's book. "It always works out." I thought she was going to cry.

"Thank you, Ms. White. You've been wonderful."

My feet should definitely feel hot because hell's fires were surely nipping at my toes for lying. The burning should really be close in retribution for the whoppers I'd just told.

---

I didn't have long to wait. Bright and early, *too early*, the next morning, Ms. White called to give me the good news. Her boss, Mr. Burcher, approved the drive-up teller position and upheld Ms. White's suggestion to hire me.

"Can you start Monday?" Lilly inquired.

"Absolutely."

---

Banker's hours are a joke, as I had to be at Idaho First National by 8:00 a.m. and wouldn't be off work until 5:00 p.m. I would, however, get an hour-long lunch break. It was weird to be on such set regular hours after my time at the Weekly. With that much time on my hands for lunch, perhaps I would go visit Maybelle at the feed store. Her company was enjoyable, and her husband, Gerald, was a sweetheart.

I needed to allow time for the fifteen- to twenty-minute drive to Harmony and the extra time it would take to put on my best banker's duds. I was going to have to get the iron and ironing board out as well. To make matters even worse, my old banking clothes were still stuffed into garbage bags. The wrinkles were going to be very set, especially since they weren't in those bags *folded*.

I selected and ironed a charcoal pinstripe pantsuit and crisp, white blouse. At least by choosing pants, knee-high stockings could be worn as opposed to the oppressive nylons required for a dress or skirt. Also in the pantsuit's favor was that the material was slightly more wrinkle resistant than the other outfits. Although I didn't plan on having this job for long—as I was determined to expose Candy for the rat she was and get my job back—I still needed to make a good enough impression to keep the job until the *Weekly* begged on bended knees for my return.

The first day at work went pretty much as I expected: orientation, meet and greet all the other employees, read and sign the handbook, and complete all the necessary new hire forms. There were also some customer service tapes I was supposed to watch, but the acting, *if one could call it acting*, was so bad and the information so basic I found myself using the video time to take a well-deserved nap. Thankfully my back was to the closed door, so I was fairly confident anyone approaching would wake me up.

The one hitch in the whole day was Lilly continually harangued me for details on my imaginary relationship with Charlie. I didn't know how much longer I could hold her off with, "It's just too painful to talk about." Lilly was determined to help me renew and regenerate my mythical relationship with Charlie.

The remainder of my first week went fairly well. I stood by the senior teller and watched her perform all the various different tasks a teller was required to perform. It took all my effort not to fall asleep standing on my feet. The drive-up window was sure to be even more boring, as it was only a paying and receiving window—make a deposit or cash a check.

Finally, Monday of the following week I was on my own at the drive-up window. My first act accomplished upon my relative freedom from Lilly or Sadie, the senior teller, was to see if Herbert Greene had an account with this bank.

Herbert Greene, mailing address c/o the 501 Ranch, had opened an account approximately two months prior to his death. *Eureka!* His account was still open and valid with Herb as the only account owner. There was no notation on the account notes indicating that Herb was deceased.

Herb's interest-bearing checking account held exactly $30,071.25. Upon looking up his transaction history, there were only two items shown: an initial deposit of $30,000 and an interest accrual of $71.25. No other deposits, withdrawals, or checks had cleared the account.

I completed the form to request copies of the deposit slip and offsetting entry. My hope was that the deposit item would be a check from Sylvia. My gut hunch was that Herb was blackmailing Sylvia, or at least if the money were from her the theory could be put forth that it might be blackmail payola. The snag to this little maneuver was the operations officer had to sign off on the request and ultimately the copies would come in the intra-bank mail addressed to Lilly's attention.

Since conniving and deceiving had worked to my benefit thus far, I decided to stick with it and signed my name where it indicated Operations Manager/Officer Signature. I placed the request with the others accumulated during the day.

*Dear Lord, this may not seem right, but it's for a good cause ... really. Amen.*

A searing thought permeated my consciousness; there was going to be a lot of explaining to do come judgment day.

---

Three days later a large, manila envelope arrived in the bank intra-system mail. It was boldly addressed to "Jimi Smith, Operations Manager / Harmony, ID Branch Office." Lilly brought the envelope to me at the drive-up cage.

"Jimi, you have an envelope from the Image Retrieval Department." Lilly continued to keep hold of the envelope, while my curiosity was killing me.

"Oh." Doing my best to feign surprise.

"It's addressed to Jimi Smith, Operations Manager. Did you get a promotion I don't know about?"

I laughed uncomfortably. "I'm sure it's some kind of mix-up."

"Hmm," was all the response I received.

"Why don't we open it and see what's inside. I'm sure there is a logical explanation," I suggested hopefully.

Lilly looked at me a few seconds longer before opening the envelope. As she pulled the papers out, I almost broke my neck trying to crane my head around to get a look at the documents.

"It's offsetting entries of a deposit," Lilly stated, "and a copy of the original request."

My stomach clenched, knowing what the form would indicate. Unfortunately, for all my discomfort, Lilly only showed me the request. The photocopies were still held closely to her chest.

"Oh, my goodness!" I declared in mock innocence. "I was practicing completing some forms. It wasn't supposed to go through though. Someone must have put it in with the rest of the requests. I'm so sorry, Ms. White. It's totally my fault for not tearing it up."

"You know to call me Lilly, but, Jimi, why did you sign for Operations Manager?"

That question had me stumped. "Is that what it said where I signed?" Even I didn't believe that lie.

There was a long, contemplative silence. "From this point forward, perhaps it would be best if when you want practice with forms or procedures, you see me first."

"Yes, of course, Lilly."

"Then we'll speak no more of it." It was evidently a relief for her that the topic was closed. Ms. White seemingly did not like confrontation.

Garnering all the gall I could muster, I asked, "Lilly, may I look at the off-setting entries? I'd like to examine the copies to familiarize myself with—" *With what?*

Lilly leveled a look at me that I could not interpret. "Maybe later, we'll see." She went back to her desk, leaving me pulsating with unsatisfied, pent-up inquisitive frustration. No wonder curiosity killed the cat. Now I would have to devise yet another plan to get the copies without Lilly knowing.

Providence was on my side, or more likely *luck* was. Sadie the head teller came to see me a half hour before lunch. "Hi, Jimi. How's it going back here?"

"Great," I said, trying without much success to sound enthusiastic.

"Well, I'm sure glad you're here. I hated running back and forth all the time. My job is so much more efficient now."

"Glad I can help." My mind was still on the photocopies, and I was barely aware of what Sadie was saying.

"It's Genevieve's birthday today, and we're all going out for lunch together. You'll join us, won't you?"

The hamster on the wheel in my brain was waking up. "*Everyone* will be going?"

"Of course. We have such a small staff. It's nice when we can all get together outside of the office. Birthdays make the perfect excuse."

"You know, Sadie, I'd love to, but I want to spend my lunch

hour here studying the operations manual for tellers. There's so much to learn."

Sadie let her disappointment show. "It'd be nice for you to get to know everyone else. With you back here in the cage, you don't get much chance to mingle."

"Truthfully, Sadie, I kinda let Lilly down this morning and want to make up for it by studying hard and not making any more mistakes."

"Honey, we all make mistakes," Sadie tried to persuade me.

"I know, but it shouldn't be from lack of knowledge. I hope to someday know as much as you."

Sadie didn't show much reaction to the flattery. "Okay. I wish you well on your studying then. Hope you don't fall asleep reading that manual. It's pretty dry."

"Oh, I find teller procedures fascinating." That might be laying it on a bit thick.

"Guess I'll see you later." Sadie didn't argue the point, so maybe she really did find teller work fascinating.

"You'll give the others my regret at not being able to attend the birthday luncheon, won't you?"

"Sure. Genevieve turned forty this year, so she'll probably be grumpy anyway." Sadie gave me a smile and went back to her station in front.

Once everyone left, I closed up the drive-thru window and waited ten minutes before venturing over to Lilly's desk. The envelope was nowhere in sight. I tried to pull her top drawer open, but it was locked, as was her credenza. Yeesh. Suspicious creature, wasn't she. Didn't she trust her employees?

I looked in all the logical places keys might be hidden and came up with nothing. Stepping back, I surveyed her work area, trying to find a hiding spot or something, *anything*, out of place. It took several minutes before I noticed the plant on her credenza was a bit lopsided. It couldn't be that easy. That was as dumb as leaving a house key under the front door mat. Well, not *dumb*, maybe just naïve.

Carefully lifting the pot, I found two silver cabinet keys underneath. The first key opened the desk. I pilfered through the drawers. *Nothing.* I looked at the clock; there was still at least a half hour before they should be returning. Once the credenza was open, the pot of gold at the end of the rainbow was there to behold. A choir of angels sang a chorus of hallelujahs. Right on top of some stacks of lined printouts was the packet from Image Retrieval.

Cautiously, I opened the envelope and slid the copies out. I turned the documents over and had my curiosity satiated. The check was drawn on a different bank; nonetheless, it was from Sylvia *Campbell's* personal account. It was intriguing to me that she had a personal account in her maiden name with these kinds of funds available.

"Jimi!" Ms. White said in loud, questioning disgust (followed by my loud gasp of surprise).

Lilly's entrance scared me so badly that I had dropped the papers to the floor and grabbed my chest. My heart was pounding as if I had just been caught committing murder or something of equally horrific magnitude.

"Ms. White, uh, um, you're back early." Not only was the comment lame; it was incriminating.

"What are you doing?" Lilly demanded.

I should have spent some time creating a scenario where if caught a plausible defense could be offered.

"Ms. White, I should have been honest with you from the onset."

"Mmm-hmm." Her arms were crossed over her chest. Her body language did not bode well for my continued employment.

"I needed those copies but was too afraid to ask for them."

"Why did you need those particular copies so urgently, not that it could be any excuse for lying or breaking into my desk?"

"Herbert Greene, the account owner, is dead. My Charlie, Charlie Greene, is Herb's only living kin. Charlie was named sole beneficiary for Herb's estate." Pausing for a moment, I then said, "I looked up Herb's name on a whim. I knew he had worked for a ranch in this area. I was actually surprised to find the account. Curiosity got the best of me when I saw the balance." It was scary how quickly I could weave and fabricate a story of lies.

"I see. Of what importance is this money if Charlie doesn't want you in his life?" Dang. She was more clever than anticipated.

"There is an experimental surgery that might restore Charlie's ability to walk. Insurance won't cover it because there haven't been enough proven studies behind it. I don't know how much the surgery will cost, but maybe with this money . . ." I started sobbing. "Maybe he could . . . I mean *we* could . . . oh, I don't know what I mean. I'm grasping for the moon, for anything really that might make Charlie mine again."

"Jimi, you can't use bank resources for your own personal inquiries and investigations." The word investigation caused me to squirm. *Had she figured out this was for a news story?* "If the money is there and Charlie is the benefactor, what difference does it make who wrote the check."

And yet another astute question was rendered. To gain some more time before answering, I looked down, pretending to wipe tears from my eyes and compose myself.

"I wanted to make sure it didn't come from Herb's business partner. It would be horrible to get Charlie's hopes up if the money was a loan from Herb's business or any other type of loan that might need paid back from estate proceeds."

"Jimi, I understand your motivation if not your methods. I have no choice but to take this matter up with the branch manager."

"I understand, Lilly. You've been more accommodating than I deserve. Whatever happens, I know you will be acting in the best interest of the bank."

"Why don't you balance out your cash drawer and go home. I'll call you tomorrow."

The phone rang sharply at 7:00 a.m. Friday morning while I was getting ready for work. The caller was Mr. Burcher, the branch manager. Basically, I was told once again to explore new employment horizons. Mr. Burcher must have gone into the bank an hour early in the anticipation and pleasure of firing me. My purpose for working at the bank had been served, so it was time to plan my next move.

I put a call in to Gunderson, Gunderson, Malcolm, and Reed. The conversation was brief, but James Gunderson III, Esq. was very pleased with the information regarding the thirty thousand dollar check from Sylvia's personal account. He told me to keep up the good work and notify him should any more interesting facts pertinent to Harriet's case be uncovered.

Now what? I was hungry. There was a bag of M&M's in the refrigerator, along with a bottle of sweetened tea: the perfect meal. Munching on the candies one at a time, I contemplated my next move. Somehow I needed to find out if Sylvia and Herb had a falling out. It might help reinforce the blackmail theory.

Sugar has amazing properties that promote excellent brain function. Since I was once again in need of employment-related compensation, why not apply at the Lux Hotel in Twin Falls? It was the only place where the connection between Herb and Sylvia had been confirmed.

Now was as good a time as any to put in a job application. Doris, the night manager at the Lux, had been dressed in a navy blazer, cream-colored blouse, and khaki slacks. Similar items of clothing could be found on my floor, so I decided to dress the part. Perhaps if I already looked like an employee of the Lux it would help my hiring probability.

It took awhile, but I found a blue blazer, ivory blouse, and tan slacks. Finding specific clothing items in my apartment reminded me of Easter egg hunting when I was a kid, except the clothes were more of a challenge to locate. With the assistance of an iron to smooth out the wrinkles, my Lux Hotel employee ensemble was complete. Thank goodness for the blazer, because there was a dirty shoe imprint on the blouse where I had apparently stepped on it at some point. The jacket adequately hid the mark on the back of the blouse.

Shortly after 3:00 p.m., I went inside the Lux with my résumé (*omitting the latest bank job*) in hand.

A man about my age was behind the counter, leering at me with intent. His name badge read "Trainee."

"May I see the manager?"

He eyed me up and down at length in a degrading, smarmy manner. "I'm sure I can help with whatever you *need*." The way he said *need* made me want to run home and take a shower using a grill brush for a washcloth and an abrasive cleansing powder for soap.

"I'm fairly certain I need to see the manager. I'd like to apply for a job."

"You want a job here? That's fantastic. If you get hired, maybe we could carpool. I could pick you up and take you home. Maybe the next morning we'd be carpooling together"—he waggled his eyebrows up and down—"after you fix me breakfast, if ya know what I mean."

Yuck! Even if trainee boy didn't have crater-sized pockmarks intermingled with ready-to-explode, fresh zits; even if his teeth were white instead of brown; and even if he weren't several inches shorter than me, his comments were incredibly rude and terribly inappropriate.

"I don't eat breakfast, and my boyfriend, Jasper Leroy, drives me to work. He's out on probation for severely beating a former co-worker of mine. Poor Eddie. Hopefully he'll be able to walk again." I smiled sweetly. "You'd think what with Jasper being gorgeous, six feet four, and 225 pounds of solid muscle he'd be more secure. Instead he's insanely jealous." I paused, looking Trainee dead in the eye. "If you're serious about carpooling, I could talk to Jasper, assuming I get a job here."

"Actually, I drive a Vespa motor scooter to work. I was just kidding about the carpooling thing."

"The manager?" I prompted.

"Uh, yeah. Let me get him for you." He scurried off like a rodent seeking shelter from a ravenous feline.

The gentleman who came out to meet me was the epitome of professionalism. The little rat didn't return with him, happily, either.

"How may I assist you?" he inquired. "I understand you wish to speak with a manager."

"Yes, sir." *That sounded too formal.* "I'm here to apply for a job. That is, if you have any openings."

"What type of hotel work interests you?" he inquired.

"I'd like to work in reservations, the front desk, or the office." *Anything that will get me near a Lux Hotel computer.*

"The only opening we have at this time is in housekeeping." This information didn't suit me well at all.

"No other openings?" There was a slight whine to my tone. *Please, please, please; anything but a maid.*

"I'm sorry. The only positions available at present are in housekeeping." He paused a moment. "Perhaps you would like to leave your résumé in case something opens up in the near future."

This was gonna hurt. "Actually, a job in housekeeping would be great."

He looked surprised at my acquiescence.

"Are you sure?" he asked.

*What? Didn't I look like I could clean a room?* "Absolutely. I'd really like a job here, and housekeeping would be a nice start." *God was punishing me.*

"Let me see if Ardith is available. She's head of the house-keeping department." He picked up the phone and punched in a couple of numbers.

"Ardith, this is Michael in the front office. I have someone inquiring about a housekeeping position." Pause. "Certainly. I'll send her right down." He hung up the phone.

"Take the elevator to the basement. Straight ahead, you will see Ardith's office."

"Thank you," I intoned, *not feeling thankful at all.*

"Good luck."

I couldn't even work up a smile in reply.

Following the manager's directions, I found myself in a cement dungeon with gray cement walls, floor, and ceiling. At the end of the hall was a room with no door. I had to assume it was Ardith's office. Passing a huge, open laundry area, there were several people working furiously, all red-faced and sweaty. It was loud and steamy in the basement. Several washers and dryers were going at once. My hair was falling flat, and I was sweltering in the blazer. It had to be ninety degrees with 90 percent humidity down there. Hopefully the maids didn't run the laundry service too.

A frizzy-haired stick of a woman with a strong attachment to henna dye sat behind a scarred desk. Her thinning hair exposed a lot of pink scalp, which had evidently absorbed some of the hair dye. She had lipstick on her teeth and a cigarette hanging from her lower lip. The cigarette was glued to her lip by the dry, caked-on lipstick. Her coffee cup had heavy lipstick marks and was badly caffeine-stained. It didn't look as if the cup had ever been washed.

"Yeah?" she growled. It was a voice that had been exposed to decades of smoking and hard liquor.

"Ardith?"

She nodded affirmation.

"Michael directed me to you about the housekeeping position."

"This is some kinda joke, right?" Ardith's tone didn't indicate humor.

"Uh. No, ma'am. I'm looking for work."

"Princess, you wouldn't last a day here, you in your fancy blazer. What do you want a maid job for?"

"I need the work."

"You got a criminal record or something? I don't hire thieves or druggies." The entire time she spoke, the cigarette bobbled up and down but never fell off her lip; it was mesmerizing.

"No, I don't have a criminal record, and I've never used drugs."

"Maid, huh?" She still didn't believe me.

"Yes, if you'll hire me." I tried to sound humble, which isn't difficult when you are reduced to begging for maid work.

"You know what? I'll do a background check, and if you're clean you can start in two days. You'll have to take a drug test, though."

"That will be fine."

"This is gonna be fun." She opened a cavernous drawer that creaked in protest and produced a coffee-stained, wrinkled application. "Complete this before you leave."

Looking around, I noticed there was no place to sit and write. Guess I'd have to complete it sitting in my car. "Do I give this to Michael or bring it back down here to you?"

"You give it to me, sister. *If* you're hired, *I am* your boss and no one else. Got it?"

"I'll be right back with the application. Where do I go for the drug test?"

"First, let's see if you pass the background check; then we'll talk pee test."

---

Back at my apartment, I was determined to find out if I was capable of cleaning. Looking around at the mess, I decided it was too big of a job and didn't know where to start. Clearing a section off the sofa, I sat down and picked up my cell phone. Why hadn't Jet called? Certainly by now he knew I'd been fired. Well, placed on administrative leave anyway, but it amounted to the same thing. Jet's dad couldn't wait to finalize the details of my demise with the paper.

Scrolling through my recent received calls, I was disappointed that Jet hadn't tried to get in touch with me. Maybe I should call him. *And say what?* I couldn't think of a thing. There was only one missed call, and it was from Daniel, though he hadn't left a message. *What the heck? Daniel was always good company,* I thought, dialing his number.

"You've reached Daniel's voicemail. Leave me a message. If you are female, leave a long message."

"Daniel, it's Jimi. You called my cell, so I'm returning your call." Nothing clever came to mind, so I hung up.

*Now what?* I was bored, lonely, and still unemployed. I didn't even feel like reading. Was 7:45 p.m. too early to go to bed? Tossing off the blazer and slacks, both items landing on the floor, I decided 7:45 was the perfect bedtime.

---

My cell phone rudely awakened me at 9:03 p.m. Trying to adjust my eyes, the caller ID screen showed Daniel's number.

"Hello." Clearing my throat hadn't helped; I still sounded groggy.

"Did I wake you?" Daniel sounded surprised.

"No. What's up?" I lied.

"I *did* wake you. Geez. Even my great grandmother stays up later than 9:00 p.m."

"It's 9:03, wiseguy."

"I wanted to check in and see how you're doing. Word around the office is you got fired for the Harry Butt obit."

"Do you honestly believe I wrote that and sent it to the printer?" I retorted, working up a head of steam. *Where were my M&M's?*

"Then who?" Daniel asked.

"Gee, maybe the new hire who formats articles for the printer?" My voice was raised to a screech.

"Oh, come on. Candace is a nice girl. Why would she do that?"

"She's a vicious, conniving witch." *Nice girl? Hah!* "Daniel, I'm hanging up now. Goodnight!"

"Wait. Don't be such a hothead."

*Click! Let him hear dial tone.*

While rummaging through my freezer for any reclusive chocolate, my cell phone rang again. After a couple of rings and a little debate with myself, I answered Daniel's call.

"Yes," came out a little snotty.

"Don't be mad at me. I'm your friend. Remember?" He did sound conciliatory. "I'll bring you some chocolate if you forgive me."

"Any friend of mine is an enemy of Candace, but I'll take the chocolate."

"Tell you what I'm going to do just for you. I'll get the offending disk back from the printer. It will show the date and time the file was last modified and which *user* modified the file."

"Daniel, you are brilliant. If you can pull this off, you're my new best friend."

"You haven't heard my terms and conditions."

"Name it." Feeling so giddy with the probability of not only getting my job back at the Weekly but also in anticipation of nailing the coffin shut on Candy's newspaper career at the same time, payment terms seemed insignificant.

"Number one: you'll accompany me to a political fundraising dinner at my parents' country club next week; number two: you will stay by my side the entire evening, looking adoringly at me at every conceivable opportunity; and number three: you will kiss me at the end of the night, *and not* a brotherly kiss either. The kiss will last as long as *I* want it to."

"Daniel, how about I concede to numbers one and two but substitute a good hug in place of item number three."

"Nope. No deal."

"I'm probably a terrible kisser. I haven't had a lot of practice."

"Don't care."

"Daniel, I don't get it. You could have any girl in town, in the county for that matter. Why me?"

"I wish I knew the answer to that question." He sounded confused yet resigned.

"I know the answer. You want what you can't have."

"No, Jimi. I want you."

I didn't like the seriousness of his tone.

"If I were chasing you, you would get bored with me in a minute," I quipped.

"Chase me then, and in fifty years I'll let you know if I'm getting bored."

"Daniel, what do you think is going to come of this?"

"A nice evening and my curiosity satisfied. Deal or no deal?"

"You don't leave me much choice," I lamented.

"Nope." He didn't sound even a bit apologetic.

"This is blackmail."

"Yep."

Darn his larcenous heart.

"Fine. Deal." My tone was definitely peevish.

"Oh, yeah. Jimi, one more thing."

"What?" I snapped.

"You'll keep the kiss in character with your personality."

"What's that supposed to mean?"

"That you won't keep your mouth shut."

*Click.* Daniel had disconnected the call without another word.

I had just made a deal for a date with a renowned playboy, so why this feeling of excitement rather than anger? It didn't make sense because it was Jet who had my heart. But Daniel certainly had my attention.

# chapter 16

After successfully passing the drug pee test, Ardith called to let me know my employment was secured at the Lux Motel. The job paid $6.25 an hour plus tips, and I was to start today. The workday for housekeeping staff began at the profane hour of 4:45 a.m., which meant my needing to leave Ditters Ferry at 3:45 a.m. The Lux Hotel would supply me with a uniform, but I was required to buy some nude-colored support hose and white nursing shoes. Ardith assured me they had a uniform to fit a size eight.

Loading up on coffee at the mini-mart in Ditters Ferry, I made the dark and dreary drive to Twin Falls. The basement at the Lux was already buzzing with activity when I made my appearance.

"Smith!" Ardith yelled.

"Yes?"

"Cutting it kinda close, aren't ya? It's exactly 4:45 a.m.," Ardith sneered.

"That's what time you told me to be here."

"You can tell a person's character by how early *or late* they arrive to work. Fifteen minutes early means *good character*. Right on time means a *don't care* attitude. Five minutes late, and you're unemployed."

"Yes, ma'am." It was too early for this crap.

"Your uniform is hanging up over there." She jerked her head in the direction of a ghastly gray uniform hanging on a wire coat hanger from a nail in her office wall. "You can change in here."

"But there's no door," I said, stating the obvious.

"Oh, you poor, little, shy baby." Her teeth were once again smeared with lipstick. She pulled a cigarette from her pocket

*susan case*

219

and lit up, blowing smoke in my face. "There's a bathroom in the laundry area. Change quick, Miss Prissy."

I was going to need a lot more coffee and a pound of chocolate to get through this day. Once in the bathroom—which had no lock on the door—I put my back to the door and stripped. While pulling the offensive garment over my head, I noticed the filthy imbedded dirt and grease ring around the collar and perspiration stains under each armpit. The uniform reeked of garlic and body odor. I took the uniform back off. Harriet Greene was not worth this much degradation. I hesitated a moment longer, but my *big story* might be worth it.

Willing my stomach contents to stay in place, I hastily donned the odious garb. Ardith was correct about one thing: the uniform would fit a size eight. Unfortunately, it would fit three size eights. I could wrap it around me twice, and the hem hung down almost to my ankles. The neckline and shoulders were made for a more much developed body than mine. If Kirstie could see me now, she'd probably forgive me for the yard sale incident.

I put my clothes in a plastic bag and exited the bathroom. Ardith was standing immediately outside the door with her arms folded across her chest.

"It took you long enough." Then she bellowed, "Nancy, new meat."

"Yes, Ardith?" A thin, pasty-looking woman with a haggard expression met us.

"Here's your new trainee. Show her the ropes until lunch."

"Okay." Nancy didn't seem too thrilled with Ardith's directive.

"Then get moving, both of you!" Ardith demanded.

Nancy got her rolling cart and proceeded to the supply area. "You need to count your stock of refill necessities for fifteen rooms."

She waited for me to nod my head in comprehension, so I obliged her.

"You gotta have enough soap, shampoo, conditioner, TP, tissues, coffee supplies, and cups."

She waited for another nod, and I gratified her with another bob of my head.

"Make sure you have all your cleaning items: toilet scouring stone, rags, spray cleaner, and squeegee."

Nancy then maneuvered the cart to the laundry area where she picked up enough sheets, pillow cases, towels, and washrags for what seemed like thirty rooms. Then she explained that each room with a king-sized bed got towels and coffee for two people. Each room with two queen beds got enough supplies for four people.

Once completely loaded, she told me to push the cart to the elevator. Nancy had a list of rooms that had already been vacated. I tried to figure out who would leave a nice, comfortable hotel room by 5:00 a.m. There must be some sick and twisted people staying at the Lux in downtown Twin Falls.

The cart weighed a ton and had a loose wheel that made it list to the right. The cart kept bumping into the wall; then I'd overcorrect. It was slow moving, and Nancy, finally losing patience with me, took over the cart.

"Only twelve of my rooms were occupied last night, so this should be a short day."

Our rooms were located on the third floor. Checking the list, Nancy pulled the cart in front of room 313 and used a credit-card-looking thing to open the door.

"Strip the beds and put the soiled linens in this bag." She pointed to the empty bag on the right of the cart. "When you're done with that, we'll put the clean sheets on the beds." Nancy sat on a chair and waited for me to do her bidding.

Stripping the bed of its spread, blanket, and sheets and pillow cases, I grabbed up the entire load to take to the cart.

"What are you doing?" Nancy demanded.

"I'm taking the soiled linens to the cart." I said, stating the obvious.

"What are you doing with the bedspread and blanket?"

"Don't they get washed too?"

Nancy looked at me as if my brain had fallen out of my ear and lay inert on the floor between us.

"No. We don't wash those."

"But what if someone gets out of the shower and sets their hairy, naked butt on the bedspread."

"So?" The meaning was lost on her that it would be a disgusting and germy thing to happen.

It was too early in the morning to argue, so I threw the pile onto the floor and pulled out only the sheets and pillow cases to take to the cart. Nancy followed me and retrieved the clean linens we would need. She efficiently showed me how to make the bed in a very precise manner. It seemed silly to go through all the tucking and corner points and foldovers for sheets that were going to be messed up anyway.

Once the bed was made, I dusted the furniture and emptied the garbage while Nancy ran the vacuum. Next, she instructed me it was time to clean the bathroom. She picked up one of the used washrags and proceeded to clean the toilet with it, *using the toilet water to rinse.* Nancy performed this lovely task with her bare hands. Then she used the same rag to wipe down the vanity and sink.

"Uh, is that sanitary?" Bile was rising in my throat. There was no way my bare hands were going into a commode, nor would I be using toilet water to clean the sinks and floors.

"You got a problem?" Nancy asked belligerently.

"Um, no. Only asking questions so I can be sure to do it right when I'm on my own."

Nancy then dried the shower with a used guest towel and spritzed the mirror with glass cleaner using another dirtied guest towel.

Nancy grumbled that the cheapskates who stayed here last night didn't even leave a tip. We made sure the coffee pot had its appropriate accoutrements, and then she rinsed the coffee mugs in the bathroom sink.

"We don't wash those with detergent?" I asked.

"Sister, if you keep complaining we are never going to be able to get done. You need to learn there are a few shortcuts. If the cups start looking dingy, *then* you take them to be cleaned."

Nancy pulled a tattered checklist from her pocket. Guest info book. *Check.* TV guide. *Check.* Drawers and closet emptied. *Check.* And so on. It took a full thirty-five minutes to complete the room.

"You are really slowing me down," Nancy complained.

"Sorry." My comment was obligatory.

"Whatever."

*I seem to have a real gift of making friends and garnering respect.*

On and on the day went. It was finally time for our lunch break. Nancy parked the cart in the last room we cleaned before going to the basement lounge area. Nancy retrieved her lunch from her locker and began unwrapping a sandwich enclosed in wax paper. Nancy's bare hands, which had been swishing around in seven different toilets, now held her tuna sandwich, which she ate with relish, literally and figuratively. She held the sandwich in both hands, hands that she had *never* bothered to wash after cleaning the rooms. My gag reflex was working overtime.

"Didn't you bring a lunch?" Nancy asked me.

"No. I thought I'd catch a bite at one of the fast food restaurants closeby."

Again, she looked at me as if my brain had formed a gelatinous puddle outside my head. "You don't have time for that," she screeched. "I'm not waiting around for you. I take a fifteen-minute lunch break so I can get out of here early. You can just go hungry."

Turning my back on her, I got a cup of stale, bitter coffee from the huge pot and put three quarters into the snack machine for a small bag of chips. That would have to do until

223

I got off work. Sitting down next to Nancy with my *lunch*, I couldn't think of a thing to say. She pulled a brown, bruised banana from her brown bag and peeled it quickly and inhaled it in four bites.

"Let's go," she said, and she was on her feet and running.

The last few rooms we cleaned had been trashed. There was half of a large pizza in one room, which Nancy asked if I would like to take home. When I said a polite, "No, thank you," she shrugged her shoulders and said it was my loss. She kept the pizza for herself, a pizza that had to have been sitting out all night. *This woman must have the germ-fighting and digestive capabilities of a goat.*

By the end of the day, I was bone weary and never had the opportunity to get anywhere near a Lux computer. Furthermore, I smelled like the disgusting uniform I had been forced to wear. It was after 3:30 p.m. when work was finally over, and Nancy was fuming. Apparently, when she worked alone, she never got off work later than 2:15 p.m.

The hour drive home didn't help my disposition any either. I decided to go to Dibbzy's and Granddad's to use their washing machine and dryer. There was no way I would go another day smelling like my malodorous uniform.

Nobody was home when I arrived, so I let myself in. Now that I was gainfully employed, Dibbz and Grandpa returned to their "never locking a door" habit.

After putting the uniform into the wash with a generous amount of detergent, I went to the kitchen to make myself a sandwich. Organic, sugar-free, salt-free peanut butter on oat bran molasses bread was my only choice. I was so hungry it actually tasted good.

I carried my sandwich and glass of vanilla soy milk to the living room and got comfortable on the sofa. Nothing much was on TV, so I settled for the local news. I brushed the crumbs of dry oat bread off my shirt and set my empty glass on the coffee table. There was a nice, plump pillow at one end of the couch and a soft, yellow blanket folded over the backrest. Perfect. Might as well get comfy while I watch the news. Probably all of about fifteen seconds passed before I was snoozing contentedly.

Something cold and wet on my face woke me up. Trying to focus, I opened my eyes and saw droplets of water coming from above me. The roof must be leaking. I sat up and looked out the sliding glass doors to the patio. The sun was shining, and there was no sign of rain. The water drops persisted and, in fact, were coming faster. Looking for the source, I noticed the stream was arcing over the back of the sofa. Getting on my knees, I looked over the back only to find Spence lying on the floor with a giant squirt gun in his hands.

"You little pest."

Screaming a war cry, I went over the sofa and landed on top of him. With a *whompf*, all the air went out of Spence's lungs, and I started tickling him. Unfortunately, I sorely underestimated the strength training that Spence had been enduring for football. In one swift move, Spence was now on top and was pinning my arms to the floor. I couldn't budge.

As only a brother will do, he let a thick stream of saliva drop from his mouth and then sucked it back in just before it could hit my forehead. Spence finally tired of the game—thankfully before any drool came into contact with my face.

"You're such a brat," I said, shoving him away.

"And you're such a dork." *His usual comeback.*

"Where are Dibbz and granddad?"

"I think Dibbz took Granddad to the doctor," Spence said.

"Nothing serious, is it?"

"Naw. I don't think so. Just a checkup and blood draw. The doc wants to check Granddad for diabetes."

That certainly sounded serious to me. I made a mental note to call in a couple of days to find out the test results.

"Well, I'm gonna pack up my laundry and head home. Why don't you come visit me sometime?" I offered.

*susan case*

"One reason, it could seriously jeopardize my standing as the coolest dude in school to be seen at your place."

This prompted me to give him another shove.

"When I'm famous and my big story breaks, you'll be begging to hang out with me."

"You can wrap a dork in a pretty, fancy package with the biggest silk bow, but when you open the package, there's still just a dork inside." Spence grinned at me.

"You're such a pest."

"But I'm smart and good-looking, so who cares?"

I needed some of his confidence and bravado.

"See ya later, twerp," I said, heading to the laundry room.

"*Hasta*, freak."

We really had such a special relationship.

---

My second day of work at the Lux I was on my own with eleven rooms to clean. I had stopped at the store to purchase some latex gloves as I was determined that toilet water would not touch my bare skin.

I used the time cleaning to plot how to obtain access to the hotel's mainframe. The thought of flirting with pimple-faced *Trainee Boy* was thrown out. Not even a sensational national story with my byline was worth that.

I'd already tried to get Doris, the night manager, to look the information up for me. However, she was resolute in her refusal; that information was confidential, *period!* Doris didn't mind giving me details about the dead guy because he could never sue or complain, but the living was something else entirely.

Perhaps after work I could hang around the front desk to chitchat. With a little luck, an opening might present itself. Doris was on duty tonight, and heaven knew how much she enjoyed conversation.

All eleven rooms were relatively clean by 3:35 p.m., and I had made a whopping $4.75 in tips. Doris didn't come on duty until 5:00 p.m. Maybe a matinee or a bite to eat was in order. I still hadn't gotten into the practice of making myself a lunch, and by quitting time I was starving. Of course, a bag of popcorn drenched in melted butter could constitute a meal. Also, a movie would help pass the time more quickly.

Changing into my civilian clothes, I headed off for the mall. The only show playing in the time frame I wanted was an animated kid's show—not my first choice in entertainment. It turned out to be kinda cute, and the popcorn was delicious. It was slightly stale and chewy, just like I like it.

Doris was reading a romance novel when I approached the front desk. I brought her a blueberry muffin, trying to ingratiate myself with her. Who's going to send someone packing that brings an aromatic fresh-from-the-oven bakery offering. I certainly wouldn't.

"What's up, Jimi?" Doris smiled.

"Not much. I'm meeting a friend for dinner later and needed to kill some time, so I thought we could visit if you're not too busy." I allowed my gaze to fall briefly on the book so she couldn't deny that she had time.

It turned out to be a wasted gesture because she smiled brightly and said, "I'd love some company." Doris motioned for me to go through the *Employees Only* door and join her behind the counter. Glancing to my left, I noticed the computer was logged on and one of the night's reservations was displayed.

"May I get you a cup of coffee?" I asked Doris.

"Coffee sounds great, but I'll get it. I love a lot of cream and sugar." Doris was a woman after my own heart. "Won't you join me?"

"I'll just have some water. Thanks."

We idly chatted while I waited for the coffee to take effect. I was hoping she would have to go to the bathroom soon and I would politely offer to watch the front desk while she was indisposed.

*susan case*

After three cups of coffee and almost two hours of stilted conversation, she had to use the restroom.

"I'll be right back. I need to use the little girl's room."

"I'll watch the desk for you," I offered.

"Thank you. Just put any calls on hold or let guests know that I will be right back." Doris excused herself.

I had been discreetly studying the navigation icons on the monitor's screen and observed Doris maneuver her way through different options while helping a couple of phone customers and one walk-in guest.

The date of Herb and Sylvia's last visit to the Lux was ingrained in my brain. I began going through several options unsuccessfully when I stumbled onto the registration archive selection. I put in the July 7 date and room number 139, which was the room directly to the left of Herb's room number 137. That room showed no history for that particular night. Using the back button, I put in room number 135. *Jackpot!* Jim and Elsa Riggins of Culvert, California, were the occupants. There was even a note that they had called in a disturbance to the front desk. They were given a coupon for one free night at the Lux Hotel in appeasement. I hit the back button, but nothing happened. The screen was frozen. Even the three-finger salute—CONTROL+ALT+DELETE—had no effect. With this screen on display, Doris would know I had been snooping into the computer system.

I couldn't even find the computer's tower to perform a force shut down. Doris was whistling a tuneless song as she rounded the corner, so I did the only thing I could do. I beat a hasty retreat with a quick good-bye thrown to Doris thrown over my shoulder. What the heck. I was going to call in my resignation in the morning anyway. Doris looked a bit puzzled by my swift departure, but there was no way I was going to wait around for her to discover my treachery.

Once at my car, I bundled up my uniform and quickly took

it to the basement to leave with Ardith. Why wait until morning to resign?

Ardith didn't seem surprised or saddened by my resignation. Her only comment was, "I'm surprised you lasted two days, Princess."

---

I telephoned James Gunderson III, Esq. promptly upon waking bright and early at 11:07 a.m. the day after my resignation from the Lux Hotel. I went through the usual procedure before Harriet's attorney came on the line.

"James Gunderson, Esquire," his smooth-accented voice crooned.

"Mr. Gunderson, this is Jimi Smith. I have some additional information you may want."

"Wonderful to hear from you, Ms. Smith. What news do you have for me?"

"Well, I got a job at the Lux Hotel so I could find out if perhaps Herb and Sylvia had a falling out."

"Yes. Proceed." He sounded bored.

"Anyway, I have the name and location of the couple who had the room connecting to Herb and Sylvia's room on their last night at the Lux."

"Mr. and Mrs. Riggins," we *both* said at the exact same time.

"That's right. How did you know?"

"Ms. Smith, surely you realized I would subpoena the records of the hotel once you informed me of Herb and Sylvia's regular visits."

"Oh, of course, I should have realized." And to think I'd cleaned toilets and worn that loathsome, stinking uniform for nothing!

"So what new information do you have for me?" Gunderson prompted.

"Uh, the Riggins filed a complaint with the front desk

*susan case*

229

because of a loud argument coming from Herb and Sylvia's room."

"Yes. That was in the hotel notes."

Now he sounded irked as well as uninterested. I felt so stupid.

"Um, that was all."

"I see. Well, thank you, Ms. Smith." With that comment, the distinguished, illustrious Idaho esquire James Gunderson III dismissed me by hanging up. He didn't even ask me to keep digging or provide any further information.

It was time for some chocolate and a nap. Unfortunately, there was no candy in my apartment. I figured I may as well go to the store and then pay a visit to the unemployment office while I was out.

---

Back at my apartment with M&M's in tow, I bent to retrieve the key from under the front mat. No key. That was strange. I had left it there before going out. Turning the knob, I found the door unlocked, which was spooky. I peaked inside only to find everything in its usual disorder and disarray, but there were stark white, expensive-looking gift packages neatly stacked on my not-so-tidy sofa. Instead of a robber stealing my few possessions, I had a generous apartment fairy leaving presents.

There was a note set atop the smallest package. It read, "You shouldn't leave your key under the front door mat." It was signed simply, "Daniel."

Opening the largest box first, inside was a black silk sheath evening dress. The dress had a high neck with a single band of choker-style, large, black pearls. The glossy pearls were of a glistening gunmetal gray color with iridescent shades of purple, teal, and blue radiating from the orbs when caught by the light. The tiny silver hook clasp at the back of the neck was all that would apparently hold the dress in place. The label read that of a world famous designer, and it was exactly my size. Shucking my clothes to the floor, I slipped the weightless, slinky garment over my head only to realize that it had absolutely no back. The dress closely followed the curves of my sides and circled down to a bare quarter-inch above the swell of my backside. Daniel's taste in women's apparel apparently stemmed from watching one too many Kate Hudson movies.

The dress, by design, ensured that the wearer could have no undergarments on whatsoever. The bathroom mirror told the complete story. It appeared from behind as if I were naked from the top of my buttocks and up. I had to stand on my tippy-toes to see if the dress actually covered my derrière cleavage. The top was loose-fitting, but from the curve of my hips down to my knees it was clingy. My eyes were transfixed to the image in the mirror. The contrast of white skin against the black silk was striking. The dress transformed me into someone exotic. Hopefully the sexy nature of the dress wasn't too revealing or suggestive.

The next box contained a pair of black stiletto, sandal-style heels with crystal stones encrusted across the bridge. The shoes were also crafted from a renowned, ultra-chic designer, and my size again. I took off my sweat socks and slid my feet into the Cinderella slippers. I felt like a princess—a six-foot-tall princess, but royalty nonetheless. Thank goodness Daniel stands several inches above six feet.

The last box was from Tiffany's. It contained a triple-strand bracelet of small, black pearls. Again, the pearls had the lustrous peacock multi-hued colors radiating over each bead. All this and Daniel only expected a kiss? Something more was afoot here, and I was darn sure whatever it was, it wasn't in my best interest.

I was more than a little disappointed in myself that there were expectant little butterflies nervously and excitedly fluttering in my stomach rather than bats wings raging in indignation and trepidation.

This Friday night I would be attending a function far out-

*susan case*

side my social class, in clothes that far exceeded my income status, with a gorgeous man who had a nebulous and nefarious-tinged reputation with women. And yet the gala couldn't come soon enough. My anticipation was palpable.

---

Daniel left a message on my voicemail that he would pick me up at 6:45 p.m. It was now 6:15 p.m., and I was completely ready but afraid to sit down. I had spent almost a full day with Kirstie to receive the works: facial, haircut and style, manicure, pedicure, and then she did my evening makeup. I never did learn how to replicate the magic that Kirstie could perform with makeup. The effect she created was striking, sultry, smokey-eyed, and sexy.

Pacing my apartment, I realized that a half an hour was an exorbitant amount of time—I wasn't even yearning for chocolate. The sad fact was I was contemplating male reaction to my transformed appearance.

I phoned Kirstie to help pass the time, but the call went straight to voicemail, so I hung up without leaving a message. Picking up the latest issue of one of my favorite magazines, I leaned back against the wall and tried to concentrate on an article about how to transform a drab living room into a cheery, cozy, inviting space. I loved the before and after pictures of home decorating magazines, even knowing I would never endeavor to attempt such a project myself. The delightful images in my head never translated well into the capabilities of what my hands could perform, having not been gifted with arts and crafts skills. All my artistic ventures had turned out looking as if an enthused five-year-old had gotten a hold of her mommy's art supplies.

Hearing a car pull up out front, I glanced at my alarm clock. It was only 6:32 p.m., but I peeked out the window expectantly anyway. A long, black, sleek limousine was pulling to a smooth stop. Keeping my gaze out the window, I was curious to see who was inside. A chauffer in a smart, crisp uniform exited the driver's door and came around to open the curbside back passenger door.

It was Daniel who stepped from the car. I assumed he would pick me up in his Corvette. Not wanting him to see the inside of my apartment, I took one last, reassuring look at myself in the mirror then shot out the door.

Daniel was midway up the second flight of stairs when he we made eye contact. An expression of shock was evident on his face, and he stumbled a bit. Daniel in a tuxedo was a sight to behold. He could easily pass for a movie star or high-paid model. Not one to usually be affected by someone's appearance, I had to admit he took my breath away. Tall, blonde, tanned, blue-eyed, broad-shouldered, square-jawed, and with dimpled cheeks, Daniel was undeniably a man who made women turn to jelly. I mentally warned myself that looks like his could potentially engender reckless, wanton thoughts, thoughts I refused to entertain for even a second.

When he reached the landing and was about ten feet away from me, he stopped. I waited. Without saying a word, he made a motion indicating that he wanted me to turn around. I debated pretending indignation but smiled instead and shook my head no. Daniel raised an eyebrow and made the motion again, this time followed by a quiet, "Please." Hesitating only a couple of heartbeats, I complied and slowly turned around. I could feel the warm blush creeping up into my cheeks, but I looked over my shoulder to see his reaction anyway. It was everything I hoped it would be.

"Jimi, you take my breath away." This comment was offered sincerely, without even a trace of artifice.

"I was just thinking the same thing about you, Daniel," I replied.

When I got close enough to Daniel, he put his hand under my elbow in a protective, almost possessive manner. We made our way down the stairs to the limo, where the chauffer tipped his cap and smiled before opening the door.

Once we were comfortably seated in the luxurious limo and on our way, I couldn't resist asking, "Why the limo?"

Daniel's intense expression caused me a moment's pause.

"Because I wanted to give you my undivided attention. It was a smart decision because after seeing you in this dress, I could never have kept my eyes on the road." He lightly touched my bare shoulder with the back of his index finger and slowly traced the length of my arm. It created a tingling sensation and caused me to shiver. "You have the most exquisite skin. I knew it would be this soft."

I wondered what he would do next, but he only laid his hand atop mine and rested it there.

"Are you cold?" Daniel asked as he scooted closer.

"No. I'm fine."

"We have an hour's drive to the club. Would you like something to drink?" Daniel opened a concealed liquor cabinet. The golden glow of ambient lighting reflected from the many different bottles. "Champagne?" he offered.

Deciding it was a little early in the evening and I wanted to keep my wits about me, I declined with a brief shake of my head. "How about some—?"

Before I could say, "water," Daniel was handing me a chilled bottle of French mountain spring water.

"I was about to say white wine, but this will do nicely." Although I was reaching for the water, Daniel pulled the bottle away from me.

"Oh no, no, no," he tsked. "Don't ever let it be said that I didn't give a woman *exactly* what she desired." I arched an eyebrow in derision as Daniel replaced the water back into the cabinet.

He carefully perused all the labels before making a choice. "This should do nicely." He poured the liquid into a beautifully etched, delicate, crystal wine glass. He filled it slightly over half full.

I accepted the glass and took a small sip. It was fruity, bubbly, and light. Even though it tasted wonderful, being unaccustomed to alcohol, I thought it best to simply nonchalantly hold the glass but not drink any more.

Daniel poured himself a glass also and looked over at me curiously. "Don't you like it?"

"Yes. It's quite good. Thank you."

"Then drink," he encouraged.

"I will." *What was up his sleeve? Was he trying to get me drunk?*

Daniel handed the opened bottle over to me. "Since you like it so much, I thought perhaps you would want to know the wine maker and vintage selection."

Now I felt more than a little silly on two different counts. The label read "Sparkling White Grape Non-Alcoholic Cider." So now I had misjudged Daniel and proved that I was, in fact, unsophisticated.

"Also, don't ever let it be said that I coerced a woman into doing anything she didn't want to do."

Point taken, I shamefully stared at the glass in my hand, regretting my unwarranted assumption.

Daniel put his arm around me and lifted my chin with the opposite hand. "Don't feel too bad. I still expect that kiss you promised."

"Have you discovered anything about the disk?" I asked excitedly. My hopes were raised. Daniel seemed disappointed with the topic's change of direction.

"No, not yet, but the printer promised to mail the original disk back to the newspaper to my attention on Monday. We'll get this sorted out soon enough."

"Oh, okay." I tried to hide my disappointment. "You'll call me as soon as you know anything though, right?"

"Yes. You have my word."

"Thank you, Daniel. I really do appreciate your helping me out."

"My motives aren't completely altruistic, Jimi. Don't put me on a white steed in shining armor." Daniel was looking at me the way a starving man would look if he had discovered the last remaining loaf of bread on earth. "Jimi, I know you weren't planning on kissing me until the end of the evening, but I want to kiss you now before anything can happen that might ruin this . . ." He didn't seem to be able to find the words to describe what it was that might be ruined.

Daniel gently placed a hand on either side of my face in a soft caress but not pressuring me closer. "Please. May I kiss you now?" He breathed the words softly and seductively.

I inclined my head in a manner that expressly granted permission without having to say the embarrassing words, "Yes, you may kiss me."

He kept looking intently at me, as if waiting for something. I was beginning to feel uncomfortable and confused by his lingering stare. I opened my mouth to ask what was wrong when a look of triumph crossed his features. Daniel pressed his lips to mine, taking complete and thorough possession of my mouth.

There were no words to describe the carnal nature of the kiss. I had no thoughts in my head at all but was filled with glorious sensations, warm, spine-tingling, toe-curling, *I can barely breathe* sensations. Daniel obviously had way too much experience. He was that good. No wonder he had such a reputation with women. A woman would remember Daniel's kiss eighty years after the fact as vividly as if it had just happened. I leaned into Daniel to deepen the kiss, as if that were possible.

Daniel abruptly pulled away. He handed my glass of sparkling cider back to me and picked up his own. Then, with a grunt of disgust, he put the cider down and reached for a decanter of what I assumed was hard liquor. He poured about two fingers worth of amber liquid into a short, thick, heavy-bottomed glass and downed it quickly.

Although trying hard not to cry, I could feel hot tears welling in my eyes. Looking away from Daniel and out the window, I rapidly blinked in an attempt to dry the tears before they could spill down my cheeks and ruin my makeup. Daniel had pulled away from my kiss the same as Jet had.

"Jimi?" Daniel said softly, trying to get my attention.

"Hmm?" I continued looking out the darkly tinted window.

"Look at me." It was a soft request, not an order.

"Why?" Even I could hear the hurt in my voice, and it really ticked me off.

"Please."

I turned toward him but kept my gaze lowered.

"Jimi." Daniel put a hand under my chin and forced my gaze upward. "Why are you crying?"

"I'm not," I lied.

We sat there in uncomfortable silence for what seemed like an eternity.

"Do you want to know why I ended the kiss so quickly?"

"No, not really." I thought back to Jet and his quick departure from my presence after he kissed me. "A girl really doesn't want to hear the list of details as to why she's found . . . *lacking*." A blush of embarrassment rushed from my chest up to my scalp.

Daniel snorted an incredulous laugh. "You've got to be kidding." He waited for me to look squarely at him. "I ended the kiss because my thoughts were heading down a path that you would not approve of. The truth is, Jimi, you are dangerous."

"What do you mean? I'm such a terrible kisser that I could actually inflict harm?"

"No. You are dangerous because you make a man think about buying a house, trading his sports car in on a minivan, and spending his Saturday afternoons coaching little league baseball."

"I'm not following you." *Was I as predictable and boring as an old housewife?*

"What I mean is that you're not the sort of woman to treat casually."

"It was only a kiss."

*susan case*

"The hell it was." He sounded annoyed.

"Well, regardless, you've had your kiss, and now we can get on with the evening without having to think about it anymore."

"Jimi, I won't be able to think about anything else, except perhaps an encore performance if your hurt pride will allow it."

Serendipitously we were pulling into the circular drive of the country club. The chauffer parked the car at the portico-covered entrance and came around to open my door.

I exited quickly, but Daniel was right behind me and took my arm. "Don't forget to look adoringly at me every chance you get," he whispered on a laugh into my ear.

"I'm not sure my acting skills are up to it." I couldn't resist adding, "You better hope you are able to prove me innocent when you retrieve the disk considering what I've had to endure to keep my end of the bargain."

"Yes, I could tell how much you hated kissing me," Daniel drawled out with a smile.

Darn his hide. Another hot flush infused my face. Daniel was never going to let me live down my reaction and obvious desire to extend and deepen the kiss. In fairness to me, Daniel's kiss could resuscitate a dead woman, so what chance did *I* have what with being so painfully alive?

The foyer had an expansive ivory marble floor with striations of gold. The domed ceiling was at least fifty feet high. The curved staircase was wide and impressive. The finest plantation home in all the Deep South couldn't equal the beauty and elegance of this staircase. The thick, plush carpeting absorbed all sound. We walked arm-in-arm to the mezzanine.

The room was circular and massive. Round tables were covered in crisply ironed linen and glistened with elegant place settings, heavy, gold-plated flatware, and crystal water glasses. Everything was set in tones of ivory and gold. The centerpieces had large, white, fragrant flowers and ivory candles floating in crystal bowls that were rimmed in gold. I counted ten pieces of silverware for each setting. I was way out of my depth and wouldn't be able to eat a bite until first determining the appropriate utensil to use.

Daniel followed my gaze and noticed my consternation. "You'll do fine. In that dress, no one is going to notice what fork you use. You could eat with your hands or peel a banana with your feet and every man here would still want to be your dinner partner."

I didn't like being compared to a monkey, but his comment was somehow reassuring anyway.

"What about the women? What will they be thinking?"

"They will be busy picturing me without my tuxedo on, of course."

I had to laugh at his arrogance.

"Would you like something to drink?" Daniel offered.

"Yes, please. Pick something to help me blend in and look sophisticated."

"Once again, you underestimate the dress and what's beneath it. But to make you feel better, I'll get you something that sparkles. Have a seat here or feel free to mingle. It looks like quite a line at the bar."

When Daniel left I sat down and let my gaze slowly peruse the room. Every person, male and female, carried an aura of wealth, power, and entitlement. The waiters looked more at home than I did. What kind of life had Daniel led? It was certainly far removed from anything I had known.

Music softly played in the distance, and I found myself drawn to the source. A small orchestra and fair-sized dance floor were situated behind an ivory silk partition. The music conductor was attired in a formal white tuxedo. There was a violin and stringed instrument section, brass section, an enormous black polished grand piano, and even a six-foot-tall gold harp.

Appropriately, the harpist looked like an angel. Her blonde hair was set in a halo of curls, and she wore a long, loose-flowing, white gown accented with gold brocade. Her pale loveliness was the epitome of serenity. Perhaps playing the harp did that for a

*susan case*

239

person. Between the rainbow-refracting crystal, glossy marble columns, and gold accoutrements, it felt like I had entered a dress rehearsal for heaven.

Daniel came up behind me and whispered in my ear, "You'll dance with me later."

"We'll see."

"It wasn't a question." His easy smile took the sting out of the remark. "Here is your *sophisticated* Champagne cocktail." He bowed slightly as he presented me with the tall, fluted glass.

"Why thank you, kind sir," I said, using my best belle of the ball Southern accent. "I do believe I was about to get the vapors and perish of thirst. You are my hero."

"Why, Miss Scarlett," Daniel played along, "you may have the vapors, but not from thirst. You're feeling faint in anticipation of the ungentlemanly advances I am sure to make before evening's end. We Rhett Butler types are known for our rakish *yet skilled* behavior with the opposite sex."

This discussion needed to stop. I *was* getting the vapors. Just thinking about the kiss in the limo and my desire for a replay made me blush. It was all very confusing. I still didn't trust Daniel; my heart belonged to Jet, and yet I was inexplicably drawn to Daniel's more than obvious charms.

"Dinner will be served soon, and then we'll have to sit through the boring political fund raising speeches. Let's find our table." Daniel led me to a directory with an alphabetical listing of names and corresponding tables. We found our table, which was very close and centrally located to the long-festooned speaker's elevated table and dais.

Within a couple of minutes, the seats at our table were full and introductions made. It was an interesting mix of people, and the dialogue was animated and stimulating. I was enjoying myself more than I could have believed. Dinner was sumptuous, with every course served on gold-rimmed fine China by white-gloved waiters with linen napkins folded over their forearms. I never took a single bite until I saw which utensil Daniel used first. It didn't matter to me in the slightest that he was discreetly laughing at me.

All was well with my world until I heard the noxious sound of fake, sycophant giggling. *It couldn't be. Dare I turn my head?* I couldn't stand it any longer. Casually glancing to the table behind me, my worst suspicion was confirmed. Candy Kane, her bosom overflowing in a gold-sequined, tight mini-dress, was seated at a table with none other than Jet and his parents. Candy's double-D assets were on full display tonight. Her cleavage bore a remarkable resemblance to a mail slot for oversized FedEx envelopes.

I hated the fact that Jet in a slim-fitting tuxedo that accentuated his broad shoulders took my breath away.

Jet's surprised gaze was mirrored by my own. Realizing his mouth was agape, he firmly shut it and nodded a curt acknowledgment of my presence. I turned back to the table, fuming with repressed anger. Jet was back in town and hadn't even called me. He must have known that I had been fired, and yet he hadn't even bothered to find out my side of the story.

Daniel was laughing at something said by one of the other diners and then happened to glance my way. As established by prior history, my expression was an anathema to a properly-schooled poker face. My anger was right on the surface, but Jet's apparent betrayal and choice of dinner partner was more than I could bear. Even with that realization, I still noticed that Jet was devastatingly handsome in his tuxedo.

Candy cackled again. Daniel and I both turned at the sound just in time to see Candy clinging to Jet's arm and leaning into him. She was trying her best to angle her cleavage for Jet's optimum vantage viewpoint. He didn't seem to notice though. His stare was locked onto Daniel. They gave each other the Pez head guy nod acknowledgment gesture, and Daniel turned back to the conversation at our table.

Although I couldn't be sure, it felt as if someone's gaze was burning a hole into my naked, exposed back. I couldn't concentrate on the conversation flowing around me, and my appetite was completely gone. Even the chocolate soufflé presented at the end of the meal held no appeal. Well, perhaps I could manage one bite. Why should Jet and Candy be allowed to ruin my dessert?

Introduction of the guest speaker was made with fanfare followed by pretentious compliments, and we were regaled with an embellished political history. The featured guest was none other than incumbent Governor Crewson Seals. Truthfully, I never cared for the governor. He was too fake, too polished, too oily, too tanned, and usually too inebriated to take seriously. His opening line made me sick.

"At five hundred dollars a plate, everyone present must believe I will again go all the way." The governor made an exaggerated show of winking at his wife in a desultory sexual manner. "I'm sure my wife hopes I will *go all the way*"—a smattering of uncomfortable, polite laughter followed— "back to the governor's mansion, of course." The governor's wife masked her expression well and set her rehearsed, adoring gaze upon her husband with the dewy-eyed expression of a college freshman harboring a crush on a professor.

Daniel or his parents paid five hundred dollars for a dinner I was about to regurgitate. Maybe they could get their money back and slip it to the competing candidate's campaign fund. Candy cackled loudly at the governor's attempted humor, and it took every ounce of my restraint not to turn around and hiss at her like an angry cat. I was clenching my fists in an effort to retract my claws.

Finally, the tipsy governor finished his slurred speech, lightly touching on a couple of sober, albeit non-controversial, social issues, which was no small task given his nonsober condition. Seals concluded by encouraging guests to carryout the three *d's* of his campaign: *drink, dance,* and *donate further to his already well-funded political crusade.*

The orchestra began playing a tranquil song, which soon

swelled into a melody that made one feel as if they were transported back to the glamour and elegance of golden-era Hollywood. As the music continued, hushed waiters removed dirty dishes from the tables without so much as clinking a glass or rattling a piece of silverware. Couples filled the dance floor and were soon circling about in a smooth, rhythmic manner.

"Would you like to dance?" Daniel put his arm around my shoulders, his fingers lightly caressing me.

"Daniel, I don't know how."

"I'll show you. Just relax in my arms and follow my lead."

Somehow *relaxing* in Daniel's arms didn't seem possible. All I could think about was that stupid kiss.

"You're flushed. Are you thinking about our *exchange* in the limo?" Daniel asked with a smile.

"No. I'm thinking it's hot in here."

"Liar." Daniel stood and held his hand out to me.

I couldn't resist him, and didn't want to.

He led me to the dance floor and twirled me around with a flourish. The warmth of his hand was low, *very low*, on my bare back as he pulled me close. We swirled around the other couples, and I didn't falter once, somehow able to relax in his embrace and trust his lead.

"You're supposed to look adoringly at me," Daniel reminded me with a smile.

I batted my eyelashes and gave him a simpering gaze.

"You look like one of those dolls that when you tip the head back the eyes open and close; it's creepy."

Glancing down at my feet, I tried to think of the most sexually charged moment ever played out in a movie. When the perfect scene came to mind, I set my expression from simpering to simmering. I mimicked the dreamy-eyed movie star expression and slightly parted my wetted lips in provocative invitation and looked Daniel square in the eye.

Daniel didn't speak for a few moments. Then he leaned in close, his lips only a hairsbreadth from mine. "Look at me that way again, and I'm going to forget my resolution to act the gentleman and will immediately take you back to the limo."

*Fear. Anticipation.* Combine the two and that summed up my current feelings.

"Ah. That's much better. I like it when you're off guard and fighting your emotions and obvious attraction to me."

"I am not attracted to you."

Daniel laughed in arrogant disbelief. "Keep it up, Pinocchio, and we'll see how long your nose gets."

"You are so full of yourself."

"And you are a liar. Your face mirrors your every emotion, *including desire,* in plain, easy-to-read language."

I decided to change the subject. "This has been such a lovely evening; the elegant club, the heavenly music, the wonderful meal, and, of course, this dress. In case I forget to say it later, thank you, Daniel."

"What about the shoes, the bracelet, *the limo ride?*" he said with meaning.

"Thank you for those too," I said sincerely.

"May I cut in?" Jet sounded as if he were unsuccessfully trying to control rage.

*Why was he always so angry around me?*

Daniel let go of my hand and backed away. His body language indicated permission, but his face denoted irritation.

Jet maneuvered us to the far edge of the dance floor without uttering so much as one word. It felt more like a military march cadence than a dance. My anger was equal to Jet's and bubbling barely beneath the surface.

Separating his body from mine—not that he was all that close to begin with—Jet pulled me none too gently out the terrace doors. The night was turning frigid, and I could feel the evidence of the cold nudging against the silk at the bodice of my dress.

"So, lover boy bought you that *dress.*" Jet practically spat the word out in disgust. He must have overheard my conversation with Daniel.

"Daniel, *my friend,* purchased this dress for me, yes."

"That's not a dress. It's a blatant invitation." He looked at me as if he were a street preacher and I was a hooker parading for business on Main Street.

"What a horrible thing to say." It felt like a knife was twisting in my heart and making gaping holes in my lungs. All the breath left me in a whoosh. I no longer felt pretty; Jet's comment made me feel cheap. Jet had ruined this magical evening, and I hated him for it.

"*Horrible?* It's the truth," Jet ranted on. "Every man in this place knows that you have nothing on under that tiny scrap of silk.

"It's a designer gown."

"Yeah. It's designed to entice avarice in men. If you wanted to be leered at, I wish you would have asked me sooner." Jet slowly let his gaze run up and down my body in a way that made me feel dirty.

"I think I'll go back inside now." I hated the fact that his comments hurt so badly.

"So what does lover boy want in return for the designer gown and accessories?"

"He's trying to prove my innocence and get me my job back at the paper, not that you would care."

"He's not trying to prove your innocence; he's trying to *take* it."

"For heaven's sake, Jet. I'm twenty-four—hardly a child."

"You may be twenty-four, but you are as inexperienced as they come." Jet paused then tried to substantiate his remark. "I've held you in my arms and kissed you, remember?"

"Why, of all the ... *insulting* comments! I apologize that my kisses were so amateurish and not up to your standards."

"I didn't say that!" We were getting so loud it was a wonder no one had come out to see what all the shouting was about.

"I'm going back inside. Why don't you go find your date? Her kisses are sure to be much more professional. She probably garnered her experience on the Las Vegas strip."

Jet caught hold of my hand and turned me around to face him. "Jimi, you are completely misconstruing my meaning."

"Jet, you've ruined my evening and cast unwarranted dispersions on Daniel." I took a deep, controlling breath. "At least Daniel is trying to help me. Where have you been the last few miserable weeks?"

"I got back into town this afternoon. I didn't know about what happened at the paper until a couple of hours ago. I still don't fully understand what all transpired." Jet was trying to regain his composure also. "Did you promise Forsythe anything for his *assistance?*"

"This conversation is completely ridiculous," I said.

"Answer the question. Did you promise Daniel something for his help?"

"I told him I would attend this party and that I would kiss him at the end of the evening." *There. I hoped he was happy.*

"Here's the difference between Forsythe and me; *I* would have helped you for *nothing.*"

"Yeah, well, *I* would have kissed him for *nothing,*" I lashed out, regretting the words as soon as they escaped my lips. *Why does Jet bring out the very worst in me?*

"Touché." Jet saluted me. "Too bad Forsythe had to shell out a few thousand dollars for a sure thing."

"You, you . . ." I couldn't think of a word evil enough to describe Jet at the moment.

Jet roughly pulled me to him, pressing the length of his body against mine in a blatantly suggestive manner. One of Jet's hands put heavy force at the base of my spine and the other was pressed between my shoulder blades. Jet's hold effectively ensured I could not move, and the pressure points left nothing to the imagination as to the intimate act Jet was trying to imitate.

Jet kissed me hard and then abruptly released me. "You can bill me for the kiss." He looked me up and down again. "But it sure wasn't worth the price of that *dress*." Jet mocked a bow and said, "Enjoy your ride home."

With those parting shots, Jet left me alone on the terrace and retreated back into the sanctuary of the club. Although it was freezing out, I wasn't ready to go back inside. Opening my eyes wide, I faced the icy breeze, ensuring any tears would dry before they could fall.

I don't know how long I was out on the terrace embracing the solitude, but Daniel finally came out looking for me.

"There you are." He saw my face. "What's wrong?" Daniel put a hand on either of my arms and rubbed them up and down. "You're freezing." He took his tuxedo jacket off and placed it around my shoulders. The warmth of the jacket paired with the faint scent of Daniel's expensive cologne was soothing.

"I want to go home."

"Sure." He didn't even ask why I wanted to leave. "Come inside, and I'll have the limo brought around."

"I'd like to stay out here until you come back for me." No force on heaven or earth could make me stay in there alone and incur a chance meeting with Jet. The fairy princess had turned back into the peasant girl, a peasant girl who was way out of her league both socially and sexually.

The limo ride home was long and quiet. I wasn't very good company, and Daniel respected my mood. He turned some soft music on and left me alone to my thoughts. As we neared my apartment, I could tell he wanted to say something but hesitated. Finally, his desire to speak outweighed his indecision.

"Jimi, I'm glad you kissed me at the beginning of the evening."

He deserved the truth. "I'm glad too. It's not a kiss I'll soon be forgetting."

"It was a kiss I will never forget."

Where was my charming, untrustworthy bad boy? Where

was the Daniel that I could dismiss with a laugh? Evidently, that Daniel Forsythe had disappeared and in his place was a gorgeous, vulnerable man whose sincerity tugged at my heart.

The limo stopped, and the chauffer came around to my door.

"I'll walk you to your door."

With no pretenses left, I didn't even bother to decline. We walked hand in hand up the stairs.

"Daniel, it was a wonderful evening. I'm sorry it was spoiled toward the end."

"The evening wasn't spoiled. Stuff happens, right?"

"You went to a lot of trouble and expense to give me a fairy-tale evening, and you need to know how much I appreciate it." Not even waiting to see if Daniel would kiss me, I stood on tiptoe and kissed him. It was a soft kiss from the heart, no motivation or expectation behind it.

Daniel seemed to recognize where the gesture came from and didn't push for the kiss to linger.

I didn't know what to say. Suddenly the moment became awkward. "Daniel, I . . ."

"Jimi," he said, halting my attempt to fill the awkward silence, "go clean your apartment. It's a pig sty." He smiled and walked away.

Daniel certainly knew his way around women, or at least this woman. I walked into my messy apartment with a much lighter heart than I would have imagined possible an hour ago.

# chapter 17

The insistent unwelcome buzz of my cell phone awakened me at 7:00 a.m. What type of inconsiderate idiot places a call this early on a Saturday morning? It took a moment to clear my vision and read the caller ID. It was someone from the newspaper office. *What could this be about? Do they want to fire me a second time?* Curiosity got the better of me, and I answered before it could go to voicemail.

"Hello."

"Jimi, it's Jet. Please don't hang up," he rushed out.

I was considering my choices. Jet was the last person I wanted to speak with. It was beginning to feel more like Saturday *mourning.* Pausing, I let him wonder if I had hung up.

"Jimi?" I could hear Jet's frustrated sigh.

"Yes?"

"We'd like for you to come into the office this morning."

"We?" Was he bringing in Candy to take notes?

"Yes. My father will be here as well."

Well, that certainly cleared up the other partner in "we."

"Swell." My sarcasm was clear and evident.

"Jimi, we really need to speak with you. I promise it will be worth your while."

"Can't you just tell me whatever it is over the phone?"

"No. It needs to be in person."

"What time do you want me there?" That question made it sound as if I were actually considering acquiescing to his request.

"Can you be here at eight?"

"Do you have coffee going?" I snapped the question out.

"I'll do you one better. I'll have a white chocolate, caramel, triple-shot latte with a generous dollop of real whipped cream waiting for you."

*Geez. Jet must really be serious about my coming to the office, because if I were on death row the coffee he described would be my request for a final meal.* My mouth was watering at the thought of the latte.

"I'll come," I said; then I added, "Should I wear protective armor?"

"Funny." Jet wasn't quite finished. "And Jimi, I want to see you alone after the meeting with my dad."

"I'll be there at 8:00." With that I hung up, refusing to make any further rash promises.

---

After a quick shower, I chose to wear the most unfeminine outfit possible: baggy, faded jeans paired with an oversized Universal Studios T-shirt and the clumpiest shoes I could find. Not even bothering with the most basic of makeup enhancements, I allowed my hair to air dry. The comments Jet made last night still stung, thus my determination to look as sexless as possible.

Realizing Rhonda wouldn't be at the reception desk on a Saturday morning, I went around to the back door and knocked. Jet answered the door. He looked as if he hadn't slept in a week. Even his usually perfect hair had a weird cowlick thing going on.

"Why didn't you just use your key?" Jet asked, looking confused.

I tilted my head, put my hands on my hips, and gave him my very best *are-you-some-kind-of-idiot* look.

"Yeah. Right. Sorry. I'm kinda out of it this morning."

Candy Kane and her professional kisses must have kept him up late. The thought made my blood boil and my stomach feel nauseated, which did absolutely nothing to improve my disposition.

Not bothering with cordial civility, I demanded, "Where's my latte?"

"It's in my office waiting for you. I just got it, so it should still be hot."

A snitty *humph* was all the reply he received.

Jet led the way to his office. His father was seated behind the desk. Mr. Mitchell looked as disgruntled as I felt. Jet indicated for me to sit while handing me the steaming latte. It smelled wonderful. Although I didn't want to, my eyes shut and a smile curved onto my lips. I recovered quickly but not quickly enough. Jet caught my smile and was grinning at me. I gave him a scowl in return, but to my chagrin he just kept smiling.

"Jimi, *we* have done some investigating and *we* realize that you had nothing to do with the errors in Pastor Hutt's obituary. Furthermore, *we* want to extend *our* apologies and offer you your job back."

It was annoying how Jet kept emphasizing the *we* and *our* because Jet's dad still wore a scowl that matched my own.

"Dad," Jet continued, giving his father a meaningful look, "I believe you have something to say to Jimi?"

Mr. Mitchell cleared his throat and hemmed and hawed around before reluctantly saying, "I made a mistake. I shouldn't have jumped to conclusions before getting all the facts."

It was obvious that it really pained Mr. Mitchell to say those words. However, it wasn't nearly enough to placate my injured pride.

"We really want you back at the paper, Jimi. What do you say?" Jet offered.

"I'll have to think about it. I worked a lot of long hours without breaks and never even heard a *thank you* and then was summarily dismissed without benefit of a proper investigation."

Jet's dad looked shocked, as if he had just met the most ungrateful being on the planet. Sticking my chin out, I leveled a gaze at Mr. Mitchell that said, '*I really don't care what you think*'.

After a moment's hesitation, Mr. Mitchell's expression changed to one of grudging respect.

"Miss Smith, as stated before, I was in error, and I do hope you will consider resuming your position with the Weekly." This sounded considerably more sincere than the first forced apology.

"Is Candace Kane still employed here?" If you're going to gain a backbone, go big.

"Ms. Kane is no longer a member of the Weekly team." Mr. Mitchell stood and came around the desk, extending his hand to me. "Miss Smith, I have underestimated you and errantly questioned your ethics as well. I won't make either of those mistakes again." His grasp was warm and firm. His handshake seemed to say, '*my word is my bond*' and I trusted him.

I gave him my most confident, conciliatory smile. "I will be at my desk 7:00 a.m. sharp Monday morning."

He nodded his approval and released my hand. "By the way, Miss Smith," Mr. Mitchell said as he headed toward the door, "you looked stunning last night."

My thank you was directed to Mr. Mitchell, but I was looking directly at Jet when I said it. Jet's shocked expression indicated that he felt his dad had become a traitor.

Mr. Mitchell left without further comment, and I got out of my chair to make my departure as well.

"Jimi, I'd like for you to stay a little longer."

"Why?" I wasn't going to make this easy for him.

"Please, just sit down for a moment."

I hesitated awhile before complying. I plopped down into the chair and folded my arms across my chest, and my jaw was locked into place as well.

"Say what you have to say." If my body language didn't convey my irritation, my snotty tone certainly did.

"I want to say that I am very sorry about last night. I said some uncalled for, truly nasty things—things you didn't deserve."

Jet squatted down in front of me, resting his backside on his heels. He placed a warm hand on each of my knees. A nervous fluttering sensation was beginning in my stomach; the effects of too much caffeine probably.

"Jimi, I truly am sorry for everything. If I could take last night back, I would." He sounded sincere. "I'm asking for your forgiveness."

"Where have you been the last few weeks, Jet, while my world was falling apart? You didn't even call once." I hated the fact that I sounded so hurt.

"I've been in Arizona overseeing one of my dad's construction projects. We're building a golf course and man-made lakes. Eventually there will be retirement housing put in." He paused, I assumed, trying to figure out how to say why he hadn't called during the time he was gone. "I thought we needed some time apart. It seems one or both of us are always exploding in anger every time we're together."

I guiltily remembered slapping Jet's face, but at this particular moment I still couldn't bring myself to apologize for it.

"Fine. You have my forgiveness." My response sounded flippant. "Anything else?" I asked, starting to rise, but the firm pressure Jet was now applying to my legs kept me seated.

"Jimi, we have to work together. Can't you find it in your heart to honestly forgive me?"

"*Honestly*, I don't know, but our working relationship will be fine." I stood up, and Jet followed suit. "Are we through?"

Jet shrugged, clearly unhappy with my reply.

I was almost to the door before Jet stopped me with a question.

"Did you kiss Forsythe at the end of the evening?"

"You have no right to ask that question." And I had no intention of answering.

"No, I don't, but I'm asking it anyway." He repeated, "Did you kiss Forsythe at the end of the evening?"

The friendly kiss at the end of the evening wasn't the type of kiss Jet was referring to.

"No. Daniel didn't kiss me at the end of the evening." The barest hint of arrogant smugness flashed across Jet's face, so I added, "I kissed him at the beginning." With that parting shot, I left Jet's office. Why could I never leave well enough alone?

———————————

Monday morning was all business, and I never once encountered Jet. Most of the morning was spent putting my desk back to rights and reloading the files that had been deleted from my computer. I wondered what happened to Candy. Although no longer an employee of the newspaper, speculation still swirled through my mind as to whether Candy continued to be a part of Jet's life. It shouldn't have mattered, but it did.

A few Weekly staffers came around to welcome me back, but each time it was an awkward, fleeting conversation. The only thing that kept the office from feeling like a tomb was the excitement over Mrs. Greene's impending trial. Her October 12 trial date was only two days away.

The remainder of the day went as expected, and I received a couple more assignments to cover local events. By 5:00 p.m. I was strained and fatigued. Although there wasn't much to eat in my apartment, I was too drained to bother going to the grocery store. There was some peanut butter in the cupboard anyway.

Barely home ten minutes, my cell phone rang. It was Daniel.

"Hello."

"Hey, Jimi. It's Daniel. I wondered if you wanted to go out to dinner tonight."

"Daniel, I appreciate the offer, but I'm beat. It's been a tough day."

"I heard you got rehired. Guess you won't need my help or that disk after all."

"I still appreciate what you tried to do."

"Have you had dinner yet?"

"No. I was just going to make myself a peanut butter sandwich." A sandwich without bread, because the last two slices had been eaten a few days ago.

"How about I bring a pizza and a movie over?"

Lately everything about Daniel was pure temptation. Surveying the destruction of my apartment, I decided it would be best not to have any visitors.

"No, not tonight, but thank you anyway," I replied reluctantly.

"Apartment too messy?" he guessed.

"Yes, and I don't have a DVD player either." Why bother lying? He'd seen my place when he dropped off the dress and shoes, so he already knew I'm a slob.

"All right. Here's what we're going to do," he informed me as if I had no say in the matter. "I'll order a pizza, rent a movie, and then pick you up. We'll have dinner and a movie at my place. I promise to have you home at a decent hour too."

My resistance, such as it was, vanished.

"May I have some sweet tea too?"

Daniel laughed. "Yeah. I'm sure the pizza place has tea."

"Sweetened tea," I corrected.

"I'll make sure it's sweet."

"All right. I'll concede, but you should know I probably won't be very good company tonight."

"I'll deal with it. See you in forty-five minutes." He hung up.

Why did everyone in my life end conversations so abruptly without saying good-bye? Truth was it was probably the only way to get the last word in.

I brushed my teeth and finger-combed my hair. Daniel wouldn't like it, but I changed into some comfy sweat pants and an unflattering long-sleeved T-shirt. I certainly wouldn't be taking his breath away tonight or causing him to stumble in a dazed sexual haze.

It wasn't long before I heard the toot of Daniel's Corvette horn.

*So thinks he can just honk his horn and I'll come running? Pizza. He thinks right!* I left my apartment in a hurry.

Daniel didn't make any comments on my appearance. Picking up the hot, fragrant pizza box from the passenger's seat, I handed it to Daniel just long enough to sit down. It was going to take all my restraint not to sneak a slice before we reached his place. This morning's chocolate doughnut paired with my eighth cup of coffee was all I had eaten today.

"Where do you live?" Why hadn't I asked before?

"Hamlet." Hamlet was a small town about five miles outside of Ditters Ferry.

I was a little disappointed in the distance from town, as the aroma wafting from the pizza box was killing me.

"Oh."

"If you are that hungry go ahead and take a slice, but don't spill any sauce on my custom leather seats," Daniel said, reading my mind.

"What makes you think I'm hungry?"

"You're staring at the pizza box the way you should be staring at me. Besides, you're drooling." He laughed.

My mouth was watering in anticipation of the pizza, but looking at Daniel could induce the same effect. A fear spread through me that I might be turning into a shameless hussy. Because, although Jet infuriated me, he could still engender the same thoughts and desires that I was currently experiencing for Daniel. This is probably what happens when a girl waits too long for her first real kisses and dating experiences. I should have gone through all this in high school and college, certainly not starting out at the ripe old age of twenty-four. Daniel and Jet must both think I'm a backward buffoon.

"Why are you frowning at the pizza box? A minute ago it looked like you were in love with it."

"I was just thinking."

"Must be something deep," he guessed.

"Daniel." I paused, waiting for him to look at me.

He finally glanced my way. "Yes?"

"Why do you want to spend time with me?" I truly needed to know, desperately needing some form of encouragement that would build even the slightest amount of confidence in me as a woman.

"I don't know. I just do." He made it sound so simple, but it didn't alleviate my self-doubts at all.

We were pulling to a stop in the driveway of a beautiful brick home with a perfectly manicured lawn. The trees surrounding the home site were large and stately. Daniel reached across and unbuckled my seatbelt in a thoughtful gesture. He gave me a quick kiss on the cheek and asked me not to get out of the car. Daniel came around to open my door in another considerate action.

"Can't have you dropping that pizza trying to get out of the car."

Well, it was still a considerate action—just directed to his car instead of me.

Daniel's home was tidy yet in every other way typically masculine. Not much on the walls, no plants, and all the furniture was soft, black leather, and the few tables were chrome and glass. There wasn't even a television in sight. The only other piece of furniture was stationed against the wall opposing the sofa. It was a massive black lacquer cabinet that stood at least five feet tall and six feet wide. Nothing sat atop it, not so much as a single photograph or a spot of dust. The house was spotless. What must he have thought when he saw my place?

Daniel took the pizza box and the small bag that had been sitting by my feet in the car to the kitchen. He returned with two plates, each holding a large slice of pizza and a couple of napkins.

"I'll be right back with your tea. Would you like it over ice?"

"Yes, please." He really was thoughtful.

By the time Daniel returned with his beer and my tea, I had already eaten all the pepperoni off my slice of pizza. He looked at it and smiled.

"A little hungry, are we?"

"As a matter of fact, *yes!*"

I didn't wait for Daniel to sit or take his first bite. Without realizing it, my eyes were closed and there was a look of complete rapture on my face. I took a huge bite and didn't open my eyes again until it was time for the next mouthful. Between bites, I didn't even bother to set the slice of pizza down onto the plate, instead choosing to keep it at-the-ready for the next hunk I planned to gnaw off.

"You do know there is more pizza in the kitchen."

Choosing to ignore the comment, I asked what movie he had rented. The title he quoted was for the latest chick flick released to DVD.

"Is this the usual genre of movies you rent?" I asked curiously.

"Not exactly, but I didn't think you'd be in the mood for blood and guts."

"You are right." I looked around the room again. "Where's your TV?"

"There's one in my bedroom." He looked sideways at me.

My pizza dropped onto my lap and left a huge blotch of sauce on my sweatpants.

"Of course, I have this TV also." Daniel picked up a remote control from an end table and pointed it toward the black lacquer cabinet. The top of the cabinet opened, and a huge screen began to slowly rise. It was the coolest thing I had ever seen. I didn't even care that Daniel was still laughing at me.

"The bathroom is down the hall to the left if you want to rinse the tomato sauce off your pants."

As any grown-up, sophisticated woman would do, I regally

stood and stuck my tongue out at Daniel before heading down the hall.

I didn't have much success getting the stain out. My pant leg was soaked, and all I had accomplished for my efforts was to spread the stain. Shrugging my shoulders, I headed back to the living room.

I ate two more slices of pizza before the opening credits could even finish rolling. Taking my shoes off, I tucked my feet under me and leaned onto the plump, cushiony arm of the sofa. Now that my hunger was satiated, it was time to get comfortable and concentrate on the movie.

---

The smell of fresh percolated coffee and early morning rays of sunshine roused my senses a little. I was too warm and comfortable though to open my eyes yet. *Just another few minutes.*

*Coffee?* I cautiously opened one eye then quickly closed it with a groan. This was truly embarrassing. I had fallen asleep before the movie had even barely begun. Daniel had covered me with a large, heavy afghan and placed a small pillow under my head. *How did I sleep through that?*

Hearing some rustling sounds coming from the kitchen, I scrunched my eyes shut even tighter.

"Good morning, sleepyhead."

He made it sound as though I were a child.

Opening my eyes, I saw Daniel holding a large mug out to me. "Three sugars and extra cream."

My caffeine-starved brain managed to send a signal for my hand to reach for the steaming cup. "Bless you."

"Sit up first; otherwise you'll spill." Daniel certainly was a persnickety housekeeper.

I sat up and took the warm mug, cradling it between both hands. "*Mmmm.*"

The coffee cup was almost empty before I spoke. "I'm sorry I fell asleep. I can't believe you covered me with a blanket and put a pillow under my head without waking me up." Looking at Daniel, I continued. "Thank you for doing that."

"Yeah, well, I was afraid you might get cold. The pillow didn't work, though."

"Huh?"

"You still snored like a lumberjack after a bender."

"I do *not* snore."

"*No?* Then I better get animal control out here because evidently there are pigs rooting around for truffles under my sofa."

The way he said it, I couldn't help but laugh out loud, regardless of how unfeminine the comment made me seem.

"Come on." Daniel reached for my hand to help me up. "I imagine you'll want to change clothes before going into the office." He continued looking me over. "Your hair is all squished flat on one side with some weird vortex thing going on in back, and there is a pillow crease down your cheek."

I set the mug onto the coffee table and held my hands up in defeated conjecture. "Then I guess the attraction is over now that you've seen me at my worst."

Daniel pulled me close and laid a long, lingering kiss on my lips. Still not releasing me, he said, "If this is the worst it gets, I'll buy earplugs to get through the night and wear a blindfold until you've had your morning coffee and shower."

"You're such a horse's behind," I said, giving him a playful push. "Take me to my apartment, please."

Since I wasn't starving, it seemed a short drive back home. "Will I see you at the office?" I asked getting out of the car.

"No. I've got a freelance job in Boise today."

"Okay. See ya," I said, waving good-bye over my shoulder.

"I'll call you later." Daniel raised his voice to be heard over the engine.

I didn't even turn around. Instead I lifted my hand in a gesture that let him know I had heard him.

I opened the door and froze. At first glance I thought everything in the place had been stolen, but on further inspection it had been *cleaned*. My apartment absolutely glowed with cleanliness and order. And people wonder why I don't lock my door. *Gifts. Now maid service . . .*

The kitchen was not only spotless; the cupboards had been filled with goodies like cereal, mac and cheese, canned goods, and crackers. Moving to the fridge, I opened it to find milk, cheese, eggs, deli meats, and fresh veggies, fruits, and condiments.

*Is there a noise like running water coming from my bathroom?* I couldn't decide if I should check it out or run from my apartment screaming. What kind of sick whacko breaks into someone's home to clean and supply it with groceries?

I stood frozen as the bathroom door began to open. I couldn't scream. All I could do was put a hand to my rapidly closing throat in terror.

I finally eked out a sort of yelping dog sound, and Jet jumped a good two feet in the air.

"*What the . . . ?*" Jet gasped.

"*Jet,* what are you doing here?" I didn't mean to yell at him, but my heart was still beating wildly in fear.

"Where have you been?" Jet's face turned red. "I've been worried sick." He picked up my cell phone from the now shiny, dust-free dresser and waved it at me in accusation. "How is someone supposed to get a hold of you if you don't carry your phone with you?" He paused only long enough to catch his breath before continuing his diatribe. "Your car is here, your purse is here, your phone is here, and by the looks of your apartment, no one would ever know if there had been foul play or a scuffle."

"Let me get this straight. You were worried about me, so you cleaned my apartment and then went to the store for supplies."

"I got tired of pacing the floor and tripping over debris. Besides, I needed to burn off some energy. And then I found that there was nothing to eat."

"You've been here all night?"

*susan case*

"Yes, *I've* been here all night!" Jet shouted. "Where have *you* been*?*"

"I could state the obvious—that it's none of your business—but to simplify things I'll answer. I went to a friend's house to watch a movie and fell asleep. End of story." I put my hands on my hips. "Satisfied?"

"*No.* Not until you tell me who the *friend* was." The man had more than his share of nerve.

"Jet, why are you here? What is it you want?" I needed to derail him from his current line of interrogation.

"I thought we could review your notes on Harriet's trial, see if anything was overlooked." That sounded suspiciously weak.

"We could do that at work today," I pointed out. "Why the urgency to see me last night?"

Jet paced the floor. Frankly I got tired of waiting for an answer.

"Tell you what. I'm going to take a shower and get dressed for work. You may stay or leave. It's your call."

I looked around the room. Now that there was nothing on the floor or couch, I didn't know where to look for my clothes.

"They're in the dresser," Jet said distractedly yet still reading my mind. "Top drawer: undergarments and socks; second drawer: blouses; and third drawer: pants."

My face heated up. *Jet touched my undies?*

Keeping my back to him and purposely blocking his view, I opened the top drawer and quickly wadded a thong into a ball in my fist. Then, just as Jet said, I found a neatly folded blouse in the second drawer and a pair of khakis in the third drawer. My humiliation was complete. I was a slovenly, snoring, selfish catastrophe.

I locked the bathroom door. While in the shower, I wondered if Jet were still on the other side of the door. Towel-drying my hair and using a little gel was going to have to be sufficient grooming for the day. I dressed quickly and took a deep breath before peeking out the door. My cheeks were still rosy from the steam of the shower.

Jet was still there. He was standing by the window, staring out in a daze.

"We need to get to the office," I said, unable to think of anything else to say.

Jet turned around. "You asked me why I was here, so I'll tell you." He sat on the sofa and gazed at his interlaced hands resting between his knees. "First, I am so sorry about the awful things I said to you. Second, I'm sorry for the way I kissed you at the country club."

"You're sorry you kissed me?"

Jet got up and walked over to me. Standing toe-to-toe, I had to tilt my head back to look up at him. Finally, he broke the silence.

"No. I'm sorry for the *way* I kissed you. How I really wanted to kiss you was like this."

Jet held me as he had at the club—pressure points at the base of my spine and between my shoulder blades—but this time the effect was quite different. With my head already tilted back, it gave Jet perfect access to my mouth. I didn't even put forth the weakest effort to push him away. His kiss caused my brain to fog and my heart to pound. The kiss was as thorough as Daniel's had been in the limo, and my reaction was the same. *More, more, more.* Jet finally ended the kiss, but not because I wanted him to.

"If you can't figure out how I feel about you, I'm going to have to start being more direct." With that comment, Jet left my apartment.

*Yowza. How much more direct can he be?*

Leaning heavily against the wall for support, I realized an adjustment needed made to my previous self-description. In actuality I was a slovenly, snoring, selfish catastrophe who was also apparently a shameless hussy. Not one man for the first twenty-four years of my life, and now there were two. I couldn't

*susan case*

do anything right. A disturbing question entered my brain: *Why does being wrong feel so deliciously enticing?*

---

The intercom on my phone beeped. "Bring your notes on the Greene investigation to my office." This curt demand came from Jet.

Where had the man who kissed me this morning gone?

All I had accomplished so far today was to make a list of pros and cons for each man: Jet and Daniel. Unfortunately, the only *con* I could think of for either was that they were both attracted to me. Daniel was a tall, blonde, blue-eyed, square-jawed, dimple in the chin, muscular, mischievous, fun Adonis. Jet was tall, broad-shouldered, olive-skinned, dark-eyed, dark-haired, muscular, seriously macho man who had owned my heart since high school and possessed a smile that could stop traffic—well, female traffic anyway. Both were wealthy. I couldn't help feeling that some cosmic joke was about to be played on me. Both men seemed to want me, but I feared simultaneously both would soon reject me. I'd just have to enjoy the ride until the time came to choose or jump ship altogether. But somehow I knew that when the time came to jump ship, there would be an anchor tied around my ankles.

My notes on the Greene investigation were already printed out, in order, and neatly contained in a manila folder. In the margins of my notes were conclusions, theories, or question marks. Collecting all the documentation on the Greene case, I headed to Jet's office. I rapped softly on the door with the back of my knuckles while pushing the door fully open with my other hand.

Jet was on the phone but waved me in. I'd never seen him look so disheveled. His hair was mussed on either side as if he'd been running his fingers through it in exasperation. The cuffs of his sleeves were rolled back, and his crooked tie had been loosened to the point that he may as well have been wearing it as a belt.

Once Jet hung up the phone, he cleared a long section off his desk and pulled his chair around to my side of the desk. "This way we can look at it together," he said.

I opened my notes, and we started going through them from the beginning. Jet asked several intuitive questions and, he seemed pleased with my responses. There were notations also as to the discoveries I had forwarded on to Harriet's attorney. When Jet reached the part about the furniture dolly receipt, he noticed there was no memo entry about having sent this information to the attorney.

"Did you inform Mr. Gunderson about the receipt?" Jet asked.

"Well, no. Actually, it didn't seem significant."

"But you have in your notes that it seemed 'out of place.'"

"Yeah." I had to think back. "Harriet kept all of her receipts neatly gathered together by month and filed away. That receipt was under the corner of her desktop day planner, and it seemed odd at the time."

Jet sat back to digest this information and possible ramifications. "What did Harriet say about the receipt?"

"She claimed to not know anything about it."

"Do you think it's possible someone may have planted it there to cast further suspicion onto Mrs. Greene?" Jet asked.

Shrugging my shoulders, I said, "Anything is possible."

"I've already looked over the state's witness list." Jet stood up to locate the papers from Harriet's attorney. He found what he was looking for on top of his filing cabinet. Jet began rifling through the pages of court documents. "Here it is under 'witnesses for the prosecution.' Jason Hahn, Boise Rent it All."

"Jason?"

The name definitely sounded familiar. I went through my notes and confirmed that Jason was the person I had spoken to at the rental place. There was a further notation in the margin

265

of my notes. It contained Jason's description of the woman who rented the dolly: nervous, must lift two-hundred-plus pounds by self, five feet four, slim, brown hair, and between fifty to sixty years. I read these details off to Jet.

"That sure sounds like Harriet," Jet said, discouraged.

"That's what I thought. Do you think I should have mentioned this to Harriet's attorney?"

"Probably. Full disclosure to an attorney is always best. You never know what they might come up with for countering a witness's testimony." He didn't sound critical when he said this, so my feelings were slightly spared.

Jet phoned James Gunderson, III, and they had a brief discussion about the receipt and my notes regarding my call to the rental store. I heard Jet say, "Just a minute. Let me ask her."

"Jimi, did you get a copy of the rental agreement?"

Looking further into my notes I read, 'call back 2 days if fax agmt not rec'd'. It didn't show that I had ever called back or received the copy of the agreement. I slunk into my chair as Jet relayed this information to Mr. Esquire the Third.

"Do you have any other notes pertinent to the conversation with the rental agency?" Jet asked.

"Nothing much." Then I saw some barely decipherable scribbling. "Wait a minute." I turned the paper this way and that, trying to make out my own handwriting: "nt sgn ner sig lyn" and the words "weird/nervous/hurry" in quotes. It jogged my memory enough. "Jason said that Mrs. Greene must have been in a big hurry or very nervous because she didn't sign anywhere near the signature line."

Jet gave this information to Harriet's attorney. Then he said, "Will do." A short pause followed. "Good-bye."

"What, 'will do'?" I asked Jet.

"Um, nothing." I could tell it was something Jet didn't want to discuss.

"You may as well spill it, or I'll nag you to death until you do."

Jet seemed to weighed my words and determination to follow through on the nag threat. He sighed in defeat before finally answering my question.

"Mr. Gunderson said to inform you, for future reference, these are the types of details which could make or break a case, and it was not very astute to withhold such information. He added something about letting the person with the client's best interest at heart determine what facts are useful or not."

Now I knew how a bull felt when stabbed and seeing red. What hurt worse was that Mr. Gunderson was probably right.

For the remainder of the afternoon and into early evening, Jet and I poured through all the investigation materials at our disposal. We bounced ideas back and forth. It really was stimulating working with Jet. He was incredibly bright and very discerning about filtering through facts and coming to logical possible conclusions.

Jet looked at his watch. "It's 6:45. I think we've covered everything here." His hands gestured to encompass the massive pile of paperwork on his desk. "Let's call it a day. Besides, I'm starving. We worked right through lunch."

Jet was reiterating what my stomach had been silently complaining about for the past couple of hours.

"I'll see you in the morning." I got up to leave the office.

"How about having dinner with me? We could go to Maude's Diner," Jet coaxed. "I'll even let you eat my salsa with a spoon."

My faced flushed in remembrance of that horrible night during our high school years. It was the evening I had arranged the fake interview with Jet and he had brought Candy along. To make matters even worse, I had eaten Jet's salsa thinking it was my soup. I couldn't believe he remembered the incident or, more importantly, that he would bring up such an embarrassing topic.

"Thank you for the offer, but I'm tired." I chose to ignore the salsa reference. "Also, since the food fairy stopped by my place last night, I can actually go home and fix myself something to eat in the comfort of my sweatpants and bare feet."

"Do you know how to cook?"

Jet was smiling. The sight of his smile made the pit of my stomach go all gooey. The contrast between Jet's dark olive skin and stark, white, even teeth was striking.

"I was thinking about an omelet and a salad," I said, somewhat confident I could at least manage that.

"Sounds like heaven." With the barest hesitation, Jet continued. "At the risk of being rude and presumptuous, how about cooking an omelet for two, please?" He didn't sound as if he cared that he was being presumptuous.

I was trying hard to hide my smile. *Well, he did buy all the food, after all.* It didn't take much self-coaxing to concede to his request. "Okay, but you are on salad detail."

"Deal." Jet went around to the other side of his desk. "Go on ahead. I'll meet you at your apartment in about fifteen minutes. I have some things to take care of here first."

"See ya in a few," I responded.

Once at home, I immediately took my socks and shoes off and changed into my comfy pink jogging suit. I began scavenging the fridge for items used to make an omelet. Eggs; that was a given. Ham and cheese sounded good. I located my one and only frying pan and dusted it out. It had been sitting unused in the bottom cupboard since I moved in. I set some butter out onto the counter to use to grease the pan. There. All set. I congratulated myself.

There was a knock at the door. "Come on in, Jet."

Jet didn't come in. Instead, a very confused and displeased-looking Daniel entered, carrying a package.

"You're expecting Jet?" he asked very nonchalantly, perhaps a little too casually.

"Oh. Hi, Daniel." I felt guilty but wasn't sure why. "Jet and I worked late and didn't have time to eat lunch, so I invited him over for dinner." The words came out in a rush.

"I see." Daniel hesitated before continuing. "I came over to give you this"—He handed me a package from an upscale clothier— "and to see if you would like to go out to dinner, but since you have other plans . . ." Daniel started to leave.

"Why don't you stay and have dinner? I'm making an omelet and a salad. I'd love it if you stayed." I don't know what part of my brain the invitation came from, but it was a part of my brain in desperate need of a lobotomy.

His face registered surprise. "You're sure I wouldn't be intruding."

*Someone please hand me a gun so I may have the option of a quick death.* In truth, the thought of Daniel and Jet both being there for dinner made me feel sick. Before I could even answer Daniel's somewhat rhetorical question, there was a knock at the door.

"I'll get it," Daniel said. Unfortunately, he was closer to the door, and I couldn't head him off in time.

"Come on in. Glad you could join us for dinner," Daniel greeted Jet, making it sound as if Jet were the interloper instead of himself.

Now it was Jet's turn to look bewildered and unhappy. He recovered quickly though and looked at me. "Uh. I just came over to tell you that I won't be able to make it for dinner after all."

Daniel's face lit up in elation and victory. I walked between the two and said to Jet, "Are you sure you won't stay? The more the merrier." *Who coined that stupid phrase anyway? And where is my lobotomy surgeon?*

Jet looked at Daniel's face and then set his jaw in cement. "I guess my plans can be postponed. I'll stay."

The beginning twinge of a headache was coming on.

"Jimi, aren't you going to open the package?" Daniel asked, pointing to the elegant bag in my hands.

"Oh, I'll open it later."

*susan case*

269

"Come on. Open it now." The look in Daniel's eyes was one I had never seen before. He was actually challenging me.

"Go ahead, Jimi. Open the package," Jet insisted.

I gave up in defeat. "Fine," I snapped. "Since we're all so curious." I opened the bag and pulled out the softest, prettiest buttercup yellow flannel pajama pant set I had ever seen. The sleeves and pant leg cuffs were hemmed in the same shade of muted yellow, but in silk. It was the type of outfit teenagers wore to school and the mall these days, but much more stylishly elegant. The pounding in my skull was definitely a full-fledged headache.

"Since it was my fault your pants were ruined last night, I wanted to make it up to you. I thought these would be a comfortable replacement. I'm confident they're your size."

This was said to me, but Daniel was looking directly at Jet. I turned to see Jet's reaction. Predictably, Jet looked ready to explode. There was too much electrically-charged testosterone flying through my apartment, and I was tired of looking back and forth between opponents. I wanted out of this tennis match. A championship tennis slugfest is a pleasure to watch, but it is not pleasant when *you* are the ball. The pain in my head had escalated to a screaming intensity.

Daniel looked confident and relaxed as he leaned against the kitchen counter. Jet looked tense and territorial, as if every muscle in his body had tightened in a predatory pose ready to pounce on the enemy infiltrator. Perfect. Just what I needed: a bad boy and a mad boy. Both were unquestionably acting like boys.

"Guys, I'm not feeling well," I said, pinching the bridge of my nose, as if that was going to keep my hammering brain from bursting through my forehead. "Let's have this dinner party another time."

"Jet, maybe it's best if you leave," Daniel said casually. "I'll take care of Jimi."

"Daniel, why don't you run along home?" Jet countered. "*I'll* take care of Jimi. I know where she keeps her aspirin."

"Out! Both of you *out!*" Raising my voice caused the vicious pulsations in my head to increase.

"But . . ." Daniel and Jet said simultaneously, each looking at me imploringly.

"Goodnight," I said to both with irrefutable finality. I opened my apartment door in a not very subtle invitation for them to leave. Beyond any doubt, my body language declared this was not a request but an ejection order.

Only because I couldn't help myself, as soon as my door shut, I ran to the window and peeked out. Each went directly to his own vehicle and left without saying a word to the other.

Not even a minute went by before my cell phone started buzzing. It was Jet's number on the display. I let it go to voice-mail. My curiosity got the best of me, so I called to retrieve the message. The computer voice indicated there were *two* new messages. The first was Jet.

"Jimi, that was embarrassing. You need to decide whom you wish to spend your personal time with. I will not play second to a philandering womanizer." End of message.

I listened to the second message. "Jimi, it's Daniel. Regardless of my reputation, *I* only date one woman at a time. Call me when you pare your dating list down to just one." End of message. And might I say, *Ouch!*

Six extra-strength pain-relieving tablets and a candy bar later, I crawled into bed. As surely as an ostrich will bury its head in the sand to avoid confrontation or decisions, I will devour anything made with chocolate and then slumber my way through the dilemma in a sugar-induced temporary coma. Unfortunately, morning always comes too soon.

*susan case*

# chapter 18

The office was again abuzz with frenzied conversations of speculation and anticipation for Harriet's trial. Jet and I had already discussed that we both would be present in court for the duration of the hearing. We were to head over to the Addel County Courthouse in Hilltown around 1:00 p.m.

It was close to noon, and I still hadn't seen Jet in the office. I assumed we would be traveling together, but perhaps after last night Jet would not appreciate my company in a confined vehicle. The trial was slated to start at 2:00 p.m. Opting to pretend nothing untoward had happened between us, I dialed Jet's cell phone number.

"This is Jet."

"Hi, Jet. It's Jimi. I was wondering if we were driving to Hilltown together or if I needed to use my own vehicle."

"I'll pick you up out front in a half hour. Be ready," was Jet's abrupt response.

"Fine. See you then." The last was said to dead air because Jet had already hung up.

Going through my briefcase, I made sure there was a note pad, several sharpened pencils, Post-It notes, and a highlighter. That should do. While I was thinking about it, I put my cell phone on silent mode. It would be too embarrassing to have it go off in the middle of the hearing.

I went to the restroom to use the large mirror. After taking special effort with my hair, makeup, and outfit, I wanted to check to see if any refreshment was in order.

I'm not sure why it mattered, as the judge had declared, "No cameras or video equipment allowed in the courtroom," and all eyes were sure to be transfixed on the courtroom players. Truthfully, it wasn't the court's opinion that counted. I wanted to look nice for Jet.

Satisfied with what I saw reflected in the mirror, I glanced at my watch. Jet should be here in about five minutes.

My timing was perfect. As I walked out the front door, Jet was pulling into the parking lot. He rolled the Navigator to a smooth stop. Jet's dad was in the front passenger seat, so I got in the back.

"Good afternoon, Mr. Mitchell."

"Good day, Miss Smith. Are you looking forward to the excitement of the trial?"

"This is the first trial I've ever covered, so I guess in that sense I'm looking forward to it."

"With Gunderson as an attorney, Harriet is in good hands, don't you think, Son?" Mr. Mitchell directed this question to Jet. "Jarret?" I had almost forgotten that Jet's real name was Jarret. No one used it—other than his parents, I supposed.

"Sorry, Dad. What was the question?" Jet sounded more than a little distracted.

"I said that Harriet is in excellent hands with James Gunderson for an attorney."

"Absolutely. Best attorney in the entire northwest."

There was some additional idle chitchat, but conversation was strained due to Jet's inattention. Finally, conversation ceased altogether, and we were each left to our own thoughts.

Reaching Hilltown by 12:45 p.m., we still had more than an hour before the trial was due to commence.

"How about some Chinese food?" Mr. Mitchell offered. "My treat."

Jet mumbled something, which must have been interpreted as acquiescence.

"Sounds great. Thank you," I offered, trying to work up some enthusiasm and gratitude. Jet's mood was definitely putting a damper on my own frame of mind.

The only Chinese restaurant in town was just a few short

blocks from the freeway exit. Jet carefully maneuvered his Navigator into the only empty parking space at the front of the restaurant. It was a popular place to eat, but the lunch crowd usually thinned out by 1:00 p.m.

We were seated in a russet orange high-backed booth, and I sat between father and son. Conversation was still awkward and intermittent. Jet's mind was definitely someplace else. Mr. Mitchell ordered an appetizer of pork and seeds and requested hot tea.

When the waitress returned with ice waters, a pot of hot green tea, and three small, thick, handleless cups, we placed our lunch orders. Mr. Mitchell finally succumbed to Jet's nonresponsive and subdued behavior and ceased trying to initiate any further discussion. We sat in uncomfortable silence for the duration of the meal. It was impossible to enjoy my chicken almond ding with spicy sauce. I was tempted to have my leftovers placed in a *to-go* container just so it would stink up Jet's car. Chinese food left in a hot car for several hours can really leave behind a distinctive aroma.

Like a reprieve from prison, Mr. Mitchell looked at his watch and announced it was time to get over to the courthouse. He quickly paid the bill in cash. In single file formation, we went out to Jet's car. We looked like a line of mournful ducks.

The courthouse was packed with locals in every manner of dress imaginable, all hoping to get a seat in the rapidly filling courtroom. Fortunately, the media had first access, and we were ushered in without delay and given front-row seating directly behind the prosecution's table. I doubled-checked to ensure my cell phone was on silent mode and retrieved my pad, pencil, and highlighter from my briefcase. Closing the briefcase, I was about to put it under my seat when I realized it would work great as a lap table. It was a little wide and hard to balance but did, in fact, make a great surface to write on.

The jury members filed in and sat in an elevated, cordoned-off section to the left of the judge; there were seven women

275

and five men. There was a wide range of ages. I'd guess anywhere from the youngest being around twenty-five to the oldest being well past seventy years old. Some appeared nervous, others bored, and a couple looked like they couldn't wait for the excitement to begin.

At precisely two o'clock, the bailiff announced for everyone in the courtroom to rise for the Honorable Judge Essich. The judge was a short, jovial-looking man who was completely dwarfed by his throne (a.k.a. the bench). Magistrate Essich was aglow with pink, sweat-shined cheeks, voraciously taking in the expectant stares of the courtroom players. He had little wisps of silver hair puffed above his ears, but the rest of his very round head was completely hairless. Without a doubt, this had to be the most high-profile case ever adjudicated in Addel County, and he wanted to make the most of it and leave a lasting impression. Judge Essich forced himself to school his features to appear stern and called for quiet in the court. An immediate hush fell, but the atmosphere radiated heightened anticipation.

The charges filed against Harriet A. Greene were read aloud, and the drama began to unfold. Harriet didn't have a stitch of makeup on, and her hair was worn in a severe, tight bun. She wore an outdated, polyester, hunter green, button-up suit that was at least two sizes larger than her current frame.

Sylvia sat in the front row immediately behind Harriet. Considering Sylvia's leanings toward Harriet's guilt, I was surprised to see her sitting in a place where one would expect to find support for the defendant.

The prosecuting attorney, Sheila Christianson, made her opening remarks to the jury. The D.A. was completely unfeminine and lacked any spark of personality in her bland face. Although probably only in her early thirties, attired in a shapeless gray pinstripe pantsuit with pasty gray skin and mousy brown hair haphazardly pulled back in a tortoiseshell clip, she could easily be mistaken to be in her fifties. Even her gray vinyl shoes with worn tassels were masculine and squared off at the toe. This was a woman who wanted to be taken seriously as an androgynous trial lawyer.

Although her voice was soft and low, it somehow commanded attention and could be heard throughout the room. Sheila Christianson listed all the circumstantial evidence that had been compiled against Harriet. There was Harriet's letter opener found impaled in the decedent's chest. There was the recent million-dollar appraisal of the jointly-owned acreage and home. And finally, the prosecutor hinted at recent contact between Harriet and her estranged husband, the murder victim. Sheila Christianson effectively outlined motive, method, and opportunity. She knew exactly when to pause for effect and make eye contact with a particular juror, and used nuances of tone to indicate how guilty Harriet *had* to be, and then used a cautionary tone to inform the jury of the tricks the defense would use to cloud and distort the facts by use of smoke and mirrors to confuse the jury. By the time the prosecutor completed her opening remarks, the jury looked ready to hang Harriet without benefit of hearing from a single material witness.

James Gunderson III, Esq. looked nothing like his voice on the phone. I had pictured a tall, distinguished-looking English gentleman in a tweed houndstooth suit with an air of nobility about him. Instead he looked like a Mafioso with slicked-back, black hair. One thick, hairy wrist sported a garish gold watch and sausage-shaped fingers, three of which sported gold rings set with large jewels. He was short and round and moved like a bantam rooster. I kept expecting him to peck at a worm on the floor or claim a prize hen at any moment. Although impeccably dressed, he resembled an Armani-clad road construction caution barrel. Gunderson strutted to the jury box and halted. He leaned against the railing and turned toward the prosecution table with his arms folded across his rotund chest.

"Ladies and gentlemen of the jury,"—he looked each juror in the face individually—"my esteemed colleague gave you an accurate list of details. However, please note she was and will be unable to tie a single piece of evidence directly to the wrongfully accused. All the facts you will see and hear entered into testimony are circumstantial at best in their connection to Harriet Greene. I don't need smoke and mirrors, nor do I need to caution you as to the tricks the prosecution is sure to employ. Through the jury selection process, I noted intelligence and intuitiveness from each juror."

Again, he paused to engage each jurist in eye contact. The sound of Gunderson's voice was hypnotic, and his words of praise to the jury panel caused each member to sit a little straighter and become just a bit puffed up due to their notable *and noted* intellect. There is something in the American psyche that leads us ignorant Yanks to believe that anyone with an English accent must be of superior intellect and honesty. This would explain why infomercials in the United States predominantly choose English-accented hawkers to expound on the virtues of their latest and greatest gadgets and wares.

"The prosecution will deluge you with data but will be unable to provide a single witness or fact that cannot be disputed by reasonable doubt. Attempting to disparage the defense of this fine woman you see seated before you was the prosecution's own feeble attempt at smoke and mirrors and misdirection."

Sheila Christianson's head looked ready to explode. Her pasty face momentarily flushed red with anger as Gunderson continued.

"I simply ask that you use your God-given intelligence to decipher what, *if anything*, can be directly attributed to Harriet Greene. After all is said and done during this trial, you will have no recourse but to acquit her of all these erroneous charges mislaid at the feet of an innocent, hardworking woman." Gunderson strutted back to the defense table, again reminding me of a cocky rooster.

And so the trial began with the prosecution striking first blood but the defense inflicting the deepest wound. The prosecution called its first witness: Clint Markham, ME, a forensic doctor who would relate in graphic and gory detail precisely how Herbert Greene died. He concluded that Harriet's letter opener was definitely the murder weapon, then went on to explain how long the body had been in the water and gave the approximate date and time of death. It was also brought to light that there were no defensive wounds found on the victim, which probably indicated that Herbert Greene knew and/or trusted his attacker. One would think this questioning would only take a few minutes, but the forensic expert was on the stand for over two hours. The defense would pose only three questions to this particular witness.

Gunderson politely asked his first question. "Were any fingerprints or DNA, other than the decedent's, found on the murder weapon?"

The fine doctor spoke in circles until Gunderson demanded a yes or no response. Put this way, the forensic expert was forced to admit that there were, "No fingerprints or any DNA other than the victim's found on the letter opener."

Gunderson asked his second question: "Precisely how much strength would it take to drive a dull blade, such as a letter opener, through a muscular male body that would cause the murder weapon to not only break a breast bone but then imbed itself deep into the heart?"

Quince Markham, ME looked a tad uncomfortable with this question. He answered that it would take measurable force.

"*Measurable force.* What does that mean?" Gunderson turned to look at Harriet, effectively drawing all eyes to her.

At that moment, Harriet Greene was conveniently reaching for the water pitcher with shaky hands; her bony, frail wrists decorated with multiple age spots were on display for the jurors inspection and retrospection.

The doctor responded that given *enough rage*, anyone could potentially drive the murder weapon through bone and heart muscle. Clint Markham, ME may as well have been speaking to the carpet because all eyes were still on Harriet's fragile, thin frame. Gunderson thanked the good doctor and excused him from the witness stand.

The last witness of the day was from Barnes Appraisal. The appraiser took the stand and confirmed that he had indeed performed the Greene property and home appraisal. The land and home appraised for $1.4 million market value. Under further questioning, the witness stated that Mr. Herbert Greene requested and received a copy of the appraisal for a $150 fee.

James Gunderson asked the final question of the day: "Does it indicate in your file who paid for the copy of the appraisal?"

"We keep copies of all checks." He flipped through some pages. "Here it is: a copy of the check for $150. The payee was Sylvia Whitworth."

Gunderson excused the appraiser, and the court was called into recess for the day. Court would be resumed at 10:00 a.m. tomorrow.

Sylvia squirmed in her chair, but only a few pairs of eyes were on her. Not many in the courtroom knew Sylvia Whitworth. Her anonymity would be short-lived.

---

After the quiet ride back to Ditters Ferry with Jet and his dad, I had devised a plausible excuse to drive my own vehicle for the second day of court. I told Jet I wanted to do some shopping and run a few errands in Hilltown after the court recessed for the day.

The prosecution called Jason Hahn of Boise Rent it All as its first witness of the day. Jason recounted what he had told me. The woman who rented the dolly seemed excessively nervous and needed to know that she would be able to lift two hundred pounds on her own. The name on the contract was Harriet Greene. Plus, the rental of the heavy duty furniture dolly timed out to match the approximate date of death for Herbert Greene. It was a lot of damning evidence against Harriet.

Sheila Christianson asked Jason to please point out the person who rented the furniture dolly. Jason pointed toward the defense table.

"Let the record show that Jason Hahn has identified Harriet Greene, the accused, as the person who rented the furniture dolly." Sheila Christianson said this with authority and enthusiasm and a slight smile of triumph. The DA felt the furniture dolly was the key piece of evidence indicting Harriet.

"No," Jason Hahn said.

"No what?" The prosecutor asked, confused.

"No. I didn't point to *her*," he said while indicating Harriet Greene. "The woman sitting directly behind the accused is the person who rented the dolly."

He pointed again, and there was a collective gasp from everyone in the courtroom as all eyes, except mine, locked onto a shell-shocked Sylvia. Abruptly swiveling to turn toward where Jason was pointing, I dropped my briefcase onto the floor. As I picked it up, I inadvertently made eye contact with Harriet, who was looking down and away from Sylvia. To my amazement, Harriet Greene didn't appear the least bit surprised when the furniture dolly rental information was revealed. Instead, for just a fleeting moment, she wore the evil smile of a devil who had collected yet another soul for eternal residence in fire and brimstone.

Harriet caught my gaze and immediately wore an expression of shock and dismay.

*Was I seeing things? That momentary wicked smirk, had it really been there? Did Harriet know before the testimony was even given that Sylvia would be implicated as the person who rented the dolly? Had I been played for a fool? Could Harriet have preplanned and masterminded the entire series of events? Were Sylvia and Harriet in on it together? Why else would Sylvia have rented the dolly? But why would Sylvia incriminate herself? Judging by Sylvia's face, she definitely was not in on any plan with Harriet.*

Nothing made sense.

All of these suppositions seemed ridiculous and far-fetched, especially since Harriet herself would be aware that she would

*susan case*

281

be arrested and jailed. But what a brilliant plot it would be; Harriet kills her husband and then subsequently points the finger of guilt at her husband's lover for the murder. Talk about poetic justice. It was sheer freakin' genius, if in fact it were true. If, as I suspected, the evidence began to point in another direction, reasonable doubt would be assured and the jury would have to acquit Harriet of all charges.

When the judge was able to get the crowd to quiet after several harsh raps of the gavel, the prosecution asked Jason if he was absolutely certain that the woman he had pointed to, Sylvia Whitworth, was the person who had rented the dolly using Harriet Greene's name. Jason gave an emphatic yes and went on to state that he distinctly remembered this woman and the large, one-of-a-kind ring she wore on her index finger. The prosecution called for an immediate recess as melee erupted in the courtroom.

My mind was reeling with questions and possibilities. I wondered if anyone else saw the quickly passing evil grin on Harriet's face. Looking around the room, all eyes seemed to have been, and continued to be, affixed to Sylvia. Sylvia was in a dither trying to get through the crowd and hustle out of the building.

"Bailiff, detain her," Judge Essich barked and nodded toward Sylvia, "until we can sort things out."

Sylvia stood like a statue and wore the proverbial deer-staring-into-the-headlights expression as the muscular bailiff headed her direction. Gunderson approached the bench and requested that Judge Essich issue an immediate search warrant for Sylvia's home and vehicles. The judge didn't hesitate even a second before granting permission for the warrant.

Prosecutor Sheila Christianson appeared ready to pass out. It was as if she had just heard the death knell ringing a close to her case against Harriet Greene. If Harriet were found innocent, she was surely going to look like an idiot. The prosecutor thought about the wasted time, money, and media exposure already spent on this case, not to mention the fact that her term was nearly up and she was in the midst of her re-election campaign.

I felt sick, used, and *stupid.* There was only one answer for Harriet's malevolent sneer: the cunning witch had laid out a trail of crumbs for me. I had not only followed the trail, devouring every crumb; I had hungrily begged for more.

Judge Essich granted a recess, stating court would resume at 10:00 a.m. on Monday, October 17. Acknowledging this information, we all went our separate ways. In the depths of my being, I knew that Harriet Greene was indeed a clever, manipulative genius and had thought of every contingency. *How long had she been planning Herb's murder?* I racked my brain for an idea, *any idea,* to find some evidence to prove Harriet's guilt, but came up empty. Perhaps another trip to Harriet's house was in order. There had to be something there, something Harriet may have carelessly forgotten.

I stopped to fuel up my car and get a cold drink and then went straight to Harriet's place. It was a forty-minute drive from Hilltown to Harriet's home on the far side of Ditters Ferry. Pulling into her long driveway, I spotted two county sheriff cars. The deputies were probably already dusting for fingerprints in the office where the dolly receipt had been found. Talk about moving fast. In my gut I knew they would find Sylvia's prints. Harriet would have thought of everything. I headed home defeated, without a plan of action.

When court resumed on Monday, I knew the defense would mount and build evidence against Sylvia Whitworth. *Smoke, mirrors, and misdirection; Prosecuting Attorney Sheila Christianson had been as right as rain.*

I needed to talk to someone, but whom? Jet would never believe me. He had trusted and assumed Harriet's innocence from the beginning. It never even occurred to Jet that she might be guilty. So my interpreting a *look* from Mrs. Greene was not going to sway him whatsoever. I was actually beginning to doubt myself. Then my mind recalled Harriet's malevolent celebratory sneer, and I knew in my heart that she was guilty of Herb's murder and responsible in framing Sylvia for his death. The million-dollar question was *how to prove it.*

# chapter 19

Awakening bright and early Monday morning, after less than two hours of sleep the night before, I determined that caffeine in huge quantities was essential. A quad-shot of espresso with cream and chocolate syrup from the Java Hut drive-thru was definitely in order. Four shots ought to wake me up.

The weekend had proved to be a colossal waste of time, as I couldn't come up with a single idea to gather any indictment against Harriet. I still didn't have anything definitive *or even speculative* to take to the prosecuting attorney's office to help ensure a guilty verdict for Harriet. You can't convict someone for a facial expression. It was too bad that cameras and video equipment hadn't been allowed in the courtroom. At least then I could confirm what I had seen. But even with that, what would it amount to? Facts, even manufactured facts, were all that mattered.

*Where's the proof?* I didn't believe for a minute that Sylvia had rented the furniture dolly. Or if she had that she did it for Harriet and without knowing the intended purpose. Questions kept screaming in my mind over and over again, demanding resolution. Instead of being on a fact-finding mission as any good journalist would have endeavored, I instead had set out to prove Harriet's innocence.

I didn't even bother to call Jet for a ride. At some point we were going to have to call a truce or at least figure out a way to work together, but the feelings were still too raw. I'd just leave things be for now. Besides, I needed time to think.

At the courthouse, there were triple the number of people seeking admittance to the Greene trial. Several Idaho television stations had sent camera crews and reporters to interview anyone willing to talk to them on the courthouse steps and lawn. After Friday's surprise revelation, they decided to begin active coverage of the trial. Cameras still weren't allowed in the courtroom, but sketch artists were permitted. All the media was ushered in first. This time, however, preferential treatment was given to the recognizable television faces. I was given a seat in the second row from the very back. Fortunately, the judge, jury, and witnesses all had raised platforms and the acoustics in the building carried sound to the far reaches of the room superbly.

The state decided to rest their case, as each of their scheduled witnesses had already taken the stand. The faces at the prosecution table looked subdued, but they were careful not to appear defeated. They still had a case to win.

No one except the judge, defense council, and prosecution were aware that a closed meeting in the judge's chambers had taken place earlier in the morning. The judge was leaning toward dismissing Harriet's case. Surprisingly, it was defense attorney James Gunderson who most strenuously objected to this idea. Seeing the handwriting on the wall, he had already spoken of the possibility of dismissal with his client. Harriet had vehemently indicated that since she had been falsely accused, arrested, spent numerous days in jail suffering all its indignities, and had her good name slandered, she demanded justice by seeing the trial through to completion. Harriet wanted her good name restored with a full acquittal. The prosecution still held onto hope that the circumstantial evidence already submitted against Harriet Greene might still warrant a conviction. It was determined and mutually agreed upon that the trial would resume and run its due course awaiting jury verdict.

Gunderson called his first witness: forensic specialist Lucinda Beecham. The prosecution objected, as the witness was not on the list. But Gunderson provided evidence that he had faxed the DA a request to add Ms. Beecham in light of the details that had come out in testimony last week. The notice of revision to the witness list had been faxed to the prosecution's office shortly after 1:00 a.m. this morning. Judge Essich over-ruled the prosecution's objection and allowed the witness.

Gunderson requested Ms. Beecham to detail her education and work experience to prove she was an expert in forensics. Ms. Beecham's credentials began to become quite a list, so in case they might need to refute any of her conclusions later in the trial, the prosecution wisely stopped Beecham's oratory and stipulated to the fact that she was *experienced* in the field of forensics.

Gunderson was one step ahead of the prosecution. "Will the state stipulate that Ms. Beecham is an *authority* and *expert* in the field of forensics? If not, she can continue listing her academic degrees, internships, and years of—"

"So stipulated," Prosecuting Attorney Sheila Christianson snapped.

"Ms. Beecham what, if anything, was found in the trunk of Sylvia Whitworth's car by your expertly trained forensic team?"

"There were no obvious blood stains visible. However, after spraying the interior of the vehicle's trunk with Luminol mixed with an oxidizing agent, there was a rather large, striking blue glow area, which indicates the presence of blood."

"Were you able to determine the blood type?" Gunderson queried.

"It was type A," Ms. Beecham responded.

"Were you given a sample of Herbert Greene's, the decedent's, blood?"

"Yes, we requested and received a sample."

"And what blood type was Herb Greene's?"

"It was type A."

"Were you able to perform a DNA match to determine if the blood is, in fact, the victim's?"

Ms. Beecham arched an eyebrow. "No. That will take several weeks. Performing DNA testing and matching is a long and intricate process."

Unperturbed, Gunderson continued his questioning. "Did you find any hairs or fibers?"

"We found a couple of hairs, which were carefully bagged, then labeled and sent to the lab along with the blood-soaked carpet sample for DNA testing. There were no fibers other than those consistent with the carpeting of the trunk."

"Thank you, Ms. Beecham." Gunderson preened then turned toward the prosecution. "Your witness."

"Ms. Beecham, what percentage of the world's population has type A blood?" the prosecutor asked.

"Forty percent of the world's population is blood type A."

"So with a population of 6.5 billion people, that would mean that . . . let me do the math here." The DA paused for effect under the pretense of looking for a calculator.

"That would be 2.6 billion," Ms. Beecham offered immediately. "Of course, there are only approximately 302 million people in the US, which would equate to 120,800,000 Americans with type A blood."

Sheila Christiansen stood with her mouth hanging open. The jury was now extremely impressed with, at minimum, the mathematic prowess of the witness. Finally deciding to take up the slack in her incredulous jaw, the prosecutor continued.

"Well then, I guess that leaves a lot of potential people whose blood it could be in the trunk of that car, doesn't it?"

"I guess that depends on how many type A bloody people one is likely to encounter and then graciously place in the trunk of one's car."

"Move to strike," screamed the prosecutor.

"The jury is instructed to disregard the last statement from this witness."

It was difficult to hear the judge over the raucous laughter in the courtroom. Judge Essich rapped his gavel several times to quiet the court. Sheila excused the witness and stormed to her chair. Things were not going well for the prosecution.

Gunderson's next several witnesses provided extensive reasonable doubt and mounted insinuating evidence against Sylvia Whitworth. The county sheriff found only two sets of prints in Harriet Greene's home office. One set matched the accused, and the other set matched none other than Sylvia Campbell, a.k.a. Sylvia Whitworth. Thanks to a minor infraction against the law in her biker days, Sylvia's fingerprints were on file in the NICBCS (National Instant Criminal Background Check System) database.

Doris the night clerk from the Lux Hotel in Twin Falls positively identified from photos that Herbert Greene regularly stayed Saturday nights at the hotel. Jim and Elsa Riggins, the couple who heard the fight in the room next door at the Lux Hotel, saw the woman leave the victim's hotel room in a huff and get into a sporty white Cadillac. Gunderson asked each of the Riggins in turn if they saw the woman who exited the Lux Hotel room in the courtroom. Both indicated that the woman was not in the courtroom.

Sylvia was suspiciously absent from the day's proceedings. However, each of the Riggins affirmed that Harriet was definitely not the woman they saw. The couple further regaled the court with the argument details and the ensuing apparent end of a relationship.

Finally, Gunderson called his last witness: the accused, Mrs. Harriet Greene. You could have heard a downward-floating cotton ball hit the carpeted floor; such was the quiet in the courtroom as a feeble, spindly Harriet Greene approached the witness box. She looked as if she might collapse before she could even state her name and be sworn in.

Harriet sat primly in the witness box. Gunderson began his questioning with quiet concern on behalf of the witness.

"Mrs. Greene, how are you feeling?"

"Objection. Relevance," shouted Sheila Christianson. Too late, she realized how petty the objection sounded.

Gunderson softly patted the railing of the witness stand

in sympathy for the witness's unstated but obviously frail condition.

"I humbly apologize to the court for my *irrelevant* question of concern."

This comment spared the judge from having to rule on the objection. Essich looked utterly thankful for the reprieve. Sustaining the objection would have made him look like a callous jerk.

Gunderson walked Harriet through a series of questions designed to get the jump on the questions the prosecution was sure to ask.

Gunderson: "Did you recently obtain a home and property appraisal?"

Defendant: "Yes, a few months ago I had made the final mortgage payment and was curious as to our property's worth."

Gunderson: "Our property?"

Defendant: "Herb's and mine. It is"—Harriet dabbed tears from her eyes— "uh, was still *our* home."

Gunderson: "Have you recently heard from your husband?"

Defendant: "Yes. We'd recently spoken a few times over the phone. It was so wonderful to hear his voice again after all these years. The last time we spoke we arranged to meet at a local restaurant the next day."

Gunderson: "Did the meeting ever take place?"

Defendant: *Dabbing tears.* "No. I never heard from him after that last call when we scheduled to meet; he never showed at the restaurant either."

Gunderson: "Mrs. Greene, did you kill your husband?"

A visibly shaken Harriet responded with righteous indignation. "Absolutely not. I loved Herb. That's why I never sought a divorce." On the barest whisper, she said, "I still love Herb."

Although the prosecution asked all the right questions and deftly attempted to anger and rattle the accused, Harriet Greene came across as an incredibly believable witness, vulnerable and honest. Harriet answered each question in a calm, assured voice, seemingly confused as to their slanderous line of questioning. Finally, the state excused the witness from the stand.

The defense declared they had no more witnesses. I was amazed, as surely the rest of the courtroom must have been, that Sylvia Whitworth hadn't been called to the witness stand. Regardless of the curiosity, now all that was left to complete the hearing was for the opposing attorneys to make their final remarks to the jury.

The prosecution again carefully lined up all the circumstantial evidence, but it paled by comparison to the reasonable doubt that Gunderson was able to conjure up. The jury was excused from the courtroom to deliberate and determine the guilt or innocence of the accused.

The deliberation took less than two hours. The bailiff returned to the court and informed the judge that the jury had indeed reached a verdict. Judge Essich called the room to order as the jury members filed in. This had to have been the fastest adjudication of a murder case in the history of the United States, barring of course the Old West when the accused was quickly and summarily hanged immediately upon a guilty verdict.

"Foreman of the jury, have you reached a verdict?" the judge asked.

"Yes, Your Honor, we have."

"What say ye on the count of murder in the first degree?"

No surprise to anyone, he said, "Not guilty, Your Honor."

All the lesser charges were read, and on each count the defendant was found to be not guilty. The prosecution gathered up notebooks and briefcases and quickly left the courtroom. They exited through the backdoor of the courthouse to avoid the maniacally information-hungry media. Sheila Christianson would need time to come up with answers that would at least keep her in the running as Prosecuting Attorney. She also was probably in a rush to get a warrant for the arrest of Sylvia Whitworth.

My mind was numb. I still sat in the now empty courtroom, running the evidence through my brain.

1) *Sylvia's fingerprints were found in Harriet's home office.*

2) *The broken affair with Herb. A spurned lover.*

3) *Wealthy husband.*

4) *The type A blood found in Sylvia's car.*

5) *The thirty thousand dollar possible blackmail monies paid to Herb by Sylvia. That fact hadn't come out at trial.*

6) *Sylvia wanted me to believe at the onset of the murder investigation that Harriet was guilty.*

7) *Sylvia threw a lamp at my head.*

8) *A jury found Harriet innocent of the murder in less than two hours.*

I hated to admit to myself that all the evidence lined up against Sylvia as the murderer. Perhaps I was mistaken about Harriet's look in the courtroom. Maybe I had seen one too many suspense movies. Maybe Harriet's expression had been motivated by something else entirely. *Maybe, maybe, maybe . . .* Or, most probable, perhaps my distinct dislike for Harriet had clouded my judgment. Whatever the reason, the point was now moot anyway. Harriet was free and could never be charged with Herb's murder again. Why spin my wheels over something that couldn't be rectified? Even armed with all this knowledge, I wasn't satisfied. The verdict felt wrong.

Walking out into the sunshine, it occurred to me that Harriet would most likely resume her position at the Weekly. Yippee. I could hardly wait. I'd be back to covering dog shows and high school athletic events. Of course, I still had the Greene murder story to write, but most of my enthusiasm for the story was now gone. I went back to work with a gloomy attitude.

The staff at the Weekly was gathered in the break room merrymaking over Harriet's innocent verdict; donuts and coffee for everyone. Not quite up to celebrating, I went to my desk to write the latest details of the Greene saga. There would be other stories related to the Greene case, most likely about Sylvia being tried for Herb's murder. But this needed to be a splashy story. Local Editor Acquitted of Murder. A sarcastic 'woo-hoo' went through my mind. Rhonda the receptionist placed a note on my desk indicating that Jet wanted to see me in his office as soon as possible. *Golly, my day keeps getting better and better.* It was still tense between Jet and me, and a solution didn't seem imminent.

Jet's door was open, so I walked in uninvited.

"Hi, Jimi. Have a seat," he offered politely.

I sat down and waited for him to proceed.

Jet leaned a butt cheek against his desk and folded his arms across his chest. "I wanted to let you know you did a fine job covering Harriet's murder investigation. The details you uncovered were what got her acquitted. Thank you for your hard work and dedication."

Jet didn't know it, but he was twisting a painful knife in my back. He was right; the evidence I had uncovered probably did help get Harriet acquitted. This only made me feel worse because, although logic said that Harriet was innocent, I still felt that she had manipulated me from the onset and framed Sylvia for murder.

"Don't you have anything to say?" Jet prompted. "At least gloat a little. You deserve to."

"Uh, sorry. Thank you for the compliment," I replied limply.

"You don't seem too happy. You should feel great about what you have accomplished."

I prevaricated. "Well, the story isn't over yet. We still need to find the guilty party."

"Come on, Jimi. You've already done that. Sylvia's trial will be nothing more than a formality."

Not being able to stand it another moment, I blurted out, "I don't think Sylvia is the murderer."

"What?" Jet was clearly shocked.

"I think Harriet murdered Herb and orchestrated the whole series of events and set up all the evidence." There. It was now out in the open.

"Are you out of your mind?" Jet looked completely incredulous. "You're the one who uncovered most of the details, except Sylvia renting the furniture dolly, which I admit was a key piece to miss."

"Jet, I saw Harriet's face when the witness pointed out Sylvia as the person who rented the dolly. Harriet wasn't even surprised. She looked, well, evilly jubilant, as if she knew in advance who would be indicated."

"Jimi, you are either tired or looking for a more sensational take on the story. Either way, I'm a little disappointed in you."

*Join the club; I'm a little disappointed in me too!* "Jet, I know what I saw." I took a deep breath. "As much as I don't like her, I think Sylvia is innocent and was framed for Herb's murder."

"Jimi, I will not publish any *theories* in this paper, nor will I allow you to continue in this vein. You are officially off the story after you write the piece declaring Harriet's innocence."

"Fine. You are the boss, but I thought it was the duty and responsibility as a purveyor of unbiased news to discover and advise the public of the facts."

"You aren't talking about facts; you are talking about supposition based on a facial expression you *think* you saw."

"I know what I saw. I would never print supposition or theory, but you shouldn't prevent me from further seeking out the truth either."

"As I said, you are off the story once the article on the outcome of Harriet's trial is printed." Jet's tone indicated he was through with our discussion.

"I'm disappointed in *you*, Jet." I held my ground and leveled a defiant stare at him. "You need to know that while I will write the current facts of the case, on my own time I will continue to investigate Herb's murder. I fully intend to find out if the evidence found against Sylvia was real or if it was planted."

"I can't dictate how you spend your personal time or how you choose to waste it."

"You've got that much right at least." Forcing a calm tone, I continued. "She's guilty, Jet, and she's gotten away with murder. I know it, and feel sick about it because I acted like a puppet instead of a real investigator. My lack of experience in investigative work is what set a murderer free. I can't live with that knowledge." I exited Jet's office with as much decorum as I could muster. What I really wanted to do was lie on the floor of his office and throw a long, loud, kicking and screaming temper tantrum.

Once the story of the outcome of Harriet's trial had been written, albeit half-heartedly, I shut down my PC, got my slim, palm-sized digital camera out of the bottom desk drawer, and retrieved the microcassette recorder and microphone I used for interviews or making mental notes that would later be transcribed for a story. Before leaving the office, I told Rhonda I was paying a visit to Mrs. Greene's house, but I'd have my cell phone with me should anyone need to get in touch. Rhonda commented on 'how nice that was of me' to visit Mrs. Greene.

I was on a mission, not to prove or disprove any preconceived scenario but instead to find out the truth. If I were wrong, so be it, but if I were right, the truth needed to come to light.

The trip to Harriet's was short. Her car wasn't there, so she was probably still going through the process of being released and retrieving her personal belongings. I hoped she'd spend some time celebrating with her attorney also. Otherwise, there probably wasn't much time before Harriet came home. I was going to have to hurry. I tucked the micro-recorder into the waistband of my pants and ran the tiny cord and microphone

295

under my sweater and poked the tip of the mic through the top buttonhole of my sweater. This would leave my hands free while I verbally made notes to myself.

The police and I had already thoroughly gone through Harriet's house. There was only one other structure on the premises. It was a small outbuilding that resembled a pump or well house. There were no windows in the building, so what little light there was had to come through the open door.

In the stream of light, dust particles could be seen floating around. The room was actually fairly well-organized. Some tools hung neatly on the wall, and the workbenches were tidy as well. There didn't seem to be anything out of place. There were no doors on the cupboards; every item was exposed and easy to see. I walked to each corner of the room. I turned the recorder on and started detailing any observations.

The third time around the room, I noticed that under one corner of the largest workbench the floor had no dust on it. The rest of the floor had a fine layer of dirt. I got on my hands and knees and took a photo of the area. There was a two-by-two foot square of wood that didn't perfectly match the rest of the flooring. It was very similar, but less worn. It was barely discernable by the naked eye, so the photo probably wouldn't show much.

I found a claw hammer and began attempting to leverage the corners of the square of wood up. It didn't give way. I started working on the other side of the square. This was going much too slow for my satisfaction. There was a flat-nosed shovel leaning against the far wall. I dropped the hammer and picked up the shovel. Wedging the flat end of the shovel into the crevice separating the pieces of wood, I used all my weight to press down on the handle, but the shovel head only scooted out of position and scraped noisily across the floor.

Once again, I wedged the shovel into the small seam, but deeper this time. When I put all the force I could rally onto the handle of the shovel, I heard a distinct creaking sound and then a *pop*. The square of wood came clear. Under the floorboard was a shoebox. I carefully picked it up and set it on the workbench. Opening the lid, inside I found a chestnut-colored wig of long, lustrous hair and *Sylvia's ring? What in the world? I had seen Sylvia with this very ring on in the courtroom last week. I didn't think the woman ever took it off. How did the ring get here?*

There was a heavy tap on my shoulder. I screamed and turned around to find Harriet with a gun pointed straight at my forehead.

"Naughty, naughty," Harriet scolded as if to an errant child. "You do know that curiosity killed the cat. *Mee-ow.*"

Her voice was demonic. I shuddered and tried to hold my water. Somehow I was starring in a distorted version of *Psycho*. Harriet was Anthony Perkins's character but posing as her own best friend.

"You really shouldn't be poking your nose where it doesn't belong. It might end up getting shot off. Tsk, tsk, tsk."

I was violently shaking now.

"Cat got your tongue? Surely Wonder Girl the super reporter has something witty to say."

My throat was swollen shut and completely dry. My eyes were crossed, transfixed on the barrel of the gun.

"You really were too easy. I knew your first day at work that your stupidity and gullibility was going to come in handy. I don't know why Geppetto wanted a real boy when pulling the strings on a puppet is so much more fun.

"You know, I've always wondered why in movies the villain takes an inordinate amount of time to explain everything to the supposed hero instead of just killing them off immediately. But now I know. Someone, *even someone as stupid as you,* needs to be made aware of the brilliance of the plan and the mastermind behind it. It's no fun keeping one's genius to oneself.

"Poor dear. You look so confused," Harriet continued. "Let me lay it out for you. I found out months ago that Herb was back in Idaho. I'd been following his every move for years but lost track of him about five years ago. When Herb got in touch with me a few months ago, I did some investigative research and found out that Sylvia was Herb's lover. She probably always had been; I knew even during our marriage that Herb was seeing someone else. I just didn't know who.

"Sylvia was originally Herb's girlfriend, you see, but she broke it off. Even though she was with someone else, her jealousy burned over Herb's and my relationship. Anyway, I needed an edge, so I got pregnant on purpose. We dropped out of the gang and did the whole boring little suburban family thing. What I hadn't counted on was that Herb would love and adore that child to distraction."

"You mean James?" I said. *That child* seemed like a heartless reference for her deceased son.

"Yes, *James*, if you will. Anyway, Herb doted on *James* but barely tolerated me. The sun rose and set on little *James*."

I was beginning to hate the way she said his name, as if she were mocking him.

"I got wind that Herb was going to leave me and take his precious son with him, so I killed James." Harriet said this as if she had simply stated she'd just gotten a manicure.

"You *what?*" I gasped, bile rising in my throat. My knees were threatening to buckle.

"You heard me. I needed to hurt Herb in the worst possible way, and James was my only leverage."

My legs dropped out beneath me and I threw up.

Harriet made a sound of disgust. "Get up! And you're going to clean that up before you die. You're such a spineless little ninny.

"I tied a large, clear plastic bag around James's crib while he slept. He never woke up. It took a lot of time, though. I knew his death would be attributed to SIDS."

I regurgitated again.

"You're cleaning that mess up too." She tapped the barrel of the gun against my cheek. It was amazing how her arms, which had looked so frail and shaky holding a water pitcher in the courtroom, now held a heavy gun in a firm, resolute manner. "Come on now. Let's head to the well. It's nice and deep, unused and dry, a perfect grave for you, don't you think?"

*Not really.*

I assumed since we were leaving, Harriet decided she would clean the mess up herself.

"Anyway, Herb was devastated and left, presumably without his lover. So I won."

"What about all the letters he wrote you?" I asked, remembering how it seemed Herb was pining away for Harriet's love.

"You really are stupid. The man was barely literate. He'd write on a piece of paper bag or Twinkie wrapper 'sind m-u-n-n-y,' as if I would be so dense. I replaced all his letters with ones I wrote myself just in case during the court proceedings I would need to back up my story about us getting back together.

"Anyway, when I found out Sylvia was Herb's lover and that they wanted half of everything"—Harriet paused for a moment—"do you know the idiot was going to leave her wealthy husband for Herb and set up housekeeping with him using the assets she's accumulated from various husbands and from the future sale of *my home?* Sylvia didn't care one bit about Herb; she only wanted what someone else had. Her mistake is in wanting what *I* had.

"Fortunately, I'm patient as well as brilliant. I bought a designer pantsuit and shoes and a glossy wig that closely matched Sylvia's own glorious mane of hair, all paid for in cash, of course. Then I treated myself to a facial and makeover. That gaudy, ugly ring was tough, though. I sketched out a duplicate ring and had an out-of-state jeweler make one for me. I paid for the ring with a money order using a false name. The ring was sent to a temporary post office box in Twin Falls, also under a false name, which has since been closed.

"Now I could rent the furniture dolly as Sylvia, and the rest was easy."

*susan case*

299

"How did you get Sylvia's fingerprints in your office?" I asked, trying to stall.

"Puhleeze," Harriet drawled out, sounding like a know-it-all teenager. "When she was at my house for dinner, I had her go into my office and use my desk calendar to see when we could meet again and then write the date on the next month. I took all the pens off the desk, forcing her to open drawers. It was simple as pie. And of course, the night I went to dinner in Boise with her I pretended to get drunk. Once everyone was asleep, I planted the blood evidence in the trunk of Sylvia's car and then cleaned it up with peroxide and a rag. The bloodied rag is buried in Sylvia's backyard, not too deep either. Turns out Sylvia is not a particularly bright murderer.

"Enough of this. Time for you to die." Harriet ushered me out of the building, prodding me with the gun barrel.

"How are you going to explain my disappearance?" I asked.

"I won't have to. I'm sure no one knows you're here, and your car will be moved to a vacant lot somewhere in town. I'll make it look like there was some foul play. Of course, your body will never be found. After all, I'm the poor, wrongfully accused widow. The DA wouldn't dare look my way after the embarrassment they just suffered.

"See the rock well up ahead?" Harriet asked.

My throat was closing so tight I couldn't form another word. My legs were rubbery and uncooperative.

"At the bottom of that well is your final resting place." Harriet giggled like a delighted little girl who had just received her very first dress-up doll at Christmas.

"I hate that you have to die such a quick and painless death, but—" Harriet delicately shrugged her bony shoulders, indicating this particular job had to be rushed.

"Why did you demand to see the post mortem photos of Herb when you were in jail? You already knew he was dead, and it made you look guilty," I stalled, further grasping at any wayward thought or question.

"Because I wanted to see his dead, bloated, decomposing corpse. I wish I could have smelled it too. He was a real bastard for what he did to me."

"How did you kill him? Surely he saw you coming at him with a letter opener." I was still snatching at anything to postpone my death.

Harriet smiled as if remembering her fondest moment in life. "I invited Herb over, dangling the $1.4 million property split under his nose. Told him we'd have a little picnic in the yard and draw up an amicable agreement. Herb was so stupid and of course *greedy*. I laced his drink with Scolpamine. It's a lovely little black market drug which renders its victim void of any cognitive thought; it's used in Columbia by thieves and rapists. Herb just stood there with this childlike grin on his face while I plunged the letter opener into his chest. He made the most wonderful gurgling noises and never quit smiling until he took his last breath. The prosecution will also find the bottle of Scolpamine buried with the bloody rag at Sylvia's home."

"Why implicate yourself with your own inscribed letter opener?"

She looked at me as if I truly were the most ignorant person on the planet Earth. "So I could have a trial and be acquitted. It's why I wanted everything to move so quickly. Get an innocent verdict, and then I'm forevermore protected against another murder trial because of our lovely little constitutional right against double jeopardy.

"This really has been fun, but it's time for you to meet with eternity. Be a good girl and hold still while I put a bullet through your tiny brain. Not much of a loss really." Harriet raised the gun level with my forehead. *Click! Click! Click, the hammer pulled back.* "Good-bye, Miss Smith."

My life was not passing before my eyes. The image of my brain exploding from the back of my skull was the only picture I could invoke.

*susan case*

301

"Put the gun down," a loud, authoritative voice shouted from the shrubbery.

"What the . . . ?" Harriet turned toward the voice and lost focus for a split second.

I lowered my shoulder and rammed Harriet in the gut. The force of impact knocked us both to the ground. She still held on to the revolver, though. I grabbed Harriet's wrist, squeezing tightly, thinking the gun would miraculously fall out of her hand, but apparently that only works in the movies. Harriet still had a firm grip on the gun. I banged her wrist harder and harder into the packed dirt. There were rustling noises coming from the shrubbery. With one last slam of Harriet's wrist against the ground, a violent explosion ripped from the gun. A loud grunt of anguished pain could be heard from the other side of the shrubs.

"I said . . . ouch . . . ugh . . . holy mother of . . . drop the frickin' gun." Deputy Sanchez was limping toward us with his gun drawn. Jet was right behind him. "I knew your sorry ass wasn't worth saving," Sanchez growled in my direction. "First you puke on me; then you commit B&E, you tamper with my crime scene, cause no end of trouble, and now you've gone and got me shot."

Harriet had finally relinquished her hold on the revolver. I slugged her in the face just for the pure pleasure of it and had the satisfaction of seeing blood drip from her nose. Harriet groaned in pain.

I rolled off Mrs. Greene onto my back. Jet dropped down next to me and put his forearm over his eyes. His normally olive complexion was white, and his breath was coming in short pants.

"None of this matters." Harriet Greene laughed hysterically. "I can't be tried a second time for Herb's murder."

"No, but you can be tried for James's murder." I pulled the microphone and cord from under my sweater and the mini

302

recorder from the waistband of my pants. I shut the recorder off with a triumphant snap.

"You little bi—"

I slugged Harriet again, this time in the mouth.

"Did you see her twitch? She was trying to reach for the gun again. I had to hit her. It was self-defense." I looked ruefully at my reddened knuckles.

Deputy Sanchez cuffed Harriet and read her her rights. He was still copiously bleeding from the shin area and mumbling curses at me. Something about how he wasn't sure he should have saved my bothersome life . . . yada yada yada.

Jet rolled on top of me and pinned me to the ground with my arms over my head.

"What the hell were you thinking?" Jet asked with his nose pressed against mine. "Although that was a really fine tackle you made. Any professional linebacker would have been proud of it."

"You should know by now, especially since I beat you up, that I can take care of myself. Besides, I had to discover the truth."

Neither one of us said anything for a moment, each trying to get our adrenaline under control.

"How did you know I'd be here, and why bring Sanchez along?"

"Because trouble follows you and," Jet confessed, "Rhonda told me where you went." His warm breath was puffing onto my lips. He looked me straight in the eye. "I'm sorry I didn't believe you or at least listen to you. I almost got you killed." I could feel Jet's body shake violently against mine.

"When I think what could have happened . . . when I saw that gun pointed at your beautiful, empty head, I almost died myself."

I made a face at the "empty head" remark. "I'm glad you finally did believe me. Of course, if you'd gotten here any sooner we might not have learned about Harriet killing her son. Now she gets to go to prison where she belongs—hopefully for a very long time. In fact, I hope forever 'cause I think she may want to kill me."

Jet tried to smile but decided to kiss me instead. It was a solid choice of which I heartily approved.

"I'm having trouble breathing," I gasped.

"Are you hurt? Did she hurt you?" Jet looked so cute when he was worried.

"No. I seem to have about two hundred pounds of pressure on my chest."

"Two hundred? Two hundred! I'll have you know I don't weigh an ounce over 185, same as I weighed in high school and college!"

I pulled Jet in for another kiss. "Whatever you say, chunky monkey. Just get off me so I can breathe." I sat up and dusted at my shirt, sweater, and pants. "I need to give Deputy Sanchez the recorder. He deserves full credit for this arrest. He *has* put up with a lot from me."

"Haven't we all," Jet lamented in empathy for the deputy.

"I can't wait to get my story written. It's gonna be a national sensation. You'll have to give me a giant pay increase to keep me."

"Jimi, there are things we need to clear up and stuff I want to tell you."

"How about later? Now isn't the time. I still feel shaky," I hedged.

"*Later* will be soon, understand?" Jet said with a tone of finality.

"Yes, sir."

Sanchez loaded a stunned and shaken Harriet into the backseat of his squad car.

"Do you want me to call 911 for you?" I asked the deputy, pointedly looking at the bloodstain spreading down his pant leg.

"Hell no. I'm taking her in myself. It's just a scrape." He appeared kinda proud of his war wound, so I didn't argue.

"I'll see you later. I'm sure you'll have a lot of questions for me," I said.

"You have no idea," he agreed.

Jet gave me a hearty hug and then got into his Navigator and waved good-bye to me.

I got into my car and heard my cell phone incessantly beeping, letting me know I had missed some calls. To my surprise, there were seven missed calls. The first six were from Jet, mostly screaming at me and imploring me not to do anything foolish.

Then I listened to the last voicemail message: "Jimi, it's Daniel. I've got tickets to the production of *Phantom of the Opera* with the actual Broadway cast. It will be playing in San Francisco this weekend. Wanna join me? Besides, there are some things I need to tell you and something very important I want to ask you. Call me soon, okay?"

In the review mirror, I watched the trail of dust kicked up by Jet's Navigator fade away. Jet's kisses still lingered on my lips.

*Damn. I've always wanted to see* Phantom of the Opera.